THE
WICKED
AND THE
DAMNED

ALSO BY REBECCA ROBINSON

The Serpent and the Wolf

THE WICKED AND THE DAMNED

DARK INHERITANCE
BOOK TWO

REBECCA ROBINSON

SIMON &
SCHUSTER

London · New York · Amsterdam/Antwerp · Sydney/Melbourne · Toronto · New Delhi

First published in the United States by Saga Press, an imprint of Simon & Schuster LLC, 2026
First published in Great Britain by Solstice Books, an imprint of Simon & Schuster UK Ltd, 2026

Copyright © Rebecca Gilmore, 2026

The right of Rebecca Gilmore to be identified as author
of this work has been asserted in accordance with the
Copyright, Designs and Patents Act, 1988.

1 3 5 7 9 10 8 6 4 2

Simon & Schuster UK Ltd
1st Floor
222 Gray's Inn Road
London WC1X 8HB

For more than 100 years, Simon & Schuster has championed authors and the stories they create. By respecting the copyright of an author's intellectual property, you enable Simon & Schuster and the author to continue publishing exceptional books for years to come. We thank you for supporting the author's copyright by purchasing an authorised edition of this book.

No amount of this book may be reproduced or stored in any format, nor may it be uploaded to any website, database, language-learning model, or other repository, retrieval, or artificial intelligence system without express permission. All rights reserved. Enquiries may be directed to Simon & Schuster, 222 Gray's Inn Road, London WC1X 8HB or RightsMailbox@simonandschuster.co.uk

Simon & Schuster Australia, Sydney
Simon & Schuster India, New Delhi

www.simonandschuster.co.uk
www.simonandschuster.com.au
www.simonandschuster.co.in

The authorised representative in the EEA is Simon & Schuster Netherlands BV, Herculesplein 96, 3584 AA Utrecht, Netherlands. info@simonandschuster.nl

Simon & Schuster strongly believes in freedom of expression and stands against censorship in all its forms. For more information, visit BooksBelong.com

A CIP catalogue record for this book
is available from the British Library

Hardback ISBN: 978-1-3985-4602-8
eBook ISBN: 978-1-3985-4603-5

This book is a work of fiction. Names, characters, places and incidents are either a product of the author's imagination or are used fictitiously. Any resemblance to actual people living or dead, events or locales is entirely coincidental.

Printed and Bound in the UK using 100% Renewable Electricity
at CPI Group (UK) Ltd

*For Shasta—the wolf that started it all.
Thank you for giving us your lifetime;
I will miss you every day of mine.*

THE WICKED AND THE DAMNED

CHAPTER 1

He'd come for her in the middle of the night.

Footsteps sounded down the hallway of the eerily quiet prison where Vaasa could not hear even the waves. It had been like that for weeks—a veil of midnight draping every inch of space in front of her, the biting cold eating at her skin and muscles and soul, nothing to hear or see or taste or *want*.

They had torn the wanting from her.

Screams pierced the silence, the final wails of sentinels as one after the other fell to the dirty ground. Vaasa pushed to her hands first, dragging her scraped knees beneath her as her bones ached from the cold. She couldn't stand upright.

"Reid," she choked out in a hoarse whisper. "Reid!"

Weeks. She had been trapped here for weeks, listening to pleas and moans of other prisoners that she hadn't been certain were real; echoes behind iron and stone could have been people or just figments of her isolated imagination. All she had were empty, disconnected details; no semblance of a schedule, the randomization of each day preventing her body from knowing the time. She was sure this prison had been constructed to bring her to the brink: the piercing chill, the silence, the darkness.

The dark was not an unfamiliar sensation to Vaasa. A long time ago, she had made a home of it, had found a way to see shadow as a place to hide. But this dark was frigid. Empty. Infinite.

The door to Vaasa's cell screeched open, and a figure stood in the gray-washed glow. Broad shoulders, long mahogany hair, orange and black eyes that finally met her own. This moment was both salvation and dying, heartbreak and healing, it was everything, *everything*.

"Reid," she choked once more, her elbows wobbling and then giving out beneath her. Her chin smacked against the ground as her weight toppled forward.

"Here!" his deep voice boomed. "She's here!"

Reid was *alive*.

He had come for her.

Tears washed down Vaasa's face as he rushed forward to her. She lurched, using the last of her energy to throw her body against his, to let him take her in his arms and steal her away from this wretched place. His warmth enveloped her, his body feeling so much bigger than hers as his arms wound around her waist and lifted her to her feet. Her torn slippers caught traction beneath her, but it was he who held her up, who carried the weight of her broken body.

"I have you," he whispered against her blood-smeared cheek. His nose pressed to the spot just behind her ear. "I'm never letting you go again."

Hot tears slipped down her cheeks. "I'm in love with you," she whispered back, her voice only capable of that much. "I should have told you every day."

Reid's arm hooked behind her back as he gently helped her to the door of her cell. "You can, Wild One. You will."

They turned the corner, and—

And then Vaasa was falling through the floor.

She wrenched her eyes open and saw nothing but black. The mist—it covered her vision, cloaked her entire face. Spinning around her in a glittering black void, Veragi magic stuffed itself down her throat and up her nose, muffling her screams. Strings of it tangled within her body, wrapped around her organs and pulled. She tossed her body to the right with as much power as she could muster, but her wrists were bound to the table. Vaasa screamed and pulled as hard as she could—

"Dammit!" a familiar voice swore.

The straps on her left wrist snapped with a hiss as her body spun off the side of the table. A hard, cold surface collided with her cheek, something slick coating her skin as the bone splintered in pain. The sensation exploded behind her right eye where she'd landed. Her shoulder felt as if it had been jerked right from its socket. The magic before her eyes extinguished, and her vision readjusted. Her right wrist was still bound to the table, and she hung from it, the rest of her body on the grimy floor while her cheek lay against the sturdy wooden leg of the table they'd bound her to. Blood trickled down her limbs in small streams from the thin hairline cuts carved into her thighs and upper arms. Small inflictions of pain that when added together became excruciating, though never enough to kill.

She opened her eyes and saw him: Lord Vlacik, staring down at her with his lip curled in disgust.

Vaasa struck.

Magic shot from her hands toward his icy blond head, a tendril of darkness flying forward like a thrown blade.

"Shit," he cursed as he leapt to the side. "Chain her!"

Metal touched the skin of her neck, and she hissed in pain. Her magic winked out. Hands held her in place and forced an iron collar around her neck, clinking it closed. She bared her teeth and launched herself forward at the lord, but the sharp metal collar dug into her neck, secured to the table by an iron chain. She cried out as her body ricocheted backward.

"Get her back on the table," Vlacik commanded.

Bile crawled up her throat, and she began to heave, hoisting herself on her side. There was nothing left in her, yet it came over and over—slick black waste, just like what she'd vomited up in Dihrah before Reid found her. She'd been on the verge of death then, and as she expelled unused Veragi magic now, Vaasa was certain she was closer to dying than she'd ever been.

This metal collar . . . it extinguished every breath of magic within her, a smothering leash. Once they had it on her, there was no escape. She was chained to the table, powerless.

"I said get her back on the table," Lord Vlacik's voice snapped, "and secure the straps tighter this time."

Instinctual fear knotted in Vaasa's stomach as her vision spun from the floor to the wall to the ceiling. A blond-haired man in a royal blue Asteryan uniform stood beside the table that held her, and she was on her back again, too tired to fight. Too confused.

A door opened. Ozik's voice floated through the air. "Enough."

"Sir—"

"I said *enough*," Ozik repeated.

Through the haze of her pain and adrenaline, Vaasa realized where she was. Or, more precisely, where she *wasn't*.

She wasn't in Mireh. Or Dihrah. She wasn't in Icruria at all.

And Reid wasn't here.

Tears welled in her eyes. He wasn't coming to find her. His footsteps had never sounded down this hall. It was just a place Vaasa retreated to in her mind when she couldn't handle the reality around her.

Vaasa released the tension in her neck and let her head fall to the side, pounding cheek finding a semblance of relief on the cold iron table. Around her was a dimly lit chamber in the bowels of the prison, filled with exactly five other people. Ozik and two sentinels whose names she didn't know stood by the door, iron keys hanging off their hips. Lord Vlacik stood to the right next to a wrinkled clergyman who sat at a metal countertop, hunched over a notebook as he scribbled observations. On that countertop were sharp objects: Thumbscrews, pronged forks, iron hoops with protruding spikes all sat waiting for the lord's terrible touch. They gleamed in the candlelight.

Vaasa's body recoiled at the memory of each of those tools against her flesh.

They did this almost daily. It had taken only once for Vaasa to realize that Lord Vlacik was working with the Asteryan clergy to uncover the secrets of Veragi magic—seeking answers Vaasa herself didn't know. Where did this magic come from? What caused it to manifest in a person?

And Lord Vlacik's personal mission: How could it be weaponized?

Vaasa was a mouse, the sacrificial subject of their experiments.

"Unless you want what we know—" Lord Vlacik started, but Ozik cut him off.

"Careful with your words, my lord, or you will find yourself as dead as your father."

The room went silent.

Vaasa and Ozik's connection came and went like the tides since she had ceded her powers to him to save Reid; some moments Ozik was silent to her, others his oily, slick magic was all she could feel in her veins. Whatever linked them was shaky and unpredictable. Each day Lord Vlacik did this to her, she lasted longer and felt more of Ozik's magic tangling with her own. There were moments she swore it fueled the manifestations of her magic that Vlacik pried out of her. Ozik never intervened until she was at the edge of her tolerance, tipping over the side of a cliff.

As if while the lord tried to uncover what caused the magic to manifest, Ozik was building her endurance.

The treacherous advisor stepped forward to loom above her. Since the election, the traces of black in Ozik's veins had disappeared, leaving only pale, porcelain skin and a cunning smile with far-too-straight teeth. His white hair brushed his shoulders, trimmed neatly and in direct contrast to the tangles of greasy black hair upon her own head. Ozik appeared stronger. Healthier. Perhaps even younger. His appearance was far closer to how she remembered it in her youth. By linking her magic to his, he had regained something that had been lost since her mother's death.

His menacing gold eyes caught upon her cheek. Perhaps a bruise had already started to form.

"She has lasted longer than any of the other witches," the lord muttered to the clergyman, who nodded in agreement.

"Of course she has," Ozik said. "She is her mother's daughter."

Vaasa closed her eyes again. It all weighed on her weary mind; that Ozik had loved her mother—and that they'd been having an affair when he'd served as their family's closest advisor—yet he'd killed her. Vena Kozár had made some kind of twisted bargain with Ozik to murder Vaasa's father, but instead of then handing Ozik the throne, she sent Vaasa into the safety of a betrothal abroad and helped Dominik become ruler of Asterya.

And Ozik had murdered her for it.

Every day Vaasa spent in this prison, she wondered what her mother had been through. What she had faced alone while Vaasa's resentment of her only grew. It was not lost on Vaasa that her mother was a relative stranger to her; she knew little of the truth.

"Did you do this to her, too?" Vaasa croaked out. "To the woman you loved?"

Ozik stared at her, lips drawn. Just as Vaasa's magic had at the Icrurian election, it wrenched from her insides in a terrible tug. Each time he returned her magic to her, it burrowed into her bones and muscles as if hiding itself from him. Yet without even a flick of his hands or a shuttering of his eyes, Ozik took the power from her again in an instant. Vaasa groaned in pain, throat hoarse from the screaming she had already done.

"We're making progress," Lord Vlacik insisted. "Let me continue."

"No," Ozik replied, staring into Vaasa's eyes. "Your time is up."

"Ozik—"

"I said your time is up," Ozik snarled, composure slipping. "I agreed to six weeks. No more, no less."

Six weeks. That was how long she had been in this prison, then. Vaasa filed away the detail, wondering why Ozik had let such a thing slip. Did he want her to know how much time had passed?

"We have spent more time trying to keep her contained than we have learning anything," Lord Vlacik argued. "Between her attempts to escape and her striking—"

"I fail to see how any of this is my problem," Ozik interrupted. "You were promised six weeks, and six weeks have passed." Vaasa watched him as he walked to the door. He looked back over his shoulder once, eyes lingering on her for only a moment before landing on the two sentinels waiting dutifully for a command. "Take her back to her cell."

Lord Vlacik stormed out the door after Ozik, and Vaasa was left with the two sentinels and quiet clergyman who continued to jot down notes without bothering to look at her again. The sentinels undid the collar around her neck. It didn't make a difference; Ozik had once again taken away her access to magic, leaving her empty and powerless. Vaasa's wrist came free, and she let her arms sag against the table. Soon, they hauled her up and out of the room, but each step she took was a strain, knees wobbling. She fought to keep upright but lost, tripping over her own dragging feet, and the sentinels barely caught her. She came face-to-face with the iron keys at their belts, studying them, locking away every detail she could.

Now wasn't the time to hatch an escape, but that time would come.

They carried her into a dark, narrow stairwell and up two flights of stairs until they stopped in front of her cell's wooden door. She stared at the small window of iron bars upon it as one of the sentinels used his set of dangling keys to open it.

"*Witch*," he sneered at her. He threw her in, and Vaasa slammed into the dirty floor. When she looked up, both sentinels had disappeared into the unquiet tomb.

Within this cell, all she could feel was the biting cold, the musty air, and the strange sense that though she was by herself, she wasn't alone.

CHAPTER 2

Something rattled the iron lock of Vaasa's cell. Faintly, she recognized the sound as a key turning. Her vision only registered the hands, cold and harsh and far sturdier than her own, coming toward her as they found her. A sentinel gripped her forearm and neck, slamming her already-injured cheek into the grimy floor so she was face down and unable to move. She thrashed, but his grip was too tight. Another sentinel took a fistful of her dirty hair and tugged, her scalp screaming as he forced her to look up. Her wrists were bound in front of her, and once again she felt an ache in her body where her magic used to be.

Footsteps echoed against the floor. Slow and menacing, someone appeared at the entrance to her cell, stepping through the doorway into her small confinement. Lord Vlacik wore a royal blue Asteryan uniform that winked with iron brooches—none of them earned in war, all inherited from his late father. With a well-kept blond beard and beady ice-blue eyes, he looked as frightening as he had every other time Vaasa had seen him. He was only about ten years her senior, but she remembered the way he'd circled her like a shark the moment she had come of age.

She wanted to lift her head and spit in his face, but she couldn't muster the strength. As it was, it would take all she had to pull herself from the floor. Fear curled in her gut. The cuts along her upper arms and thighs stung.

"Cover her," Lord Vlacik commanded, eyes raking over her torn woolen pants and shirt. Someone draped a cloak over her shoulders, the warmth of it almost useless with how cold she had become. "On your feet," he said.

Strength wavering, Vaasa struggled to stand. Harsh hands dug into her upper arms as a sentinel dragged her upright, forcing her to balance on wobbly legs.

Lord Vlacik looked disgusted at her weakness, his upper lip curled and his nose scrunched at the undeniable smell of piss and blood that permeated the prison. He turned on his heel and started back down the hallway. The sentinels holding her ropes tugged, and she had no choice but to follow. They led her across the slick floor, out of the cell and down a cold, dark walkway lined on either side with wood-and-iron doors much like the ones that had held her captive. They plunged into the narrow stairwell and dragged her down a set of steep stairs, then through a set of double doors, bathing the hallway in bright white.

Light reflecting off snow could be beautiful, but it could also be blinding. She squinted, and her eyes watered. Bitter coldness assaulted her uncovered face as she stumbled onto one of the many iron platforms that wrapped around the prison of Mekës.

Wind lifted her knotted, greasy hair in tendrils, salt stinging her lips. Different from the salt she had known, the Icrurian scent she had come to love. The smell and taste of this salt was acrid, fishy, without a hint of warmth. Her eyes adjusted as they pushed her forward; sprawled on the horizon was Mekës's shoreline, the trade port a full and bustling thing, separated from her by the frigid ocean, which churned angrily in the wind.

The prison was built upon an elevated island in the Iron Bay. Only reachable by boat, it was as inescapable as the cold itself. The east side of the prison held the cells, three enormous towers surrounded by steep cliffs, the tops of the stone structures covered in iron spires. The west side of the prison held the offices where the prison guards, the higher-ranking sentinels, and the warden gazed over the bleak scene from a tall watchtower that jutted into the sky like an angry index finger. Today, the prison appeared empty. Only Vlacik and his trusted sentinels were privy to her movements, she presumed.

Four of those sentinels led her over an arching bridge that connected the two sides of the prison. "The Last Crossing," people called it. Jumping from this very bridge was a rite of passage for the fortress and city guards—to dive into the water and survive was one of the ways they proved themselves to their peers. Vaasa peered over the edge, a sentinel muttering a warning to her in Asteryan. She wondered if she could even escape the Iron Bay if she somehow survived the jump.

Likely not. She was already too starved, too cold. That swim would leave her as nothing more than fodder for the sharks.

But she could see all of Mekës from here—the granite and iron city covered the mountainside. The enormous trade port led into winding streets covered in snow. The city hugged the coastline of the Iron Bay all the way to the entrance to the Loursevain Gap, the untenable river route winding through the Iron Peaks. After ascending the throne, Dominik had gone to Mireh under the guise of building ships that could navigate that canyon, that would grant water access to the entirety of northern Asterya. As it stood, only pirates ever dared enter the canyon. Vaasa's eye caught on a single iron statue depicting her late grandfather, who had conquered this very bay and relocated Asterya's capital here.

The view from this bridge was both a beauty and a tragedy, because prisoners that crossed it were said to stand here and stare at the expanse of the city, knowing it was the last time they would ever see sunlight casting its colorful rays upon the smooth granite buildings of Mekës.

A sentinel pulled on her ropes again, and Vaasa stumbled after him. They plunged through a stone archway that led into the western courtyard, which was entirely empty of sentinels. The prison felt like a graveyard, ghosts dancing in the walkways, sounds echoing off the walls. Ozik must have removed any prying eyes; every hallway or turn they took came up just as empty as the last. They emerged on the opposite side of the administrative building, facing the ocean once more. Soon, Vaasa was on the pathway that led directly to the ocean.

Waiting at the bottom was an Asteryan ship.

Flurries of snow fell from the sky, cloaking the air in front of her and blurring her sight. Her legs burned as they walked. At the bottom of the pathway, she tried to halt, digging her heels into the ground to keep from going any further.

A sentinel's hands slammed between her shoulder blades and sent her careening down the last few steps of the stone pathway, knees cracking against the stone. Her chin followed suit. Jaw thrumming with pain, she thought herself no different than a sheep being herded into a pen.

"Enough," a voice snapped, the edges of it sharp, the tenor of it so frighteningly familiar.

Ozik. She looked up through her lashes to see him glowering at the sentinel who had struck her.

"She is to be your empress," Ozik snarled, taking a step forward. Vaasa heard shuffling behind her and wondered if the sentinel had . . . retreated.

Ozik reached for her, but she ground out, "Fuck you." Vaasa put her hands beneath her and pushed herself to a kneel. Ozik stood in front of her, wearing a snow-white cloak clasped with an iron brooch depicting Asterya's sigil—a single mountain with a sword plunging through it. He wore the emblem with the same pride that Vaasa's father had. His chin lifted, and an ease washed over his features. He reached for her, rings of every color decorating his fingers. Red rubies and green emeralds, even a dark black stone that didn't shine like the others.

Vaasa recoiled. Panic sprung to life in her chest. Memories of the recent weeks' torture flooded her mind, and the way Ozik was watching her, it was like he could see them, too. Rage lit within her; there was nothing else to cling to, and Vaasa nursed that heat because everywhere else was cold.

Ozik lifted his hands, palms forward. "I only want to help you to your feet."

The oily slick strings between them tugged lightly as if to say, *Cooperate.*

Whatever magic linked them, he was stronger than her right now. His fingers curled around her arm, and he lifted her to her feet, bearing her weight for a moment until she found her balance. He immediately started to undo the ropes around her wrists. The moment they slid to the floor, Vaasa took two steps away from Ozik. Across the small distance she'd created, he assessed her with keen golden eyes. No doubt he took in her tattered prison attire, which had torn at her left collarbone and down her right arm. She must have been covered in dirt and blood, a wreck compared to his royal blue finery with stark iron buttons that gleamed, catching the sun.

Ozik turned to face Lord Vlacik, who narrowed his icy eyes at Vaasa as he marched down the pathway to meet them on the dock. A group of men followed him, their steps out of cadence. These guards were less refined than Vaasa remembered of the men who earned the rank of sentinel.

Vaasa shook her head so her hair would unstick from her cheeks and forced her expression into a soft, bored apathy. Every bone in her body weighed like a ton of bricks, but she squared her shoulders anyway.

The lord didn't mutter a word, but the two sentinels who had helped Vlacik torture her day in and day out stepped back when they realized she was no longer tied up.

"You can go now," Ozik told the lord, dipping his head in a small gesture of respect. "We'll see you when the others arrive."

The others?

Ozik gripped just above her elbow and started to guide her to the waiting ship. She wanted to frighten. To clamp her teeth down on his hand and rip through his skin. Fury burned in her chest at his audacity in touching her.

He had taken *everything* from her.

What did she have to lose?

Using the last reserves of her strength, Vaasa wrapped her fingers around a knife at Ozik's belt and pulled. She slashed it across his cheek. He loosed a pained hiss and stumbled away from her. Before she could turn and strike again, the sentinels were on her, and she hit the dock with a guttural grunt. She screamed in fury as they wrenched her arms behind her and pried her fingers from the knife.

A curse ripped through the air as Ozik's boot landed just next to her face. She struggled against the hold the sentinels had on her, but they held firm. "Up," he told them, and suddenly she was hauled to her feet once more. She panted, her ribs screaming with each breath she took, yet she curled her lip back in a defiant snarl.

Ozik dipped to bring them eye to eye, anger rippling across his normally calm features. Gone was the gentleness she was certain had only been an illusion for the sentinels who did not know the truth of Vaasa's confinement. Blood trickled down the deep scratch in his cheek. "You're going to cooperate," he said, his face within inches of hers and his voice quietly menacing. "Do you want to know why?"

Vaasa only stared as her exhales came out as steam, refusing to answer him.

"Because I have someone you'd rather see unharmed," he whispered.

Her vision faltered as his words sank in. Who could he possibly mean? But Vaasa knew better than to give herself away. Even a single word, a single expression, he could use against her.

He tsked in disappointment at her lack of emotion. His hand whipped out, fingers grasping her chin, and yanked her head to the side. Her eyes settled on the pathway that led to the prison, on a figure being hauled down it to meet them. There were at least ten sentinels surrounding the prisoner. Iron chains clanged together as they grew closer and closer.

Vaasa tried to suppress her adrenaline. Her fingers twitched at her side as if yearning to use magic she didn't have. She started to shake—with the cold, with the fear. The sentinels emptied out onto the flat stone walkway and revealed Ozik's second hostage, shackled more tightly than Vaasa had ever been.

"Amalie," Vaasa breathed.

Every ounce of hope drained from Vaasa as she watched a sentinel kick at the back of Amalie's knees, sending her careening forward onto the ground.

Vaasa instinctively tugged at the hands that held her. She broke away and threw herself off the dock onto the stone pathway, tripping and falling to her knees before her friend. The sharp stone of the walkway stung even through the fabric she wore.

Amalie looked up. "Vaasa," she whispered. Her face was gaunt, shadowed. Her eye was bruised. Icrurian fell from her lips: "Don't give them anything they want. Let me die, let me—"

Someone grabbed ahold of Vaasa's waist and dragged her backward. She screamed and thrashed, causing the sentinel to stumble, but not enough to be set free.

The sentinel behind Amalie placed a knife at the witch's throat, one of the very men who had tortured Vaasa, his striking green eyes alight with violence.

"Stop!" Vaasa screamed.

Amalie, her closest friend, was supposed to be *safe*. Vaasa had killed for it. Had slaughtered her own brother to ensure it. How were they right back in this place?

"Ozik, let her go! Please," Vaasa begged, throwing all her weight against the sentinel to turn and face Ozik. The man's grip was so tight, but he faltered just a step, and it was enough.

Ozik must have known everything Dominik had done in Icruria, right down to whom he had used for leverage against Vaasa. *Of course* Ozik knew. Vengeance, thick and angry, flowed onto her tongue. Her words came sharp, the Asteryan consonants catching on the roof of her mouth as she pierced him with her indigo gaze. "You have just signed your death warrant, as Dominik did."

Ozik looked down at her, a small smile at watching her struggle against a second sentinel who'd started to dig his toe into Vaasa's calf.

"Behave, and in time, you will see her freed," Ozik said.

Vaasa stopped struggling as the sentinels pulled her away. Her limbs went slack. She only stared at her closest friend—her first true friend—who was barely still within sight. Dirt was smeared over Amalie's face, and her expression seemed lost. Broken.

Then it shifted.

All the warmth Vaasa knew disappeared.

Amalie raised her chin, locked eyes with Vaasa, and smiled. Through her tears, Vaasa saw something that made her tremble. Her friend wore a wicked, vengeful expression, completely unlike the woman Vaasa knew, and for a moment, Vaasa swore Amalie's eyes flashed moonlight-white. Just like the snake, just like the wolf that Vaasa had summoned to kill her own brother. She recalled a faint memory of the moments just before Reid's mother Melisina had found them both beneath that colosseum, before Vaasa had murdered her brother to save all their lives.

Hadn't Amalie's eyes flashed white then, too?

Ozik grabbed Vaasa's face, fingers tight on her jaw, and forced her to turn and look at him again. His other hand wrapped sternly around her throat. Vaasa bucked like a wild animal, but Ozik remained unmoved. He tightened his grip until her air almost ceased.

Desperation struck Vaasa like lightning, but she did not move. She forced herself to calm, to not utter a word or strike Ozik again. She needed to survive this moment first.

"And now you know," he warned in Icrurian, low and deadly, "that if you make one wrong move, Vaasalisa, I will forfeit that girl's life quicker than I took your father's. I will slaughter her the way you did your brother—without mercy. So you *will* cooperate. Have I made myself clear?"

He didn't want anyone else to hear those words. The truth of who—and what—Ozik was would be his unraveling. Vaasa would kill him. And afterward, she would bury his body so deep in the ground that not even the dogs would find him.

She nodded.

"Good," he said, releasing her throat as she fell to her knees, gasping for air. As he stood there like a malevolent god looking down on her, Vaasa's rage melded with powerlessness. She might as well have been bowing to him. A simple grin played upon his lips.

Hands grabbed her arms again, dragging her away from Amalie, and though she fought hard, it was no use.

Cold, salt-ridden air filled her nostrils as Vaasa was hauled onto the waiting ship.

CHAPTER 3

They loaded Vaasa onto the Asteryan vessel, nothing like the fortified transfer boats built for the sole purpose of towing prisoners to and from. This was decorative, elegant—meant for show. She sat in an enclosed glass cabin, windows wrapped around the entirety of their space and revealing the oncoming city. A boat like this was never meant for long journeys; it was one her father had commissioned, only ever used to sail around the Iron Bay. Waves rocked them as they crossed the water in silence. Vaasa pulled her cloak tighter around her shoulders, silently grateful for the warmth. Ozik sat at a bolted-down wooden table, hands intertwined atop it. Vaasa watched him from where she stood, her back pressed against the single wooden wall.

They were entirely alone.

"Why am I alive?" she asked plainly, her voice barely loud enough to carry across the cabin. Away from Vlacik and the other prying ears, Vaasa wondered if she would finally get something real from Ozik. He was brilliant in front of a crowd, entirely convincing of whatever story he wanted to spin.

Ozik cocked his head, his brows threading together. "You are the last remaining Kozár, Vaasalisa. By law, you are to be our empress."

Disbelief wove through her nerves. For six weeks, she had been in that cell, certain that if Ozik wanted her dead, he'd have killed her already. She never would've guessed this was the reason. "You murdered my father for his throne and his wife, and now you want to place *me* upon it?"

Ozik crossed his arms and leaned back, resting against the bench. "I killed your father because he was a vindictive fool who took fifteen years to realize his wife was in love with someone else. He could conquer a continent but he couldn't smell the things right under his nose, and that is what happens when someone fails to mind the four walls of their home."

Fifteen years. Ozik had been having an affair with Vaasa's mother for fifteen years? "I thought you made a bargain with my mother to—"

"I said we made a *trade*. You must begin listening closely to words; they matter. I did not need to be convinced to kill your father. But your mother and I had a thousand bargains, Vaasalisa. And she broke one. I hope you do not make the same mistake."

"Did you need her magic the way you need mine?" Vaasa asked bluntly.

Ozik seemed to ruminate on her words for a moment. He ran his tongue along his front teeth, looking smug but impressed. "Most of the nobles have denied invitations since your brother's death was announced."

"You aren't going to answer my question?"

"You haven't earned an answer yet."

Vaasa grunted, her body aching as the ship tilted and she tried to remain upright.

"Court has not been held since Dominik left for Icruria," Ozik continued, ignoring her inquiry about her mother.

What mattered was the direction the soldiers pointed their steel—and steel was only an extension of coin. So while the fortress itself had a robust system of guards and the city a coordinated force, the throne had no army without Asterya's nobles. If Ozik didn't have the support of the upper echelon, then he had nothing at all. Likely, they were all lying in wait, wondering if one of them could make a viable claim for the throne.

"That is because you are not a Kozár," Vaasa finally said.

Ozik chuckled. "Obviously. But their empress has returned. All will go back to the way it's meant to be."

Vaasa crossed her arms. "A woman has never taken the throne in Asterya."

"Neither has a witch. Yet you and I are the only people still standing."

"Do they know what you are?" she dared ask.

"Only as much as they know what *you* are."

Clearly, Lord Vlacik did, and members of the clergy. How much had her own father known? Whispers of magic had always spread about Icruria alongside its reputation for unflinching brutality, but since no one made it alive past Wrultho or Hazut, the only source of information Asteryans had was their own church. According to the Asteryan clergy, witches were agents of the devil. Vaasa's own father had claimed to be a god-fearing man, had bowed his head in prayer and worked in tandem with the Asteryan clergy. Yet it was possible everything her father had conquered had been the result of bargains made with the man sitting at the table before her. Of the very magic he had claimed to despise.

"Is the archbishop in support of the *experiments* Lord Vlacik conducts?" Vaasa asked.

Ozik scoffed. "If the archbishop knew half of what happened in this city, he would burst into flames."

Mekës was the center jewel of a bloody crown. While her father had made the city seem one of pure grandeur, Vaasa knew the maker of most livelihoods lay in the seedy underbelly of an empire—the city's slums, brothels, and gambling houses were always full, even if the streets seemed clean. Vaasa shifted her weight, her legs still weary beneath her. "So if you reveal what we are, they will hunt us down for it. The clergy will make examples of us both."

"The worst part about being an emperor is that everyone *knows* you are an emperor," Ozik agreed.

Frowning, Vaasa realized what he intended to use her for. Her eyes flicked to the approaching city, all sparkling granite and sharp iron.

"You're going to make me a figurehead. That's what you did to my father, wasn't it?"

Ozik chuckled. "It's truly a relief to be back in the presence of someone worth partnering with. Your brother had half your potential."

Frustration curled in her stomach at the mention of her late brother. Thoughts of Dominik washed over her, and Vaasa tried to shake the image of his severed head in her hand. She looked back to Ozik. "The nobility will never agree. If you place me on the throne, you're handing Asterya to the Icrurians. That's the law."

Ozik shook his head. "The archbishop has already signed and delivered the dissolution. You are no longer married to Reid of Icruria."

Vaasa froze. She hadn't been prepared for what the sound of Reid's name would do to her. What it would be like to hear an entire nation attached to him now—no longer *of Mireh*, but *of Icruria*.

He had been elected headman.

"What?" she managed through her tight throat.

"He breached his side of the marriage agreement when he attacked Asterya." Ozik spoke as if it were obvious.

A wicked pulse skipped in her chest. Reid had attacked the border. Ice threaded in Vaasa's tone. "Who gave you such authority?" Any moment she let herself think of Reid, the wider the pit in her stomach grew. She felt it deep in her bones; there was no piece of paper that could nullify the choice she had made to be his wife, even if it had taken her longer than it should have to decide such a thing. Still, Ozik wouldn't tell her this information unless he wanted her to know it.

They were at war. Ozik had used Reid's aggression to his advantage. But it also meant Reid had crossed the border. Was he coming for her? Could he even survive a full-scale invasion of Asterya?

Confidence rode the upturn of Ozik's lips. "The thing about authority is that it cannot be given. Only taken."

"Yet *you* do not take it. You plan to hide behind me," Vaasa countered.

"A future that is better than any of the options you previously had. Your father would have sold you off, your brother would have murdered you, and that Icrurian would have cast you aside the moment he got his hands on your throne."

"You're wrong," Vaasa snapped, her harsh Asteryan consonants making her sound so much like her father. "It's bold of you to quote the authority of an archbishop who worships a singular, fictitious god while you sit there with my magic running through your veins."

Ozik's smile only widened at her show of anger. "Believers give deities their power, not the other way around."

With this legal dissolution, Ozik himself was free to marry her; politically, it made the most sense. If he wanted to assure his own rise to the Asteryan throne, he would silence any naysayers if he invoked a law that already existed. "If marrying you is your suggestion, I will die first."

Ozik's nose scrunched in disgust and he shook his head, his white hair brushing his shoulders. "I helped raise you, Vaasalisa. There are certain evils I would never think to commit. You will have a choice. The lords will come, and we will remind them that you are the only legitimate path to the throne, and you will pick. Which useless son can we most easily bring to heel?"

Her arms went rigid at her sides. Resentment washed over her at this box she had been relegated to. "You're going to marry me off? Again?" Once more, then, she was to be nothing but a political pawn for the Kozár name.

Ozik shook his head in frustration, his jaw tightening. "You see the world as a chain of events that have happened to you. It's time you start looking at those events as opportunities."

She glared at him, her untamable anger rising to the surface even though she could hardly breathe. The audacity of him, to claim her subjugation as a gift.

"I won't do this," Vaasa said.

Ozik raised a brow. "Perhaps you would rather marry Lord Vlacik? He's kindly submitted himself as an option."

Vaasa involuntarily pressed herself into the wall behind her. Her voice dropped to a croak. "How *dare* you."

"He's the last living inheritor of his title," Ozik said. "And given that his first wife died before they could have children, you two could be of great use to each other."

Vaasa sealed her lips in an attempt to fight off the bile rising in her throat. She worried her legs might give out beneath her. In silence, they passed in front of the city, no doubt gathering the attention of anyone at the port, especially as their boat sailed into one of the largest public docks.

Ozik stood from the table with grace, his white cloak falling over his shoulders. "The archbishop is waiting."

Vaasa tightened her jaw. "What do you mean?"

Ozik crossed the cabin to stand in front of her. "With your marriage to Reid and the subsequent trade of salt, the floodgate between nations was opened. Along that trade route, the secrets of western Icruria spread through *both* nations. You did far too good of a job convincing the Icrurians of your power, Vaasalisa. Now, everyone in this city believes you're a witch. It is your job to convince them you aren't. To convince them it was Reid who cursed you."

Vaasa gaped at him. "I won't—"

Wretched pain tore through her abdomen, and Vaasa gasped. Through the blur of her vision and the tearing deep in her body, she stumbled forward, but Ozik used his free hand to hold her steady. That singular, tangled cord in her body pulled her up as if she were a puppet on strings. Vaasa choked down a sob of pain.

"With our bargain, I do not need any other access point to magic. I own your power. With you as a source, my abilities can be called upon whenever I want."

Vaasa grit her teeth until hurt threaded her jaw. That meant escape was impossible—she couldn't outfight a witch who wielded her own power.

"*Fuck. You.*"

The burning ceased. Disdain coiled across his mouth. "If we're to have a chance, you must be willing to work with me. In time, you will understand that everything I am doing has a purpose."

Vaasa took a breath. Ozik needed more than just her magic. He wanted to rule Asterya without the title, and she had to admit there was a layer of brilliance to his strategy. He would make all the decisions, take little accountability, and become as rich as an emperor, possibly more so.

Now that he stood so near to her, she studied his middle-aged features. He still looked youthful and alive, thanks to her powers. His skin held far more color than it had that day in Icruria, as if he had been healed from something wicked.

She rolled her shoulders back, tilted her chin up, and met his eyes, narrowing her gaze.

Ozik didn't seem intimidated. "It's good to know your spirit wasn't dimmed by a prison cell. Now, come." He turned and walked toward the cabin's exit, taking each step with grace, his white cloak billowing out behind him as he gestured to the doors.

Vaasa stared at him for a moment, the thread of magic between them still running strong. She followed, cloak wrapped tightly around her, thankful for the winter sun poking through the clouds. A sentinel took her hand and guided her off the ship, a look of awe on his features that Vaasa didn't understand.

"Heiress." He tipped his head in reverence. When the panels of her cloak parted and he saw the tattered clothes beneath, he sucked in a breath.

Vaasa covered herself again, though from the corner of her eye, Ozik smirked.

The dock led them right into one of the city squares, which sat upon the edge of the water. The winter sun beat down on the open area, the granite of the surrounding buildings shimmering in the rays of light. The Sanctum spanned one side, a large structure that held the chancery and treasury, along with other offices for influential members of the Asteryan court. The entire back half was under construction, iron scaffolding along the outer walls. On the opposite side of the square stood the cathedral, with a single spire so tall it seemed to tear right through the sky, coupled with a slightly smaller one that held a behemoth clock. The granite exterior of the cathedral was studded with statues of disciples—fishermen who acted as prophets for their Asteryan god, each one maintaining their own portion of the building.

In between those two grand structures, the ocean churning as a backdrop, was a stark iron pole.

Beneath it, a drain.

It was here, witnessed by the church and the state, that criminals were tied to a post and slaughtered. Some were kept there for days or weeks, freezing to death. The energy of the place hummed around them, the feeling of death palpable in the air. Vaasa had never considered herself superstitious, but it was as if she could feel them: each and every life that had been taken in this spot. She'd felt it since she was a little girl. As if the plaza itself held memory in the divots between its cobblestones where blood had run.

"Keep your eyes down," Ozik instructed as they walked her into the crowded city square. The city guard surrounded her, lines on both sides fending off the hordes of people who yelled and tried to push past them. Their screams and accusations poured over her. The words settled on her skin but never sank their teeth in: *whore, wasted, impure, cursed.*

It was only the last one that gave her pause.

To all of them, she was inhuman. A public being, open entirely to their criticism. They didn't care how loudly they spoke or whether they conversed about her and her family like she wasn't there.

Vaasa stumbled with Ozik as guards pushed through the swarms of people to create a path. The bellowing screams died down as word of her gaunt appearance spread through the crowd. The insults transitioned to new words: *dirty, injured, hurt.*

These people had no idea she had been kept in their own prison.

Ozik wanted them to think the Icrurians had done this to her. That Reid had done this to her.

Her eyes caught on the iron pole again—and the members of the clergy who stood beside it.

Vaasa stumbled backward in an attempt to break from Ozik, but the guards flanking them crowded in closer, containing her. Standing among the clergy was the archbishop, who watched with his beady eyes as Ozik led Vaasa up onto the platform with the pole. He looked over her in assessment with cloudy gray eyes. A man in his early seventh decade, he had a wise air about him, further solidified by his silver hair and long, brushed beard.

He stepped forward, black robes flowing around him, a jewel-encrusted blade held in his right hand. Before she could scurry back, two other members of the clergy stepped into Vaasa's space. They tore the cloak from her shoulders, revealing her tattered clothing and dirt-caked skin. Vaasa shivered immediately, her body no longer listening to her mind. The crowd began to roar, and the archbishop placed a hand over his mouth.

Ozik gripped her wrist and yanked her arm forward. "Prove to this city that she is no witch," Ozik said. "Her curse has been cleansed."

Vaasa fought the urge to bare her clattering teeth. This was a useless test, entirely misguided. Her eyes landed upon the clergyman who had scribbled notes at Lord Vlacik's behest just the day prior. He knew this would prove nothing. Witches bled the same color as anyone.

But the archbishop dug the knife into her palm and slashed.

Vaasa grit her teeth to contain a pained cry. Red blood ran over her palm and through her fingers, dripping to the stone platform below. A cut that deep would take *weeks* to heal.

"There is no curse here!" the archbishop bellowed into the crowd. "After what she has endured, we should welcome our heiress home with open arms. It takes great strength to look the devil in the eyes and refuse him."

Home?

This was *not* home.

Roaring applause and screams filled the square, but Vaasa didn't hear them at all. Bells rang out from the cathedral, the sound echoing in her weary mind. In the haze of the onlookers and the flurry of the guard around her, Vaasa's gaze wandered across the square until it reached the Sanctum, her eye catching the topmost room, which belonged to the emperor and his family. She remembered being nineteen and watching from that room as they executed a notorious pirate. As the executioner sharpened his blade, every pair of eyes clung to the promise of carnage. That evening, when the nobles and her father celebrated their retribution, Vaasa had slipped into one of the servant's halls with Roman Katayev, the sentinel she had loved for perhaps her entire youth.

I wonder if justice is ever that simple, Roman had whispered in Vaasa's ear. She'd wrung her hands, trying to forget the taste of her father's violence and disappointment. It wasn't reserved for only criminals; she had been no stranger to his cruel discipline, nor to Dominik's, but Roman's question had fueled the part of her that had been exposed to enough stories and learned to begin questioning the cruelty of the men around her.

Now, as she stared upon that building, shivering in the cold, she retreated to that tiny sliver of light and warmth, escaped into the teenage memory of Roman out of habit. After all, taking refuge in that boy had once been an unbreakable pattern. She'd tried so many times to quit, but every time he had pulled her back in, until her father's simple justice had ended in Roman's death.

"Walk," Ozik hissed in Vaasa's ear, pulling her back into the present. She stumbled down the platform, the city guard forming a wall around her as the crowd pushed and trampled to get closer. Ozik's narrative was an easy one to believe, and Vaasa heard it whispered in the crowd: He had rescued her from Icruria, from the man who had murdered Dominik Kozár. What a brutal, terrible marriage he had saved her from.

Now she was nothing but a damaged, broken victim, harmless in their eyes. Not a witch. Ozik knew something profound about human nature—in order to be considered a threat, power was a prerequisite. To convince these people she wasn't a danger, he had to strip her of it.

So here she was, their poor, beloved heiress, bruised and bleeding in the snow. Her clothing torn, dirt smeared across every visible inch of her. Never mind that the freshness of her bruises didn't line up with the time it would take to journey from Icruria to Mekës. That he could have bathed her at any point along such a journey, could have let her keep her cloak to cover it all up. No, these people didn't care.

They wanted to be fed fiction.

Behind her, the archbishop and his clergy were led into an open-top carriage pulled by two chestnut horses. Ozik remained at her side. He paraded her through the streets, forced her to walk from the public port all the way to the looming Iron Fortress. Every painful step she took, the crowd screamed in performative sympathy. Their voices closed in on her. Instead of listening to them, she went somewhere else in her mind: a new refuge, an escape from this city.

The witches' tower in the Sodality of Setar, vines hanging from swaying pots and the smell of parchment permeating every inch of the room. In her mind's eye, she gazed at each shining face of her coven. Suma's salt-and-pepper hair, her graceful smile. Romana and Mariana, the twins that never were, mischievous glances shared between them. Amalie, alive and well, her softness a strength.

Melisina, her amber eyes and deep carved wisdom. The calmness of her voice as she guided Vaasa toward healing.

And then it was a white willow tree, the Icrurian breeze passing over the veranda outside Reid's villa. *Her* villa. The home her own great-grandmother, Freya, the very founder of the Veragi coven, had once lived in. Vaasa sank into that vision, pretended she could feel the wind on her skin. The rancid smell of ocean salt turned Icrurian sweet.

It threaded with amber.

In her mind, she wasn't alone. Arms wrapped around her waist from behind and pressed her into the low stone wall that lined the veranda, surface warm from the sun. Her midriff was bare, loose breeches tied at her belly button. Her inky hair lifted in the breeze.

Reid placed his chin on her shoulder.

As they neared the fortress, she was still there in another time, another place, another world.

And in that vision, she turned her head and laid her cheek against Reid's, neither of them having anything pressing to do but stay right where they were.

CHAPTER 4

Reid spun, thrusting his polearm between the plates of an enemy soldier's armor. A hook at the end of the weapon caught in the man's gut, tangling his intestines. Reid yanked the weapon back. A scream tore from his opponent's throat before the man fell to his knees and then onto his face in the viscous mud that coated the edge of the Innisjour riverbank.

If people ran, they lived. If they stayed in their homes, they lived.

If they fought, they died.

The first village that Reid's forces took left a crimson stain upon the Asteryan map. It had taken weeks to cross the continent this way, though his initial descent into northern Asterya had lasted only days. Civilians had been displaced, the northern provinces of Asterya studded with the bodies of Asteryan mercenaries—Reid would carry that choice until the day he died. The shared border between Asterya and Icruria was now blurred, having been stretched to the point of snapping.

A scream sounded to the right. One of his men's fire lances ignited, sending flames directly into the face of an Innisjour soldier. Another man darted at Reid from the left. He turned, driving the blade into the man's gut. Sweat dripped down Reid's forehead. He'd been blinking it from his eyes and wiping mud from his face for weeks now. Asteryans functioned on organized assaults; Icrurians did not fight that way. It was madness the way Reid's men broke through the Asteryan lines all around him, weaving and turning in formations that to someone with inferior training might appear random. To his left, men fell into the water to put out the flames from the fire lances, but fights raged from vessels upon the river, too.

The dam built in Innisjour by Vaasa's father had choked the water supply to eastern Icruria. It had been the key to the late Emperor Kozár's strategy; to cut Icruria off from the water was to cut the east off from its agriculture. The resulting drought and famine had left the region in shambles and given rise to the rebellion that had almost ruined Reid's claim to headman. At the election, Ton of Wrultho had conspired with Reid's own advisor to stage a coup. Both of those men were now at the bottom of the Settara, the salt lake Reid had called home his entire life.

The fissure between Icrurian territories was still wide. Which meant that if Reid wanted to gather an army large enough to conquer Asterya's capital, he needed more than their central forces. And their navy. He needed militias—and there were no better militias than the ones trained in Wrultho and Hazut.

He needed to make amends with those cities, which meant Innisjour's dam would need to fall.

And fall it would.

There was a singular thrill that coursed in Reid's veins as he moved, sinking his weapon into the side of another man. Adrenaline beating, heart thudding against his own breastplate, mud and blood spraying upon his face; violence was easy, dancing in tandem with his anger and fear. It took energy to be gentle. Most of the time, Reid thought it worth the effort.

Not now.

Not with his wife halfway across the continent, locked in his greatest enemy's capital.

The thought of Vaasa's raven hair, her indigo eyes alight with fear, blood smeared across her cheeks and hands, fueled each thrust of his weapon. Two more men fell. A third. Reid could practically hear his father's voice in his ear as he fought, guiding him, warning him, providing him the sixth sense that told him to spin and lift his polearm, the axe blade settled beneath the protruding, deadly hook at the end of the spear slicing through the arm of a soldier with a raised sword.

With each enemy vanquished, he wondered if it was enough. If anything would ever be enough to sate his rage.

Body after body approached, and each one fell. Reid left a trail of them as Innisjour shook with his force's descent. And then whispers threaded the air, turning to a billowing white flag as the young lord of Innisjour instructed his men to retreat.

Weary and battle-worn, Reid approached Lord Rezek of Innisjour outside the grounds of his estate. The young man could only be at the start of his third decade, his inexperience only serving to make him seem younger. Fear washed over the lord's soft features—his clean, bloodless, untouched face.

Lord Rezek wore clothing Reid recognized as classically Asteryan, similar to the ones Vaasa had arrived at Mireh in, the long pants and threaded cloaks like her brother and Ozik had donned when they visited. Pristine, expensive, entirely kempt. This lord had not fought today. He'd hidden in his estate upon the river, protecting his wealth instead of the lives of his people.

Reid gestured his forces forward as the sky turned shades of red and orange, the day transitioning into night. The young lord protested in frantic Asteryan as Reid's men pulled at his arms and kicked him to his knees before the iron gate that protected his gray stone manor. Now kneeling, the man stained the front of his pants dark with urine.

Reid towered over Rezek, unmoved by his whines. "Take what you need—give every servant quarter," he instructed his men, who marched through the iron gates.

"I have a message for you," Lord Rezek said in shaky Asteryan, Koen translating quietly beside Reid. "You cannot kill me."

Reid was too tired to play games. His arms felt heavy, his weapon even more so. "Speak, or your head will roll."

Koen translated again, and the lord's eyes went wide. "I have papers," he rushed. "In my coat pocket. A delivery from Mekës itself. I was instructed to give these to you. I was told it would save my life."

Reid froze as Koen translated the words.

The lord had waited until his city crumbled, until the riverbank had turned red from all the spilled blood, before playing his final card. Reid waited wordlessly as one of his men pulled the documents from the lord's pocket, handing them to Koen.

Koen scanned them, worrying his lip as he did so. Koen was Reid's dearest friend, the closest thing he had to a brother, and would now serve as a councilor during Reid's tenure as headman. Koen's face was entirely readable at this point in their camaraderie, and it was a mixture of anguish and worry that lived in the pull of his mouth. "What is it?" Reid demanded, barely mustering the energy to speak.

"They are papers of dissolution," Koen said in Icrurian, meeting Reid's eyes. "Ozik has annulled your marriage to Vaasalisa. He claims you have broken your original agreement by marching upon Asterya."

Reid stayed utterly silent. His fingers twitched around his weapon, which sat starkly in his closed fist. This didn't matter the way Ozik wanted it to matter. Ozik had no claim over Icrurian law, and they had been married in Icruria. He was still Vaasa's husband, and she still his wife.

"These papers mean nothing," Reid said.

"They are signed by their archbishop. This eliminates any lawful claim you have to the Asteryan throne," Koen argued.

Reid grit his teeth. Fury tore through him like a knife. Flicking his eyes to the young lord, he wondered why Ozik would send this in an attempt to save the man's life—it would only serve to anger Reid.

And that's when he realized that Ozik wanted this man dead.

"I never said I would take this empire lawfully." Reid stepped forward until his boot almost hit the knee of the young lord. "What do you know of my wife?" he demanded.

Some men might have argued, or stayed silent, or displayed a modicum of courage with their words. The young Lord Rezek was not one of those men. Koen translated every desperate word the man blubbered. "She is alive, walking the fortress of Mekës as we speak. All of the unmarried lords and heirs have been summoned to the castle—she is said to be in pursuit of a husband."

Reid crumpled the papers in his hands. Turning to the general who helped lead their descent upon Innisjour, he commanded, "Demolish the dam."

The general nodded, her stern eyes holding his for only a moment before she turned to bellow commands at the soldiers waiting for her instructions.

"And the lord?" Koen asked quietly.

Reid once again tightened his fist around his polearm. The young lord had surrendered, yet Reid couldn't think past the red tinge of his vision or the roaring in his ears. Reid's father had raised him in the light of many values, not the least of which was that a leader was ultimately responsible for the instructions they gave to their forces.

"The rest of his men will live," Reid told Koen.

And then Reid turned, driving the wicked blade of his polearm through the lord's gut before the young man even realized he was going to die.

CHAPTER 5

Guards crawled all around the inner ward of the Iron Fortress, their eyes fixed on Vaasa and Ozik as the two higher-ranked sentinels outside their carriage pulled her gingerly to unsteady feet.

Suddenly, they were gentle with her.

The other fortress guards watched, and Vaasa got the feeling this was the new story. It was unlikely anyone knew where she'd been these past six weeks. This entire fortress believed precisely what Ozik had spun in the city square—she had been rescued from the clutches of Icruria. Saved by Asteryan forces. Cleansed of the curse Reid of Mireh had placed upon her.

Most of the fortress staff kept straight-faced, but a few whispered to each other, and others just dropped their jaws in awe. Ozik extended her an arm. Amalie's face flashed behind Vaasa's eyes, and fear made a home in her gut. She took Ozik's extended arm and hated herself for it.

The Iron Fortress jutted from the mountainside like claws reaching into the frostbitten air. Ten black spires grew to unprecedented heights, with dangerous iron-coated points that had graced the tops since her grandfather built the monument. It was he who had mined the deep mountains others called unworkable, he who had forged iron into steel and conquered the snow-bound bay. The Iron Fortress was a testament to her grandfather's strength, something her father had inherited—something Vaasa and Dominik were meant to inherit, too.

Stained glass windows reflected light in a rainbow of color, snow blanketing the patios and exterior walkways. All the towers were connected by stone pathways arching over a garden or courtyard. Yet within the sturdy mountain rock were carved tunnels, effectively creating a system of travel around the fortress for servants and secrets.

Her eyes caught upon the far side; a greenhouse loomed, seemingly built into the mountain itself, and behind it, the valley between peaks created a natural game park where they hunted their food.

They plunged into an empty hallway with no windows and no open air. Vaasa put one foot in front of the other. Eventually the pathway wound to the western side of the fortress, and they passed one of the hidden entrances into the servants' hallways, which were a maze of dingy, connected pass-throughs that gave the servants access to most parts of the fortress at any given time. Various tucked-away doors marked their entrances and exits. Some were entirely secret, built behind bookcases or tapestries. She'd snuck through those corridors more and more as she'd gotten older, avoiding Dominik, avoiding her father, or sneaking around to meet Roman.

Each inch of space here was a memory, her body recognizing every step she took. She couldn't breathe. Not as the air of the fortress closed around her. There was so much death, so much grief and darkness splattered along these wicked halls.

She forced herself to pull deep, calming breaths the way the coven had taught her, a desperate attempt to dismiss the onslaught of memories so vivid they could have been carved into the walls as relics.

"Is there a lead sentinel?" she asked, her voice shaking. A vice-captain, one of the highest ranks for a soldier in this fortress, and the person who would command her own personal guard. There was normally one assigned per member of the royal family, and they reported only to the captain of the guard. When Dominik took the throne, he likely instituted his own men instead of their father's.

Ozik confirmed with a sharp nod. "There is."

"And where is he?"

"Out," one of the guards said. She glanced at his brooches; a lower-ranking sentinel, but not cannon fodder.

Vaasa sighed, but didn't pry further. She didn't have the energy, especially as they came upon familiar double doors: her parents' old wing of the fortress. While this particular hallway led to a variety of necessities, like their private kitchen and game rooms, it was the door at the end that they dragged her toward.

The emperor and empress's private quarters. The very rooms where she had found her mother's body drained of color and life.

Panic flared in her chest; she couldn't go in there. She skidded to a stop, backing up, and the sentinel who escorted them blocked her path. In moments, he had her hands behind her back, restrained. "No," she bleated, trying to fight his grip. She struggled like a toddler, throwing her body to the floor, only to be caught harshly and pulled back up.

"It'll be all right," Ozik told her in such calm tones. "You'll readjust."

"Please," she begged, her voice a choked whisper so low she wasn't certain anyone could hear it. She looked to the sentinels and could tell by their drawn expressions that they would offer her no reprieve. They likely saw her reaction as nothing more than a consequence of her time in Icruria; there were so few sentinels at the prison compared to the fortress, so few people who knew the truth. Ozik needed it that way.

To them, she was broken.

"You will be the empress of Asterya," Ozik told her as if he were soothing some wild animal. "This wing belongs to you."

Ozik touched her arm gently, but she flinched.

"Please, don't make me do this," she whispered, and she wished they were alone. With anyone else around, every reaction he had would be measured, intentional, and planned. He and her father had taught her that very mechanism.

He tilted his head as if he were speaking to a child. "In time, you will have a better understanding of the strength that can be gained from remembering."

Every inch of her body was a cavern: a place where love and hope and magic had until recently resided, but no longer. That space was filling with adrenaline, agony, terror. All familiar friends.

Ozik turned away from her and wandered back down the hall. He disappeared around the corner, not bothering to stay to make sure she entered the rooms—he knew perfectly well that she would. That she had no choice.

Because Amalie was dead if she refused.

As the sentinels opened the doors, movement caught her eye. At the end of the hall was the familiar frame of someone speaking to Ozik, but they disappeared before she could catch sight of them in full. Then she was thrown into her parents' quarters, the door slamming loudly behind her.

Vaasa did not move from the foyer.

She stared down the hallway, her back pressed to the entrance door, and slid down to the marble floor. All the doors down the right hallway belonged to her mother, all the ones down the left to her father. No matter which direction she went, the outcome was the same.

Vaasa saw herself, young and afraid, hiding in her mother's closet while Dominik ran around the fortress like a malevolent king. Her mother's coolness flashed behind Vaasa's eyes.

Come out from there, she'd said. *You are too old for this childish game.*

Dead.

Everyone who once lived in these rooms was dead.

Vaasa did not move. Fear was unwilling to release her from its clawed grasp, its talons curled around her heart.

You will die here, too.

Vaasa squeezed her eyes shut. It all crested over her then.

Mathjin's voice as it cracked on "grandfather."
Amalie's screams.
Her brother's head, severed from his body.
Reid's lifeless weight in her lap.

Ozik's snarling lip as he stole her magic.
The cold of the prison.
The cut of Lord Vlacik's blade.

Vaasa tried to stand. She searched for courage or strength or rationality, but could find none of them. The only thing left in her was the faint trickle of magic that seemed to wind around her abdomen. Ozik was there on the other side. It was a simmering power just below the surface, like a thin layer of gauze over a wound curdled with infection.

Vaasa shook. She rocked back and forth. Every time she thought she was ready to stand, her body simply . . . wouldn't.

At some point, she rested her cheek upon the cold stone floor.

At some point, her body gave out completely.

At some point, she slept.

Vaasa had no taste for sunlight or crisp air or the way snow glistened when it fell. She had once known these as a reprieve, a moment of peace cut through the violence of her surroundings. But she did not long for peace anymore. She craved blood and steel cutting through skin and a cry so piercing it would bring the snow on the mountains plummeting down.

She stared at Ozik across the dinner table.

For a week now, he had forced her to hold court at the Sanctum like a pathetic stand-in for her father. She had met with the other members of her father's advisory council and judicial body. For hours, she listened to their placating compliments and slimy reaches for power, all of them wondering if they would keep their positions when she took a husband. If there was a path to the salt. Half of them looked to Ozik for answers, the other half to her. This was uncharted territory—Vaasa wasn't the emperor, but she was the closest thing to it, and they likely assumed she would have her eventual husband's ear. Yet Ozik was a man. For many of them, that mattered more.

"Eat," Ozik commanded, forcing Vaasa back into the present. His golden eyes didn't budge from her, like a hawk's focused on prey. "Take advantage of the quiet meals before the rest of the nobility arrives."

Stained glass windows covered the perimeter of the room and soaked the table in a treacherous orange and red, the sunset bleeding through the patterns that overlooked the angry, churning ocean. A small feast was sprawled across the oak table: a mild white fish drenched in a steaming broth made from golden leeks and bloodred beetroot, potatoes swimming alongside it, and a loaf of warm bread.

Vaasa picked up the fork. She speared a potato and brought it to her mouth, fighting against the urge to gag, but the taste of food made her want to vomit on the pretty plates and streaks of gold woven into the tablecloth. She did not deserve to eat so richly while her friend rotted in a dungeon.

"Have you reviewed the correspondence your brother left?" Ozik asked.

Vaasa kept her eyes on her food. She hadn't set foot in her father's office, and she wasn't sure she intended to. She had no interest in this nation, no care for what became of it. Her only hope was that Reid would manage to get an army through the Loursevain Gap and obliterate any chance Asterya had of holding its territories.

And that she and Amalie would still be alive when he did.

A disbelieving *tsk* rolled off Ozik's tongue. "If you aren't going to cooperate, perhaps I should give Lord Vlacik what he wants and marry you to him now."

She narrowed her eyes, lifting her goblet to her mouth and taking a long drink as she considered her options. The simple truth was that she would slaughter Lord Vlacik and mark herself a traitor before she spent a single moment in his wedding bed. The act might condemn both Amalie and herself to death, but if their roles were reversed, Vaasa would willingly go to a burning stake before Amalie spent one night beholden to the lust of a man like that.

"If the lord is your choice, then so be it," she muttered obstinately, standing from the table.

Without warning, her abdomen lit on fire, and magic was wrenched from wherever it hid within her. She choked on her wine and tried to move her hands, but they were caught, weighed down on the table by some invisible force. Slickness ran over her skin, the feel of Ozik's raw magic slippery and wet. Breath pushed from her lips in harsh bursts, memories of her time in the prison sliding back into place and stealing her calm.

Her hands began to shake, and the absence of her power hit her like losing air. Something in her body clawed for it, nails sinking into the sides of her stomach and digging deeper and deeper to find that magic. But as she delved into herself, what she found wasn't the hissing of a snake or the waves of the Settara or the wolf with bright white eyes.

It was just that single, shimmering cord that tied her to Ozik.

Everywhere she searched in her own body, she found the remnant of him there—attached to her, woven into the threads of her muscles and wrapped around her bones. One long string, tangled in so many places it had become a spiderweb. The deeper she pushed, the more of them there were. He had taken over the spaces where her magic used to reside and had replaced them with these . . . *things*. She found that she could run her own fingers upon them, pluck the threads like an instrument and create the wails of high and low notes, music in her mind and body. And as she did, she felt the ties between them tighten.

There was something there on the other side.

She reached for it. Something glowed crimson behind her eyes.

And then pain splintered down her spine. She was being ripped in two.

Vaasa choked, and her hands slammed against the table.

"*Enough!*" Ozik yelled.

Vaasa's eyes flew open as she gasped in a breath. "What was that?" she demanded through the haze of her pain.

Ozik's anger crawled across their connection, his emotions so clear to her, so easily perceptible. A large three-pronged serving fork that rested against the platter of meat in front of her slid off the plate. Horror sliced into her. The fork turned itself over in midair, prongs pointing downward.

And then it dropped with terrifying speed and stabbed straight through Vaasa's hand, exiting through her palm as muscles severed and bones cracked.

Vaasa screamed, and Ozik's chair hissed against the ground as he stood.

Vaasa breathed heavily through her nose, trying to will the pain away without moving further.

"I raised you to be an active participant in the schemes around you," Ozik said. "I know you are capable." His measured footsteps echoed on the rug-covered floor until he was just in front of her. Hands landing on the table, he leaned into her space. His eyes inspected the stream of blood pouring down Vaasa's fingers, catching his gaze upon the place where the utensil stuck out of her mangled hand. Tears welled in Vaasa's eyes, and one escaped in a droplet that ran down her cheek.

A carnal smile crossed Ozik's lips. "You are not strong enough to burrow that deep into our connection. Remember the consequence of breaking a bargain with a Zetyr witch."

Death.

Vaasa winced, looking down at the table again, eyes focusing on the rings upon Ozik's fingers. The jewels glared back brightly at her, and it was all she could do to keep her eyes open. In her mind, she began to count the gems on each one. Every number was a piece of her sanity, every breath a reminder she was alive. Ozik's fingers flexed. Her eyes caught upon one ring in particular: a black stone ring with raw edges that made the stone look like it had been broken off a larger piece. There was a subtle churning in the vast darkness of it, and despite herself, Vaasa committed it to memory.

Ozik tsked again, and the fork slid further into her hand, causing Vaasa to cry out in pain as the metal prongs dug deeper into the table beneath her palm. Her breath came out as a hiss between her teeth. She didn't say anything. She focused on her breathing instead, her eyes watering from the sharp tremors shooting up her hand. She swallowed back more tears, but Lord Vlacik's sharp blue eyes appeared in her mind.

The feel of iron scraping over her throat. Of blinding pain in her hands and feet.

"Brace yourself," Ozik said.

He tore the fork from her hand, and Vaasa let out a strangled scream.

Magic reared up in her stomach, immediately responding to the pain, to the pounding of her heart. Vaasa gasped as power flooded her body—her stomach, her veins, her chest. It tingled on her hands. The spider's web in her body turned to writhing serpents, hisses echoing in her ear and mind.

Black mist leaked from Vaasa's fingers, coasting over the table around her dinner napkin. It morphed in front of her, soft sibilations growing louder with each second, until snakes slithered across the table.

Ozik had given her magic back.

She tried to hold it within her, to temper the rage of the power with the calmness she needed to master. But she couldn't. Her magic was a waterfall, returning angry and unstoppable. The pain in her stomach almost matched the fork that had been in her hand. Black snakes trailed along the table in scurrying waves. They rose and rose and rose—

"Strike me, and I will strike back," Ozik warned.

Vaasa snapped her eyes to meet his. Her hands squeezed shut, blood running through her fingers.

The serpents on the table halted. They moved their heads back and forth in agitated esses, waiting, craving the violence brewing within Vaasa.

Ozik straightened. He reached for her hand, eyes catching on the blood that stained the white tablecloth. Vaasa recoiled.

"Sit still," Ozik commanded. His fingers snapped around her hand. Power pulsed forth from him, and the cords between them pulled taught.

You are in control, she whispered in her own mind.

Her fingers dug into the tablecloth, and she took note of the feel of the fabric against her skin. It was a poor excuse for grounding, but it was the best she could do. The feeling of his magic crawling through her body was almost too much to bear, but Vaasa forced herself to breathe through it. To remember everything Melisina had taught her.

Like he was a Zuheia witch all on his own, the wound on her hand sewed itself back together.

Vaasa gasped, heart thudding against her chest. She stared at the result of his unrestrained magic—a smooth, scarless hand absent of even the remnant of the cut the archbishop had dealt. It all made a mess of her mind.

"*How?*" Vaasa managed through the burning in her gut.

He only lifted his golden eyes, though there was a tinge of something there, a redness creeping into his irises. An exhaustion overtaking his frown. "You have two days before the lords arrive. Read your brother's correspondence, and perhaps I will show you."

He pulled at her magic like it was a noose around her neck. The black mist within her rushed down whatever bound her to Ozik, entering those cords and draining away as if on a whim. She was empty.

Ozik stepped away from the table, sauntering wordlessly to the door. She almost got up to follow him. Almost gave in to her younger self, who reached for whatever information he could offer. Answers were a refuge Vaasa desperately wanted.

She stood from the table and began toward her family's chambers, determination steeling her spine.

CHAPTER 6

Vaasa stood at the edge of the left hallway, eyes fixed on the wooden door she knew led into her father's study.

This side of the quarters was far less panic inducing. When her father had died in his own bed, it had looked like illness. A fever, strange nightmares, thrashing at night. Then his body had simply . . . stopped.

But Vaasa knew that wasn't the truth. That Ozik had done it.

Vaasa thought of the Settara, of the cool water and the way magic had felt in her abdomen. She took one step. Then another. Dread filled her chest. Still, she pretended that she walked along that shoreline. Thought only of that and the door.

Urgency—this desperate instinct to *run*—assaulted her. It felt as if someone stood behind her, knife in hand, ready to plunge it through her back. Like at any moment, her life would be claimed. She broke into a sprint down the long hallway, heaving down breath. It was irrational—there was no one chasing her, there was no real danger. But her body did not believe her mind. She gripped the handle and threw herself into the office.

Vaasa pressed her back to the door, taking deep breaths in and out. When she opened her eyes, her hands fell from the door behind her.

Bookshelves lined three of the four walls in the ample-sized office, a sliding ladder able to travel across them all. Black archways carved the center shelves and drew her eye, rows and rows of books studding the scene. A large russet leather chair sat next to the fireplace. The firebox had been well tended—with a flint and steel, Vaasa stoked a fire. She stood from her crouch and gazed around again, eventually staring at the dark wooden desk in the center of the room.

Her late brother hadn't changed a thing. Vaasa wondered if Dominik had silently wanted to be more like their father than he'd let on. He'd had the opportunity to make this study anything he wanted it to be, yet her father's golden hourglass still sat in the very left corner of the desk like a beacon to a life that no longer drew breath.

Vaasa ran her fingers over the cool surface, remembering a time when she had sat on the other side of this desk and spent hours translating correspondence her father's soldiers had recovered from the once-unconquered center of Asterya. The correspondence had been written in code, making the dialect even more difficult for Vaasa to recognize, but the root language had been enough to uncover at least the purpose of the letters.

That same civilization had been reduced to ruins, and now the Karev family oversaw the territory from the castle her father had built for them upon those grasslands. Lord Karev was one of many contenders who would be on his way, the smell of blood in the water bringing every shark to their shore.

Her hand grazed the bookshelf on the far-left side of the room, hand landing on an iron-hewn statue of an owl. She gripped its head and pulled, and like a lever, it cranked forward.

Vaasa pushed the shelf. It opened into a sinister tunnel, pitch-black. Her heart started to race again. Just as quickly as she'd opened it, Vaasa closed the entrance to one of the fortress's escape routes. When her father had built this new wing and abandoned the old emperor's quarters on the far side of the fortress, he'd demanded this exit be built. Should they ever be attacked and unable to hold the fortress, the passageway would grant their family a way out and eventually into a secret apartment they kept in the main city. As a teenager, Vaasa had abused the presence of the tunnel, knowing when her father wasn't here and sneaking through it to meet Roman and his friends, disguised as anyone but herself. Her heart lurched into her throat.

They were all dead now.

Sitting in the oversized black leather chair just behind the oak desk, Vaasa began to thumb through each of the drawers. They contained various papers and notes on the happenings in each of Asterya's provinces, including financial logs and the reports of their supplies. Despite herself, the gathering of information was a grounding of sorts. Her foolishness sank its teeth into her—she would need to commit this all to memory by the time the lords arrived if she had any hope of navigating the new political landscape. Most of it was boring, but she was already at a disadvantage. Given she couldn't take the throne without marrying one of them, she would have to cling to any ounce of power she could wield. She didn't know what would become of Asterya, but she couldn't let it swallow her whole.

She took her own diligent notes, resorting to a notebook that felt foreign in her hands. She briefly thought of her own notebook, the one Melisina had helped her find that still wove her and Reid together, but the memory was too sharp. Too jagged.

She forced down a deep breath, then another, then another. She could do this.

Vaasa tucked each piece of information about Asterya away as if it would save her. She had always found solace in knowledge. Knowledge was where power lay.

Tiptoeing out of the office, Vaasa peered into the hallway to check for any remaining attendants. There were none. They must have retired for the evening. She slipped back into the office and sat in the chair, taking in a calming breath.

Quiet as a mouse, she used her fingers to delicately trace over the lines on the bottom of the desk. They caught upon the faintest groove. Vaasa dug her nail into the slit opening, and with a little prying, the false bottom of the desk unlatched.

There was nothing except a dark-brown leather journal tied together with a golden string. Her father had kept his most valuable notes here—another secret between her and him. He had never shared this much with Dominik, paranoid that his own son would come to claim the throne before he was ready to release it. Andrej Kozár had not seen Vaasa as a threat, so he didn't realize when he'd turned her into one.

Seemingly, Dominik had found this drawer. He had replaced the contents with something of his own. Unsuspecting and unlabeled—if the journal hadn't been hidden in this secret compartment, she would easily have passed over it. Softness pressed to her fingertips, and she knew the notebook had been well-worn, its leather soft and supple. Tentatively, she opened the first page, eyes scanning over the worn parchment.

She knew the bold lines of her brother's handwriting, had looked upon it more times than she cared to count during their shared tutelage. But his notes were accompanied by detailed charcoal sketches, somewhat of a signature of his. Art. It began with flora and fauna found around the fortress, proof of a young boy's hand and imagination. Notes turned to fantasy—the pages were littered with things Vaasa had never seen but had read in the folklore she'd acquired from the territories her father eventually conquered. Rabbits with horns, deer with the tails of a fish, even a wolf with wings jutting from its shoulders like a mighty god.

Keep your head in the clouds, her father once hissed at a twelve-year-old Dominik, *and you'll lose it*.

Their mother had glared at Vaasa then, at the place she'd perched on the edge of her father's desk, Dominik narrowing his eyes along with her. Pride had coursed through Vaasa at being the one who made their father proud. Now it just made her feel ashamed.

With the journal in her hands, every memory Vaasa had of Dominik became tinged with something else. He'd been much like their great-grandmother Freya, hadn't he? The paintings on the second floor of the Veragi witch's tower flashed behind Vaasa's eyes. The white willow tree Freya had illustrated in every season, a mark of

Vaasa's heritage in Icruria. In Mireh. The place Vaasa had traced her maternal bloodline to.

Vaasa lowered her eyes.

This entire time, Vaasa had seen her mother's discovered lineage as her own, as belonging to only her. But Dominik shared her blood. What was hers was his, too, down to the bloody legacy of their father and the death of their mother. And in all that darkness, he'd once been a boy who loved to draw.

And she had murdered him. Severed his head and thrown it into a crowd.

Vaasa's hands shook, and she debated closing the notebook. She wasn't certain she had any right to look upon it. What she had done had been the only way to save her life, she reminded herself. He'd intended to kill her.

Hero or villain, hero or villain, her mind whispered. It was a two-faced coin, and she didn't know which side she had landed on.

Vaasa forced herself to turn the page. The further she went, the more menacing the subjects became. Where the playful lines of a boy entranced with fiction once thrived, there were now depictions of death and mindless scribbles. Angry strokes cut through sketches like jagged scars, marking the things Dominik did not like. Labeling his own work as intolerable. Vaasa turned another page.

Her breath caught in her throat and swelled.

The Miro'dag.

The creature of oil and darkness stained the paper in a perfect rendition of each curve, every snag of its wings placed precisely where they belonged. She ran her fingertips over the spikes on both of the wings that served as replacements for where arms should have been. Along the curling horns that ripped mercilessly from the top of its head and stroked downward to its waist with one flick of Dominik's wrist. Ribs poking out from broken skin like prisoners dying to escape. The drawing she looked upon was technically perfect and frightening in its accuracy.

And beneath it, one word: *Zetyr*.

She immediately turned the page again and found scribbled numbers in the harsh lines of Dominik's handwriting. There was a list of them, little scratches in sequential order. Vaasa turned to the bound files behind her, stacked upon bookshelves that covered the back wall and two sidewalls.

She turned back to the numbers. It took a moment for it to click, but this was simply a code their father had taught them once upon a time—a way to mask his notes from wandering eyes. Vaasa got to work translating the numbers into letters, falling into a somewhat cathartic routine of solving a puzzle.

Standing and perusing the shelves, she plucked out the first notebook indicated in Dominik's journal. She began to flip through it, her heart pounding as she read, bile rising in her throat. Vaasa's hands started to shake.

It was a detailed account of the torture and execution of a woman her father's men had taken from one of the inland territories, written by the late Lord Vlacik, the dead father of the very man who had tortured Vaasa in the prison. Who now vied for the Asteryan throne through a betrothal to her.

This woman they tortured had been a witch. A Zohar witch, Vaasa remembered, given the woman could manipulate water. All Melisina's teachings came pouring back to her—the secrets of the covens, how Icrurian unification had decimated the witch population to few, if any, per coven. That was the true limiter of their magic: to only inherit it after a parent's death, to only ever have one witch per generation within a family. It made weaponizing magic difficult, and understanding it even more so. Witches weren't usually young people—they were men and women in the second half of their lives who had already put down roots and had entire families to lose if they fought.

With a heavy heart, Vaasa closed the bound notebook and moved on to the next one noted in Dominik's journal, finding a similar result. It was another notebook littered in entries from the late Lord Vlacik, but this time, the victim was a witch who could heal her own wounds. Zuheia, the goddess of healing, who could be traced back to Wrultho.

They had pushed and prodded the older woman, injuring her just to see if she was capable of mending the damage. The last entry described a rope they had rubbed in a processed form of iron, and then sealed. When placed upon the witch, she could no longer heal herself.

She had not survived the torture.

They had discovered beyond a shadow of a doubt that the processed iron was capable of cutting off whatever connection the witch had to her power. A shiver crawled down Vaasa's spine. Had that been the type of rope Dominik had used to tie Vaasa up under the colosseum in Dihrah? In the prison, iron chains had cut off her magic, even when Ozik had granted her access to it. They must have been coated in that same processed metal.

Vaasa read seven more accounts, each from a different territory that Vaasa's father had conquered, five of them contributed by the late Lord Vlacik. The two accounts at the end were done by the current Lord Vlacik, and Vaasa recognized Dominik's handwriting. There was another contributor, a clergyman, which indicated the beginning of the Asteryan church's involvement. It had been under Dominik's reign. Her father had been trying to contain witches' magic. But by the time Dominik was involved, the goal of the torture had changed. It became about manifesting it.

Vaasa reopened Dominik's notebook, flipping through the pages and scanning his drawings of the Miro'dag once more. There were no more mentions of Zetyr, but Dominik had known of the god Ozik gained his powers from—the god of bargains and souls. She kept turning, turning, until something slipped out of the pages in the back.

Folded in the notebook was a small parchment envelope that had been torn open, her mother's wax seal broken. Vaasa gently lifted the seal, the envelope's parchment dry and covered in fingermarks. This had been looked at more than once.

Inside was a small letter. As it unfolded, Vaasa's breath left her body.

Vaasalisa, her mother's handwriting began. *A wedding present. There is so little I can pass down to you other than pain. But I can give you this. It is the only thing that will protect you from him. Whatever you do, stay in Mireh and do not unite the other pieces. The price is far too great.*

Vaasa stared at the writing. She reread it again and again, her mind churning, her body feeling suddenly heavy and weightless at once. Who was *he*? What other pieces?

And what was the price?

The only person she could think of was Ozik.

Vena Kozár had arranged Vaasa's marriage the summer before she died, when she'd visited Mireh and trained with Melisina. This had apparently been paired with a wedding gift, one Dominik had never delivered.

As she looked at the page where the note had been hidden, she saw exactly what item her mother had been speaking of, drawn with Dominik's expert shading and strokes. Woven iron links fastened irrevocably to a small, ominous black stone.

Her mother's necklace.

She sucked in a breath. The obsidian piece on the necklace looked just like Ozik's black stone ring. How had she not made the connection before? She couldn't recall exactly when her mother had started wearing the necklace, but it had been a decorative fixture on Vena Kozár for years. Vaasa ran her fingers over the drawing, realizing something.

The necklace was missing.

She started to paw through the hidden compartment of the desk, but it was empty. She opened every drawer. No necklace. It was gone.

Her final conversation with Dominik played on a loop in her head. *I want to understand. To know why she gave you the one thing she knew would be a threat to me.* Vaasa had assumed he'd meant her marriage to Reid—that their mother had negotiated Vaasa's arrival in Mireh, her access to the Veragi coven and an ability to overcome what he believed to be a curse. But what if it was actually this? What if he had found the necklace and known something she didn't about what it was capable of?

The *him* Vena Kozár had written about . . . was it her lover, or her own son?

Vaasa closed Dominik's notebook, unable to look at it further. She wasn't certain she could ever bring herself to open it again. But one thing was definite: Her mother had sent her away from this place for a reason. She'd wanted to protect Vaasa from whatever Dominik and Lord Vlacik were doing.

Her mother had known she was in danger.

And Ozik had sent Vaasa into this office, knowing precisely what she would find.

CHAPTER

7

Water sloshed against the side of the boat, frozen and unforgiving, as Reid's footsteps echoed on pitted wood. He gazed out at a ship in the distance that seemed to be gaining on them.

Cold wind whipped through his hair. Running his hands along the banister, he took note of each imperfection on the Asteryan vessel that guided them through the narrow passageway separating Asterya and the Sheets; the short, clumsy thing would probably sink before they ever reached the other side. The dilapidated merchant's boat could very well crack open at the next sharp curve, plunging them into the frozen depths. He felt the ice of it in his bones, the water in his lungs, the darkness of drowning.

Reid shivered. All he had done for days now was shake in this cold. His hands felt like stone, numb and painful. Yet as it stood, this was the only way forward.

The story the rest of the continent would hear was clear: Reid of Mireh had been injured in a battle on the far side of the Iron Peaks just a few days ago. News of his retreat would arrive in Mekës in no time, and so his lack of appearance wouldn't raise any red flags to the Asteryans. They would mark him a coward and likely have a laugh.

Reid, on the other hand, would slip in under their noses. He'd taken a branch of the Sanguine that emptied into the icy ocean on the eastern side of the continent, on the trade route between Asterya and Zataar. This particular sea was littered with cays and infested with pirates, but this had been their only hope.

Meanwhile, Kosana moved their forces to strategic locations throughout northern Asterya—ready at the drop of a hat to resume the carnage and plunge into the Loursevain Gap. He was certain the Icrurian vessels could navigate it, or at least that his forces were skilled enough sailors to make it through. All they would fight were the pirates, but Kosana had assured him it was a task she could handle.

All Reid saw was raven hair and eyes a darker shade of indigo than the midnight water he had sailed across to get to her. Vaasa had told him she loved him, had *chosen* him, and now she would be no one else's so long as she wished it.

He was going to find her.

The captain of their ship rattled something off in Asteryan as the vessel in the distance grew even closer. It was gaining on them. Each moment it seemed to come nearer—and nearer—and nearer. Red sails whipped in the wind, no insignia upon them to mark who they sailed for. The vessel had speed, more so than this ship, and something about the look of it caused Reid to furrow his brows. Oars broke the surface and then plunged below.

An Icrurian vessel?

Reid turned to find the merchant dipping below deck—hiding, he realized—and as Reid gazed around, the mood of the crew shifted. Apprehension threaded the deck. Reid followed the merchant down the steep ladder to the cramped crew quarters, where the man spat off rapid-fire commands at people as if the crew had no real meaning to him.

Reid's mother sat with Koen at the only bolted-down bench, wrapped tightly in what little fabric the stingy merchant had to spare. It was too cold here for his mother. Her older bones were born and raised in the Icrurian heat. Koen's lips were a perpetual shade of blue as he eyed the desperate merchant who sat on the edge of the bench. The *warm* merchant. His beady gaze never shifted to Reid's.

The man's proximity itself was a warning—he usually didn't come near them. Only Reid's payment, salt by the pound, was going to save the boat beneath their feet. It was the reason the man had discreetly let their group board, Reid's "ailing" mother another part of their guise. So far, it seemed the merchant hadn't pinpointed who they really were. Their considerable resources depicted them as wealthy and lucky, someone with enough money and reason to travel to Mekës—and desperate, given his mother's supposed illness and the fresh border war. But their accents and Reid's lack of language revealed them to be anything but Asteryan, so the only hope was that the merchant believed them victims of the war Reid himself had started rather than a high witch, a councilor-elect, and the man who would be Icruria's headman in a matter of months.

The boat came to a halt. Scurrying footsteps sounded on the main deck, and then thud after thud after thud followed. Most of the crew members still in the hull raced toward the deck, only three staying, locking the hatch behind them.

That was when the screaming began.

Reid's mother rose to her feet. Reid started forward, but Koen gave one sharp shake of his head. He pushed his spectacles up his nose, his hand shaking slightly.

The merchant sat uselessly upon the bench and made no effort to stand. He only rocked back and forth. Reid reached for a dagger at his waist. He would have given anything to be on one of his own ships, with compartmentalized spaces he knew like the back of his hand. To be wearing warmer clothes that prevented this ache with each movement. His ear bent to the sound of voices, muffled and speaking a language he didn't understand.

Asteryan.

Another thud against the deck caused everyone below to go quiet.

The snapping of wood broke the silence: the lock on the hatch.

Boots appeared and slammed against the crew deck floor, carrying someone with them. A body unfurled of medium size and feminine build, and Reid was met with an audacious smile. A woman stood in front of them—light-red hair braided over both shoulders and sharp eyes the color of moss. She tilted her head. She wore animal furs and leather armor, looking warmer than all of them. Sharp blades, long and small, settled into sheaths on her thighs, waist, and arms. Full lips pursed as she looked them over, gaze landing mercilessly on the merchant. Raising her sword and pointing it at him, she spoke in Asteryan, a slight accent riding her words.

The merchant began to shake.

He looked their way, then back at her. Desperation flooded the merchant's response, and Reid didn't need to speak the same language to know the tone of it. He picked up on a few key words, *debt* being the most notable. Koen stepped in front of Reid's mother; Reid edged just slightly closer to Koen.

The red-haired woman snorted at the merchant, sliding her green eyes to them in what Reid thought might be disappointment.

Koen, who knew enough Asteryan to get them by, began to speak, and the moment he did, the woman furrowed her brow. She gestured her sword at the merchant, speaking in the common tongue of Icruria, sending shock into the pit of Reid's stomach.

"Did you know he would sell you out so quickly? He's just offered to let me have your entire party in exchange for me leaving his wares on his ship. A shame, I've been chasing this fool for months. He owes me a debt."

Reid stepped forward. "Who are you?"

"A pirate?" Koen ventured.

The woman grinned with the sharpness of a dagger. "Call it what you will."

"One who speaks Icrurian?" Reid asked.

"Apparently."

Behind him, his mother shuffled. Out of options, Reid felt himself being backed into a corner. He turned, gripping the merchant on his shoulder and spinning so he was behind him. He placed his dagger at the hollow of the merchant's throat.

The remaining men around them began to react, but before they could counter Reid, something hummed. Rattled, Reid realized. The vessel vibrated beneath his feet. A dozen or so rusted nails pulled from the wood making up the hull of the ship, lifted by some invisible force. The boards to his left shifted. Panic seared through Reid as the nails turned all at once, sharp edges pointed at them, and his eyes widened when he realized what had moved them.

Or who.

The pirate stood with her hands raised, the iron nails at her command. She said something in Asteryan, and the merchant shook uncontrollably in Reid's arms, seemingly more afraid of her than he was of the knife at his throat. He began to blubber in Asteryan, and Reid pressed his knife harder into skin.

"You're a witch," Reid said in Icrurian. "An Imros witch."

Hailing from Sigguth, Imros was the goddess of ore. Reid had met a few of the Imros coven in his life, but none as powerful as this woman seemed. To manipulate metal with such precision was more than magic—it was a gift.

The woman narrowed her eyes at him. "And you are?"

Reid's mind ticked like a clock. He had two options: Stay and die or find a way off the ship. Without another word, Reid sliced his knife across the merchant's throat. The man sank to the ground with a wretched gurgling sound. Blood oozed along the rickety wood at Reid's feet. The three men around them began to react, but before their screams could fill the air, black mist covered their noses and throats, plunging down their airways until the remaining crew fell wordlessly—lifelessly—to the deck.

The only person Melisina spared was the Imros witch. The confidence in the pirate's green eyes stuttered for only a moment, but the flash of fear had been there. She did not release the rusted nails, her fingers growing wider in what Reid thought was an attempt to contain the magic. He realized she shook with the effort. Untrained, then.

"*Who. Are. You?*" she demanded. This time, there was an edge to her voice.

"Icrurians," Melisina said, stepping out from behind Reid and raising her chin with pride. Mist still danced along her wrists and arms, spreading to the floor below and coating it like fog.

The two women filled every crevice in the space, their magic pulsing around the vessel like music whorling through the air. It was a sight to behold; Reid had scarcely seen Veragi magic intertwine with that of another coven. Only the witches of Una, and even that was a rarity.

"Drop the nails or we all drown," Melisina said.

The witch paused, but within two breaths, the nails clanged onto the floor.

"You paid him salt. She wields Veragi magic. Mirehans?"

Reid nodded, but didn't expand any further. Piracy was a wicked game, and he knew better than to reveal himself to someone who only honored a code among their crew.

"Well, best of luck," the pirate said casually, then she swung with one arm back onto the ladder and climbed.

Reid's jaw dropped, and Koen burst forward, hollering for her to wait. Reid followed him up onto the main deck, eyes widening as multiple people pilfered through anything available. Reid scanned his surroundings until he finally found the red-haired pirate. She swung from rope to rope like the ship was nothing but a playground, preparing to leap to her boat. Behind Reid, his mother emerged, hands grasping the bags of salt that Reid had given the merchant for his discretion. Blood was smeared on the outside of the canvas, but Melisina didn't seem to mind.

"Hey, you want these?" she called to the pirate.

The woman turned over her shoulder, dangling from one of the ropes, her braids flying in the wind. She swung loosely for a moment, as if unsure, but then turned her body and swung her weight back, the rope propelling her toward them. She landed and uncurled to her full height. "What exactly is your proposal?"

"Take us into the Iron Bay," Koen said, "and this salt is yours."

The pirate lifted her brow. "I'm not a guide."

The boat tipped, and Reid had to grip a stanchion in order to stay upright. Urgency stole his better senses. "What do you want?" Reid said, stepping forward. "If you get us there safely, whatever it is, it's yours."

Scrutiny seemed to come easy to the witch. She looked Reid up and down, the telltale signs of plotting swirling in the green of her eyes. "What sort of person makes a promise like that to the likes of me?"

"Someone who can make good on it."

A slow smile spread across her face. Deliberation didn't stain it, though, her eyes catching again on the bags of salt. "Why don't you come aboard and we can discuss terms?"

Gripping the rope, she swung with more grace and agility than Reid had ever seen across the gap separating their boats, not bothering to wait for further words. Her boots thumped on the boat opposite them. She sauntered across the deck, weaving through the swath of people darting this way and that.

"You know she'll likely kill us and keep the salt, right?" Koen said.

Reid only pursed his lips. He finally got a good look at the pirate's vessel across from theirs. It was Icrurian by design, no doubt fabricated in Sigguth like the rest of their ships. He was familiar with the hull and oarsbank, his fingers itching to get ahold of one of the oars that would help propel the ship forward. At least fifty stuck out, half in each direction. Except it wasn't *exactly* the same; there were mechanisms on it that he'd never seen before. Metal fixtures on the oars that attached them to the ship. Furrowing his brows, he inspected each inch he could see, making a note of the iron hinges.

"I'll go first, then," Reid said.

"Reid—" his mother tried.

"Stay. Here."

She huffed, muttering something under her breath. Reid avoided the body of the dead captain and grabbed ahold of the same ropes the pirate had used. In one graceful jump, he swung onto the opposite deck, his shoulders burning with the familiar motion, his numb hands scraping on the rough texture. He kept his eyes to himself, but a few of the pirate's crewmates whispered something at his arrival. He'd grown up on ships, had sailed them through the rivers in Icruria with his father, but this striking cold lent to a different kind of endurance. His body ached. He needed new clothing.

Koen and his mother waited across the platform the pirates were using to offload the ship. The pirate was nowhere in sight. People moved in every direction. Men and women both worked the vessel, so un-Asteryan in nature, and added further to the confounding puzzle in Reid's mind. A man with sharp, onyx eyes and broad shoulders sauntered over to them. He had dark-brown skin and a sturdy build, seemingly honed from his work on the ship. Others moved out of his way as he approached. He gestured toward the hatch. "Captain says you'll stay down there," he said in Icrurian, and Reid almost sighed in relief. He'd felt out of place listening to the indistinguishable Asteryan earlier and had an even greater appreciation for Vaasa. He was grateful to be back in the company of a language he understood.

The man placed his hand on Reid's shoulder. "The captain will see you in her quarters."

Reid turned to where Koen and his mother stood.

"We don't kill without reason," the man said. "Especially not another witch."

Reid met the man's eyes. He extended an arm, an Icrurian gesture, and Reid thought the show of it was pointless if he didn't mean it.

"Will you help my mother across?" Reid asked, taking the man's arm and giving one strong shake.

He nodded as if he truly meant it. "I will."

Reid turned, gesturing for Koen to start the journey across the narrow board. Reid walked the main deck and climbed until he found the low entrance to the captain's quarters. Heat wafted through the air, emanating from a firebox next to the desk. Reid almost sank to his knees in relief.

Warmth.

He wanted to walk up and hold his hands to it, but instead he surveyed the room. Inside was anything but simple—ornate silk curtains hung along stained glass windows, and oak furniture stood bold with carvings of leaves and roses in each piece. The lushly dressed bed boasted bright pinks and yellows. *Cheery* was the word that came to mind, so at odds with Reid's predetermined image of a pirate. But it was ostentatious, and he realized that whatever price this woman demanded would be large enough to make him blink.

Covering the opposite wall, there was artwork made entirely of iron, except as he gazed closer upon it, he realized it was a map. It depicted the entire coast and the Loursevain Gap, and then every river in Asterya and Icruria. It was the most accurate rendering he had ever seen, the offshoots perfectly scaled, the Sanguine curving until it hit the Settara and opened to the salt lake he had called home his entire life. Whoever these people were, they had sailed the entirety of this side of the continent. Had successfully navigated both warring nations and made it out alive.

The pirate sat behind a redwood desk, her knife out and spinning along the flat surface. She looked up, white teeth flashing as she asked, "So tell me, Reid of Mireh, do you have a plan for seizing the Iron Fortress, or are you just going in blind?"

CHAPTER 8

When the lords arrived, Vaasa did not curtsy or shake hands like the men; she lifted her chin and waited for them to bend at the waist.

Only one did not: Lord Vlacik. He reigned over Pryviske, a region not far from Mekës that wore its arrogance like a badge of honor. His family maintained access to the mines along the coastline that delivered much of Asterya's construction resources, and they were gifted Barken Palace, the old capital of Asterya before her grandfather had built this fortress on the Iron Bay. They'd held favor with the Kozár family for generations. There had been a time she was worried about being married off to the Pryviske estate, but Ozik had assured her of the impossibility. *We do not want them to grow any bolder*, he'd told her years prior. Now, as she gazed upon Lord Vlacik, she fought a shiver. His father was dead, and his younger sister had already borne an heir, making her and her husband a threat to Vlacik. He needed to marry, and quickly. Given what Vaasa had learned from Dominik's notes—that Vlacik's late father had been studying magic with her own father, that Vlacik and Dominik had carried on the tradition—he was a prime candidate.

Of all outcomes, a marriage to him was possibly the worst.

He stepped away from the dais, chin raised, and took his familial seat. It was one of the closest to the throne. They were surrounded by the other families just like them. Old Asteryans, they called themselves, a designation those families swung like hammers in a war room. They were one of two major political factions, always opposite the New Asteryans—the younger families who governed the northern territories her father had conquered. The New Asteryan families had been powerful merchants and sentinels, people who had not inherited their land, but instead had been given it in exchange for their assistance in her father's endeavors.

The Asteryan throne felt as sturdy as sand beneath her.

Vaasa ran her hands over the wooden armrests, the tips of which were dipped in iron. Now cold. Sharp. This had been what everything revolved around. This seat had been the catalyst to the learning of six languages. The purpose of her schemes and the tarnishing of her soul. The very reason her brother set out to kill her. The reason she had been sent into an enemy country and left there for dead.

It was only a chair.

She pictured her magic curling over the edges in tendrils of smoke, yet the power wouldn't stir within her. One after the other, local nobles and wealthier members of the middle class filed into the Sanctum while Vaasa sat and listened to them complain. Once upon a time, she'd had a taste for this sort of afternoon: one where the wine flowed and she sat near her father, taking diligent mental notes to better understand every predicament. *Be useful*, she would tell herself. *You must always be useful.* She would review it all with her father afterward, some twisted consolation prize where he turned her into both the son of his dreams and the daughter of his nightmares.

What a waste that you are a woman. What a tragedy that you will never rule.

For a moment, she felt horribly stupid for ever believing she could change his mind.

Ozik stood just one step down from her, dressed in his royal blue coat and black breeches. He analyzed the room just as closely as she did, weighing the tension between families that seemed to fill the room to bursting. Vaasa looked to the rings upon his fingers, catching upon the black stone that seemed to beckon her gaze. The similarity to her mother's necklace was uncanny. Filing that detail away in her mind, she plastered a smile on her face to greet the next family.

They approached, and the next, and the next. It was a parade of young sons, one after the other, cattle brought to slaughter, none of them any wiser. While they all maintained the same title, some lords had more land, more people and merchants and armies, than others. Those lords sat closest to the throne and seemed to draw the attention of the entire room. Old Asteryans and New Asteryans split the gallery like borders on a map. But as one lord entered, the entire room leaned forward—Lord Karev, whose footsteps echoed all the way to the throne as he approached the dais.

Thick black hair curled around his ears and fell just to the base of his neck, an equally plentiful beard framing his jawline. He was midway through his thirties but looked more like a man in his twenties, six years older than Vaasa. There was no denying that Lord Karev was handsome. His thunderstorm eyes coolly assessed everyone in the room with no particular care for their approval or thoughts, a sort of confidence that Vaasa believed was genetic: Some people were born with it, and others simply weren't. While the room watched his smooth gait and broad, drawn-back shoulders, Vaasa couldn't help but think to herself, *I've seen broader. Felt broader. Dug my nails into broader.*

His gray gaze locked onto her, then raked up and down the throne with approval. He dipped deeply at the waist. "Heiress," he said by way of greeting, her title rolling off his tongue with such ease.

She wondered if he'd practiced this in the mirror.

"Lord Karev," she responded, keeping her tone as demure as she could manage. It was precisely what these men expected.

He looked up through his eyelashes, still bent at the waist, and gave a knowing, haughty smile.

Vaasa held her weight comfortably in the chair. Stepping forward, Ozik extended a hand to Lord Karev, who readily took it. All feigned signs of respect as the gaggle of Old Asteryans looked on like vultures. Yet behind them, the New Asteryans thrummed with approval. It was then Vaasa realized that what this entire choice boiled down to was a battle between the old kingdom of Asterya and the more modern lifestyle of a young empire.

And that was something Vaasa could play off of.

"If I may be so bold," Lord Karev said, "it is a gift to have you back in this city where you belong."

Vaasa tilted her head. He'd come with intention, that much was clear in the strategic lift of his lips, but bold wasn't quite enough of a word to categorize him. It was outright brazen to make his perspective so obvious on a dais in front of every single one of his enemies.

If Lord Karev kept this up, she wouldn't have to sow discord herself. He would do it for her. Her eyes flicked to Lord Vlacik, who watched the interaction with a deep scowl.

"How charming," Vaasa said, talking like the chameleon she'd been raised to be. Her eyes trailed back to Lord Karev. She gave a graceful lift of her lips that didn't leave the impression she was thinking much at all.

He bowed deeply once again and sauntered off to his family's seats. Peculiarly, she noticed, he sat alone. No wife, no heirs, no cousins. She knew he had extended family, but why hadn't they come with him?

He struck her as capricious, which was perhaps more dangerous than his competition. At least Vlacik's violence was predictable.

The formal welcome took all the patience she had, and by the time dinner arrived, Vaasa had little interest in conversation. Still, she let her smoothest Asteryan out to play. These lords only spoke her native language; the languages of the areas her father had conquered had since become a rarity. With each smile and bat of her lashes, she felt the slick of her skin as if she had shed it; this grimy pandering made her feel exactly like her father. She cared for half of what she said and meant none of it. Her responses were shallow and predictable, just as these men expected her to be. She couldn't present herself as a threat; she needed to win some allies before she became an enemy.

A violin wept notes from the corner, music filling the room as the master of strings plucked and pulled. Wives and daughters of wealthy merchants cascaded about, their hungry eyes taking in the possibilities. Vaasa thought that maybe, for some of them, this was the opportunity they'd waited their entire lives for. It wasn't just her hand in marriage that would be dangled like a carrot. Any of these women held the potential to find themselves a match—particularly from the crop of men who did not leave this city with a throne.

Vaasa waited in her seat for a few minutes past appropriate. She itched to be anywhere else. It felt a betrayal to sit here and drink and dance while Amalie was trapped in the prison, while a war waged just past the snowcapped mountains.

When she had no idea where Reid was.

Vaasa's heart beat loudly in her chest. She swallowed another mouthful of water from the silver goblet in her hands. No one knew it wasn't wine—another small detail that would work to her advantage. Sobriety was the only option in the center of a lion's den. She stood and stepped down from the raised platform, pausing at the front of the room while everyone seemed to watch the dancing couples in the center.

One lord stepped closer and invited her to dance. Vaasa swallowed the urge to run. Hands met her waist, and the music drawled in a slow embrace, and at first Vaasa kept her breath. But the more she moved her feet, the quicker the music played, the further the ground seemed to slip from beneath her. If she closed her eyes, she was right back in Reid's arms, back in the Lower Garden with the steel drums and every pair of eyes on her and her foreman. She closed her eyes and swore she could hear Reid's voice, his rolling Icrurian. *Dance with me like lovers do.*

Vaasa's heart twisted. How could she have ever thought this world of pandering would be enough? That some ambassadorship would fulfill her? Gut empty, magic just out of her reach, she wasn't certain she'd be able to keep her dinner down. She wanted her husband. She wanted Mireh. She wanted community and the witches and the Lower Garden and the smell of salt in the air.

Vaasa forced herself to take in a breath. She wouldn't survive this if she didn't get it together. She could not break Amalie out of this prison, couldn't return to Reid and the place she wanted so desperately to call home, if she couldn't make it through one dinner. She considered every person in the room; she had been raised to do this. To predict every intention, every need, every action of those around her.

She settled her eyes on Lord Vlacik. He wielded far too much power in the space, seeming to maintain a gravity all his own. People circled around him, rotating like stars, or moths to a flame. Vaasa hovered by the wall. As she kept tabs on the lord, a man slithered to the space next to her. His presence pulsed around her, and her body picked up on its own instinct—she fought the urge to tighten her jaw or slink away.

"Lord Karev," she greeted without removing herself from the wall.

"Heiress," he greeted her back, pulling his fingers through his dark tresses. "Not a fan of dancing?"

Vaasa schooled her expression, refusing to allow her face to give any of her thoughts away. "I'm not particularly good at it."

"Strange." He leaned back against the same wall as her, turning his dark head to peer down. "I vividly remember you dancing until the last song when we were younger."

A map of their continent unrolled in Vaasa's mind, and she located his territory upon it. Just below Innisjour, and a key stretch of valleys that Reid would inevitably have to bring armies across. To unsettle Lord Karev's territory would make that task a whole lot easier; he had one of the largest mercenary armies in Asterya, and to unravel that strength would clear the path for the Icrurian Central Forces to reach the Loursevain Gap.

And he might well be the only person in the room capable of remitting Lord Vlacik.

"I didn't realize you were paying attention," she said, turning just slightly to face him. She looked up and down his tall frame like she couldn't help herself, then down at her feet for a moment as if to hide her bashfulness.

Lord Karev's mouth curled up at the edges. He turned to face her completely. "It would have been difficult not to notice you. The emperor's only daughter."

She met his intense gaze then, twisting her expression into one of pure delight.

"Perhaps I could change your mind," he said. "About dancing."

Vaasa sighed with a softness she had never once possessed. "Perhaps."

He extended her a hand, and Vaasa took it. Uncalloused. Smooth. He didn't touch rough things, so his hands should burn when he touched her. As the music hummed, Vaasa focused on the role she played. It was the only thing that kept her from falling apart.

Everyone watched them, none more so than Lord Vlacik, who stood on the edge of the room like he had no need to dance or socialize or impress. Vaasa fought the compulsion to shiver once more.

"He's rather . . . assuming, isn't he?" Lord Karev asked.

Vaasa snapped her attention to him. "He?"

Lord Karev smirked. He subtly gestured with his head to where Lord Vlacik looked on, dropping his voice to a whisper. "I hear his bed is already plenty warm. Surely you aren't considering him as a candidate for your hand?"

Vaasa met the bold lord's gaze. Sheep's clothing, she reminded herself, though her father's voice played in her ears. *To make an ally, all you must give someone is a common enemy.*

Dropping her voice to a thrilled whisper, she said, "That's quite the rumor."

"I don't speak rumors, only truths," he maintained. "Most of the nobles know about his frequent visits to The Lady Fortune."

Vaasa lifted a brow. It was the single most upscale brothel in the city, though for most, it functioned as much more than a house of pleasure. She'd been there many times and knew the owner. The Lady Fortune was known for the discretion of its staff, only made more secure by the requirement that all visitors don both a mask and costume while in the common areas. And those areas were popular: Some came for the company alone, never sneaking away to private rooms or terraces. Others employed those rooms for a variety of things; sometimes it was their own desires, other times it was a more formal, if not more legal, sort of business. To meet there had once been a game between her and Roman. She distinctly remembered sneaking out with him and his friends—she'd loved the thrill of blending in with every other debauched soul in Mekës.

Vaasa asked, "If the reputation of that establishment is true, then no one could know for certain, correct?"

Lord Karev grinned like the devil. "Men like him are easy to spot. Their pompousness gives them away."

Vaasa let out a small chuckle, making it seem like she couldn't help herself. It took only one song for Lord Karev to ask for another. He struck her as the sort of man who got his thrill in the chase, and he likely believed the luxuries of his life hadn't come easily, even if they had. So she flashed him the same mindless, dazzling grin he'd given her at the start, politely declined, and set her eyes on another eligible bachelor.

Competition only made men work harder.

The next lord, while relatively young, was already in control of his territory, his father having died sometime under Dominik's reign. The man was kind and easy to speak to, and a good enough dancer. It was the same pattern for the next hour, the entire room watching each man who touched her, while she felt like a fish being circled by sharks.

Especially when Lord Vlacik approached and extended his hand.

If she'd had access to a blade, it would have taken a monumental show of restraint not to reach for it. As she accepted the gesture, she fought her own nerves, which might make her shake if she didn't keep them in check. But it all came rushing back against her will—the cut of her skin, the agony of her magic overused. The cool sting of that iron collar.

Lord Vlacik pulled her into a dance, their bodies too close and the song too slow. He looked down his nose at her. *Pompous* had been a keen word choice from Lord Karev; Lord Vlacik held himself with the sort of confidence only generational power could muster. And everywhere his hands rested upon her felt like ice. Images of him looming above her in the prison, of him dragging a blade down her arm and her writhing in pain on the table as Ozik used her own magic to heal her, played mercilessly behind her eyes.

Lord Vlacik spun Vaasa, forcing her out of her own mind and bringing her right back to where she stood. They moved around each other as if they were on a battlefield, the very air around them shifting with tension.

"Tell me," Lord Vlacik said as they turned, "how long have you known the little witch?"

Vaasa swallowed. He was speaking about Amalie. "Talking is not a requirement of dancing," she said.

"And here I thought you would want to know how she is faring," he said.

Vaasa met his gaze, eyes narrowing.

He grinned wickedly, knowing he had her. All teeth. His voice dripped venom. "She is alive. Ozik won't let me play anymore, though. Pity, considering he isn't the emperor of Asterya—I'm confused why he's giving me orders at all."

Lord Vlacik was well aware of why Ozik had control; he had watched the man use Vaasa's power for weeks in that prison. Undoubtedly, the lord knew more of magic than anyone else in their proximity.

His hands tightened on her waist. "I'm sure Ozik has told you about my proposal. Wouldn't all of this just be easier if I were the emperor? I'd take you to see your little friend as often as you like, and no one would know the truth of what you are."

Vaasa's breathing quickened. He couldn't tell the world of her magic without facing the wrath of Ozik. In fact, it seemed Ozik was the only thing keeping Lord Vlacik at bay. This poor excuse for blackmail was simply that: a failure. But he was a man with far too much access, far too much information. Dominik had spent so much time worrying about Vaasa while a threat like this had been sitting right beneath his nose.

Their father would have had a man like Lord Vlacik killed.

She couldn't help herself from hissing, "I will die before I marry you."

He scoffed at her words, loud enough for people to hear, loud enough to draw attention. His breath coasted over her ear as he whispered, "I don't need an Icrurian brute's whore to get what I want."

Something fisted in Vaasa's stomach, insult or rage or some terrible combination of them both.

Loud enough for everyone around them to hear, Lord Vlacik said, "Whose son do you intend to squish beneath your feet, then?"

Vaasa slowed to a stop, and the music screeched to silence. Their conversation was no longer meant for only their ears. "Excuse me?"

"Oh, don't play dumb, Vaasalisa," Lord Vlacik crooned.

Every pair of eyes and ears focused on them, stares like hot iron on her back. "Heiress," she corrected. This level of disrespect was an inexcusable choice on his part, and no matter how unthreatening she needed to seem, she had been born to the continent's most ruthless conqueror. It would only be expected that she correct him.

She tried to pull away.

Lord Vlacik sneered, still holding her hand and her waist firmly. He turned to the rest of the room and lifted his arm, displaying her for the crowd to perceive, practically crushing her hand within his. "It will take more than dinner and dancing to convince me of this woman's intentions."

Lord Karev pulled himself from the wall, and Ozik lifted his chin, watching the interaction closely. A guard at the edge of the room started forward, hand on his sword, eyes moving between where Lord Karev approached and where Lord Vlacik touched her.

Vaasa ripped her hand from Vlacik's, stepping back from him as if she'd been burned.

"Ungrateful," one of the other Old Asteryan lords hissed from his position on the side of the room. The man's eyes met Lord Vlacik's, seeking approval.

This display of outrage was fabricated, she realized. Vlacik meant to gain favor, to look strong and immovable in the face of all these families. Perception was the only thing that really fueled them; the truth had always come second to the way they could tell it.

Vlacik looked down his nose at her. "Tell us, why should any of our men be forced to marry you for a throne we could take for ourselves? A woman who has already been *ruined* by an Icrurian?"

Ozik stood from his chair abruptly, insult carved into the lines of his face. As she peered around the room, it seemed that plenty in the crowd agreed—to them, it was blasphemous to have to work so hard for a woman. In their eyes, the throne should go to one of their men by default, regardless of the law. Regardless of who deserved it.

Vaasa took note of their faces. She categorized each one, considered their threat levels and where their territories lie. She had escaped this. She had fought for a life worth living. Yet in the absence of anything else, this instinct was as natural as breathing. Every expression painted a picture in her mind—of what they thought, what they felt, what they were capable of. She could practically feel every single thing in the room, some innate instinct.

Anger.

Fear.

Pride.

Lust.

Ambition.

Her eyes met Ozik's for the briefest of moments, and the cords in her body tangled and tightened. *Do something*, he seemed to say. Icruria had shown her a new path, but as she gazed around the room, she found herself entirely capable of becoming what Reid had once called her.

The most insincere woman he'd ever met.

They were trying to put her in a cage, and she was going to make them pay.

So, despite it all, Vaasa fought a smile. *This* was familiar. *This* was a landscape she had been raised in.

Each of these men was about to be ruined, too.

Her eyes met Lord Vlacik's with the most ridiculous sadness, false tears springing at her command. One slipped down her cheek. She visibly swallowed. He wanted to make himself seem powerful, but in that moment, she knew he was being perceived as cruel. Impolite. Asteryans were nothing if not politically correct, and Ozik had already sold them a story of some desperate rescue, their heiress saved from the clutches of a violent warmonger.

They already believed her a victim.

"If you'll excuse me," she said flatly, not bothering to snap back. Let them think her meek. Easily offended. That was their mistake to make. She always had been a snake in the grass.

Vaasa fled the room through double doors, stumbling into the stone hallway beyond. She didn't look back at the dining hall. She slammed into a body, stumbling backward, and forced her eyes up.

Vaasa gasped.

Before her stood a phantom. She stared into the face of a boy who had grown into a man—hair that had once been golden but had darkened into a burnt honey, a sparse beard that had filled to frame a sharper, wiser mouth. And though he had grown taller and certainly more handsome than the young soldier she'd known, his eyes remained exactly the same. Like the sharpest edges of a cliff, a brown so layered with yellow it had seared itself into her mind the first time she'd seen him. She had memorized him. There was a time when she could have drawn his every last feature with her eyes closed.

And now those phantom eyes flashed with fear.

"Heiress," a voice called, and warning bells chimed in her head.

Vaasa spun back toward the ballroom, contorting her features into the overwhelmed, insulted heiress she had just pretended to be. Her heart was still pounding hard in her chest as she looked upon Lord Karev, his handsome face soft and concerned.

Vaasa looked back over her shoulder to find the hallway empty. No one was there where the phantom had been.

"Heiress?" came Karev's voice again, closer now.

Vaasa pivoted. She lowered her eyes, playing the embarrassed lamb, and pretended to wipe a tear. The moment of covering her face allowed her to contort her expression back into what she needed it to be.

Lord Karev took a few steps toward her but stopped at a healthy distance. "He never should have spoken to you like that."

"He is impolite," Vaasa said, her voice cracking just a touch.

Lord Karev stepped closer. "You have not been ruined," he said. Something conspiratorial marked the way he smiled, the way he lowered his voice to secrets whispered just between them. "I would argue you know more about our enemy than any of them could dare guess. Given the right partner, you could be a brilliant weapon against Icruria."

Inauthenticity dripped from each of his words, so carefully positioning himself as the natural choice for that partnership. Yet it was the slightest of openings. Despite the way she could never underestimate Lord Karev, he was a far safer choice than Lord Vlacik. So she lifted her eyes to meet his and curved her lips into a small grin.

He tilted his head, peering around to check that they were still alone. It took every ounce of her control to stay focused on Lord Karev. He said, "Would you like to see the little scheme Lord Vlacik thought up while your brother reigned?"

That was all it took to get her full attention. Vaasa's breath swelled in her chest as she silently nodded.

"Then I'll send word in a few days. Join me for an evening out."

"Where will we be going?"

"And here I thought you liked surprises, Heiress."

She became the vision of rebellious excitement. Just a vapid little heiress who was in over her head. "A surprise it is, then."

Lord Karev dipped at the waist, sketching a well-practiced bow, and then started back to the doors of the dining room. As he opened them, he looked over his shoulder at her. "I'll send word," he promised.

This was precarious. The closer she allowed Karev to get, the more capable he was of turning on her. She was under no illusions that he intended to be her partner in anything; he was the sort of man who took what he wanted, even if he made the exchange feel like a sound deal.

Yet what better choice did she have? At least for now.

"I'll be waiting," Vaasa agreed, and Lord Karev gave her a dazzling smile.

Through the pounding of her heart, the doors clicked shut.

Vaasa turned in a full circle, gazing around the empty hallway of the Sanctum, not a soul in sight. Where had the guard gone? Had she hallucinated a ghost?

The door opened again, and this time, it was Ozik.

"Brilliantly done, Vaasalisa," he cooed, patting her elbow. "I think that's enough for tonight, don't you?"

He led her through the Sanctum, and Vaasa didn't have the wherewithal to argue. She scanned each hall they went down, every turn they took. Even as they plunged into the night air and loaded into a carriage, she searched.

She knew she had seen him.

Roman.

The soldier she had loved when she was only a girl—and the first thing Dominik had ever taken from her.

CHAPTER 9

Sleep was a futile endeavor. Vaasa tossed and turned on the couch, the fire raging in front of her. It thawed her frozen limbs. Still, her body twitched with restlessness.

She swore she had seen Roman. Had it just been some figment of her lonely imagination? Some cruel twist of Ozik's control over her?

"This is useless," she hissed to herself, sitting up and throwing the blankets off the side of the couch. All the attendants had retired for the evening. Why should she sleep? These were the only hours she was truly alone. For a moment, she thought about entering her mother's room, but the idea immediately summoned a wave of panic.

And then she wondered . . . who guarded her door at night? During the day, there was a rotation of guards she had already memorized, but she hadn't yet gotten the nerve to explore the fortress under the cover of darkness. To look for the necklace her mother had left for her in other parts of the castle.

Perhaps now she would have the freedom to.

Vaasa pulled herself to her feet and quickly changed into a warm wool dress and boots that wouldn't make noise on the blue runners situated throughout every major hallway in the fortress. She tucked a dagger into her belt and threw her cloak over her shoulders. Silent as she had ever been, she slipped out her door and gazed down the dark hallway of the emperor's wing.

A body stood up straight. "Heiress," the guard said.

So she *was* being watched. The insignia he wore identified him as a higher-ranking guard, though not quite the lead sentinel she had yet to meet. "I can't sleep. I'm going to the kitchens," she told him, sauntering past him.

"What do you need? I'll have it brought to—"

"Please," she said, tilting her head innocently. "There's no need to wake anyone up. I'll fetch it myself. I just need a walk."

"Heiress—"

"Is the fortress unsafe?" she asked. "Have the rest of our guards left their posts?"

The man immediately shifted his tone from concern to defensiveness, just as she assumed he would. "They are right where they should be."

"Then I'm safe, unless you doubt the competence of the men you work with?"

The sentinel bristled at her insinuation. "Of course not."

She smiled sweetly. "Good."

Vaasa turned on her heel and strode to the end of the hallway. She exited the emperor's wing of the fortress and plunged into the main rotunda, taking the stairs to the second floor. Everything was exactly as it had been before she left. She knew each inch of this fortress like the back of her hands. Yet it was an assurance she couldn't rest upon; predictability was not a guarantee. Faintly, she heard the footsteps of the sentinel behind her. Others were placed throughout, though none of them stopped her. The one who had been posted outside her door kept a healthy distance, but dutifully followed her down each corridor.

Vaasa approached one of the older wings of the fortress, the one her grandfather had lived in before her father had demanded a new, larger wing be built. She placed her hand on the knob, turning to face the sentinel and leaning back against the door. "This wing was my grandfather's," she reminded him. "It's private. Please wait out here."

He pursed his lips, but then said, "I thought you were going to the kitchens."

Vaasa sharpened her tone. "I've changed my mind."

The sentinel nodded, taking a step back. "I'll wait out here."

Frustration grew within her. He was too suspicious; she lowered her eyes and swallowed. "I'm going to read some of his old books. It . . . makes it easier to be here without the rest of my family. I may fall asleep. Please don't disturb me."

The sentinel's expression turned sympathetic at the mention of her late parents and brother. He handed her his oil lamp. "Of course, Heiress. I'll move my post here for the time being. Would you like me to send an attendant in the morning?"

Vaasa tightened her grip around the handle of the lamp and shook her head. "I'll return to my rooms when I'm ready. Thank you, though. Your compassion is appreciated."

The man nodded.

Vaasa slipped through the doors, closing them behind her, finally alone again.

If the necklace was hidden somewhere other than the emperor's wing, this was her next best guess. So she scurried to the end of the hall, a fugitive under the cover of night, her entire body thrumming. None of the sconces were lit. She entered one of the conversation rooms. Everything was exactly as she'd remembered it—untouched, unsullied. In here, art hung on the walls, covered now by fabric sheets in order to maintain their exact state, as if someone was afraid of allowing a single day to pass where *what used to be* could end up tarnished. Settees gathered around each other in the center of the room, all facing a hearth that she pictured raging with warmth. There were still blankets folded neatly in the corner, still end tables prepared to hold wine. Still a fluffy white rug sprawled in the center, tying everything together.

She set down her lamp, eyes landing on the books settled atop the mantel of the fireplace. Her father had grown up in warmth like this, and he had chosen differently for Dominik and her. Resentment tingled in her veins.

"You came," a voice said from the doorway, and Vaasa practically jumped out of her skin. Instinctually, her hand curled around the knife strapped beneath her cloak. She could just see the outline of him, of trousered legs and a coat—formal, especially given the time of night.

And then he stepped into the light, and it felt for a moment like time had stopped.

Vaasa lowered the dagger. "Roman," she breathed.

The corner of his lips turned up. "Vaasa," he said.

She threw herself across the room, something desperate overtaking her better senses. His arms caught her and scooped her up against his body—no longer sculpted like in youth but hard and corded like that of a man. He held her so tightly she thought it might keep her together. She breathed him in, adrenaline rushing through her veins.

Was there anything left of her to break?

She'd watched as Roman left. Cried when she pictured him at the front lines. Followed each and every battle with a meticulous scorn, waiting, knowing, and when the news had come that his entire squadron had been killed, she had mourned in silence. Raged in the shadows. It was the first true moment she'd thought herself a chameleon, because to hide the way her heart broke had felt like learning an entirely new language; it took practice and an extraordinary amount of thought to translate every move of her body. She'd sworn to herself then that her father was right: Love was a useless thing.

Yet here Roman was, alive, and—

Vaasa broke from him, realization pummeling her with a ruthless edge. She stumbled away until her back hit the wall, her hand snapping to her knife again.

Instinct pulsed. This was too convenient. Too coincidental. Roman was not here by accident. No matter which way she considered it, Ozik had his hand in this moment.

And yet she couldn't bring herself to run.

"Vaasa—"

"You're alive?" she demanded.

Roman nodded, though something that looked an awful lot like pain flashed in his eyes. "I wanted to give you more time. To let you settle in before I sprung this on you. But then you saw me earlier, and I just thought that if you were going to look for me anywhere, it would be here."

Her palms pressed against the wall with the same force as her back, like if she tried hard enough, she could push right through it and disappear. He was mere feet from her. She could feel the proximity as if it were a living thing. Stolen moments hung in the space between their bodies, memories it seemed they were both conscious of: the first time she'd ever noticed him in the inner ward, how he had whispered to her in the abandoned servant's kitchen over a piece of cake, the string of nights she had met him there afterward. The moment he had finally backed her into the counter and put his mouth on hers. It had been hot—on fire the way young things were, fueled by the *firsts* of it all.

The nights they had snuck into these very rooms. Had slept tangled with each other in one of the many beds in this part of the fortress.

Breath didn't come easily to Vaasa, and as she tried to take a deep inhale through her nose, her heart beat faster. "Why are you here? Why are you dressed like . . . a sentinel?" she asked. She scanned his attire again, and her eyes caught on a set of iron keys dangling off his hip.

What did Roman have access to?

His smile deepened. "Because I *am* a sentinel. Your lead sentinel, actually."

Vaasa's lips parted. She forced her gaze to stay up instead of looking at those iron keys. This meant he had control of her guards, her schedule, her transportation. Her rooms. Everything. Suspicion flooded her. What had he done to be put in charge of her personal guard? Her pained whisper cut the quiet air. "I thought you were dead."

His shoulders softened, and carefully, he stepped forward. "Until Dominik's death, I had to be."

I'm so sorry. The words she had never gotten the chance to say built upon her tongue, but she choked them down, her eyes stinging. Alive. Roman Katayev was *alive*.

She slid down the wall, farther away from him.

He paused and tilted his head, yet no hair fell into his eyes the way it would have years ago. It was cut short now, not a strand moved out of place. Perhaps she would have once thought such a style clean. Now it seemed restricted. There was something so different about him, the rebellious glint of youth hidden behind the stoicism of his gaze.

He didn't dare come closer. Instead, he plucked a few candles off the wall, bringing them to the lantern and lighting them himself. She watched each step he took. He lit the room until even the cobwebs in the corners glittered when the candlelight hit them just so. All the while she breathed, grounding herself with the feeling of the wall against her palms. Practicing every subtle breathing technique Melisina had ever taught her.

"The hearth has been tended," Roman said as he inspected the firebox. He gestured to the pile of fresh wood that had likely been replaced sometime within the week. "The attendants are keeping it usable."

"Light it," Vaasa said, gaining control of her voice again.

He pursed his lips. "Are you sure?"

"There's a fire in every room."

Roman bit his cheek, but then nodded. In minutes, warmth and light spilled through the space, coating it with more life than it had likely seen in years.

Vaasa stood up straight and squared her shoulders, careful of her composure. "How are you alive when the rest of your squadron is dead?" she asked him.

His hands rested on his knees as he knelt next to the hearth. "Still so direct," he muttered. It held a tenor it hadn't before, of either age or pain, even as he used a metal poker to shift the logs in the hearth. Fluidly, he pulled himself to standing and gestured for her to sit upon the couch.

Vaasa shook her head.

Roman sat upon the arm anyway, crossing one ankle over the other, but he accepted her refusal. His eyes met hers across the minimal space.

"I never got along with my commander. He insisted we take one of the boats into the fighting, but I refused."

"You abandoned post?"

"I was warned not to enter the rivers, so I didn't. They were all killed, and I was assumed to be on the boat."

Pride bloomed in Vaasa—of course the Icrurians bested them on the water. But it was also a testament to Roman's cunning and perception. He had known better than to put himself at the disadvantage. "When did you resurface?" she asked, turning her body more to face him.

Roman waited to speak, perhaps gathering his thoughts, but when he did, his voice came shaky. "I was a prisoner. Rounded up like cattle and forced to work in the outskirts of Wrultho."

Vaasa sucked in a breath and fisted her hands into her dress. Her heart ached for him, truly, as she thought about the life he must have faced. All because he had loved her.

It seemed to be a pattern.

She looked down at the floor, trying to come to terms with the renewed guilt of it all.

"The prison there is built under the ground. It's within a set of twisting catacombs that spreads beneath the city like roots. Prisoners run into those catacombs, and no one stops them. If you escape, you live freely. Very few have ever escaped," Roman continued.

Vaasa couldn't quite breathe. "But you did?" She picked at a thread on her dress, desperately trying to focus on the little knot.

"Vaasa. Would you please look at me?"

Shit. Vaasa held her breath as she lifted her eyes. His gaze was tentative, searching, and if she wanted to, the look might have made her trust him.

She breathed out heavily.

Grief carved tightly into his jaw. "You're looking at me like I'm a stranger."

She contemplated the right words. "In many ways, you are."

"And in many ways, I'm not."

Biting her lower lip, Vaasa returned to the semblance of honesty they'd always shared before, thinking that in the ounce of familiarity, she might win his truth. "Who do you report to? Ozik or me?"

"You," he clarified. "And then whoever is emperor next."

Vaasa looked squarely at him, leveling her tone. "Lie to me some more, Roman."

Lips pursed, his shoulders drooped. "All right. I escaped Wrultho a year ago and made my way down the Sanguine. News of your marriage spread, and I just . . . had to leave Icruria. I worked for a merchant who traveled all the way to Mekës. When I heard Dominik was dead, I returned, and Ozik showed me mercy. He's asked that I make sure you're safe and comfortable. That I keep you entertained."

If she'd been in a mood for humor, Vaasa would have tilted her head back and laughed. Ozik had sent Roman as a carrot to dangle in front of her? Something to take a bite out of that might give her reason enough to cooperate? "He's going to force me into another marriage, so he's given me a lover to soften the blow?"

Roman rubbed the back of his neck, redness crawling up his skin. "I believe he's given you an old friend. And a lead sentinel whom you can trust."

Vaasa stepped away from the wall, slowly regaining her sense of self. Was he loyal to Ozik, or simply naive? "You believe I trust you?"

"No." He watched as she walked closer and dropped his hand into his lap. "Not yet. I know it will take time. But I hope you come to realize that I did come here to keep you safe. That I serve at your word beyond all others'."

Time was one of the many things she didn't have. If there was an opportunity to search the fortress and surrounding city for her mother's necklace, it was here with Roman. He was in control of everything. She walked past him and to the opposite side of the couch, sinking into the cushions. "What do you make of this? The visiting lords and my impending marriage?"

Though Vaasa was careful with her body, he wasn't careful with his. He didn't seem to mind the space he took up or the way it created a palpable proximity between them. He leaned against the arm of the couch, lifting a leg until he was seated casually and could rest his elbow against his knee. "I can't seem to see another way forward. If you don't marry someone, the lords will plunge Asterya into a civil war as they fight for the throne. It'll destabilize the entire empire."

Precisely. But that was the first time the gravity of the situation plummeted down her spine. There was only so much time before she ended up walking down another aisle, before she was back in the same position she'd been in after her mother's death, except far worse. Yet without a doubt, there was room to pit the Old Asteryans against the New. The brimming tug-of-war between Vlacik and Karev was enough to do most of the work for her.

Could Vaasa survive a world in which she was forced to stand opposite Reid on a battlefield? She had originally hoped she could free Amalie and somehow make it out of this city before Asterya could work through this transition of power. But if she was strategic, she might be able to win this war from the inside.

She could say none of this to Roman, though. Vaasa sighed. "Then I suppose I'm left with no choice."

Roman took a deep breath as if he was gathering courage. "There is a reason I have tried to keep my distance."

Vaasa lifted a brow.

"I have heard things about you . . . about magic. That Reid of Mireh cursed you."

Her ear couldn't help but bend to that name—*Reid of Mireh.* What would it sound like to hear it fall from a nation's lips and not just her own? To hear his new title on full display? *Reid of Icruria.* Yearning flooded her body, but she pressed it down and tried to focus on the details of what he'd said. "He did no such thing."

"So it wasn't him, the Wolf?"

Vaasa scoffed, folding her arms over her chest and trying not to twitch at that nickname. *The Wolf.* Her wolf. The man who reflected the very creature her magic had become. "He does not possess magic."

"Do you?"

Tilting her head, she asked, "Would it scare you if I did?"

"Yes," Roman admitted.

Holding his gaze, Vaasa pieced together his level of knowledge as she did with every opponent. Yet she wasn't certain he *was* an opponent—not yet. "It was my mother," she said, spinning a half-truth to gauge his reaction. "Her curse passed down to me when I found her dead. Ozik has ways of keeping it hidden."

Roman moved ever so slightly away. It was fear, she knew. "It's under control now?"

She couldn't explain why hurt threaded up her spine and around her chest, but it felt like a ribbon had been tied in knots throughout her. "For now. Lord Vlacik wants to weaponize it. That's why he and Ozik tortured me."

Roman sat up straight. "They *what?*"

If he was questioning Ozik, he didn't do so out loud. Vaasa wasn't certain what to say next. What could she? "Yes," she finally managed.

"Vaasa, I—"

"You didn't know?"

"I didn't know. I swear it." Roman leaned forward again and took her hand, looking at her now with new understanding. That touch sent awareness down every nerve she possessed. But she didn't let go—not yet.

He scanned every inch of her with his brown eyes, probably looking for signs of injury. Those had all healed or were hidden beneath her heavy wool dress. Even the marks on her face had disappeared. He seemed satisfied with what he found, and then she realized that perhaps he was looking for traces of the curse. If what he said about Wrultho was true, he'd likely witnessed magic in some form.

What had they done to him to make him so afraid?

"I knew you'd been kept in one of the cells," Roman said, "but Ozik assured me it was to keep you and everyone else safe as you fought the curse. You have to believe me. If I'd known what they were doing to you—"

"What would you have done?" she asked candidly.

Roman paused. Then, "I would have figured something out."

A lackluster response, she thought, but scolded herself. What *could* Roman have done, truly? He'd have risked his own life and maybe the lives of others in order to do . . . what? Send her back to Icruria?

"Tell me you believe me," he pressed, tightening his grip on her hand. "Please."

Vaasa didn't know if it was truth or fiction that fell from her lips when she said, "I believe you." It was simply what he wanted to hear.

Warmth returned to the depths of his brown eyes, like a lamp had filled them with light. He stayed close to her, and the proximity confused her, caused her stomach to turn over on itself with an unexpected anxiety. She pulled her hand back, running it through her hair.

But she couldn't bring herself to scoot away—this was *Roman*. He was alive. Not once did she believe she would ever get the chance to see him again, to look upon him in adulthood, and know he was safe.

A smile split his face. "We have all the time in the world tonight." He leaned his side against the back of the couch, again hitching a leg beneath his other one and settling in like no time had passed since he'd last sat here. Their knees almost touched. "Please, don't go yet. I . . . want to know about you. Tell me everything that has happened since I last saw you."

There was far too much to tell, too much life that had passed by. Yet her emotions stirred at the sound of a voice she had thought with certainty she would never hear again. She had spent a decade wondering how his features would have shifted. She had thought the sight impossible, and now she wasn't quite ready to give it up.

Love is a useless thing, her father's voice floated in her mind.

But it's not, her own whispered back. *It's worth it to care for someone.*

"Tell me a story first," she requested.

With a small chuckle, Roman obliged. He relayed the days after he'd been assigned to Innisjour. Some memories were painful, others lighthearted. Most, he insisted, were absent of anything worthwhile. She told him of the months after he'd left. Of the new languages she had learned and the books she'd read. She did not tell him of Icruria or Reid or the life she had chosen in another nation. Something about his eyes told her he couldn't bear it. And it made her wonder what pieces of his life he was leaving out, too, because if she had strategically chosen what to tell him, certainly he'd done the same.

"You're afraid of him," Roman said eventually, referring to Ozik. The light outside began to chase away the moon, bathing the carpet in a red glow and signaling the end of their time. The fire had long died. She rebelled against that fact, wondering how much more of the night she could squeeze from this very moment. "But you do not need to be afraid of me. He may have brought me here, but he's not the reason I'm staying."

Vaasa inspected Roman's pristine coat and pants, all the way down to the leather of his boots, his Asteryan blue coat glaring back at her. The set of iron keys hanging near his hip bone was the only break in the blue.

They were too close; she was tired and losing her grip on her composure. She stood from the couch. "If I am truly to be an empress, I should be afraid of everyone. And if you are truly my lead sentinel . . ." She sighed, shaking her head. "So should you."

Roman pursed his lips but didn't argue.

"I should go," she whispered.

"You should," he agreed.

She paused, not entirely sure how to let the moment go. "When will I see you again?"

A soft smile spread across his lips. Even wary from no sleep, he'd never broached haggard. Still sturdy. Still handsome. Bits of the expressions she'd once known leaked through, and his youthful excitement shone again on his face. "I suppose there's no use in hiding from you any longer. I'd thought you needed time with the lords, but . . ." he trailed off.

"I don't need time with the lords," she said.

He nodded contently. "Then you'll see me soon. Good night," he told her, though she knew the night was long gone.

"Good night," she whispered.

It was the last thing she said before she turned and fled the room. A new guard waited outside, and she knew Roman would have the better sense to find a way out of the old wing that didn't lead to anyone thinking they'd spent the night alone. They were well practiced, after all. When she entered her mother's and father's quarters again, she curled up on the couch beneath a blanket and breathed deeply. Her mind whirled with everything she had just come to know.

Ozik had placed Roman strategically, had given her this crumb for a purpose. It was another piece of this puzzle she couldn't quite put together. Yet she had seen those iron keys dangling at his waist, and she was willing to bet one of them led to Amalie's prison.

He had held her hand.

She looked down at it, and shame washed over her.

She had gotten a taste, had heard the sound of Reid's name, and suddenly she was breaking—the carefully crafted dam of her feral longing cracked. Desperation filled her like a well. Every cut she had tried and failed to stave off opened in a chasm. Vaasa buried her head into her blankets, tears streaming down her face. It may have been warm, but the very depths of her still felt cold.

Where was Reid? Did he know the merchants were the only way he'd survive the cays, and that they would betray him the moment they heard his Icrurian tongue? Did he think he could make it around the Sheets or navigate the Bay of Innisjour with its mysterious fatal tides?

Did he know that he would not reach her, no matter how hard he tried?

CHAPTER 10

Reid stared at the pirate, torn between lying and telling the full truth. Strategy, at least between people, had never been his area of expertise. On the battlefield he could maneuver soldiers like chess pieces, yet conversation had always gotten the better of him. In hindsight, it was foolish to assume he could keep his identity concealed for long. But what he hadn't expected was for a pirate to be the person to uncover it.

For her to have a map of the continent more accurate than any of his armies.

She smiled as if her ability to be two steps ahead thrilled her. "I'm not as ignorant as that merchant. If he'd known who you were, he'd have brought your head to Mekës."

Reid pursed his lips. The warmth started to seep into his body, providing a disarming relief he was suddenly terrified to lose. "Is that your plan? To turn us over to Asterya?"

Leaning back, the pirate held his eyes firmly as she said, "I would rather set myself on fire than give that empire something it craves."

Perhaps she was closer to an ally than Reid thought. The corners of his mouth tugged into a smile. "If you know who I am, then you know I can make good on my deal."

She tilted her head. "Can you?"

"I told you: Name your price."

She gestured to the chair in front of her desk. "Take a seat."

Reid settled in as the pirate's knife clattered on the desk. She used a torn green cloth to wipe her hands of the acrid-smelling polish covering her fingers, then tossed it down next to the knife. "Your blades must be wrecked," she said, extending a hand.

"Are you asking me to hand over my weapons?"

She gave a one-sided grin. "You're smarter than you look."

Reid scoffed, crossing his arms, waiting for her to continue speaking. Instead, she passed the polish and the green cloth to him. "Have at it yourself, then."

He slid a knife from his belt and began to polish it, waiting patiently for her to tell him what she wanted.

For a long moment she was quiet, discerning. It reminded him of the times he had sat in silence, waiting for Vaasa to collect her thoughts and tell him something worth hearing. He had never pushed her into speaking, but it was a testament of patience, just like waiting for this pirate was now.

She let out a sigh. "I want a pardon."

Reid looked up through his lashes, only taking his gaze off his weapon for a moment. "I'll give you letters of marque. You can pirate the rivers all you wish."

"It's not for me," she clarified. "And I don't need some useless document giving me permission to do what I already do. I need an Icrurian pardon for someone; he will need asylum."

"Why?"

"Six months ago, my brother was imprisoned by Dominik Kozár."

Reid's hand didn't miss a beat as he continued to work the polish into the blade, yet his mind reeled. She was asking for a pardon for her brother—a seemingly selfless act. It contradicted his initial impression of her. "Done."

She quirked a brow. "You don't even know what his crime was."

With a shrug of his left shoulder, Reid said, "I don't need to. Done. What else do you want?"

The pirate pursed her full lips. "I need help freeing him. I know a lord who has a connection to the prison, but it's going to cost far more than I can ask my crew to afford. That's where you come in."

Reid ran his tongue along his teeth, but the truth was that he didn't care what it cost. He set down the green cloth, still holding his blade in his hand. "Give me a figure."

"I want access to your salt."

Reid remained composed, trying not to give his shock away too quickly. These sorts of deals were not his strength; he did far better with a battlefield than he did the economy. But his predecessor had laid a blueprint he could follow. He could, at least in his mind, pretend to be Marc. The man's impassive face shone behind Reid's eyes. That was one of the ways Reid had gotten through the more difficult economic decisions in the past five years—he asked himself what Marc would have done.

"Access to my salt?" Reid asked.

"A line of trade will be enough to sate the lord I'd like to work with," the pirate confirmed. "He has a friend who works closely with the lord of the prison. I'm confident he can get us answers about how to break in, perhaps even assistance from his men."

Reid was not usually one to make a false deal or bargain something he didn't actually intend to give. Truthfully, he had no interest in working with the lord in question, though he needn't say as much. This deal was temporary. Icruria couldn't guide forces through the Loursevain Gap just yet, but Reid believed that someday they would. Someday soon. And when that happened, when Asterya finally fell, he saw no need to keep delivering salt to some lord he would inevitably remove.

For now, Reid had one goal, and one goal only: to get his wife back. Whatever it took to accomplish that goal was worth doing. "Fine. I'll facilitate some kind of trade agreement."

The pirate gave a firm nod. "I have one more demand."

"I'm listening."

"I want your witch to train me."

The floor might have slipped out from beneath his feet. He narrowed his eyes. "You want her to . . . train you?"

"Yes. In magic. It's the only thing left I don't already have that your party can offer me."

Could a Veragi witch even help someone from another coven? Knowing his mother, she would try. She would do it out of the goodness of her heart. If he knew anything of magic, it was that left untrained, it became incredibly painful.

Luckily for him, he wasn't as kind as his mother. "Only if you bring my party to the Iron Bay and then take us *back* to Icruria, all of our loved ones in tow."

Reid got the feeling this woman had never done anything without a backup plan, and the thought concerned him. Especially as he glanced at the iron-wrought map along her wall. She could very well lure them into the Iron Bay, slaughter them all, and dump his body in front of the gates to the fortress. She could demand her lost prisoner as her reward, and surely Ozik would grant it to her.

It all hinged on the thread of rage—of *hatred*—that sparked in the pirate's eyes at the mention of Dominik. The greatest problem for conquerors was that they had no shortage of enemies; whatever had been stolen from this woman needed to be enough to make her an ally. Given her flawless use of Icrurian and the magic that soaked her veins, she must be from a bloodline native to Icruria. To Sigguth.

But if she was here, it was possible Icruria had made an enemy of her, too.

Still, the woman balanced her blade in her fingers, letting it tip from left to right as she stared at him. "I want asylum for the members of my crew who choose to take it. All the best comforts in your capital. When this is over, they won't be able to return to Asterya."

"And yourself?"

She merely shrugged. "Sure."

The pirate confounded him, but she was right. If they succeeded, without a doubt this crew would never make it back in and out of Asterya alive. This would be the end of her pirating—it would sever any relationship she had with Mekës.

"Deal," Reid said.

"Deal," she repeated.

Reid reached out his arm, the Icrurian way of greeting and symbolizing trust, but the pirate looked at it. She scoffed. "I'm not your friend, Wolf."

He chuckled, perhaps nervously, and dropped his arm. "What is your name, then?"

Power threaded the room as the pirate—or witch, whatever the hell she was—said, "Sachia, captain of *The Red Corsair*."

With each moment Reid spent above deck, he got a better understanding of the long stretch of sea that led into the Iron Bay. Cays littered the ocean between Zataar and Asterya, and their ship carefully avoided coming too close to any of them. "Each island belongs to different crews," Sachia told him one morning as they stared out at the open ocean. "Kings in their own right, some even have castles to prove it."

The entire way of life confounded him. "They're like individual nations, then?" Reid asked.

"No." Sachia stared out at the water, her hands curling around the gunwale. "Everyone gets in bed with Asterya or Zataar at some point. Some whore themselves to both. Those people wind up rich or dead."

At that, Reid went rigid. He wondered if that was what had happened to Sachia's brother.

The enormous glaciers and icebergs of the Sheets lent to tumultuous, freezing-cold water. Assurance rode his bones; the Icrurian army could not navigate this side of the continent *and* avoid the pirates in time to conquer Mekës.

They would need to go through the Loursevain Gap.

Dressed in warm leathers, a fur-lined cloak, and thick gloves, the numbness of Reid's hands had ceased, the ever-present trembling of shivers long gone. Sachia had made their entire party comfortable, had treated them like members of her crew. They'd been given one of the private quarters in the hull to share. They slept on hammocks that were strung from the ceiling, and though it was nothing like his bed at home, it was far superior to the floor and thin padding they'd slept on in the merchant's boat.

"Off the stern!" the quartermaster, who Reid had learned was named Jonáš, alerted.

Reid and Koen turned at the same time. Behind them, a set of white sails billowed in the wind, a ship moving with incredible speed. To keep up with Sachia's boat was a feat itself, but to overtake—

"She slowed down," Koen whispered from beside Reid, realizing how this ship had caught up to *The Red Corsair* in the first place. Sachia had wanted it to. She'd been standing here, waiting for this very moment.

How long ago had she spotted it?

A loud boom sounded.

Something splashed in the water just off the port. From beside him, Sachia laughed into the wind. "I love when they want to play!" she mused, sprinting back up the steps to where Jonáš waited by the helm. Reid wasn't certain how Sachia moved so nimbly in the cold, but it was as if the ice in the air didn't affect her.

Reid's mother was below deck, and he silently hoped she'd stay there. Another boom sounded, and this time, Reid watched as a cast-iron cannonball hurled toward their ship, his adrenaline pounding—

Midair, the ball flew to the left and slammed through the surface of the sea. Somewhere near the helm, Sachia, arms raised, cackled with pride.

The boat lurched to the side, and Reid stumbled, grabbing ahold of a mast as the ship turned at what felt like an impossible angle. Within moments, their boat was sailing directly at the opposing ship.

"Sachia!" Reid yelled in warning. He took two steps at a time as he ascended to the helm.

She stood with her eyes glued to the Asteryan vessel. Wind lifted her red hair, and a vengeful grin crossed her face.

"Sachia!" he yelled again.

It was a futile endeavor. Sachia was glued to the Asteryan ship, her body taut with rage, her hands shaking as they waited for the next onslaught of cannon fire. A loud boom rang through the air, and another cast-iron ball flew toward them. Sweat accumulated on Sachia's brow, but she lifted her arms and it was as if she'd caught the ball in midair. She flung her strength to the side, and the cannonball followed, drifting past their ship with a splash into the water.

Magic. Over the past few days, he'd learned that Sachia's strength lay in maneuvering large objects. It was the smaller details she couldn't manage with precision—locks, buttons, the clasp of a necklace.

Jonáš sprinted up the steps at the same time Reid yelled over the wind. "What am I looking for?"

"Cannons!" Jonáš confirmed.

"I don't understand!"

"What do they need to power those cannons?" Jonáš asked, his voice booming across the deck just as Koen ran up the stairs to join them.

Reid stared at the boat for a moment, his mind turning. He looked to where the cannonballs fired from and considered the Icrurian weapons he could equate to their Asteryan cannons. They ran on . . . "Black powder," he muttered. Then, "Black powder!" he yelled.

"Black. Powder." Jonáš repeated each word like it was its own sentence, giving a thrilled, toothy grin. "There's only one thing more valuable during wartime!"

"What's that?" Koen asked.

Jonáš's expression darkened. "Revenge."

Sachia kept her eyes on the opposing vessel. "Don't you want to know what else is on board, Wolf?"

A part of him felt deeply ashamed at the thrill that coursed in his veins. Yes, he wanted to know. Their boat grew closer, and with each inch, Reid held his breath. They barreled forward, too close now for the cannons to be of any use. *The Red Corsair* slowed next to the ship, sliding into a parallel position. The men on the rival ship scurried like ants, their shouts echoing in the wild air.

"Let's go!" Jonáš yelled.

And just like that, members of Sachia's crew swung from ropes and boarded the mercenary vessel, and the men aboard didn't stand a chance.

Every member of the mercenary crew fell.

Sachia slaughtered the captain last. He bleated in fear, but she showed no sympathy as she lifted a knife and thrust it into his gut, twisting the blade.

Pirates carried chests of provisions and luxuries across a makeshift bridge. They were incredibly careful with the large wooden barrels that Reid knew contained the explosive material so difficult to find outside Zataar and Icruria. It was one of the advantages they had against the Asteryan forces: The main ingredient in the explosive powder could be sourced along the Sanguine, which Reid had long suspected was part of Vaasa's father's attempts to infiltrate eastern Icruria. This substance fueled the most terrifying weapons Reid had ever laid eyes on.

Standing near the edge of the boat, Reid pulled the top off one of the barrels and sucked in a breath, sticking his fingers into the black powdery substance. Far too much of it for the number of cannons aboard. At his side, Koen silently darted his eyes from barrel to barrel, likely doing estimates in his head.

"They were bringing it back to Mekës, weren't they?" Reid asked.

"Likely from Zataar," Sachia confirmed as she ambled up next to him. The boat swayed with the tumultuous sea, though the sky itself was merely overcast. Small drops of snow fell in soft movements. Vindication dripped from her easy posture as she looked upon the bodies scattered across the deck. Reid was numb to such a thing, but he knew Koen wasn't. When he glanced at his friend, Koen stared down at the body of the captain that Sachia had slaughtered. Reid could imagine what went through Koen's constantly whirling mind—perhaps the nature of violence or the worth of justice. Koen had ponderings about the world that Reid couldn't shoulder, and he wondered how his friend kept his spine straight with the weight of all those questions.

"They were one of Sutherland's crews," Jonáš said, bringing out papers from the captain's quarters. Reid only got a glance, but he noticed a torn wax seal of what appeared to be an adorned key.

"Hired by Vlacik?" Sachia asked.

Jonáš gave a sharp nod. "I have no doubts."

Sachia skimmed over the papers, jostling them in her hands as she switched from one letter to another.

"Who are they?" Reid asked. Neither name was familiar, but given they still spoke in Icrurian, Sachia and Jonáš weren't hiding anything.

"Lord Vlacik of Pryviske," Sachia said with a lip curled in disgust, not bothering to take her eyes from the papers. "In these waters, it's always Vlacik."

She said nothing on the other name: Sutherland. Instead, she handed the papers back to Jonáš and sauntered to the other members of her crew. As if it were second nature, she helped them transport goods across the gaping drop between ships.

"Who is Sutherland?" Koen asked.

"A pirate king," Jonáš explained. "One of the nastiest. Neither Sachia nor I have ever laid eyes on the man, but he has more control over the trade in these waters than just about any other crew. The day he dies is the day Sachia and I beach that ship and live our lives on an island somewhere away from this wretched continent. Somewhere warm."

"Is he the reason Sachia's brother is in the Mekës prison?" Koen asked.

Jonáš glanced at Reid from the corner of his eye, though he seemed unsurprised that Reid had told Koen of the details of his and Sachia's agreement. He stared directly at Koen as he answered the question. "Yes."

Reid wasn't sure if it was any of his business or if Jonáš would spill a word of truth, but he asked, "What for?"

"We left his crew," Jonáš muttered before walking away. "And now it's him or us."

CHAPTER
11

Vaasa woke in the early afternoon and stood at the edge of the right hallway, staring at her mother's door down the dark corridor.

Was the necklace inside?

She took a step forward. Her body felt disconnected from her, like she was floating above it and staring at herself. The seed of her panic sprouted.

She could see her mother's body. Could smell and taste the acrid magic. The quick rewinding of time brought her right back to this place, staring at the remnant of her mother's life, Vaasa's future hanging in the air and suffocating amid all the wicked power.

It was my mother. Her curse passed down to me when I found her dead.

Vaasa's breath came quicker.

Like roots bursting from a shell, they plunged down, an invasive species, this panic strangling all the life inside her. She could feel it again—her magic bursting like a dam inside her body, spreading like blood in the water, sliding down each muscle and winding around her bones. The visceral fear of that moment. She'd believed she was dying. She had been convinced of her fate.

Her legs wouldn't move. This paralysis was entirely against her will. She tried to lift her leg but she couldn't, she—

Vaasa turned away, gritting her teeth. She let out a frustrated groan and covered her face with her hands. Her chest rose and fell with her breaths. "It's okay," she whispered to herself, pretending her voice was Amalie's or Melisina's. Pretending for a moment that she wasn't alone. "It's okay to be afraid."

She stood there for minutes. Maybe more. Everything swirled in her mind—Ozik, Lord Vlacik, Roman.

Reid. Amalie. Her coven.

Vaasa retreated to the couch and buried herself beneath her blanket, shutting out the sunlight, shutting out anything and everything at once.

She didn't emerge from her rooms for the rest of the day.

She didn't see Ozik. She didn't see Roman.

And when Lord Karev called on her, she told the attendants she was ill.

The next day, Vaasa followed the path her body had finally deemed safe into her father's office down the left hallway of the emperor's quarters. Sleep had evaded her, though she'd known better than to go seeking Roman again. She had been too close to her past.

She would need to rest today, to reserve her energy for more pandering with the lords. She couldn't fake ill with Lord Karev for long, given what was at stake.

She parsed through every single thing Dominik had written, and in a file deep in a drawer, she found the letters he'd exchanged with Mathjin, Reid's traitorous advisor. The man's face flashed behind her eyes—the ice of his irises, the twist of his mouth. The sheer terror she'd felt at finding herself tied up beneath the colosseum of Dihrah, left for dead at the hands of her brother.

And yet she could still see it—the pain etched into the wrinkles of Mathjin's skin as he spoke about his daughter and unborn grandchild, who had been slaughtered by an Asteryan soldier. His was a death she hadn't allowed herself time to process, either. She wondered silently if Reid missed him, if he was experiencing the same churning, tumultuous emotions she was.

What she wouldn't give to ask him.

She devoured every word of the letters. Every detail of the steel Dominik and Mathjin had smuggled to Ton, of the rebellion they'd stoked in Wrultho that had ultimately bled all over the Icrurian election. She couldn't believe that the late foreman of Wrultho had been foolish enough to make deals with the son of the very Asteryan emperor who had scorned him the first time. Ton must have been desperate, more so than ever before.

Dominik's notes made it clear that the brazen invasion of Icruria had been in pursuit of precisely what he'd been working with Lord Vlacik to uncover: magic. Vaasa understood now; that was why he'd gone to Mireh. The night he'd tried to poison her, Vaasa had all but given him a show, thinking he would believe she was struggling to control a curse. Had he already known what her magic was? Had that been the real reason for arranging her abduction, possibly even her death?

Vaasa shuddered. Even though Dominik's journal of drawings sat open on the desk beside her, stark proof of his humanity, the evidence of his evil glared up at her in the form of these records. He had tortured other witches. Had likely intended to torture her. With Lord Vlacik and the clergy involved, conspiracy was a crack in the foundation of this city. Of this empire. They wouldn't stop until they had decimated what was left of Icruria's already-dwindling covens.

It wasn't enough to escape Mekës. She would find a way to stop them.

Which begged the question of why Ozik had left something like this for Vaasa to find. Why would he want to turn her against the very empire he intended for them to rule in tandem?

Locking everything back in the compartment in the desk, Vaasa set her head down for just a moment, just to rest her strained eyes.

"Long night?" a voice asked, and Vaasa shot up from the desk, stray hairs plastered to her face.

She sucked in a sharp breath as she stared at Ozik across the office. He stood in the doorframe, and she looked around, wondering how she hadn't heard him enter. She peered at the clock standing in the corner. Hours had passed.

Vaasa smoothed out her wool dress and nodded. She didn't feel inclined to speak to him. Part of her wanted to come right out and ask about the necklace, about all the witches he had let die, yet she knew better than to show her cards immediately. It was an assumption that he knew the secret drawer in her father's desk existed at all. She had no intention of giving herself away this quickly—not until she'd managed a real search for her mother's last gift.

He gestured for her to stand. "Come with me."

"I'd rather not."

He tilted his head predatorily.

She swallowed. The feeling of a fork driving through her hand was fresh in her mind, and Vaasa tensed. She breathed in through her nose and curled her fingers against the desk, pressing down in a subtle form of grounding. Then, Vaasa indignantly crossed her arms over her chest. "Tell me why you brought Roman here."

A small pause. "Empresses have lovers all the time, Vaasalisa."

Bile threatened to push up her throat. He would know. *He* had been the empress's lover—her mother's torrid affair. She curled her lip in disgust. "I have no interest in a lover."

"Then don't have one," he suggested.

Vaasa narrowed her eyes, though she didn't get up from the desk.

Ozik gave a heavy sigh, as if she were nothing but a petulant teenager. The sound of it was so familiar, a relic from the days he had tutored her. "I thought if you could see yourself here, perhaps you'd be more willing to rule. It is nothing more than that. I've known he was alive for quite some time, and when he arrived here, I agreed to let him stay. It was the least I could do, considering your brother and father sent him off to his death."

"I don't believe you," Vaasa said. "What's his bargain?"

Ozik arched a brow. "Not everyone I come across is a person I waste magic on. Sometimes, old-fashioned politics are enough."

Again, she said, "I don't believe you."

He pursed his lips like there was a thought caught between his teeth, then relaxed his shoulders. "Your skill for observation is a gift, dear Vaasalisa. Don't ever underestimate it."

Vaasa wasn't certain why she'd asked the question in the first place. Ozik was never going to give her a straight answer. She looked down at the desk for a moment, composing herself.

"I've answered your question. Now, come," he said.

The cords between them circled one of her ribs and gave a sharp tug. Pained breath pushed out through her lips, a reminder that his willingness to answer her questions at all wasn't a compromise; it was a gift. She fell back into whatever version of herself she had been before Icruria, pliant and obedient and afraid. Uncrossing her arms, her body moved without much thought. She stood from the chair.

She hated herself for the way he grinned.

They exited the emperor's wing without a word, neither of them speaking to each other as they walked. Sun poured through the stained glass windows, throwing color all over the floor and walls in particularly well-lit passages. A cold gust of wind bit at Vaasa's cheeks as Ozik opened the door to the courtyards at the back of the fortress, all placed at different levels on the mountain and connected by large stone bridges. Snow piled on the capstones in soft white, a few flurries falling harmlessly from the red and orange sky.

Ozik took one set of stairs after another, reaching a new level each time, until he led them to a familiar stone walkway on the far side of the fortress near the entrance to the game park, which sprawled in a valley behind the fortress. She realized quickly where they intended to go.

"The greenhouse?" Vaasa asked.

"It's warmer there," Ozik said as if it were explanation enough.

She hadn't considered the intensity of being back here in Mekës, of what it would mean to see everything from a time in her life that she had become so good at making hazy. Every place her father had stepped, every hallway she'd seen Dominik in and then spun on her heel. Her mother. Roman.

She hadn't grieved, not in the way that provided closure. She had simply pushed it down as far as it could go. In Mireh, her exploration of magic had felt like ripping off all the carefully placed bandages she'd used to staunch the bleeding of her youth. She had bandaged it over with something new. But now every time she rediscovered a memory, that wound ripped itself back open.

"Vaasa," Ozik called.

She looked up. Towering on the other side of the fortress, the sloped roofs of the greenhouse poked out from behind walls of berry-colored holly. Built of iron and half-silvered glass, the building comprised three major rooms, two in the front and one larger chamber in the back. The glass gave the illusion of light bouncing, making one see their own reflection instead of whatever was inside. Each chamber of the greenhouse felt like a world of its own. Being embedded into the treacherous cliffside with no expansive path to the main fortress, it was an impregnable area, and an assault from the water was fundamentally ill-conceived. It was one of the few places that stood mostly unguarded.

Vaasa quickly followed Ozik inside. He walked along the glimmering gravel pathway that wound through the greenhouse, providing access to all three chambers. Heat wafted around them, a perfect balmy temperature to grow the sorts of things that could not thrive in the snow. Vegetables and legumes grew in the front two rooms, yet the room tucked at the back, closest to the ocean cliffs, was covered in flora so unlike the daphne and primrose that burst through the snow along the courtyards. It would be impossible to see from the outside, even with the floor-to-ceiling glass walls that provided an unobstructed view of the ocean, given the peculiar glass they'd used to build it instead of the stained glass most of the fortress utilized. It was unexpectedly refreshing to gaze out at the world without viewing some artist's rendition of her family's sins.

Stone-hewn statues of people Vaasa did not know, set into the ground sporadically as the path intertwined on itself, guarded the greenhouse. Veins of gold and silver threaded through black stone, and when the light hit them just right, those lines seemed to pulse. Sometimes she wondered if they were frozen there in time. When she was younger, she'd made up stories about them—each a character in the life she'd planned to live.

Like Icrurian air coasting along her skin, she reveled in the heat for a soft, stolen moment. Warmth mingled with her memories of Mireh, and it became a cavern in her chest. She shed her cloak as she entered the farthest room.

Vines hung from the ceiling with purple and pink buds exploding from them like droplets of rain about to slip off the leaves. Vaasa entered slowly, eyes trailing over every detail. The gravel pathway continued, lined on each side by flowers in pink and white and lavender. Bushes filled the empty spaces and iridescent stones decorated the pathways, all of which led to a gnarled olive tree in the back.

Vaasa stopped.

Roman stood there, waiting.

Vaasa's heart slammed against her chest. "What—" she started.

Roman stepped to the side, revealing a bench beneath the olive tree and a woman who immediately stood from it.

Amalie.

CHAPTER 12

"Amalie!" Vaasa kicked up gravel around her feet as she sprinted, tossing her cloak to the floor. She ignored everything else in the room, her eyes only on her closest friend. Amalie stepped forward just as Vaasa slid into the space in front of her, shaking, inspecting her, running her hands over Amalie's shoulders. She had been cleaned, given new Asteryan clothes, her brown hair brushed. There wasn't a trace of wounds or cuts on her olive skin. Nothing like what had been done to Vaasa in the prison. The only indicator that Amalie was a prisoner were the two iron shackles clamped around her wrists, bound together by a thick chain.

Undoubtedly, they were made of that same magic-stifling material as the collar Lord Vlacik had forced Vaasa to wear in the prison.

"I'm all right," Amalie said quietly.

Vaasa looked up at Roman, who observed Amalie suspiciously. His shoulders were taut, like he was prepared to move at any second, to intervene if Amalie revealed herself to be a threat. Vaasa couldn't place what he knew and what he didn't, but he had brought Amalie here. He had access to her.

"As you can see, she is recovering from her curse," Ozik said, his voice coming closer. "Your lead sentinel was kind enough to retrieve her."

Vaasa looked over Amalie once more, frustration mingling with her relief. Ozik was still selling this curse narrative, even to Roman. Her words slipped through gritted teeth. "What do you want, Ozik?"

"Don't give him anything," Amalie snarled in Icrurian.

Ozik whipped his head to her, eyeing her suspiciously. Like he anticipated a fight. "To remind you that it is worth it to cooperate," Ozik finally said. "Thank you, Katayev. You're dismissed. Return the girl to her cell."

Amalie froze.

"Stop," Vaasa begged, turning to Ozik. She had no magic to strike, nothing to fight back with. The powerlessness of it seeped into her bones. Her fists balled at her side. "I'll give you whatever you want. Just let her stay."

"Don't," Amalie warned. "You should run, Vaasa. Whatever you do, flee this place."

Ozik tsked, gesturing toward Roman that he should remove Amalie. He held Vaasa's gaze sternly. "Cooperate. That's what I want. Do that, and you will see her again. *Unharmed.*"

Vaasa looked back at Amalie, tears welling in her eyes. Roman hesitated, confusion marring his features, but finally stepped toward the witch. Amalie recoiled, snapping, "I can walk on my own."

Roman grabbed ahold of her arm anyway.

"I'm sorry," Vaasa choked. "I'm so sorry."

And then Amalie met her eyes with a burning fury. Something new seemed to emanate from her, this otherworldliness that Vaasa hadn't seen before. This *rage*.

"You aren't the one who will pay for this," Amalie said. She slid her eyes to Ozik.

And he stepped back. "Now, Roman."

Vaasa's breath caught as she watched Roman drag Amalie out of the greenhouse, the entire exchange marking itself upon her. She swore she'd just seen trepidation in Ozik's tight grimace. Vaasa watched Roman's back as he exited the room with Amalie.

Was everything Roman had said to her a lie? He had cowed to Ozik within seconds.

Vaasa turned to face Ozik, prepared to argue further or at least attempt to pry information from him, but softly, gently, there came a whisper of something in her body.

Magic sprang from wherever it was hidden inside her, curling around her muscles and bones, fortifying her like armor. It sloshed into her gut and burned in her chest. Magic poured from her fingertips in tendrils of black mist, cloaking the ground around her feet. Vaasa stumbled back in shock, finding Ozik standing just a few feet away.

"I can and will take your magic back, should you get any futile notions of attacking," he drawled. "You've always been a good student, Vaasalisa. Do not prove me wrong."

The advisor held the same confident air about him that he had when she was young; he appeared as though he'd come to teach her something. Their daily lessons, sometimes multiple times a day, flashed before her eyes. The stern pull of his mouth, the crinkle of his brow when he found himself disappointed in her—all touchstones of her childhood. Building blocks of the woman she was now, who questioned the motivations of every person around her. Who had never been safe enough to trust anyone. So much so that when she'd finally been faced with authenticity, she had spent months convincing herself the people who loved her were lying.

Except Melisina had begun to banish that fear. Amalie, too. Her entire coven. They had taught her magic because they loved her, which made it far more difficult to look Ozik in the eyes now.

He had never taught her a single thing for her benefit. It had always been for his.

"What are you doing?" Vaasa choked out.

"You're weak," Ozik said, as if that was an explanation.

"What do you mean?"

"What do you know of your magic, Vaasalisa? What has your coven taught you?"

Vaasa could hardly process his questions. She focused instead on the snake, on the shifting of magic once again within her body. It was like something came loose within her, the power itself burrowing into her organs and tissues. It lapped against her insides as she transformed it from snake to water to bird of prey. Though it still felt different, this was closer to herself than anything she'd felt in weeks.

Cooperate. That's what I want. Do that, and you will see her again.

"What do *you* know of my magic?" Vaasa asked, emboldened by her renewed connection to Veragi, the goddess of witchcraft herself.

"I know that in order to make the most of it, you must learn to *wield* it, even through pain," Ozik said.

"Is that why you let Lord Vlacik torture me?" she dared to ask.

Ozik pursed his lips. "Your mother survived for years because of what I could show her. Did you think she got lucky? Veragi witches are the most tumultuous, the most haunted, of the bloodlines. Your magic is an art form that has been sorely lost."

Silence coursed between them. There was nothing Vaasa could say in response to him, only listen. Only absorb. Once again, she saw the man she'd known as a teenager. Harsh, sharp, but incredibly intelligent. Though she feared him, she in a strange way trusted her value to him. There had been a time when Ozik's tutelage was the one thing she clung to, desperately hoping the skills he taught her might lead to an ambassadorship instead of a marriage.

And now Vaasa was forced to reconcile that man with the one who stood across from her—who had murdered her mother, killed the love of her life, brought him back in a twisted bargain, and then locked her up in a prison to be tortured.

The one who still held Amalie as leverage.

"I saw the wolf," Ozik said, crossing his arms over his chest. "You've at least uncovered the most basic thing your magic can do: manifestations. You know mine well enough."

Realization dawned upon her. "The Miro'dag." A *manifestation*. "What does that mean? Manifestation?"

"It is an expression of our magic, of our souls. That is the way with sentimental magic."

Sentimental magic. His words swirled in her mind, connecting with everything she'd learned thus far. Admittedly, there were large gaps. Things Melisina and the rest of the coven hadn't taught her, things they perhaps didn't know themselves. *Focus on what you do know,* they'd repeated over and over. Sometimes those words had set her free, other times they had felt like a consolation prize for the fact that most information about magic had been irrevocably burned away.

Vaasa tilted her head. "Your manifestation is a demon. What exactly does that say about *your* soul?"

Ozik remained deadly serious as he said, "That it is dark and wicked and was lost long ago."

Vaasa stared blankly, hoping her impassive grimace would be interpreted as a result of her deep-seated hatred for the advisor, not her own incompetence.

He sighed. "There is only one person in this world who can teach you what has been erased from history, and that is me. The question is whether you are willing to learn, or whether you are going to waste this opportunity."

"Opportunity?" she shot back, poison on her tongue. "You are holding me hostage and torturing my best friend."

Ozik merely chuckled. "The witch is alive and has not been harmed. Lord Vlacik hasn't touched her. We are . . . trying another way."

He had put a stop to the torture? Vaasa crossed her arms. "Fine. Let me see her."

"Earn it."

"Why? Why teach me anything at all?"

His severe gaze could have turned her into one of the statues that guarded the greenhouse. "Because soon you're going to do something for me, Vaasalisa. And in order for you to accomplish it, you will need to become a more formidable ally."

Vaasa narrowed her eyes. "I will never do *anything* for you. Not willingly."

Ozik shifted his weight, frustration coating his features. She hadn't been this obstinate with him since she was a teenager. Her magic tugged in her abdomen and then leaked onto her hands. She startled, stumbling backward a step, shaking her wrists like they were covered in water. "What are you doing?"

He began to walk, circling her. "What do you know of the Witches' War?"

Vaasa hesitated, unsure if she wanted to engage. The magic tightened, and she sputtered, "I know that before it, Icruria was ruled by magical bloodlines. The Witches' War extinguished most of them and made way for Icrurian unification."

He nodded, his steps slow. Her magic calmed, and she let out a small sigh, her shoulders going slack.

"The covens used to rule Icruria," he said. "But during the Witches' War, most of the old texts were burned. And when the common tongue replaced the old dialects, it was the death of oral tradition. Therefore, the relative death of the gods and goddesses that the independent city-states worshipped."

It had always surprised her that the Icrurians did not have deeper religious traditions; most of their deities were now fables or fuel for celebrations. The gods and goddesses that the sodalities were named after were the only real landmarks left. The deities had become cultural; the witches were the last remaining remnant of the gods' and goddesses' power.

The information curled in her ears and settled there, giving her that same inextinguishable hunger she'd had from a young age. She gathered history and languages like weapons because that was what understanding them could turn someone into. *That* was the weapon her father and Ozik had created. So she couldn't help herself—she leaned in to listen, and by the subtle curl of Ozik's lips, he knew he had her.

"What the Icrurians refuse to speak about is that the deities were wicked, evil creatures," he continued. "They need witches in order to keep their foothold in this realm. Without their covens, they can be sealed into tombs scattered across this continent. But even then, their bloodlines still pop up in unexpected places, and so if even one witch emerges, the deity has a foothold again."

Vaasa leaned farther forward, memorizing every word he said, even if she didn't entirely believe him. There was no telling whether this version of history was true.

"What is sentimental magic, then?" she asked.

"Begin wielding your magic again, and I will tell you."

Vaasa pursed her lips. She shouldn't obey. She knew the right choice. Yet the allure of knowledge pushed her forward, magic spilling from her fingertips. It coated the floor around her once more, spreading like fog on the water.

Ozik began again. "There are two types of magic, two types of covens, just like there are two classifications of deities. Ones that rule the outer world, the physical; and ones that rule the inner world, the emotional. Corporeal versus sentimental. Veragi is a sentimental deity—the most powerful one, as her witches have a skill unlike any other."

Vaasa swallowed. Her magic slithered at her feet, then spread out into the greenhouse. She tried to bring it back inside herself, but Ozik shook his head. As the black tendrils coated the stones marking the pathway she stood upon, Vaasa tried not to rear back from her own power.

"Push it forward. Use everything around you instead of everything within you," he said.

Vaasa's eyebrows slammed together, his words not making sense. She stared down at the magic, hesitating, and then it reared forward out of her control. Knots in her body tightened and tugged, an outside force now guiding her power. She gasped and stumbled as it burst out in sharp tendrils, one of which snapped against an iron bench to her left. It knocked the bench sideways with a crash, and petals flew into the air, drifting softly to coat the ground.

"Stop," she said.

Her magic slithered back up her dress, the wolf nowhere to be found. Vaasa's heart beat faster, fear growing within her as the magic curled around her body. Her waist. Her chest. It consumed her arm, then her shoulders, brushing the nape of her neck. She knew better than to let the power reach her face. As it brushed her throat, terror slammed against her ribcage. "Stop!"

"It is a void because you don't know what else to make it, but that doesn't have to be its final form," Ozik said, voice unbelievably calm as he watched her panic. "Your mother saw a spider, so afraid of being crushed beneath everyone else's feet. What is it you're so terrified of becoming?"

This information about her mother sank its teeth into her. Her mother, a woman afraid of being powerless, of being too small to fight back. Vaasa heard it again, the hiss of the snake. Felt the ridges of scales as it wound around her throat.

Ozik tilted his head, enamored by the creature. The gold in his eyes was swallowed by the black snake that slithered along her skin. The manifestation rose to rub against her cheek. It was cool to the touch, its sharp sibilations a warning in her ears.

"A serpent," Ozik said. "The very thing they called your father."

"*Stop*," Vaasa whispered, this time tasting the power as the snake slid across her lips.

Ozik inspected Vaasa, saw how her hands shook. His eyes narrowed upon the magic circling her throat, and all of Vaasa's emotions played upon his face. However their bargain linked them, they shared the intensity of this moment. They shared her fear.

"I am not controlling this any longer. You are."

Vaasa forced herself to suck down air, and the hiss of the snake rattled in her ear. She met Ozik's eyes, and he stared at her, his hands clasped behind his back.

"All magic needs fuel," he said. "*Think*. When did you see the wolf? When did it finally make itself known to you?"

The look on his face seemed to say he already knew the answer. There was ancient wisdom behind his eyes, and she wasn't certain how she'd never seen it before, how she'd never recognized the churning of power within him or the unnatural years that stared back at her. It was as if his own magic had grown unruly in the time she was away, in the time her mother had been dead. No longer able to be masked, to be hidden.

Perhaps it was all a trick, some mind game. Yet she thought back to the height of her own magic, to the times it had felt utterly out of control. At the beginning, in the Library of Una when she'd searched desperately for a clue as to what this magic was. With Kosana, when she'd found herself outmatched by the warrior as they trained next to the Settara. Again when Reid had told her that Dominik was coming to Mireh. Most notably, when she'd looked at her brother and decided she'd lost enough, when she'd accepted her death and let go of that . . .

Fear.

Every time the magic had reared to the surface in an uncontrollable wave, it had been a reaction to fear. Fear she would never find answers. Fear Kosana would prove her worthless. Fear Dominik would harm all the people she had just begun to love. Fear that she would die, that Amalie would die, and the greatest tragedy of her life would be not having enough time.

Her magic churned in her gut, a ruthless force once again as she stared at Ozik across the pathway. Fear of him. Fear of everything, always. The very thing that had given the snake its shape, that had made a monster out of her.

Fear of herself.

But she didn't need to be afraid any longer. She was not what they had tried to make her.

Something tangible and powerful poured out of her body, mist and magic and everything she had ever felt up until that moment. To her left, the wolf took form as naturally to her as breathing. Its smoky edges curled into the air, white eyes shining from a shadowy face. One paw swiped at the stones beneath it.

The corner of Ozik's lips curled into a knowing smile as he gazed upon her manifestation. "Your magic was never out of control, Vaasalisa. It was feeding, because *that* is what sentimental magic does. It's what makes Veragi magic so spectacular, so threatening. You are starving, and so you are feasting on yourself, the closest and easiest source. But what would happen if you feasted on everything around you instead?"

Vaasa looked to the wolf, felt every edge and subtle sway of it. Felt the desire to send it forward and strike. The manifestation took a step, lowering its nose to the ground and letting out an audible growl.

Ozik watched it closely. "Think. *Observe.* You have always perceived the emotions of those around you. Perhaps now is the time you start weaponizing them instead of internalizing them."

Vaasa stared at him, and despite what she wanted to believe, she swore she could *feel* his subtle fear. She could taste it. It slid across her tongue in satiating breaths. The relief it brought was palpable, instantaneous.

The wolf grew sharper. More defined. No longer were the edges glimmering tendrils of smoke; she could see and feel the texture of hair, of claws, of teeth.

Her eyes snapped to Ozik.

She was feeding off him.

This was unnatural. Perverse and wrong.

Vaasa dismissed the magic, obliterating it into mist that dissipated in the air. Ozik frowned as he stepped forward, hissing, "What are you doing?"

A memory threaded her mind of the day her coven crawled beneath a table with her. Melisina's soft voice echoed. *Just cry. Let it out.* And Vaasa realized: Ozik's tutelage wasn't one she was willing to accept. Not anymore. Her coven had shown her the power of gentle love, and she would no longer squeeze a stem of thorns for the sake of the flower. "I won't twist magic this way. I never asked you to train me."

The look on his face was stifling—fury and grief carved into the pale lines of it. "A bargain goes both ways, Vaasalisa."

Vaasa's fists tightened. "So, if I don't let you train my magic, you'll murder me like you did my mother?"

Ozik's grimaced. "I did not kill your mother. She broke a bargain.

I don't control the rules of magic. And how do you intend to survive if you refuse to learn them?"

"Then why not release my mother from the bargain?" Vaasa demanded. "Why not release me? Are you so powerless that you cannot free your own thralls?"

Ozik's voice rose. "You cannot handle the answers to your questions until you learn to use your magic. I will tell you what you need to know when you are ready, but you are *not ready*."

"How could I be?" she barked back. "I am not my mother. I am not so desperate for love or power that I'll eat it off a dagger. I am not afraid of being crushed—I'm afraid of being *you*."

It was as if a sharp blade cut directly through her muscles. Her magic severed from her body once again, this time immediately and without rebellion. Ozik walked forward. Gasping, Vaasa lifted her hands to her throat as if to defend her own life, an innate reaction. Her knees buckled and scraped against the stones beneath her.

"You are an ignorant child with no understanding of who your mother was or what she gave to keep you alive. So long as you are in my presence, do not speak of her as if you knew her. You didn't."

Vaasa wanted to spit at him, to remind him that it was his fault that she'd never known her mother. That all she'd gotten was the cold, aloof version of a woman fighting to stay alive in a place that hadn't kept her safe.

And if Ozik had loved her, he would have saved her.

But he hadn't.

He released the hold he had on Vaasa, and she fell forward, hands catching her just before her face hit the iridescent stones. Nausea tightened her throat, but she didn't give in. She was at least tolerating their connection, tolerating the use of her magic. No darkness lined the edges of her vision this time.

"I said I was trying things a different way," Ozik said. He picked up his cloak from the bench he'd draped it over. "Every morning, you will come here, and I will train your magic. Each time you make enough progress, I will have the witch brought to you."

Vaasa looked down at the stones cutting into her knees. He had all the leverage in the world, and she had nothing. Any grasp on the life she had found in Mireh was smothered now.

No.

Even in darkness, even on the verge of death, Vaasa had never been helpless. She had an arsenal in her mind, and it was time she started using it.

You cannot handle the answers to your questions until you learn to use your magic.

Ozik wanted her to grow stronger. Each time he'd allowed Lord Vlacik to cut at her skin or for her magic to overtake her, it had been in pursuit of her endurance. He was *training* her. Teaching her, just as he had done when she was a child.

The question was why. What was it that Ozik wanted her to become? To accomplish?

"I will see you tomorrow morning," Ozik said.

He disappeared into a different room of the greenhouse, and Vaasa was left staring up at the olive tree, the words of her mother's letter playing out in the back of her mind.

Whatever you do, stay in Mireh and do not unite the other pieces. The price is far too great.

The following day, Vaasa found Ozik waiting beneath the olive tree.

He stood at her arrival, striding forward with ease. Like it had yesterday, her magic unfurled in her gut, melding to the snake she had thought about all night. She swallowed down her fear, prepared to do things his way if that was what it took. She didn't like the idea of the magic he claimed she could access—to feed on other people's emotions instead of her own—but what choice did she have?

For now, her breath came easier. She let the power flow through her veins and leak onto her fingertips. Dark smoke licked the air, then curled around her hands and wrists.

"Are you ready to begin?" Ozik asked.

Vaasa met his eyes. Everything about him was calmer in here. Brighter. As if, with the flora and the late morning sunshine filtering through the glass walls, he was a different person. The warmth brought relief, and with it, the space for curiosity. For her to focus everything she had on finding out precisely what this man needed.

So she could take it all away.

"I'm ready," Vaasa said.

Ozik grinned.

CHAPTER 13

It was almost morning when Vaasa woke, gut clenching and burning, the feeling of her magic being torn from her bones pervading every nerve she had. She cried out, turning over and pulling her legs up to her chest, rocking in agony. The pain seared down her neck and spine, spreading to every inch of her body, as if her very core was being flayed in two. Magic writhed beneath her skin.

Vaasa tried to breathe. She couldn't. Tears streamed down her face as Ozik used Vaasa's magic for something she couldn't name. Couldn't see. She dove into that pain, tried to connect with it, to find some thread to grasp between her fingers and give her access to whatever it was Ozik was doing.

It pulled her in as if it were her own body moving, her will manipulating the connection. The pain began to ease as she followed that feeling, as she gave into the connection that guided her. And then behind her eyes, she was staring at the shimmering string between them that threaded down what looked like an underground tunnel. Everything was blurry, but there was something along the walls that sent a shiver down her spine. She couldn't quite make out the shape of it, but her body knew to keep its distance. Her instinct told her not to look closer. She stared down that shadowy corridor until she came upon a massive archway, the stones ivory white.

Despite herself, Vaasa walked inside. Everything except for the space immediately in front of her was blurred, the edges smoked and details indistinguishable. But glowing in front of her was a red pool of *something*. It swirled in on itself, too bright to be blood. The longer she stared, the longer she felt the sentience of what existed within it. Breathing. Writhing. Waiting.

The red pool began to ripple.

Something terrible, something ancient.

Death.

She felt it. Someone was dying. She smelled the metallic carnage, the fear. She experienced it as Ozik did, as if she were him and he were her. Connected. Intertwined. His horror and agony were hers. Every moment of it was miserable. Their magic was one and the same, and he was the fuel while she was the fire. It was oil on her skin. The rancid smell of burning hair and flesh pervaded all the air around her.

And then she was falling. Something crashed.

The magic extinguished, and everything in her mind went dark, and she was thrust back into her own body as it hit the ground. Her eyes flew open as her heart thudded rapid-fire against her chest. She'd rolled off the couch, and to her left, an end table had fallen over, the small iron figurines that graced it scattered on the floor.

Black mist coated the blankets around her. Vaasa scrambled to her knees and gasped, this magic making sense to her. It was familiar and kind and *home*. Black tendrils rose and dipped playfully around her. Some wrapped about her wrists. Cool to the touch. Mist on her skin.

Veragi magic.

It was *hers*.

Vaasa breathed in deeply, savoring the feel of it around her.

And then it snapped back into her body, buried once again in her bones and sinew.

Gone.

Just as quickly as she'd had it, the force disappeared. An emptiness conquered every spot where hope had just bloomed.

The door to the emperor's quarters burst open, and Vaasa tried to move, tried to defend herself. She turned just in time to see Roman with his sword drawn, staring at the room empty of anyone but her.

"What happened?" he demanded. He must have been standing outside her door, must have been waiting that entire time. He'd likely heard the table crash.

"I . . . had a nightmare," she choked out.

His shoulders fell sullenly at the words. He looked at the table, at the figurines scattered on the floor. "You're sleeping out here?"

Vaasa bit her lip. She didn't confirm or deny his assumption; her placement did that for her, with the blankets strewn across the rumpled couch. "Why were you outside of my door?"

"The sentinels rotate; tonight was my turn to guard your door. I've . . . debated coming and speaking with you."

Vaasa scowled.

Roman walked past her to the spilled table and lifted it with ease, kneeling down to pick up the iron figurines. His eyes drifted to the couch. After a moment, he asked, "Is there anything I can do?"

Her heart still raced, concern lingering in each of her nerves as she considered exactly what Ozik had been doing with her magic. She didn't understand any of what she had just seen.

And she didn't know whether she could trust Roman.

"I need to see my friend," she whispered.

Roman paused his cleaning. "She's still dangerous. I don't think Ozik has been able to break her curse. He made it clear that seeing her without him present could be extraordinarily dangerous for you."

Vaasa didn't believe that for a second; it was a lie Ozik spun to keep her from seeing Amalie. She almost came right out and told Roman everything, but the voice in her head told her not to give an inch. Roman had never been deeply religious, but he'd bowed his head and read the teachings of the clergy without much question. If he found out her magic wasn't some curse she wanted to expel, would he turn on her? Would he wish her locked back up in that prison in hopes of finding some impossible cure?

"I . . ." she trailed off. She had to think of something. Anything. The idea of lying to him was a knife in her gut, but she didn't have another choice. "How much do you know of Ozik?"

Roman pursed his lips. Even with both of them on their knees, he was still taller than her. He placed the figurines back on the table but didn't lift from his place on the floor. His soft brown eyes were shielded, though that didn't strike Vaasa as stemming from loyalty. They were still wider, more fearful.

"I know I won't survive disobeying him," he finally said. "Not until you are formally the empress."

Was that his plan, then? To obey Ozik long enough to make it to her wedding? "I think you know as well as I do that a title won't save either of us from him," she whispered, the two of them staring at each other in the dark.

"You believe he will kill you?"

Vaasa knew Ozik wouldn't. Not as long as he needed her magic, and given the strength and youth he had gained from their bond, she suspected Ozik would do just about anything to keep her alive. "No," she said. "But he intends to rule with me as a puppet for life. Likely, once there are heirs, he will kill whoever I marry."

Roman didn't move. His expression melded to one of impassivity, even more guarded than he had been before. "Is that why you accepted Lord Karev's invitation for tomorrow night? To move forward with one of your suitors?"

Vaasa sat more upright, trying to keep her composure. "I don't see what other choice I have." It was the best she could do to create the illusion of a real competition for her hand, for the Asteryan throne, and delay an actual marriage. She wasn't certain she could outmaneuver Ozik, but if she had the opportunity to sow discord between the lords, it might be enough to damage any chance they had at gathering an army strong enough to outlast the Icrurian Central Forces. Perhaps that was her only way to escape—to lie in wait. "I don't want to marry any of them," she confessed.

At those words, Roman crawled to the fire, stoking it, and the flames roared back to life. Light flooded the room as he turned to face her again. With the fire at his back, his face was still shadowed, making him look almost ethereal. Truly and wholly a ghost. "I—" He paused for a moment. "I don't know what to do. Who to trust."

"Trust with what?"

Roman pursed his lips, then started to crawl toward her again. The closer he came, the more her body recognized him. He had snuck into her rooms countless times before. They had been in similar positions as this. He stopped just before where she sat, her back against the couch, his knees only a few feet from her.

"Did you love him?" Roman asked so quietly. "The Wolf of Mireh."

The wolf. *Her* wolf. The person her magic had seemed to model itself after, as if it, too, wanted to be more like him. Her soul and his, similar enough to reflect in her power. The thought of Reid caused a knot to form in her throat. This was the first time they had spoken of him, had acknowledged that she'd been married to another man.

She and Roman were incapable of casual conversation, she realized. It was impossible to know someone and then unknow them. Without trying, they would pick up where they'd left off, because that was what people did. She saw the anger in Roman's eyes. He had always been a jealous creature. And she couldn't bring herself to break his heart—not yet. She pulled her blankets over her lap, careful to keep the majority of herself covered. "Being in Icruria saved my life," she said. "Dominik would have killed me."

Roman pursed his lips. "I don't think you would have stayed anywhere you were in danger. That's why I find this whole story about Icruria difficult to believe."

"That Ozik came and rescued me from the clutches of a violent warlord?"

A pause, and then: "How did Dominik die?"

Vaasa kept silent. She kept waiting for that serpent to coil, for the wolf to raise its head and howl, but was left with an utter sense of emptiness that was almost more consuming than the magic had been. Whatever trickle of it she'd felt earlier had gone.

Roman waited, eyes burning into her. "Was it Reid of Mireh? There are so many rumors."

Her defensiveness reared up—it was instinct. "*I* killed Dominik."

Roman raised his eyebrows and then looked her over like he was seeing her for the first time. His gaze dragged up and down her, to the line where her nightgown met the blankets. "You are not who you used to be."

"No, I am not."

"Neither am I."

She bristled. "No, I am nothing like who I was, Roman. You can't even begin to fathom."

"Do you believe me afraid of you? With one death on your hands?" He chuckled with a desperate lilt. "I went to *war*, Vaasa. I was a prisoner. You have no idea what I have seen and sacrificed to be sitting here next to you."

Vaasa glanced at Roman's hands as if the blood would still be there, but they looked the same as they always had. And though she could tell him everything, of the magic she had gained and the lives she had taken with it, she didn't. "You're right, I'm sorry," she said instead. Vaasa didn't tell him the other things she had pieced together here or the questions that plagued her. She didn't quite know how to breathe correctly in his presence, like there was still a part of her reaching backward, seizing at her chest.

Roman ran his tongue over his teeth. "The Wolf. He was . . . kind to you, then?"

Vaasa fiddled with her hands. Yes. Kinder than any other person had ever been to her. But what good did it do to reveal such a thing to Roman?

"Does it matter?" she asked.

"Of course it matters." He gritted his teeth and looked away from her, staring into the fire once more. "When I found out you were marrying him, I was sick, Vaasa. Terrified. And when I heard he was parading you around his city and that your brother was opening trade with Icruria, it just destroyed me. I know what kind of man Reid of Mireh is."

Vaasa paused. It was odd to hear of hers and Reid's escapades, their games of love that had blossomed into the real thing, from someone who heard the whispers they had purposefully stoked. Icruria had always been a secret, yet upon her marriage, the curtain had fallen. Trade had assured it. Still, it was personal: the flicker of hatred that marked the way Roman tightened his fists. "What do you mean, you know what kind of man he is?"

Roman finally lifted his chin, a muscle feathering in his jaw. "He often passed through Wrultho. His father was the head of their squadron, but I noticed him the first time he arrived, young to be the leader of anything and brutal. People whispered about him, about the sheer amount of Asteryans he killed along the Sanguine. He . . ." Roman shook his head. "It doesn't matter. Each time he returned, he was decorated with something new, earned from yet another mass slaughter on the river. He was a cruel man. There's a reason they call him the Wolf of Mireh."

Stoic as the stone around her, Vaasa didn't dare breathe. *Cruel* was not a word she would ever use to describe Reid.

"I . . ." Vaasa looked down at her hands. The choice to lie to Roman fully, to spin some mistruth about her marriage—it was a choice she couldn't undo.

"Did you consummate the union?" Roman asked outright, leaning forward as if he'd been anticipating this very line of conversation since the moment they found each other again.

What an outdated Asteryan concept, Reid had once said to her.

Vaasa parted her lips, then snapped them shut. Each moment she'd spent with Reid had set her on fire, no matter how hard she'd fought it. When she'd finally had him, had his mouth on hers and his bare skin against her own, she had never wanted anything more. It wasn't a consummation. It was a choice. And if the world hadn't done exactly what she'd predicted it would do, if Dominik and Ozik hadn't ruined everything, she knew with certainty she would still be there with Reid, sleeping next to him now.

But what of that could Roman understand, especially after what he'd just told her? She sighed. "I did."

Roman closed his eyes. Shook his head. "Of course you did. I . . . I don't know why I thought otherwise."

"But it upsets you," she noted.

Roman shrugged, leaning back onto his hands. "It was foolish to believe you hadn't been with someone after me. That I'm the only man to know you that way."

Vaasa couldn't explain the anxiety that welled in her at this line of conversation. The insurmountable guilt for having lived when she thought he hadn't. "I mourned you for a very long time, Roman."

He stared at her for a drawn-out moment. "I don't believe I've stopped mourning you, Vaasa."

Breath stilled in her chest. How many times had she wished for the chance to see him again? To hear his voice? Yet he was looking right at her, and she would trade just about anything to be staring at another man. What kind of person did that make her?

"Reid of Mireh sacked Innisjour," Roman said, changing the topic before Vaasa had the opportunity to say more. "Slaughtered the young lord there and hundreds of civilians. He tore down the dam and demolished an entire city, claiming his marriage to you makes him emperor of Asterya."

"Ozik told me he crossed the border," Vaasa said.

Roman narrowed his eyes just slightly. "He's been injured. He retreated from battle."

The world seemed to stall on its axis. That word stole the air from the room. *Injured.*

Roman's eyes searched her expression more closely than he ever had before.

She pushed it down—the wanting. The panic. The pain. Now was not the time. She had already given away too much.

Roman stood abruptly, taking a few steps away from her. "Vaasa, are you in love with him?"

"Roman, I—"

"He's already killed hundreds under the pretense that he has a claim to your throne. To our empire."

She saw Roman so clearly now, saw the betrayal written in the lines of his face at the thought of her having fallen in love with an Icrurian. With his enemy. But it was more than that.

There, in the depths of his eyes, was a glimmer of desire.

Our empire.

Suddenly, he morphed into someone entirely new before her. Gone was the remnant of the boy who had loved her, of the rebellion she'd found in him. He had been the safest thing. A man who couldn't take anything real from her. It wasn't like she would have ever been allowed to marry him.

And now there was a throne dangling above all their heads, and she wondered . . . was it enough to tempt Roman, too? Was that why he was here? To make himself a contender?

It hurt to think about Reid, even more so to pretend he wasn't the love of her life. That each inch of her didn't ache for him now. But survival demanded the worst of people, and she had always been capable of deception. A voice in her head whispered that she must lie, that she must spin whatever tale she needed in order to keep this inextinguishable truth from coming out: She was in love with the man who should be her greatest enemy, and if given half the chance, she would tear her home apart in his name.

"I was *married* to Reid of Mireh," Vaasa clarified, voice growing sharp. "He became my only political ally while Dominik was two steps away from taking my life. If you're asking if he was cruel or if I hated him, the answer is no."

It was purposeful, to twist his question and then to say the word *no*. He was waiting, hoping, *craving*, that exact word in response. It gave the appearance of disagreement—manipulated a palatable answer and put the onus on him to continue demanding further truth.

Roman pursed his lips, digesting her words slowly. Likely, he would interpret them to mean what he wanted to hear because that was far easier than stomaching reality. "And what did he want, then? Your throne?"

Vaasa shook her head, falling into the same wretched version of herself who could tell a part truth and call it whole. "It is what *I* wanted, Roman. I wanted my freedom. I wanted my life back. I wanted Dominik to pay for each time he took something from me, and I was willing to trade anything to get it. To manipulate Reid, if that's what it took."

Truth. That had been exactly the place she'd started in when Reid had brought her back from Dihrah.

"And what did that manipulation entail?" Roman demanded.

Bold—he was so very bold. She pulled the blankets further up her body and basked in the seed of rage simmering in her gut. His words reminded her of Lord Vlacik and the claims he'd made about her, of the things she knew they called her behind closed doors. *An Icrurian's whore.* Her competence would always be reduced to this: The world could not imagine a woman clever enough to outsmart a man, so they simply labeled her a temptress. "Are you asking if I fucked him to get what I wanted? If I let him play out his little fantasies so he would start a war for me?"

Roman's jaw flickered with anger. "I suppose I am."

"No," she snapped. "I didn't have to do a damn thing to convince Reid of Mireh to attack the border. Dominik and Ozik did all the work for me. But I suppose I should be flattered you think I'm a good enough fuck to incite a war."

Roman's eyes caught fire, but he seemed to notice the deep insult that had elicited her poison and reined in whatever response he'd conjured in his mind. "Vaasa, I never should have said that, I—"

"No, you shouldn't have," she seethed. "The Icrurians never would have crossed the border if Dominik and Ozik hadn't stoked a rebellion and tried to murder the major leaders of every city-state. My brother caused this war, and it had nothing to do with whose bed I was sold off to."

He was more tense than she had ever seen him. Yet his shoulders fell, breath coming back to him. "You're right."

"I know."

He hung his head. "You were always smarter than Dominik. Always a better choice to lead."

"Yet I still need a husband to do so."

He shifted his weight, still standing near the fireplace a few paces away from her. "And that's not what you want? To marry?"

There was a part of Vaasa that wanted so badly for Roman to be on her side. It thrummed in her chest, that wretched hope. But though she had wanted to trust him, to take a chance, she was not naive enough to let it come at the expense of her freedom. "No. I want the throne I sold my soul for—not because some husband is too stupid to outwit me, but because it has always belonged to me."

As she said the words, she realized there was truth woven into them. There was a part of her that *did* want the Asteryan throne. She *did* believe it belonged to her now, that she had sold her soul a thousand times over each time she learned a new language only for her father to bring those people to their knees. She had lied because of it, betrayed her own heart because of it, killed her brother because of it. But it did not belong to her just for the things she had done—it was for the things that had been done to her.

"They took everything from me," she hissed. Rage, authentic in its origin, spewed from her. "First they took you, then my mother, then they sold me off for bags of salt. So I want the throne because I have sacrificed enough for it, and I will not stop until it is mine."

Until I have torn it apart, and it can take no more from anyone else.

Roman squared his shoulders, lifting his chin and inspecting her face for any sign of mistruth. He wouldn't find it. Her confession held too much honesty, even if an omission lived between the words. Resolution crossed his mouth in the form of a firm line. He stepped forward and sank to his knees again, this time closer to her. Tentatively, he reached out, fingers extended and brushing softly along her cheek. She tried to look away, but his hand slipped behind her neck and his thumb held her jaw, forcing her to meet his eyes. The brown of them burned.

"I never should have spoken to you that way. I'm sorry."

She wanted to forgive him—that was the worst part. "Don't do it again," she whispered.

"I won't." He pushed a strand of her hair away from her face, tucking it behind her ear. His hand hovered there, still holding her cheek, though less forceful now. "I must be the one person you don't lie to. Promise me that, and I'll give you whatever you want."

It was a dangerous line to walk, a terrible tearing of her soul, but she needed access to Amalie more than she needed anything else. If Vaasa could find a way to get to Amalie, she could begin plotting an escape.

The lie slipped out as naturally as breathing. "I promise."

This place did not breed honesty. She had been born into lies. And anyway, secrets were what her relationship with Roman was built upon.

"You want to see your friend?" he asked. "You believe it's a risk worth taking?"

She nodded silently.

"All right. On a clear night, I'll take you." Roman looked around the empty room. "I should go. I've already stayed too long. Will you be able to sleep?"

"Yes," Vaasa said. "Thank you."

His touch slid from her cheek. Roman stood from his place on her floor and walked to the entrance of the quarters, looking over his shoulder at her. His hand hovered over the doorknob.

"What is it?" Vaasa asked.

Roman held her stare for a moment longer than he should have. "I hate him. The Wolf. For many things. But if he has known you, and you are not the reason he went to war, then I hate him even more."

Vaasa's lips parted, but no words came to her. What could she say? How could she explain the way her chest tightened in anxiety when she'd heard Reid was injured, the way she wanted to pull the blankets over her head and hide from it? Because she knew—she knew she was exactly the reason Reid had crossed the border.

He didn't want the Asteryan throne. He wanted *her*.

And here she was, staring at the previous love of her life.

Vaasa whispered good night just as Roman closed the door. The moment it latched, she leapt up from her makeshift bed and pressed her ear to the wood. Footsteps moved down the hall, away from her, and she let out a long breath. She replayed the entire interaction, simultaneously enraptured and disgusted with herself. Quietly, she settled on the couch once more.

Vaasa stared at the fire as it crackled and considered all of what Roman had said tonight.

Thoughts of Reid being injured enough to retreat from battle haunted her. And then Amalie, eyes flashing white with something unknown, the rage with which she'd stared at Ozik. Her mother's necklace, a puzzle piece she certainly needed to find.

Lord Karev's invitation tomorrow night.

Vaasa's fear turned her empty stomach into a pit. She hadn't wanted to lie to Roman, but her choices felt narrow. Another piece of her disappeared as she became exactly what she'd been raised to be. Manipulative, a backstabber, someone who believed their own lies, or at least their reasons for telling them.

But what if she wasn't the only one? A larger question lingered in her mind, one detail Roman had yet to mention. How did a man who was supposed to be dead earn the very position that put him in proximity to her?

At the *exact* moment the Asteryan throne hung in the balance.

Lord Vlacik was trying to use force. Lord Karev was trying to use charm.

Was Roman trying to use her heart?

CHAPTER 14

"I don't believe we need to stand watch tonight," Koen confessed, leaning against the railing of *The Red Corsair* and staring out at the vast, churning sea.

Reid didn't disagree. Splitting the night between Koen and himself was a pointless endeavor. Even if Sachia's crew did turn on them, their group was pathetically outnumbered. A single guard wouldn't make a difference. "If they wanted to kill us, they would have already," he agreed. "Or perhaps they're waiting until we make port."

"Perhaps," Koen mused.

Reid turned to get a better look at his friend. The closest thing he had to a brother. Koen's adoptive father, Kier, Reid's predecessor as headman, had been a close family friend to Melisina. It only lent to a closeness between Reid and Koen as well. They had never once been able to escape each other, but the truth was that Reid had no interest in escaping Koen. In fact, he wasn't certain anything could separate them for long.

Which was why he knew when something troubled his friend. "You're worried," Reid noted.

Koen slid his eyes to Reid and adjusted his spectacles. "Only a fool wouldn't be."

"Neither of you needs to be out here," Sachia said, sauntering down the stairs from the deck where she and Reid's mother had just been training. Her shoulders had dropped and her jaw had unclenched; Melisina was teaching her to release the magic slowly instead of allowing it to build to a breaking point. So far, it seemed that many of the techniques his mother knew applied to Sachia. Yet the feel of their magic was vastly different; Sachia's made the air around them sharp, whereas Veragi magic felt more like prying, seeking threads. "You should get some sleep. It takes energy to infiltrate the capital of Asterya."

"You speak of treason, Pirate," Reid said. "It is not infiltration when I am the rightful emperor."

She scoffed. "You're a jilted divorcé at best, Wolf."

Reid shook his head, though Koen let out a small chuckle at the pirate's boldness. Sachia would have gotten along swimmingly with Kosana, had the commander been here. A calm comfort had overtaken the crew at the group's presence. Even Jonáš had already begun to spend time with them willingly.

Reid didn't know how to explain it, but he had a gut feeling that trust could be found here.

"We need to cut your hair," Sachia said. "And shave your beard."

Reid furrowed his brow, and Koen snorted. "Good luck," his friend said.

"You look Icrurian," Sachia reminded him. "You look like Reid of Mireh."

She had a point. Reid ground his teeth. "How much farther do you estimate?"

Sachia pulled a spyglass from her waist, extending it to Reid. When he took it, she pointed to the horizon. "Do you see those mountains in the distance?"

Reid peered through the glass, seeing the dark shadow of something along the line where the sky met the sea. The moon was bright enough tonight to illuminate the dark and give him vision. Even the persistent snow had halted. "Yes."

"Those are the Iron Peaks. We'll make port tomorrow."

Koen stood up straight, hand snaking out to steal the spyglass right from Reid's hands. "Where is the prison?" he asked.

Sachia's tone went cold. "On an island deep inside the bay, off the shore of the main port. You won't see it until we're much deeper in."

"Do you have an escape plan yet?" Reid asked.

"I will." She rolled her shoulders as if she needed to revel in the calmness while it lasted. "I can cut your hair now, or I can cut it tomorrow."

Reid released his hold upon the gunwale, sighing. "Now is fine." He tried to exchange a glance with Koen, but his friend's attention was still occupied. Still entirely glued to the spyglass, pointing to the Iron Peaks. He stayed like that, perhaps trying not to laugh.

Faintly, Reid knew that he and Sachia weren't the only fools sneaking into this port in order to find someone. While Koen would have come here in service to Reid, in service to Vaasa, these circumstances were different. Reid understood infatuation. He himself had been transfixed by Vaasa the moment he met her, even in the nights when he'd tried not to be. There was nothing that would have kept Koen from this city. Not with Amalie still missing and not a single word about her whispered at any port. It had been confirmed that Vaasa was alive.

The same couldn't be said for Amalie.

"You can take the first shift," Reid said, though both he and Koen knew they had just agreed to end their separate watches. Koen simply wanted quiet. A chance to think.

Koen glanced at him for a moment, a readable gratefulness in his eyes at the fact that Reid had not yet asked the question, hadn't tried to pry information from Koen about the depths of his feelings for the young witch.

Perhaps Koen didn't know the extent of it. Perhaps Koen not knowing something made it all the worse for him.

With a strong breath, Reid sauntered after Sachia.

Mekës was more massive than Reid had ever imagined.

"Are you prepared?" Reid's mother asked. He looked to where she stood beside him, and his heart sank. The weeks on the water had worn her down; darkness shaded beneath her eyes, her usual warm smile replaced with a downward tilt of her mouth. The hammocks did no favors for her older limbs. A bit of magic darted around her hands, a telltale sign that she was too tired to contain it.

"You should have stayed in Innisjour," he whispered.

She shook her head in resounding disagreement. "They are my girls," she said, voice softly cracking. "And they are in pain."

His jaw clenched. Reid had asked a few times whether his mother had heard the voice of Veragi again, but each time he asked, she only shook her head in defeat.

"I'm prepared," he told her instead of asking another time. He couldn't manage to hold his voice steady. Fear plagued him, and though he did his best to swallow it down, the truth of it still lingered.

He had no indication as to what waited for him here.

His mother turned to him, and when she looked at him like that, he realized it wasn't just Vaasa and Amalie she had come for. He was foolish to suggest she stay in Innisjour; his mother, no matter his age, was never going to let him walk into danger without her.

The most powerful Veragi witch in history. A fact that had complicated their relationship at times, but that had taught him to live with the nuances of others' identities. People were hardly ever the singular version he wanted to see them as; his mother had made it easier for him to accept people for who they were.

"I'm not certain I can get used to you with short hair," she confessed. "And no beard. Just like on your wedding night."

At that, Reid conceded a small chuckle. Sachia had taken the lengths down to what she assured him was an Asteryan style; it no longer hung to his shoulders, and instead was cut much closer to his head, with the locks of it framing his ears. "I look less like Father," Reid confessed.

The auburn color of his hair had come entirely from his father's side, and Reid had grown it out the moment he could.

"Ah, but you will always look like you," his mother said.

She rested a hand on his shoulder, and they stood quietly together, taking in the granite-built silhouette of the city. Somewhere in that cluster of buildings, Vaasa lay in wait. Amalie lay in wait.

By the time the sun had fully risen, they had docked in the Mekës port and unloaded the silks and fabrics they'd pilfered from the dead merchant Reid had first paid to bring them here. The barrels of black powder stayed aboard, and Sachia confirmed it was best they remove those when night blanketed the port once again. Reid's gait adjusted to land, even with the sway of the docks beneath his feet. This transition had become like breathing to him. Five years working in the High Temple of Mireh had not taken the river from beneath his feet.

The smell of fish rode the air, so different from the crisp salt and light breeze of his home. This scent was rancid and cold, painful to the nostrils. Up on the slope leading to the Iron Peaks, the fortress of Mekës loomed. He gazed at the many towers, at what appeared to be patios and bridges connecting them all, and wondered exactly how much black powder it would take to send them cascading down the side of the mountain. It took considerable restraint not to storm up to the gates at that very moment and begin looking for his wife.

"Come," Sachia said, gesturing with her head toward one of the narrow streets. Koen stayed at his side while his mother stayed aboard the ship. The less they traipsed about the city, the better—their language would place a target on their backs. Members of Sachia's crew stayed aboard the ship at all times, and though it pained him to leave his mother, she'd assured him that she felt safe.

Reid trailed behind Koen as if he were a guard, his hand on the sword Sachia had loaned him. This was their agreed-upon disguise—to present the man who could speak Asteryan as a wealthy merchant and relegate Reid to what they already believed about him: an Icrurian brute.

They meandered down a pathway, snow pushed to either side as if a young boy had just worked a shovel down the center of it. The route led them to a teeming fish market, which smelled just as pungent as the sea. It seemed all roads led to the north side of the port, where Reid could see the spire of their Asteryan cathedral. He turned, narrowly avoiding slamming his shoulder into a scurrying fisherman in dingy clothes that didn't seem nearly warm enough. On the other side of the square was a large building that could only serve as their house of government. Between those two buildings was a stark iron pole, and when Reid flicked his eyes to the cobblestone, he noticed a drain.

It was meant for execution, then.

Sachia gestured with her head for Reid and Koen to follow her down a narrower walkway to their right. It led to a seamstress's shop, unassuming and settled nicely on a less crowded street. Sachia ducked inside, and Reid followed, cloak pulled around his shoulders, his face covered and his sword ready. Koen kept just in front of him, playing the powerful merchant well. A bell sounded at their entrance, and two older women came shuffling out from behind a row of fabric. All around them were sewn dresses, cloaks, pants, and other intricate winter garments. Reid scanned a display of ladies' intimates, eyes catching on black lace.

Sachia exchanged words with the owners, one of whom scurried out to see the loads of fabrics she brought in, the other going in a separate direction in a hurry.

The bells of the door rang.

"Sachia," a voice threaded through the air, causing Reid to turn and peer around the fabric, coming face-to-face with a dark-haired man. Dressed in a decorative black coat and pants, the man appeared nothing short of a lord, though seemingly young to command so much from his presence. His gray eyes were daunting, analytical, and keen.

Reid immediately distrusted him.

The man looked over both Koen and Reid, then spoke again in Asteryan. Reid wasn't able to understand much past the basic topic of their discussion, until Koen leaned in and translated. "He said that he heard her ship was in the port. He's inquiring as to who we are."

The man fixed his eyes upon them. Striding forward, he extended a hand to Koen. "Lord Patrik Karev," he said, and that much Reid understood.

Koen gave some kind of nicety back, taking the lord's hand and shaking it in the strange Asteryan gesture, though not offering up his own name.

"Icrurian?" Lord Karev asked.

Koen spoke quickly and with a direct, matter-of-fact tone. Frustration bloomed in Reid at his inability to understand. Sachia dragged the lord's attention back to her, and the two started to walk down one of the rows of fabric. He gestured to a row of dresses, and Sachia nodded, the two falling into easy conversation, yet Reid was able to discern a few key words. *Heiress* being one of them. One of the seamstresses came scuttling out and joined their discussion, waving her expressive arms toward a row of velvet dresses at the front of the store. Sachia led the lord away from them, running her finger over the different garments as she went.

Koen turned on his heel and walked away, looking utterly bored, and Reid took it as an invitation to follow him. "What are they speaking about?" he whispered once they were down a different row and out of earshot.

"The two seem to have done business before. He's inquiring about the pirate Jonáš told us about, Sutherland. And the other lord he mentioned, Lord Vlacik." Koen hushed for a moment, listening, and then added, "He said something about Sachia running her own crew now."

Reid bent to listen, desperate, but within a few words he was lost. Each time he thought he caught on to the topic of their discussion, the words jumbled together into something unrecognizable, and Reid sighed.

"He claims to need a dress for Vaasa," Koen said.

Reid went rigid. Why would that man need anything for Vaasa? "She's helping him pick one out?"

"Sachia offered to have it sent on his behalf to the fortress."

Breath caught in Reid's throat. *That* was how he could reach Vaasa. If he could just sneak a letter into that box—

The bell dinged, signaling the lord's departure.

Reid spun, finding Sachia as she wound around the garments and came to meet them at the back of the store. She leaned against the fabric stacks, but kept her voice intentionally low. "That's the lord I told you about. He's interested in the black powder, for starters, but he's more interested in you two. I said I would explain later, so he's invited me to come see him tomorrow night. He said he would be with the heiress, but it didn't mean we couldn't speak."

"We're going," Reid asserted.

"Don't be a fool," Sachia practically hissed. "There are far too many nobles where he's going, and it will make him suspicious. The goal is to gain access to the prison, not find ourselves locked inside of it."

Reid considered her words, hating how quickly he had to agree. It was a knee-jerk reaction to try and get closer to Vaasa, to find any path to her he could.

"Are we sending her a dress?" Koen asked.

Sachia nodded.

"I need a pen and paper," Reid managed through his gritted teeth. He started to turn, but Sachia shook her head.

"It's too dangerous for you to put something as obvious as a letter in that package. You have no idea if the fortress guard is searching her deliveries," she reminded him. "Think of something else."

Shit, Sachia was right. It would be foolish to risk this. Reid's shoulders slumped in defeat. Yet Koen tapped his foot, a sign he was moments away from something brilliant.

"What about the leather tie you used to hold your hair? Do you still have it?" Koen asked.

Reid reached into his pocket where he'd stashed the leather tie. At one time, it had belonged to his father, and he just hadn't found the strength to leave it on the ship. "It's here."

"Sew it into the dress," Koen suggested.

Reid's lips parted in shock. "That . . . might work."

"Indeed," Sachia agreed. "We just need to pick a dress. He said he didn't care which."

To not care . . . Reid bit the inside of his cheek. He stared at the velvet dresses lining the back wall, his heart clenching and searching for just a taste of her. Just to *see* Vaasa, to know she was okay.

What would he do when he found her? How would they escape Mekës? Escape Ozik?

Would she come with him at all?

That last question was the strangling one. The thing that welled in his body like a pool of fire. He had only had her one night. He'd heard Vaasa tell him she loved him, but she had never promised him that she would stay. Even if she had risked her life for him. Had sacrificed her magic for him.

That was the worry that haunted him.

He wasn't sure that was a worthwhile sacrifice at all.

"May I?" Reid asked.

"Pick the dress?"

Reid nodded.

Sachia shrugged, and Koen looked at him with understanding. Reid split from them, venturing around the rows of fabric and premade garments, his eyes scanning the smooth velvet he saw at the back.

Each of them was richly colored, so soft to the touch. Such depth in the starkness of the fabric. His eyes landed upon a dark navy dress with no extra decorations or appliqués. It was so simple in its design, yet his eyes couldn't leave it. She would look stunning in a dress like this.

"This one," he said, running his index finger along the fabric.

Sachia stared at him like he was a lovesick fool, and perhaps it was an apt description. He didn't care. He clenched the leather tie tightly in his fist.

Sachia merely nodded, walking to find the seamstresses. In moments, the navy blue dress was pulled down from the wall, and Reid handed Sachia the tie.

CHAPTER 15

On the morning of their first outing, Lord Karev sent Vaasa a gift. It came in a large box, one the sentinels hauled into her rooms after Vaasa had finished training with Ozik. When Vaasa opened it, she came upon a pile of deep navy blue velvet. Carefully, she ran her fingers over the soft fabric before pulling it from the box. It was a long-sleeved dress, so stark in its simplicity, the real decoration of the dress being the fabric itself. With a narrower skirt that didn't hoop out from her waist, she was silently grateful for a more utilitarian shape that didn't feature such useless grandeur. She lifted it from the box and inspected the dress, her heart racing.

It was stunning.

For a moment she paused, wondering if this was all more than she could handle. Still, she slipped the dress over her chemise and adjusted how it hung on her body, admiring the fit. There was a small scrape against her hip, and she felt along the dress, noticing a bump. She slid the dress off again, turning it inside out to get a better look.

Her breath hitched.

There, sewn into the inside lining of the dress, was a leather tie.

She knew such a leather tie. Had run her fingers over it, had watched it in the heat of an Icrurian summer, had fought the temptation to pull it from Reid's hair and run her fingers through the strands.

It looked a lot like Reid's leather tie.

Vaasa's hands started to shake. How had Lord Karev gotten this? Was it a threat? Was it possible the lord was more than what met the eye? She held the tie to her chest and breathed deeply. Every nerve she had went on high alert, and she did not calm by the time evening arrived.

Roman waited for her outside her door. She greeted him politely, his eyes lingering on where the dress clung to her. "A gift?" he asked.

Vaasa nodded.

As they walked through the fortress to the main entrance, Roman whispered, "It's a clear night. After you're done with *him*, I'll take you."

Vaasa almost stumbled to a stop. He was going to take her to see Amalie? "Tonight?"

"Tonight," Roman confirmed.

Vaasa's chest tightened ruthlessly. All she had to do was make it through the evening, and then she could see her closest friend. It gave her the courage to lift her chin and walk as if she were already an empress.

Lord Karev waited for her at exactly the time he'd promised. Dressed in a black petticoat that was cropped at the top of his waistline in the front, the lord was once again the image of new wealth and status. The iron buttons on his coat were a nod to Asteryan strength. Despite what she wanted to think of him, his looks were enough to sway a room. With his sharp jawline and thick brows, Lord Karev was far more handsome than he deserved to be.

He waited in the main courtyard next to a large, ornately decorated carriage that held his family's seal. A coronet sitting upon a spool of fabric, two stars above the scene. It was drawn in honor of the Karev family's humble beginning as fabric merchants. Lord Karev smiled at her as Vaasa approached, dipping at the waist much like he had done the night prior. This time, however, she wasn't alone. Roman trailed her. He had come out into the daylight, now taking the full responsibilities of her lead sentinel. She wasn't certain of his schedule, but he had been standing guard since the early afternoon.

Lord Karev flicked his eyes to Roman, looking the sentinel up and down. He seemed to measure the distance between the guard and Vaasa, brow furrowing. "And who is this?" he asked.

Roman dipped his head in feigned respect, though Vaasa noticed a tenseness in his posture. "Roman Katayev, the heiress's lead sentinel, Sire."

Lord Karev pursed his lips for a moment, then nodded sternly. Ever the polite Asteryan. "Well, thank you for escorting her to me. My guard will take over from here."

Roman shook his head. "With all due respect, the heiress won't leave the fortress without me or my men."

"Hmm." Lord Karev looked to Vaasa, and she nodded in resignation. In Roman's defense, it was utterly foolish for Lord Karev to believe he would be allowed to take her from the fortress alone. "So be it. I would have brought another carriage had I known. I apologize."

"No burden," Roman said, and just as he did, a small group of men on horseback entered the courtyard. With their group was a riderless horse that could only be for Roman. The sentinel turned on his heel and walked to the men, quickly loading onto the horse and adjusting his royal blue cloak. They all spoke with affability, a few of the men laughing.

"Where we're going, they'll have to wait outside," Lord Karev told her quietly.

Vaasa looked up into his gray eyes apologetically. She wasn't sure how to play their interactions now, given the leather tie. "I'll order them to stand the perimeter."

Lord Karev watched Roman carefully, not bothering much with attention on her. "Does he always follow you like a lost puppy?"

The truth was that this was the first time any of them had been in this position. Yet, that wasn't the safe answer to give, so Vaasa resorted to nodding, deciding it was best that Lord Karev not believe they could be alone. Perhaps they truly couldn't. This arrangement with Roman was uncharted territory. "Yes."

"Hmm" was all he said.

Then he opened the door to his carriage, and though she thought it was akin to stepping right into a spider's web, Vaasa gracefully took the step and crawled inside.

They arrived at the Emperor's Theater, and Vaasa couldn't help but stick her nose to the window to stare out at the massive building. One of the jewels of Mekës, the theater had been built in her father's honor when she was just a child. It was one of the few places in the city that Vaasa had never looked upon with disgust—untainted, lively, innocent. Most of the city was dark by the nature of the iron and granite used to build it, but this building had a stained glass window almost as large as the ones within the fortress that seemed to shed light upon every shadow of the exterior. It was anything but plain; scenes from famous plays had been carved into the exterior walls, statues of legendary characters walking along the sloped roofs.

She'd made a habit of visiting the theater frequently before her parents had died. If she closed her eyes, she could almost see her father walking up the beautiful granite steps. Could see his royal blue cloak billowing out behind him and the calmness of his indigo eyes—a perfect match to hers and Dominik's—as he looked over his shoulder and beckoned her to follow.

Father's fucking favorite, Dominik's voice slithered in her mind.

Vaasa looked down at the leather seats of Lord Karev's carriage, stealing her gaze away from the crowded theater. It was a strange thing to remember two conflicting sides of a person like the dual faces of a coin: one that made her ache with loss, one that made her glad of it. In the absence of her family, she was no longer certain what was real and what was amplified by specific memories. Did she miss them, or was she clinging to a story she could now tell herself because they were no longer there to prove her wrong?

Her heart twisted in on itself, each memory a thorn. She turned her body to face the lord, putting on her best surprised grin. "We're seeing a show?"

Lord Karev leaned back in the seat, taking as much space as he pleased. "You could call it that."

Her brow furrowed, but the carriage came to a stop. Lord Karev quickly exited, then held his hand for Vaasa to follow. Before she got the opportunity, the lord turned to Roman, who had dismounted from his horse and followed them up the snow-covered steps. "Hold the perimeter, we'll just be inside," Lord Karev commanded.

Roman stared at him for a second, seemingly dumbfounded at having received a command from the lord, then turned his attention to her as if to ask *What are my commands?*

Vaasa could see it there in his eyes: a desire for her to undermine Lord Karev. Yet she knew better—she couldn't, not if she wanted to keep her and Roman's history between them. It would do irreparable damage if anyone else was to learn of the ways in which they'd known each other. The line she walked with Lord Karev was precarious enough already. "The perimeter is fine," she confirmed.

Roman's jaw clenched for only a moment, but he didn't challenge her. Instead, he walked away quickly, like none of it mattered to him. Like *she* didn't matter to him. It was a fair, even appropriate, response. Still, it stung somewhere deep within her chest. This was precisely what their world would have been—them only knowing each other intimately under the cover of night, having to pretend that they didn't matter to each other when other people looked on. It was momentarily infuriating, how seamlessly that same potential future had found her.

Vaasa followed Lord Karev up the rest of the steps and into the theater. Yet the moment they entered, he veered left, away from the stunning chandelier and the three levels bustling with people. They trailed around the main corridor until they came upon a servants' hallway that had a guard standing in front of it, though once again, he was less at attention, less disciplined, than she remembered the city guard to be. As they approached, the guard gawked at her presence—a gesture entirely out of character. Quickly, he sketched a bow.

Beside her, Lord Karev remained tense, keeping watch on the sentinel. He kept his posture closed, controlled.

Either Lord Karev didn't trust the city guard, or this sentinel wasn't who he pretended to be. Without another word, he opened the door he stood in front of, revealing one of the many servants' passages built into the theater. Every building the nobles frequented had been designed with these small corridors. Vaasa watched each step Lord Karev took as they descended into the dark, dingy hallway. When they arrived at a staircase that would lead to what Vaasa assumed was the basement, she stopped hesitantly at the top. "Where are we going, Lord Karev?" She peered down the shadowy descent, her stomach turning.

Karev grinned as he placed one foot on the first step. "Do you need a sentinel to protect you, Heiress, or will a lord do?"

It was a strange mixture of flirtation and condescension, though Vaasa knew enough of men to know she needed to look charmed. It was once again difficult to ignore how blatantly perfect he might have been for her so many years ago. Bold, scheming, witty. In another life, this man would have driven Dominik to the point of insanity.

With a rebellious little smirk, she gestured for him to go on. "I suppose a lord will do."

They climbed down the stairs into what she realized were likely storage spaces. Costumes, candelabras, and other props littered the room. Yet, the raucous sounds of laughter floated through the walls. The clamor grew louder with each step. Before long, they arrived at yet another door, which was guarded by a different sentinel. This time, the guard didn't speak to them; he simply opened the door.

Loud cheering and the banging of fists on wood echoed around a large crowd. Eerie yellow light emanated from the enormous basement that Vaasa hadn't even known was there. People stood on all available sides of the room in a horseshoe, their loud screams pointed at a lifted platform in the center.

Upon that platform, two men, both with chains on their wrists, dove at each other. Vaasa almost gasped as she watched them swing fists and elbows. They tumbled to the ground and spun, swinging punches, blood spewing. It was disorganized fighting at best, like a street brawl between boys. And one *was* a boy—red hair, no older than sixteen.

Beside the platform, even the guards remained absorbed in the fight. They congregated together, no formal positions around the room. Who had trained these men?

Vaasa gazed around and watched as men exchanged coin while their wives or other escorts whispered under the hush of the crowd.

"They're betting on the outcome," she said quietly.

Lord Karev nodded. "They're prisoners, Heiress. The ones who win tend to live longer than the others. From what I hear, their cells are more comfortable, too."

Nausea immediately swept over Vaasa. It was an underground fighting ring. "Who is responsible for this?"

Lord Karev gestured with his head to a group of people standing on the opposite side of the room. Within it were a few merchants or other nobles, but Vaasa recognized the warden of the prison. She froze. Beside him, the two high-ranking sentinels who had played an active role in her torture stood there casually, as if they were guests instead of on duty.

And in the center of the crowd, Lord Vlacik.

Vaasa tried to keep her composure, swallowing against the feeling of bile rising in her throat. "The city guard. They work for Lord Vlacik."

Karev flicked his gaze to her, looking smugly impressed. "You're quick, aren't you? Those aren't guards at all, though."

Anxiety kept its chokehold on her, but Vaasa forced herself to tear her eyes from Vlacik and instead look up at Karev. "Who are they, then?"

Karev leaned forward with his gray eyes glimmering. His voice caressed her ear. "They're pirates, Heiress. Your entire city is infested with them."

"How?" Vaasa hissed.

He remained close to her, his words still a conspiratorial whisper, and she paid attention to every twitch of his body. Every movement. "Because the infamous Captain Sutherland is deep in Vlacik's pocket. No one has seen the pirate in months, but his crews have infiltrated the prison, and thanks to your brother, the city guard. They are high-ranked officers now, hardly distinguishable from the men who rightfully earned their status."

Vaasa contorted her face into a smile as if Karev had just told her a joke. Anything to make it seem that their closeness was a flirtation, not gossip. But she knew of Captain Sutherland and his empire on the sea; he was a pest her father hadn't been able to quash, or perhaps he'd never felt it worth the resources. Sutherland's name had only begun to circulate a few years ago, as if he'd just popped up out of nowhere.

Too long had passed between the lord's words and Vaasa's reaction. Karev offered his arm to her, picking up on her intention to seem as though they discussed something else. She took it, once again pulling close so their sides pressed together. "This started under my brother's reign?" she asked on a whisper.

"Your brother was content to allow Vlacik more power," he told her. "To give his council positions, and the greatest exemptions and trade opportunities to the Old Asteryans. Beneath this theater, he made Lord Vlacik quite a lot of money."

Dominik's connection to Vlacik unfolded in Vaasa's mind, made more complicated by the torture they had been conducting in the prisons. To allow Vlacik that close to the throne had been a mistake that was so unlike Dominik. He had always consolidated power, not given it away. Her brother must have desired knowledge of magic more than just about anything else. But why? Was it because he'd wanted to wield that magic himself, or was it something more desperate than a race for power? He'd found the necklace their mother had left Vaasa and chosen not to deliver it to her. He'd needed it, then, or felt threatened by the idea of Vaasa having it. The necklace meant something, *did* something. And it seemed like Ozik was guiding her in that same direction—like he wanted her to find the necklace.

Then it occurred to her that perhaps Dominik hadn't just hidden the necklace from Vaasa. Maybe he'd been hiding it from Ozik, too.

Vaasa fought the urge to close her eyes, if only to avoid having to see her brother's sharp features behind her lids. Another stark reminder that the line between who she wanted her family to be and who they actually were really was sharper than she thought. "Do *you* bet on this?" she asked.

Lord Karev merely shrugged. "From time to time. But pick any noble from our dinner the other night, and you'll find the same answer. This is how Lord Vlacik keeps his foothold now that his father is dead. Plenty of families are indebted to the Vlaciks. His connection to Sutherland on the seas and his infiltration of the prison and city guard have made him the most powerful man in Mekës."

That was the sort of economic power that no noble should hold, especially not one with sadistic tendencies like Lord Vlacik. Yet it made her situation even more perilous; he was a true contender for the throne, even without her. He could likely use such debts to take control of the empire, and all he would need to face down was Ozik. In fact, his awareness of Ozik's power was probably the only thing keeping Lord Vlacik at bay.

Perhaps that was why the lord was so hell-bent on understanding magic. It wasn't just to weaponize it, but to defeat the Zetyr witch who stood between him and the throne. Maybe Dominik's partnership with Vlacik had been in service of that same goal.

Vaasa turned to the fight still ensuing on the platform. The younger boy had a peculiar fighting style, one far wilder than the older man he faced. It was almost . . . Icrurian. Quick. To the point. Deliberate gaps in his defense led his much older opponent into his next strike, leaving the boy always one step ahead. This was how Kosana fought, how Esoti moved. Longing almost broke through Vaasa's careful composure—for the sight of those Icrurian warriors, for that salt lake in Mireh, for a place and a people that felt so much more like home.

The boy gave a quick combination with his hands and caught the older man on a right hook, which sent the man barreling down. The boy jumped on him, digging his elbow into the man's throat, and the fight was over.

City guards jumped on them both, tearing the fighters apart. The young boy was escorted by a few guards out of the room, one of whom had assisted Lord Vlacik during Vaasa's confinement. Her fists tightened. She remembered the sentinel's dirty blond hair, his patchy beard.

She searched the crowd, eyes passing over each face she recognized. Once again, she found Lord Vlacik. Dressed in his Asteryan blue coat and black pants, iron broaches stark against his chest, he proudly displayed his identity. His vile, sharp blue eyes met Vaasa's from across the room.

He grinned with all his teeth.

She could feel his hands on her. Feel the sharpness of a blade as he dragged it across her palm. As chains bit into her wrist. Cold iron chafed against her skin. The visceral memory of it might never leave her.

She had to control her breathing. Fight the urge to shake.

Vlacik bid the men around him goodbye, and Vaasa went still. Fear curled in her gut. Though she knew her father and brother to be capable of cruelty, she didn't believe them quite capable of *this*. Her flashback haunted her as Vlacik approached.

"Lord Karev," he greeted the man next to her first—an expected gesture that reminded her just where she was. "Surely, this isn't the place for an heiress."

Lord Karev chuckled with an artificial friendliness, and the space between them grew tense. Two beasts at the top of a mountain, prepared to sink their teeth into flesh if it meant being the only one there. "I believe you underestimate her, then," Karev said.

The way both men spoke about her as if she weren't standing right there, as if she didn't have a mouth to speak with herself, lit a fire in her. It took true restraint not to let a remark slip from her lips. Just as she had the night prior, she felt like a snake, shedding anything true or decent or real about herself. She was shrinking right where she stood.

But that fire didn't die. The throne did not belong to either of these men. Not yet.

Another group of men was brought to the ring, and the raucous crowd picked up volume again. Vaasa's heart wrenched. She remembered the combat circles she'd been a part of in Icruria, remembered how the training and fighting felt empowering when consented to. When it was done with people she trusted.

But this . . . it made her sick.

"I don't believe she's enjoying herself," Lord Vlacik noted.

"I'd like to see you up there," Vaasa suggested, narrowing her eyes on him. "Against anyone who's lost a fight tonight. Betting on that is something I'd enjoy."

Lord Vlacik's eyes flared in anger, but he kept his mouth shut. Lord Karev, on the other hand, let out a barking laugh. The sound caused a few people to look, which turned Lord Vlacik a particular shade of vermilion.

"A pleasure, as always," Lord Karev said before extending Vaasa his arm in a clear gesture that the interaction was over. That *he* was closest to her, and no one else.

Vaasa lifted her chin, taking Lord Karev's offer. In this room, she needed to show no fear. No disgust. These people could turn on her quicker than she could think to stop them.

As Lord Karev guided her through the crowd, people turned to stare, watching them with shock in their features. Just by being here, she was signaling approval. If she had acted as she wanted, if she thought it would have made a difference, she'd have stormed out. But as she gazed around, she realized that an act such as that—to try and change people's minds—was an act of love. Of grace. Of an attempt to save them.

And she did not want to save these nobles. She wanted to burn their houses to the ground.

Vaasa held herself with an air of power and dignity, shedding all signs of weakness. And Lord Karev lifted his own chin to match her posture. To the crowd, they likely looked in cahoots. And she realized that was Lord Karev's intent all along. He'd brought her here for the specific purpose of undermining Lord Vlacik.

She had a begrudging respect for his political prowess.

She thought of Reid then, and a small voice in her mind whispered that the woman he'd found was still inside her. Sewn into her being, much like his leather tie sewn into her dress.

But where was he?

"Lord Karev," a voice said over the reverberating sounds of the fight reaching a climax.

The lord spun with Vaasa still on his arm, pulling her with him. She came face-to-face with the owner of that voice—a woman, hair a stunning shade of red that was braided over one shoulder. Eyes of moss looked at them both, catching upon Vaasa for a visceral, stolen moment. There was only a flash of an expression, something Vaasa couldn't read, and then the woman was all business again. "Heiress," she said, dipping her head in respect.

"Meet Sachia," Lord Karev said, taking interest in the woman. "She is a fabric merchant, much like my parents once were. In fact, her family created your dress this evening."

Vaasa controlled each breath she took, but she memorized every detail of the woman. Sachia was sharper around the edges than most other nobles. Though she was dressed as richly as any of the other women in the room, there was a harshness about her. A strange air that spoke of a life beyond a rich merchant's daughter.

"My family owns the shop in the market square," Sachia said, gesturing to the fabric. "My father is abroad."

Vaasa plastered on a smile. "It's lovely to meet you. The dress is beautiful."

"It suits you. At least that's what he said when he picked it out," Sachia said, her words seeming to carry some undertone that Vaasa didn't understand. When Vaasa furrowed her brow, Sachia gestured to Lord Karev. "The lord, that is."

Lord Karev smiled down at her. "And wasn't I correct? The dress is made far more beautiful by the wearer."

Vaasa snapped back into the version of herself she needed to sell. "You're too kind," she said with just enough sugared sweetness that it sounded casual, like she heard such compliments all the time. "You'll have to come visit the fortress," Vaasa added. "Since coming home, I'm in need of a new wardrobe."

"I would be honored," Sachia said. "I've just come back from a journey myself. I'm in need of a new friend."

Lord Karev chuckled, turning his attention to Sachia and moving his body so he blocked most people's view of her. "I would love to discuss the wares you've returned home with."

The woman moved an inch, putting herself entirely in the shadow of Lord Karev, like she was hiding. "Silk, velvet, the likes," she confirmed. "And a few other things."

Lord Karev raised his brow. This held his interest, as if he already knew the answer to his question and was just seeking confirmation. "Other things?"

"I was lucky enough to come upon some resources that are . . . rare," she said.

Vaasa tilted her head.

The woman looked around them to ensure they weren't being listened to, then leaned in closely. Her eyes held Vaasa's as she whispered, "Salt."

Vaasa's heart leapt into her throat.

"You don't say?" Karev smoothly leaned forward, his interest apparent. Trepidation seeped from him, though, especially as he flicked his eyes to Vaasa. "From the men I met earlier today?"

The men? Who had Lord Karev met?

Sachia nodded. "I'm also here to follow up on my brother's deal."

He gave a carnal grin. "Well, perhaps we do have something to speak about, then."

"Perhaps," the woman replied in a less concealed tone, no longer keeping a secret between them. "I thought we could meet tomorrow night at the Lady."

The Lady Fortune, the brothel in the city that Lord Karev had accused Lord Vlacik of frequenting. If they intended to meet at that establishment, then whatever business they were doing was not the kind that should be so openly discussed in a room such as this, surrounded by nobles.

The woman was no regular merchant's daughter. Vaasa was beginning to wonder if she was a merchant at all, if instead she was like the other people who masqueraded about, wolves in sheep's clothing.

Lord Karev glanced at Vaasa, seeming to gauge her reaction. She didn't dare give one. Instead, she looked out at the crowd and to the stage as if this entire interaction bored her. Like his entrepreneurial interests weren't anything that could keep her fickle attention.

"Send word in the afternoon," Lord Karev said.

The woman nodded, then dipped her head once more. "Heiress, it was lovely to meet you."

Vaasa looked once more at the woman, taking the full picture of her in. Memorizing every single detail she could. "I hope to see you again," Vaasa said.

"I'll be in touch about a wardrobe," the woman said with a smile.

And then she walked off without another word, her gait strong and commanding. She crossed the room and immediately ducked out the door. Vaasa went still.

Had that woman sewn the leather tie into Vaasa's dress? She said she had gone on a journey, that she had returned with salt.

If Vaasa hadn't known better, she'd have thought Lord Karev was doing business with a pirate.

A pirate who knew something about Reid.

CHAPTER 16

Reid paced in a back room of the fabric shop where they had been sleeping, Koen's analytical eyes trailing every step he took. Sachia had been gone all night, and all Reid had been left with were the whispers he had picked up on in the fish market. Though he did not speak Asteryan fluently, the soldiers he'd served with in eastern Icruria had at least taught him enough to understand what their Asteryan prisoners were saying to them. The first words he'd learned had been the obscenities. It didn't take much to put two and two together, to reveal the general point of what people were claiming, and Koen had confirmed his translations.

The heiress was a whore.
The heiress was their savior.
The heiress was cursed.

Reid's sense of calm had entirely left him; he was certain Koen had left out some of the more choice rumors and opinions. While Reid had known it would be difficult to be here, he hadn't imagined how different this city would be from his own.

"You must stop pacing," his mother said.

"It does not make time move faster," Jonáš insisted.

His mother gave a gentle smile to the quartermaster, the two having become familiar with each other so quickly. His mother had that effect on people, something Reid wished he'd inherited.

Just then, the door rattled. Sachia came in, and Reid furrowed his brows. He had spent an unusual amount of time with this woman for weeks now, and there was something in the sharpness of her gaze that gave Reid pause. "Did you find Lord Karev?"

Sachia crossed her arms. "I did." She turned to Jonáš, who seemed to analyze her body language with the same intensity that Reid did. "He's willing to meet."

"Of course he is," Jonáš replied.

Sachia was so rigid she almost appeared to vibrate. "I found your consort, too," she said suddenly, turning to Reid.

Reid's heart hammered in his chest, his knees growing wobbly for the first time in as long as he could remember. "Was she hurt?"

Melisina stood from the bed, and Koen moved to the space next to him as if he were ready to catch Reid, should he lose his balance.

Sachia shook her head. "She appeared uninjured."

"She's safe?" Melisina asked.

Sachia scoffed, leaning against the ladder. "Oh, I wouldn't go that far. She's on the arm of Lord Karev, who's as much of a double-dealing bastard as Vlacik. In their pissing match for Asterya, they will send her to an early grave."

Reid's brows slammed together. "What do you mean?"

"Both of them are courting her," Sachia said. "It's all the room could talk about. But Vlacik has control of the prison and the city guard."

"How?"

Sachia clenched and unclenched her fists. She and Jonáš had what seemed like a silent conversation, and she appeared to nod a concession. Jonáš sighed, turning to face Reid and Koen. "When Andrej Kozár died and his imbecile of a son took the throne, Sutherland leveraged his connections to Vlacik and infiltrated the city guard. When we defected from his crew, Vlacik turned on Sachia's brother as punishment. Threw him in the prison. It must have been a favor Sutherland called in."

"And was he there tonight?" Koen asked. "The captain you once served?"

"If I'd found him, he'd be dead, or I wouldn't have returned," Sachia said, her voice more of an angry croak than the sturdy tone Reid had come to expect from her. "But it's possible I missed him. He masquerades as a high-ranking sentinel, one of Vlacik's own personal guard."

Jonáš took a small breath, like he was suffocated by the enormity of Sachia's emotions. Even Reid could feel them from where he stood. He knew this of witches; their intensity echoed around them. Sometimes, his mother could be felt so completely that the room became too small.

"*Very* few people know Sutherland's identity," Jonáš finally said. "Only the people in his inner circle. But they all know his name."

"So, you were in his inner circle, then?" Reid asked.

Sachia pressed her lips together. It was Jonáš who replied, disgust riding his tone. "He knew of Sachia's magic, and so our defection was more than a severing of loyalty. It was the loss of his greatest commodity."

Sachia shook her head, raising her hand in a clear gesture that she wanted this line of conversation to end. "I just hope the heiress is as clever as you say because I told her where I would be meeting Karev tomorrow night to discuss my recent acquisition of salt."

Reid couldn't breathe fully, his chest burning. If Vaasa did figure it out, would she go there? Would he be able to flee with her then? "She's the cleverest woman I know. She will understand."

"We need to be there," Koen said.

Sachia nodded. "I agree. Lord Karev already knows I have an interest in gaining access to the prison, so he wouldn't have offered unless he intended to give that to me."

Reid realized then that their interests weren't entirely aligned; if he found Vaasa, could see a way to get her out, it might delay their escape to wait for Sachia to gain access to the prison. He wondered if Sachia had considered this, too. But as he looked over at her, Sachia grit her teeth, and he realized she was holding back tears.

"What happened?" Reid asked.

At first, it seemed as though Sachia wouldn't answer. But then she batted at her cheeks, the tears falling despite all the effort she had put into holding them back. "My brother was there tonight. He was in that fucking fighting ring."

"Sachia," Melisina started, speaking for the first time since the witch had arrived.

She scoffed. "He won, and he's alive, so at least there's that. Tomorrow night, Vlacik will get exactly what he deserves."

Reid furrowed his brows. "What do you mean?"

"Karev believes his only competition is Vlacik." Sachia turned her knife in her hand, nimble fingers narrowly avoiding the blade. "So, in exchange for my brother, I'm going to remove the opposition."

CHAPTER 17

"This way," Roman said, gesturing to the end of the hall. Vaasa had changed from the dress Karev bought her into the warm clothes of a fortress guard, prepared for the shocking cold of the Iron Bay at night, for the way wind whipped around the prison. Clear skies served as an omen or an irony—it all depended on whether they could get out of the fortress unseen.

They slinked through the corridors on quiet feet, dipping into the servants' halls in order to avoid the other guards. Roman knew their placements and schedules by heart. The costume Vaasa wore would only work from afar; if any guards came too close, they would immediately know she wasn't one of them.

She couldn't shake the fear that one of those guards would alert Vlacik—it was possible any one of them worked for him, after all.

Roman was truly her only ally in this city.

They took a narrow passageway into the bowels of the fortress. The gray stone walls mirrored the ones built in the old wing on the far side that she and Roman had gone to the first night she found him. They were built at the same time, before Vaasa's father had expanded the fortress to even greater heights and architectural miracles. He'd built around the original structure, so it often ebbed and flowed, old to new, much like Asterya itself.

This part of the castle was warmer, further in the depths where heat was trapped. They took a wide staircase decorated on one side by a statue of the monotheistic Asteryan god, arms raised in triumph. Vaasa stared at it for only a moment before sliding around the corner. She collided with something—some*one*.

Ozik.

He looked at her, lips drawn. At the bottom of his neck where his cloak clipped together with an iron buckle, black crept up his veins. Vaasa didn't dare gasp or make any indication of what she'd noticed. There was something deeply different about Ozik in this moment— he was far closer to the advisor she had faced upon the platform at the Icrurian election. Dressed in his usual blue regalia with his bright-white cloak, he looked ready for an important dinner, not for the stroke of midnight.

Roman rounded the corner next. His footsteps halted, and the air in the stairwell shifted.

"My, my, my," Ozik crooned in Icrurian, voice dripping like the oil of his magic. Slick. Dark. Fury lit in his gaze, dragging between her and Roman. Threads of crimson bled into the brilliant gold of his irises. This was doubtlessly different than how he'd been that morning at training. The tight control with which he'd held himself was missing. "If it isn't a perfect rendition of the past. Just history repeating itself."

"Sire—" Roman tried, but Ozik lifted a hand to silence him.

"You're using your position a little too liberally, aren't you?" Ozik snarled.

Roman paled.

But Ozik turned his fury only on Vaasa. "If I were a lord?" Ozik asked, stepping into her space. "If I were Lord Karev?"

Vaasa narrowed her eyes. Roman said nothing—an act that felt like a betrayal. Vaasa sneered, "You aren't a lord."

The red of Ozik's eyes grew, no longer whispers of color, but a full claiming of his irises that bled into the whites. Hand snaking out, he gripped Vaasa's throat, cutting off her airway before she could draw another breath. "You think you are so clever," he growled, his voice taking on a tenor it never had before.

This was not the man who had helped raise her.

Panic tore at her body from within, and she had no chance to stifle the choked plea at her lips. She couldn't breathe. Ozik tipped back his head and laughed, the veins in his neck growing darker beneath his pale skin.

"Sire—" Roman tried.

"Silence," he boomed, voice echoing around them.

Ozik lowered Vaasa to her knees, power swirling in his angry expression as his fingers loosened on her throat. Breath filled her lungs painfully, and she took in whatever air she could. "You are just as meddlesome as your mother," he whispered. His eyes were on fire, a bloodred glow emanating all throughout them. And just behind him, the Miro'dag took form. "You will die like her, too."

Vaasa froze. Panic overtook every instinct she'd honed, stealing away her usual ability to keep her composure. She thrashed, but he only gripped her neck tighter, his other hand snaking out to take hold of her shoulder.

The creature screamed. Fury twisted Ozik's mouth into an angry frown.

Faintly, she heard the sound of Roman's sword unsheathing, a command falling from his lips for Ozik to let her go. Fear clawed its way through Roman's shaking tone.

Yet Vaasa couldn't take her eyes off Ozik. There was something in his gaze—some rebellion, some spark of logic or recognition or consciousness that hadn't been there a moment prior. It was like she was looking at two different people. His eyes flickered once more, gold fighting for dominance in the red.

"What are you?" Vaasa gasped with what little air she could manage.

Ozik's hand upon her throat shook with strain. One finger lifted, then snapped back down. He seemed at war with himself. His fingers tried once, twice, and finally they released her with a spasm. He drew back, releasing her entirely. Vaasa buckled over and put her own hands around her neck, desperate to protect it. Her knees dug into the hard staircase beneath her.

The Miro'dag approached, the smell of rotting flesh and burning hair stuffing itself up her nose. She looked into its crimson eyes, the same color that had seeped into Ozik's, and the churning of power within them was a living thing. Magic, raw and unfiltered, shone back at her.

"Vaasalisa," Ozik said, suddenly back to the professorial tone that he'd held with her just that morning. Every morning so far. He took two careful steps back, left foot finally reaching the bottom of the staircase. Desperation stained his gaze as the crimson winked in and out of his irises.

He was silently asking her for something, she just didn't know what.

Roman's footsteps sounded as he ran to her side. He bent to where she knelt on the staircase, trying to pull at her arms to help her stand. Silver glinted at the corner of Vaasa's eye, and her hand snapped out like a snake biting prey. Grabbing the dagger sheathed at Roman's belt, she pulled, and using all her strength, she struck upward, the sound of her boots sliding on the stairs.

She stabbed the hooked blade into Ozik's throat, cutting through skin and sinew, and tugged it back out with a ruthless grunt.

Blood oozed from the gaping wound on the advisor's neck, the color of it tainted by streaks of black. It ran down the column of Ozik's throat and soaked the neck of his white cloak. As he choked, Ozik's eyes flashed with rage and pain, and then they bled entirely to gold, all the red gone.

Pain lanced through her core, her magic activating once more. Wide-eyed, Vaasa stumbled back and tripped, falling to her rear on a step. A twinge shot up her spine.

But Ozik didn't fall. His knees didn't buckle, and the floor didn't welcome him in a slump of lifeless bones. The wound at his neck began to sew, skin stitching back together in a seamless line. A smile graced his lips as color returned to his mouth and cheeks. Even though black blood still stained his skin and cloak, there was no trace of the wound anywhere.

"Your effort is noted," Ozik said, perfectly level and controlled. And then he turned his attention to Roman. "If you disobey me again, I will put your head on a pike."

Roman went pale as a ghost.

The burning within her ceased. "Please," she begged, "let me see her."

Ozik simply shook his head. "Earn it," he said. He gave Roman a withering stare. "And do be more discreet."

Ozik turned on his heel and walked away like the entire interaction had never occurred.

Breath pushed in and out of Vaasa's lungs: hot, heavy, desperate. She was certain the floor would give way beneath her, that the fortress would swallow her whole. The gravity of her situation settled in her stomach, her suspicions from the moment he'd healed her hand fully confirmed.

Ozik couldn't die. Not like a mortal could.

As she stood, she tried to take a step, but Roman grabbed her wrist, pulling her back and catching her off guard. She rammed into his chest, and he hauled her up the stairs. Her feet caught purchase, and she ran with him. The moment they were out of the stairwell, he turned and caught her shoulders, inspecting her fully. "Are you all right?"

It all played in a loop in her mind—Roman had simply watched, so terrified of Ozik that he couldn't move. For whatever reason, his lack of interference stung. She hadn't ever needed someone to protect her, but she wished there was someone to help her keep this fear at bay. She wanted Reid.

Roman's jaw clenched. "We need to get to the old wing. I need the truth. Now."

Adrenaline still fogged her mind. They couldn't be alone; she was going to lose her grip on herself, let something slip without a plan—

"Vaasa," he said, trying to calm her down. "I'm here for you. To protect you. But I need your honesty—"

"You call that protecting me?" she whispered.

His features contorted in insult. "I am your only partner in this," he reminded her in a curt whisper.

She twisted her shoulders and broke his grasp, careening down the hallway as he hissed for her to stop. She burst into the servants' hall, and Roman ceased trying to speak to her the moment another guard came into view. It was too much of a risk. Vaasa kept her quickened pace, mind turning in an unstoppable loop, until she slipped back into the emperor's wing using one of the hidden passageways.

And then Roman pounced.

His hand caught her wrist, and he tugged her against his body. She struggled against him, but he didn't release his vise grip. Instead, he dragged her toward the wall, attempting to pin her against it. Instinct told her to twist the wrist he held and break his grip, yet exhaustion crested over her in a dizzying wave. She stumbled and fell, back slamming against the wall. Weeks of pain caught up to her in a flash—*weak*. She was so fucking tired and weak. Tears welled in her eyes, but she bit down on her cheek to hold back any noise.

"What. Happened," he said, each word its own sentence. "What the hell did Ozik just do to you? Why didn't he die?"

Anger caught fire within her, swiftly replacing her desperation with something more familiar: rage. "You know why." She wrenched her wrist free and slammed her hands into Roman's chest, pushing him off her, her strength finally enough to demand space.

Roman stumbled back, eyes going wide. "Vaasa—"

"Why would I trust you? You've all but come back from the dead, and you are lying to me."

"I haven't lied—"

Vaasa spun on him. "You *know* he has magic! That's he's a witch."

Roman paused. Words seemed to dance on his lips. Finally, he asked, "Will it be truth between us, or should I question everything you say?"

"You have no right to ask me that."

Her chest bone seemed to splinter. It was as if the light from his lantern revealed a side of him that Vaasa had never met, a terrible spinning of everything she'd once believed about him. There was a time in her life that Roman had been one of the only people who hadn't lied to her. Hadn't used her. She remembered the sound of his voice as he whispered those promises in her ear: *I am here. I want you. I will never betray you.*

Those words provided her the opportunity to see him as she had once seen him, this younger version of her reaching across the hallway, hoping those promises still held true. "My friend," she said, stepping forward. "Take me to her. Now. *Please.*"

As Roman gauged the distance between them, he shook his head. "I can't. You heard him, Vaasa. He'll kill me."

Magic. He was scared of magic, and he was going to let it stop him from helping her. Just like he had when Ozik had wrapped his hand around her throat on the stairwell.

Roman had done *nothing*.

Vaasa closed her eyes. Disappointment slithered through her, and she realized she might actually have told him everything if he'd given her a reason to.

She lifted her chin so she could meet his gaze with all the malice she could conjure. "I was under the impression *I* was the future ruler, not him."

Roman stepped forward, but Vaasa shook her head, pulling swiftly away from him down the hall that led to the emperor's private rooms. "Go back to your post," she spat.

"You are my post," he argued.

"Just go," she said without looking back.

"Vaasa—"

She stopped and turned, dropping her voice to a clinical neutral, as if he were any guard in the palace. As if his lips had never touched hers, his body had never twisted in her sheets under the cover of night. "I can't risk this throne on the rumor that I'm having an affair with my lead sentinel, and as the current holder of that position, you shouldn't either."

Something broke on his face. Something awful and deep.

He set off down the hall without another word, and Vaasa stood there alone.

CHAPTER 18

As Vaasa walked to the greenhouse the next morning, it was hard to keep her hands steady. Quietly, she worked out what she had seen in the stairwell the evening prior. Ozik should have died, and yet he didn't. And the way he had spoken about her mother...

It was a direct contradiction to everything else he'd said about Vena Kozár. Those were not the words of a man who had lost someone he loved; they were the words of a murderer.

The red of his eyes haunted her while she slept, the battle between gold and crimson. There was something Ozik wasn't telling her about his magic, and she got the feeling her mother had died trying to figure it out. That perhaps Dominik had been working toward that answer, too.

It must have been tied to the necklace her mother had tried to send her. Vaasa had torn apart the office again, but to no avail.

When she walked into the back room of the greenhouse, Ozik greeted her with his usual professorial demeanor. "Good morning," he said, as if nothing had happened the night prior.

She wasn't certain if he was ignoring it or if he had no memory of the altercation. Her eyes dropped to his throat, which showed no sign of injury. Not even the faintest remnant of a scar. "Good morning," she muttered.

He gave a puzzled tilt of his head but said nothing else. Instead, the lid on her magic opened as if blown by a strong wind, and the force shot into her with a terrifying velocity. Vaasa steadied herself, digging her feet into the ground, and Ozik caught sight of the movement. "Good," he said. "Ground yourself."

Vaasa fought the urge to double over. She forced her face into a stoic neutrality instead of the pained scowl she'd taken to in the mornings they worked together.

"Calm it," he commanded.

Vaasa tamed the intensity of the force as if she had a tide all her own, smothering its power with a wave.

"Now, summon its physical form."

Vaasa did as she was told, the two of them moving through the beginning exercises as if this was no different from strength training or blade work. Magic pulsed in the air, and the connection between her and Ozik grew steadier with each manipulation of the black mist around her. Their connection was strongest when she wielded Veragi magic like this. Mist danced up her arms and made it to her shoulders in seconds. It curled around her neck, and this time she didn't flinch.

"Now summon a manifestation," he said.

The magic in her body obeyed her will; it was easier than ever to call upon the wolf, to let it out of her body and into the world around her. Every day they trained together, she distinguished more of Ozik on the other side of their bond. His emotions coursed across it. She had never felt anything so intense—this sadness, this overwhelming grief. It was a feast to her starving power. Magic rang in her ears as the canine took shape, each tuft of fur defined, teeth sharp as knives. It growled, head low, nose almost touching the stony pathway. Tendrils of black mist licked the air around it.

She looked upon Ozik. Her rage grew in her, reaching for new heights, spreading into each of her limbs and up her throat, begging to get out. The wolf stalked, step by step, across the distance between them.

Ozik didn't move.

The wolf sniffed at his feet. More details took shape: different shades of black and purple and blue and green, all shifting on the wolf's fur as it circled Ozik's legs. A corner of the wolf's lip raised on a low growl. Sharp teeth with fatal incisors. She could *feel* it. In her mind, she pictured it lifting on its haunches, front paws slamming in Ozik's chest and dragging him to the ground. The wolf widening its jaw, fangs gleaming as it clutched Ozik's neck and sunk its teeth—

"Vaasa," Ozik said calmly, drawing her attention back to where she stood.

The wolf was poised to strike, positioning itself with its head lowered and back raised, prepared any moment to leap at him. Razor-sharp teeth poked out as it growled louder. She wanted the wolf to attack him. She wanted to cause harm.

But she knew what leverage he held, and it didn't matter what pain she caused him.

He wouldn't die.

Vaasa dismissed the magic, and the wolf disintegrated into nothing but tendrils of smoke that floated on the air like a lost wind.

Ozik frowned. "You should have struck."

He yanked Vaasa's magic from her body, and she cried out, this time unable to stop herself from doubling over as his own manifestation took form. She could feel the Miro'dag in the greenhouse, feel where its taloned feet sat on the stones of the pathway, before ever looking up. But when she did, she saw those crimson eyes, and something in her cowered.

She was right back on that platform, Reid's lifeless body in her arms, the blood of both their nations wetting the dirt.

"Stop," she gasped.

But he didn't. Ozik stalked forward with an angry expression, the Miro'dag just steps behind him. "From now on, you strike," Ozik said, voice churning with words unspoken. Like an echo. He stopped just in front of where she stood and grabbed her chin, forcing her to lift from her cowardly, protective pose. With her core exposed, panic sluiced down her spine. She tried to pull away, but he shook his head in irritation. "You gave up your opportunity, didn't you? This is the price of hesitation."

"Ozik—"

"Do you want to end up like your mother?" he growled, then shook his head like a dog. His eyes held hers starkly, and then a red glow emanated from behind the gold as his face contorted in rage. Their connection dimmed, and Vaasa felt herself breathe, felt the pull on her own magic lift, as if Ozik had lost his grip on it. Whatever bound them was suddenly moving in both directions, an energy humming along that cord that she wondered if she could grasp. The strings that bound them were simply an instrument, so she strummed.

And there she was again—standing in that dark tomb, staring down at a pool of red. It churned and writhed, the water rippling, the glow of red growing brighter. It was precisely where she'd been the first time she pushed their bond this far. Power and rage simmered on the other side of the water. And then from within it, something wicked and ancient pulsed, and she saw . . .

Eyes.

They peered up at her as if she were staring at her own reflection.

"What is that?" Vaasa whispered.

Then gold spread like a stain through the pool, extinguishing the crimson. Their connection clamped down on her, and her vision of the dark tomb fractured.

"Get out of my head!" Ozik's voice boomed.

He slammed his hands against her shoulders and sent her rocking back. Gravel cut into her hands as she landed on her back, and her own magic rose to choke her, black mist smothering the windows and snuffing out the light in the greenhouse. "Ozik," she called out desperately, gaping up at him.

His eyes were a brilliant gold again.

"You should be afraid, Vaasalisa," he warned, walking toward her. "We are running out of time."

"Running out of time for what?"

He shook his head again, clenching his eyes closed, and the cords between them ignited in flames. She kicked her legs at the gravel to back away from him, struggling not to cry out in pain. This was no natural magic. This was nothing of what she'd read in Dihrah.

There was something terribly wrong.

Vaasa eyed the door, prepared to run, but he blocked her exit. There was no way out. Fear struck her and—

Fear.

It was his fear. She felt every inch of it in the room, his rage and terror and grief grown so large they could have cracked the windows.

She didn't want it. She didn't want to wield magic this way, to give in to the version of herself that he wanted her to be.

Ozik leapt, and then he was on her. Vaasa slammed into the stones and rolled, his body weight more than she had anticipated. He caught her there, pressing her arms into the small stones beneath her. It was possible he'd drawn blood, but there was no time to tell. Not as he dug his knee into her gut and leaned near her. His voice dropped to a low warning. "There is a part of you that is capable of great horrors to get what you want. If you don't let her out, *I will tear her from your bones.*"

Rage curled in the air; it slid along her lips, her tongue, her throat. It joined everything within her. Vaasa reacted upon pure instinct. Her wolf snapped out of her again on a loud howl, and then an ear-shattering wail escaped Ozik's mouth. He was dragged off her, black oil splattering everywhere as the wolf feasted. Gravel flew through the air as the wolf dragged Ozik farther and farther away, his new fear and pain only giving Vaasa more to feed off of.

She forced her feet beneath her and snapped up to a fighting stance. Ozik screamed in pain, and for a moment, Vaasa worried someone would come for them. But then the sound of his agony filled her with such delight, she couldn't make herself care. "You may not be able to die," she snarled down at him. "But you *can* suffer."

Bloodied and pinned beneath the wolf, Ozik . . . laughed.

Through injuries that Vaasa knew were fatal to anyone else, Ozik shook with a raucous fit. The wolf disintegrated, and Vaasa stepped back closer to the olive tree. Slowly, Ozik turned onto his back, his chest still convulsing with his hysterics. His arm fell to the side and calmed, laughter fading to a chuckle.

He turned his head so his golden eyes met hers. Voice imbued with pride, he said, "There she is."

She had done it again—had fed upon him instead of herself. Her hands shook.

Vaasa started toward the door, unable to gaze upon his torn skin or bloodied features. The magic snapped back inside her, and as she walked, she savored every moment her power stayed. It was only temporary, she knew. At any moment he would take it back.

As she reached the door, he coughed, and his voice drifted between them. "Good. You must be willing to save yourself at all costs."

Vaasa stopped. Had she just heard him correctly?

Whatever you do, stay in Mireh and do not unite the other pieces. The price is far too great.

Her magic slipped away like the wind, but when she turned, there was nothing but sprays of blood upon the gravel.

CHAPTER

19

Despite the weariness she felt, Vaasa dressed carefully, strategically, for her task. She tugged on her boots and pulled her cloak over her shoulders, dressing for warmth. She untangled her hair and used a hot iron rod she'd warmed with the fire to twist her hair into a different curl pattern. As she stared into a mirror, a drained indigo stared back. Shadows had grown around her eyes, an incurable tiredness, so she patted cosmetics over them in hopes of counteracting the dullness. She dragged kohl across her lid and darkened her lashes, doing everything she could to seem different from how she normally looked. Finally, she wrapped a scarf around the lower half of her face, leaving only her eyes exposed.

Vaasa scurried into the hallway and took one last look at the door she knew a guard stood behind, hoping desperately they wouldn't try to come inside and speak to her. If they found her missing, they'd alert Roman immediately. Her best hope was that the attendants had all retired for the night and no one would know she'd gone.

She slipped into her father's office and approached the iron owl statue, letting her hand drift over the cold trinket. She pulled, then pressed, and the door swung open. The eerie, dark tunnel beyond waited. Lifting her lantern, Vaasa stepped inside.

She needed to be at The Lady Fortune tonight.

The passageway wound out of the fortress and into an apartment in one of the richer districts of the city. So many merchants and lords spent time away that these dwellings were often left empty when not loaned out to close friends. Burglary was a blight, but to Vaasa's surprise, the apartment was untouched. She wondered silently if Ozik had been using it, but there was no sign of him here. She didn't linger inside; it was only fond memories that lived in these walls, and Vaasa had no space for them.

The streets next to the fortress bustled with only Asterya's richest families, and tonight it was busier than usual, given the sheer number of nobles who had come into the port. They kept homes here so they might be more comfortable upon visiting. The streets, at least in this part of the city, were fairly safe to walk through. Coldness bit at Vaasa, even her warmest attire not enough to sate the snow. Stone buildings were built along narrow walkways, some of which were steeper than others, the ground slick in places it had been worn down or along staircases. Snow coated the narrowest ones, as no one bothered to guide a cart or horse-led carriage through those alleyways, and therefore no one shoveled them. Those were the streets Vaasa stuck to. Every once in a while, she passed a rich noble or merchant who was returning home, but they didn't make much of her, and they were shielding their faces from the snow, too.

Vaasa veered into one of the town squares, which during the day held the fish market. The stench of fish still lingered in the air, but at this time of night, the only people braving the cold were boat captains too drunk to feel the chill, or the women who made a splendid living from those men's darkest desires. Though several brothels studded the city in different neighborhoods, there was one in particular that most of the nobles frequented: The Lady Fortune.

As Vaasa entered, scarf still covering her face, she tipped her head at the beautiful hostess. The tawny-skinned woman gestured to the wall behind her, dotted with masks, each of which hung on pegs that went all the way up to the ceiling. There were hundreds of options. Vaasa pointed to one, and the hostess climbed a ladder and plucked it from the wall. She led Vaasa into one of the many changing rooms, where Vaasa picked a costume from the closet, chuckling at her choice. White as snow, a tight bodice hugged her hips and breasts, then fell in sweeping fabric to the floor. It paired with a set of white wings. An Asteryan angel—something Vaasa assuredly was not. White fabric framed her eyes and cheekbones, silver swirls of thread covering the intricate thing, and small crystals were strung on clear line that hung in different lengths along her cheeks, making it seem as though the mask itself was crying. The hostess retrieved her. Vaasa held her breath as they walked through a set of double doors.

Laughter echoed off the walls, music threading through the air, the raucous sounds of a party teeming around her. The main receiving room had a different theme each night. Some nights, Vaasa remembered, it was set up to look like a tavern. Others it was a lounge, others a theater. Tonight, it looked exactly like a high-end art gallery. Duplicates of famous paintings were hung along the walls, and the women themselves were dressed as exhibits. They draped themselves over chairs, clad in little but silks or thin chiffon, the many rooms heated by enormous fireplaces that blazed along the walls. Vaasa meandered from room to room without making conversation with anyone, eyes on the masks and costumes that hid their identities. Privacy was paramount, given the status and riches of the patrons. People didn't come here just for the sex; the mistress had turned this brothel into as much a social club.

In the third room she entered, there was a group of five people in the corner, four men and one woman, all with their heads close. The woman had red hair the same as Sachia's. Two of the men had their backs to Vaasa, but one was thin and the other had broad shoulders. Her heart lurched at the thought—for a moment, she let herself dream it was Reid. That something like that could be possible.

And then she noticed the white-blond hair of one of the men facing her.

Though she couldn't confirm it, she had a sinking feeling it was Lord Vlacik. It had to be. He sat next to the final man at their table, one with dark hair, who raised gray eyes to her.

Lord Karev?

As naturally as she could, Vaasa scurried into the next room. The owner of the brothel sat in a chair, chest bursting from her beautiful gown, her head tipped back in laughter as she sipped on a goblet of some kind of sparkling liquor. The woman took one look at her and tilted her head. Her mask was thin, no real attempt at hiding her identity.

Vaasa pushed her hair from her shoulder and touched the side of her neck—an old signal of sorts.

The woman stood, excusing herself from the group of people she spoke to, and grabbed ahold of Vaasa's elbow as she led them up to the third floor and past a roped off hallway into what Vaasa knew was the private quarters the woman kept for herself.

"Regína," Vaasa said as they entered the woman's receiving room. Adorned with ornate wallpaper and large, red sofas, the space was meant to host only those Regína wanted near.

"I was wondering if you would come back here," Regína said, giving her a tantalizing smile. The woman had coiled brown hair and pale skin that was taut around her eyes. Silver earrings dangled from her lobes, matching the circular pendant she wore, inlaid with a fat ruby. Voluptuous hips rocked with each step she took, and despite herself, Vaasa relaxed a little.

"Did you think I wouldn't resume our business arrangement?" Vaasa asked.

Regína slipped off her fox mask, revealing her entire face to Vaasa. "I did not, but a woman can hope."

The women who worked the port were some of the highest earners in Mekës, maintaining one of the largest industries in the city. Though the fish market and the spices and jewels all had their place in the sunlight, these women were trained in the art of desire and were paid quite well for it. Moreover, they knew *everything* in the city, and Regína did more than trade in sex; she traded in secrets. It was here that deals were struck, that men truly bartered and made their fortunes. That had made Regína one of Vaasa's closest allies, though she had never been foolish enough to consider the madame a friend.

Vaasa reached into her pocket, pulling out a gold coin that immediately caught Regína's eye. The weight of it was enough to cover far more than Vaasa asked, but to reveal the identities of her patrons was a cardinal sin for Regína. Vaasa knew the only reason she'd ever gotten information out of the woman was because of her title; Regína wanted the full protection of the crown in case the clergy ever came knocking. "Lord Karev and Lord Vlacik are meeting downstairs, aren't they?" Vaasa asked.

Regína raised her brow.

"If I'm to marry either of them, I need to know the truth," Vaasa said.

Regína's eyes went wide at that insinuation, and Vaasa thought for a moment it was fear she looked into. Regína took the coin from Vaasa's fingers. "Long live the Empress," she said, tucking it into her bodice. "Yes, during your brother's reign of terror, Vlacik and Karev would meet here regularly. Tonight, however, they're at odds. I overheard them speaking about a missing shipment of black powder."

"Black powder?" Vaasa hissed.

Regína furrowed her brows. "We are at war. The woman at their table . . . I believe she's a pirate. She reserved two rooms on the second floor. Vlacik reserved his usual suite."

Vaasa crossed her arms, tucking away the information. "What else?"

"The two other men at their table, I've never seen them here. They speak Icrurian."

Vaasa's heart slammed against her ribs. "What?"

"I overheard them whispering the language earlier. The lanky one called himself a salt lord."

An Icrurian salt lord was *here*? That was a blatant disregard for the economic sanctions at play in Icruria—no one traded with another nation without the headman and councilors' consent. Ton of Wrultho, the now-dead foreman of Wrultho, had made that error years ago, and it led to a dam erected in Innisjour that had choked eastern Icruria's water supply. It had defined the election and ultimately fueled his attempt at a coup.

Given the controversy the Icrurian election had undoubtedly stirred in the nation, this salt lord was either profiting off a war and risking his life to do it, or he was lying. Vaasa had met many of the salt lords, and she filed through each of them in her mind, trying to pinpoint one with such a lanky build.

Not a single lord came to mind.

But two men, one tall and thin and the other with broad shoulders . . . no. It was impossible. Wasn't it?

"Was one of them wearing spectacles?" Vaasa asked.

Regína seemed to take careful note of that detail, leaving Vaasa anxious at the thought. But when the madame nodded, Vaasa could hardly breathe.

"Thank you," Vaasa said.

Regína pursed her lips warily. "You be careful, you hear? Those lords, they're no regular monsters."

Vaasa nodded, her adrenaline reaching a peak. "I will," she said, then hurried back into the main rooms, desperate to catch another glimpse of the Icrurians at the table.

CHAPTER 20

Vaasa went from room to room until she found them again, though by the time she returned, there were only three people remaining: Sachia, Vlacik, and Karev. Her pulse quickened, entirely out of control. The full view of them was covered by drapes that hung from the ceiling, looking like an art exhibit all on their own. She found a couch and stretched herself across it comfortably as she spoke with a few of the patrons. A merchant's daughter, they probably assumed. Spoiled. Immodest. She made up some story about her recent travels to a coastal territory, having assumed these men had more in common with the Old Asteryans than the New.

A few of the women joined the lords' table as time passed. One slid her hand down Lord Vlacik's chest, fingers drawing circles on his shoulders. He was lost in the trance of it, and soon enough, the two excused themselves through a set of doors that led to one of the staircases Vaasa knew granted access to the private suites on the upper levels. Perhaps Vlacik's room was reserved for that exact reason and nothing more.

Sachia leaned in closer to Karev, the two now whispering. Vaasa forced herself to look away, to maintain some semblance of nonchalance.

This place and its norms weren't unfamiliar; Vaasa had snuck here quite a few times during her young adult life, mostly with Roman and his friends. She thought of their fight for only a moment, not allowing herself to get caught up in the memory.

She bided her time, conversing with the women, who had grown more comfortable in her presence, though when they realized she was unlikely to pay them herself, they moved on. She kept her secret glances at Sachia as subtle as she could, doing a few turns around the main room and gazing upon the gallery portraits as if they were real and she was nothing but an admirer.

Someone sauntered up to Vaasa's left, the way he held himself distinct and familiar. Gray eyes looked down at her. "I don't believe we've met," Lord Karev said quietly. It was certain—his voice and his eyes were too recognizable, even beneath a red opera mask. "You don't look like any of the women who work here."

Slipping into another accent was second nature for Vaasa, and she did so with the same gusto she once had used to convince entire rooms of her father's guests that she was able to confidently speak their language; that she was *just like them*. The way she spoke concealed her true voice. "Don't you think it's a bit pathetic that you've memorized all of the women who work here?"

Lord Karev grinned, only half his mouth visible beneath his mask. "Apparently, not all."

Out of the corner of her eye, she saw Sachia scurry toward the double doors that led to the stairs. For only a single moment, the woman looked up, and their gazes locked.

Vaasa looked away.

She wanted to kick herself. Her entire plan seemed to crumble through her fingers. If she followed Sachia now, it would tip off Lord Karev. If she didn't, she might never know who those men were. She'd hoped Karev would excuse himself and give Vaasa the opportunity to speak with Sachia at the table first.

The sound of a door opening drew her attention immediately, and she almost cursed under her breath. A man walked through those doors. Though he wore a costume coat and had even changed his boots, Vaasa knew damn well who it was. He donned a familiar mask made of crow's feathers. Each time they'd met here, he'd disguised himself as that very bird.

Roman.

Someone must have found her gone.

"If you'll excuse me," she said, turning to leave. Shit, shit, *shit*.

"Here for someone, then?" Lord Karev asked, eyes lifting to where Roman had just entered.

"We all have our hidden tastes," Vaasa purred, shielding the sound of her voice once more and moving out of his orbit. If she had any luck, he would believe her some random woman waiting for a forbidden love she couldn't have in the daylight.

Vaasa fled the room through the double doors and ascended the staircase in a hurry, hiking her dress up so she could run faster. Her only choice was to try and explore the second floor, to—

A hand gripped her arm, pulling her away from the stairs while another covered her mouth before she had a chance to speak. She'd only caught a glimmer of him—a hard body and short hair, his features covered by a full face mask. Her back fell harshly against his chest, and the door next to them opened. The two of them went spilling into the room. She tried to pull away, but his grip on her was too secure, and then he pressed his back against the door, holding it closed, still locking all of her against all of him.

A voice rose and broke on her name, so quietly spoken in her ear. "*Vaasalisa.*"

Her body froze. It had been so long since she had heard her name in his voice, and this time it wasn't unfamiliarity or anger that rode the words. It was salvation, thick and piercing, in how he let the entirety of it spill from his lips.

His hand released her mouth at the same time the scent of him registered. Salt. Amber.

Home.

"How?" she breathed.

The sound of his Icrurian accent curled in her ear. "Not even death could keep me from you."

"*Reid.*" Her voice cracked, and then she spun and threw herself at him. Her arms wrapped around his neck at the same time his own dragged her against him. She fought a wretched sob, forcing herself to stay quiet, afraid someone might hear them through the door. But she felt him. Felt his heart beat wildly in his chest, felt the intensity of each thud.

She tore at his mask. It fell from his face and revealed the stunning lines of his jaw, lips, and cheeks. Orange eyes and dark auburn hair, cut short now, his broad shoulders a beacon of home. He looked so different without his long ponytail and dressed in Asteryan clothing, yet there was some instinct in her that recognized him perfectly—the one that yearned for every part of him.

His fingers gently lifted her own mask, and her heart rose as she watched him take in the sight of her unobstructed face.

"Finally." He traced her cheek with his thumb. "I found you."

"You were never injured?" she asked.

It earned her that confident smirk of his, pride in what she now realized was his own small scheme. "No. Just on my way to you."

"Reid," she said again. Because she could. Because she wanted to. Because it was hers to whisper. She leaned into his large hand, the roughness of his skin a breath of fresh air, a relief of disproportionate measure against the deceiving softness of everyone else in this city. She could stand no farther distance. Vaasa wound her hand around the nape of his neck and pulled his mouth down to hers in a searing kiss.

The intimacy seemed to unwind him, to confirm something for Reid that Vaasa didn't understand. But she felt the loosening of his body beneath her hands as he kissed her back. He backed them further into the room, his free hand trailing behind him for only a moment before he twisted it into her hair. His tongue pressed against the seam of her lips, and she parted them, deepening the kiss. Her hands clawed at his shoulders, dragging herself against his body as tightly as she could go.

"Run away with me, Wild One," he whispered against her mouth. "Let me take you home."

For a stolen breath, she pretended that it was that simple. That they could sprint down the stairs and out into the snow and steal a boat from the harbor, rowing all the way home. But then reality returned, and Vaasa remembered exactly who was searching for her downstairs. Fear yanked her upright; it caused her world to tilt and shatter.

"You have to hide," she said, head whipping around and looking for a good spot. There was a closet on the far side of the room, but would Reid fit into it?

"What is going on?" he asked, his thick Icrurian accent weaving between them. His body had gone stiff again.

Vaasa didn't know how to explain. Nerves racked against her ribcage. To contextualize everything with Roman would take far longer than they had. "My lead sentinel didn't give me permission to leave. He's trying to find me downstairs. If he sees you, if he—"

"I've locked the door," Reid assured her, inspecting her frightened gaze. "There was no one behind you on the stairs."

"Are you certain?"

"Positive."

Vaasa stared up at him. Perhaps Roman would think she wasn't here and just leave. If she waited it out . . .

They were alone.

"How did you know it was me?" she whispered.

The very edge of his mouth turned up into that amused grin, the same one that had at one time sent anger rushing through her. His Icrurian accent played with her, all soft vowels and strung-together words. "Did you think I wouldn't know you through a mask? I've seen through every one."

Her entire being reached for him, as it always seemed to. Her hands rose to touch his jaw. His cheeks. To trace the lines of his face, just to be sure it was all real.

But it was real. Reid was here, in Mekës. Roman was right downstairs. Karev and Vlacik were under the same roof.

Yet all she could focus on was him. Her body knew, and the tautness in her muscles loosened. She could finally let fear fall. This was the undeniable effect Reid of Mireh had upon her; before him, no one had ever brought her peace.

"How are you here?" she asked.

He loosened his grip upon her, gesturing toward the window. "I'll tell you everything later. For now, we need to find Amalie and run. We've gotten luckier—"

"He has Amalie," Vaasa interrupted. Her hand wrapped around his wrist. "Ozik has her in the prison. If I go, he'll kill her."

Reid's eyes darkened, anger playing on his clenched jaw, and he cursed through his teeth. The hand she wasn't holding raised to rake through his short hair. He looked so strange in Asteryan fashion, his borrowed clothes one of the costumes all attendees wore. Gone were the sweeping, jewel-toned fabrics of Icruria, and she missed them.

"All right, what's your plan?" he asked. Measured. Strategic. Calm. The same as she had always known him.

Vaasa bit her lip. "I don't have one yet."

His thick brow raised. "Oh."

Vaasa stepped away just long enough to undo the ridiculous wings that covered her shoulders. Reid took them from her and placed them upon the bed. It caused her chest to tighten—in affection, in agony. It was the simplicity of him wanting to help her: a small task, yet something they could do together.

He approached again, his eyes scanning over her. "I—" He went utterly still. "What are those?" Reid demanded, hand raising to trail over her upper arm. Vaasa didn't need to look to know he was referring to the small silvery scars that Lord Vlacik had left her with. The ones Ozik had allowed to remain on her, a subtle reminder of what could be inflicted upon her if she misbehaved. A story he could spin about what had happened in Icruria. "Don't worry—"

"Do *not* avoid the question," he demanded.

"Please," Vaasa whispered.

Reid's voice shook with grief and hatred. "Who cut you?"

"I don't want to discuss it."

"Was it Ozik?"

Vaasa shook her head. "Please—"

"Do they still live?"

Vaasa nodded.

His finger caught her chin and lifted her eyes to meet his, refusing to allow her to hide. "One more thing, and then you never have to speak of it again. A name. Just a name."

Vaasa swallowed. "Lord Vlacik."

Reid looked up at her, something blooming to life in his gaze. A familiarity. Of course—he had just met with the man. Vaasa went stiff, and by the way he pressed his lips together, she knew he hated to see her afraid. His composure melted then. Gone was the anger and the violence and the wolf. He replaced it with that gentle simmer—still a fire, yet one that was meant to keep her warm instead. He kept to his word; he didn't speak as he checked both arms for the marks. "Did you get my message? The leather tie?" he finally asked.

Vaasa closed her eyes for only a moment, her heart thudding in her chest. "Yes," she whispered, opening her eyes again. She reached into her pocket and extended the tie to him. "I did. I thought . . ." She gritted her teeth as she breathed in. "I thought it might be a trap. Is she really a merchant's daughter?"

Reid shook his head. His fingers glided over the leather like it meant something precious to him, and then he pocketed it. "Sachia is a pirate and a witch, too. Her brother is in the prison. We're trying to break him out. Koen is downstairs negotiating with a man named Lord Karev. Are you familiar with him?"

Koen was the other man, the lanky one. She had been right. "You're masquerading as salt lords? Smuggling black powder?"

"How do you know that?"

"Lord Karev is meeting with an Icrurian. We're at war, Reid. You had to know that would gather attention." She raked a hand through her hair. "You have to stop. If Ozik catches wind—"

"Breathe, Wild One," he murmured. "I know. We're going to have to be careful, but there is no other way forward. I've considered my options all day. There are a hundred underhanded deals happening in this city as we speak. Hopefully we'll just be another one. "Koen is using the name Remi LeTorneau, my grandfather. I'm supposedly his bodyguard."

Vaasa pursed her lips. She had to tell him the truth of who he was bargaining with—about why it would never be just another deal. "Lord Karev is a frontrunner for the throne. Him and Lord Vlacik."

Reid's face darkened. "Sachia told me. Ambitious, aren't these men? To try and steal someone else's wife?"

Vaasa lay her hand on Reid's cheek. "Can we communicate through Sachia? Do you think she would be willing?" A pirate witch. Vaasa could hardly wrap her mind around it. What she didn't say floated between them: *Can we trust her?*

Reid's jaw stayed tight, but he let out a small breath. "She will help us. She and Karev have a plan to seize control of the prison."

Vaasa frowned. "Vlacik can get you further into that prison than Karev ever will."

"Not after tonight."

"What do you mean?"

Reid paused, though concern flickered in his eyes. This knowledge of something Vaasa didn't yet understand. "Do you know of the pirate Sutherland?"

Vaasa could hardly breathe. "Do *you?*"

He gave a stern nod. "Sachia defected from his crew. Vlacik imprisoned Sachia's brother as punishment."

Vaasa sucked in a breath. "Sachia's brother is in the Mekës prison?"

"Yes," Reid said. "These pirates are all indebted to your nobles in one way or another, but it seems Vlacik has more control than most. In order to cut Sutherland off at the knees, we need to remove Vlacik."

Remove Vlacik? Vaasa stood frozen, staring up at him. "Reid, what are you going to do?"

"He dies. Tonight."

"Reid—"

"Those scars on your arms are reason enough, Wild One. This isn't something we can negotiate."

"Or she and Lord Karev are setting you up," Vaasa said, heart suddenly in her throat. "If you have any hand in Vlacik's murder, it's a trap, one that ends in your execution. Are you sure he doesn't know who you are? That Sachia hasn't told him?"

Reid shook his head. "That would be a waste of Sachia's time and effort. If she wanted to bargain for her brother by turning me in, she would have simply gone to Ozik or kept us hostage on her ship."

"She has a history with these lords. She's been trading with them for years," Vaasa said.

"She hates them. I have a gut feeling, I just—"

"A gut feeling?" Vaasa pressed her fingers to her forehead, trying to stave off the headache that her own panic was causing. "You don't know these people, Reid. If Sachia went to Ozik, it would be just as likely that he'd have her executed along with her brother. She's avoiding being arrested by making an underhanded deal with Karev."

Reid's shoulders remained steady and loose. "If that were true, she never would have signaled for you to come here. She would have told me that she hadn't found you, and she'd have led me into this trap tonight without any chance of seeing you. She's a witch, Vaasa. An Imros witch. My mother is training her."

A pang of jealousy hit Vaasa, foolish and out of line. Yet she centered on one truth that caused her entire stomach to drop. "Melisina is here? In Mekës?"

"We're sleeping in a fabric shop, but she's waiting for you. We all are. We're going to get Amalie and Sachia's brother out, and then we're going to flee."

An old, unwelcome friend, anxiety, grew teeth in Vaasa's body. She wanted to be grateful, to feel some kind of relief, but it didn't come.

There were so many people to lose.

She wanted to crawl out that window and never look back, just as she thought she'd do in Mireh on the night of her wedding. But this time, she would be running toward her coven, toward her husband, instead of escaping them. All their lives were at risk here, and for what? For *her*?

"You should break into the prison and get Amalie and Sachia's brother. You all can leave, you can—"

"Don't you dare finish that sentence," Reid warned her.

Their eyes held, and he saw to the core of her. It was as if he'd already memorized every piece of her puzzle the way she tried to do to others. She uncovered the rest of the world, yet he was the only person who seemed able to uncover her.

"All right," she said. "I have an idea, but you may not like it."

Reid furrowed his brow but tilted his head to listen.

Vaasa took a deep breath. They needed access to the prison, a way to see each other again, and a distraction to hold off the nobility. "I'm going to let Lord Karev court me. Officially. Lead him into a proposal."

Reid stared at her. "No. Absolutely not."

"I don't know what else to do," Vaasa argued. "Ozik is going to make me accept someone's proposal, and it may be the best chance I have of seeing you again. If I can convince Lord Karev of my intention to marry him, that I can help him with these trade negotiations, I can stay close to you." She thought of what Karev had insinuated the night all the lords had arrived—that she knew more about Icruria than anyone.

Reid paused for a moment, truly considering her plan, but shook his head. "There has to be another way."

"Reid," she whispered, voice dropping to a scandalous whisper. "I am situated perfectly to conquer our greatest enemy. To save the continent from the ambitions of these unworthy men. I told you once I would give you the Asteryan throne. Let me take it from them."

His eyes watched her closely, and Vaasa squirmed beneath Reid's gaze. "A courtier *and* a war general," he said, repeating what he'd once called her after she finally told him the truth of his claim to the Asteryan throne through their marriage.

"You know now who you married," she confirmed.

"The most curious being in my existence." He brushed her hair from her face. His next words came in a guttural growl, a threat and a promise, a flash of violence she recognized from the day he'd cleaned her wounds after she'd baited Kosana. "Tell me it will all be pretending with him. That none of it will be real."

"Nothing of what you hear or see is real, except when I am alone with you," she said. "Everything else is a game, one I am going to make them pay for." Vaasa held his gaze, running her fingers over his cheek again. She took a breath, knowing that if she didn't say this now, she would regret it for the rest of her life, no matter how long or short that was. "I should have told you that I would stay. I *want* to stay with you. Take away the timeline, forget the three years. I want more."

Relief flared in his eyes, perhaps indicating how little faith he'd had. "When the time comes, will you run with me? Rule at my side as high consort, not as a figurehead or a chess piece?"

He'd seen the worst of what she had to offer, the poison she could leak when she was afraid or miserable or enraged. That was the version of her that he had fallen in love with—the stubborn one, the violent one, the broken one.

And Reid of Mireh had never turned away.

Vaasa smiled at him, the snake and the wolf both coming alive within her to defend him. His ambitions. His desires. "When the time comes, I will follow you to the ends of the earth."

"I am in love with you," he whispered. "I didn't tell you that enough. I should have told you the moment I realized it."

"I love you, too." She rested her forehead against his, taking in the feel of his arms and his body. *Alive*, her mind repeated. *Alive and well.* "I am your wife. Everything begins and ends with that."

He took her in his arms again, a heavy silence coursing between them. Vaasa felt the weight of time as it wound down. She needed to go, or Roman would likely alert someone else to her absence. In truth, he was doing her a favor by not sounding the alarm and shutting down the entire city. Still, if he found her at The Lady Fortune, this entire opportunity would be wasted. If the city began to search, they might discover Reid.

"Convince her not to kill Vlacik," she said. "Give me a few days to figure this all out."

Reid grit his teeth. "I'll try. But . . ." Everything around them went still. "I'm afraid we may be too late for that."

"What do you mean?"

"All of the pieces are in place. She could already be seeking him out," Reid said.

Vaasa froze, but only for a second. Just long enough for the potential outcome of this to hit her.

If anyone had recognized her tonight, they could easily pin this death on her. After their spat at dinner and her dismissing of Vlacik beneath the theater, the nobility had witnessed them at odds.

Regína had seen her here tonight, and Vaasa was not foolish enough to think she was the only person who could purchase the madame's secrets.

"I have to go," she whispered. "They'll frame me, Reid. This city is looking for any reason to tie me to the iron post."

"I'm sorry. I didn't think—"

"Goodbye," she whispered. Though it felt like ripping out a part of herself, Vaasa forced her legs to move. Forced her body to unpeel from Reid's and rush toward the door. She picked up the rest of her costume and her mask, securing it with its long white ribbon once more. She put herself back together as if she were donning armor.

"Vaasa," he demanded.

She turned back, and their eyes locked. He stood there like a statue, every muscle in his body tensed. "No title is worth the loss of you. I will give it all up. Both nations. Lest you misunderstand my priorities."

Vaasa held his gaze, longing and pain coating each of her nerves. How could she force her body to leave this room? She responded with absolute truth—a rarity in this city, especially coming from her. "I would sacrifice the world to have you."

With one last look, she slipped out the door, checking the hallway carefully, dangerous hope filling her to the brim.

Reid had found her. He had crossed their continent and infiltrated the capital of Asterya. She was no longer alone.

And she swore she felt it, even just for a moment: white eyes and sharp teeth.

The wolf.

Trembling in her bones, breaking the chains that held it.

CHAPTER 21

Cold stung Vaasa's eyes as she exited the brothel into the threshold between late night and early morning, only sparing enough minutes to change back into her clothes. The sun still hadn't started to rise, and darkness bathed the snowcapped mountains Mekës was built upon. She could just barely make out the curtain walls of the fortress. She knew the way, though, and she immediately made for the back of the building, entering one of the narrow streets that would lead her there.

A body stepped into her path, coming too close too quickly. Panic splintered her rib cage for only a moment, and she retreated, hands fumbling for the dagger she'd tucked in the interlining of her cloak. And then he was close enough that his brown eyes were illuminated beneath a thick hooded cloak.

Roman, she realized. Her adrenaline remained constant, as did her hand on the pommel of her knife.

Roman thrust down his hood and the scarf covering his face, frustration in his voice. "What the hell do you think you're doing, Vaasa? The *brothel?*"

She looked around them to be sure no one was watching, but a few people spilled from the front door of The Lady Fortune just fifty feet away. "You shouldn't have come," she whispered, scurrying past him and rounding the corner of the building down the cobblestone street.

"I am your lead sentinel. I had no other choice," he seethed, coming up behind her. "I *knew* you would be here. That you just couldn't help yourself. I should have set off every—"

"Keep your voice *down*," she hissed over her shoulder.

He grabbed her wrist to slow her, and something in her went cold. She hadn't given him permission to touch her. Even if there had once been a time she wanted him to touch her this way, a time when she would have followed his lead.

Roman stepped to cover her back, his breath warm on her exposed neck. "I know you're angry with me," he said, still so delicately holding her forearm. "But you can't leave the fortress without me, without one of my men."

His touch was different and wrong, especially as she considered where she had been tonight, who she had been with. She started to turn on him, to—

Something slammed into the ground. An awful crunching sound echoed around them. Roman jumped back on instinct, but then Vaasa's eyes landed on the source.

It was a body.

Someone had thrown a body out of the window.

Mangled, broken limbs lay strewn in the wrong direction, blood pooling around the corpse and running through the cracks between cobblestones. The head was turned, though, and Vaasa stared into lifeless, ice-blue eyes.

It was Lord Vlacik.

No.

"Run!" Roman hissed, pulling her back and away from the scene. Vaasa fought the urge to vomit, the overwhelming tang of blood suffocating the air.

Vaasa stumbled away at Roman's direction. They fled down another street, any direction that would take them away from the scene.

As breath pumped in and out of Vaasa's lungs, the cold air burned her throat, but she kept pace until they were at least three streets away. A line of horses waited outside a dimly lit building, secured to a tie rail. Roman's was among them, she realized. He'd hidden his steed there. They slowed for the first time, and adrenaline leaked into her fingertips. She felt every inch of her connection to Ozik in that moment, every place her magic no longer touched.

It would have flooded her body mercilessly. She wanted that sensation, craved it.

"Are you okay?" Roman asked, both hands on her shoulders as he looked her over.

She shooed his hands away, turning and swallowing the bile that rose in her throat. Her hand covered her mouth. "I'm fine," she insisted, though it came out breathy and strained. "That was Vlacik. That was fucking *Vlacik*."

"Look at me," Roman demanded.

She had to school her emotions, to get ahold of herself if she wanted to play this right. Vaasa turned and kept her mouth covered.

"Did anyone recognize you in that brothel, Vaasa? *Think*."

There was so much she couldn't say. "No, of course not," she decided, lying through her teeth. She pulled air in through her nose.

"Are you sure?"

"Yes."

And then as she looked at him, she realized . . . "You wore that to the brothel, correct?"

Roman went still. He looked down at his nonregulation attire and swore. "My jacket is inside."

"*Roman.*"

"We need to get back to the fortress. Now."

Roman knew precisely what she did, knew what it would mean if anyone had realized who they were. They would blame her for Lord Vlacik's death after their spat, after he had insulted her and threatened to take the Asteryan throne by virtue of his gender. She would be labeled a murderer. They'd already called her a whore and a traitor and a witch. Her credibility hung on the fragile word of the Asteryan archbishop.

The possibilities clawed at her, and Vaasa fought the tears welling in her eyes. She couldn't tell if it was fear or relief that swirled in her churning stomach. Her torturer was dead. He couldn't harm her or Amalie any longer.

But she was sure Reid had something to do with his murder.

She stayed silent as Roman loaded her onto his horse and grabbed the reins. He trudged beside the animal in the snow, guiding them all the way to the main gates of the fortress. He never asked how she had snuck out, and she didn't offer the information. The guards at the front gates would see her, but the only other option was to show Roman the tunnels that led from her father's office into her family's hidden apartment.

That wasn't something she could risk.

The sentinels at the front gates bristled at Vaasa's presence, turning to Roman for an explanation. He muttered something about her staying out late with some of the nobles, but Vaasa wasn't convinced the sentinels believed them, especially since he kept his cloak closed to hide the lack of his regalia. The pair watched them both closely, and their judgmental gazes caused her to shift her weight in obvious discomfort.

As they headed back to the emperor's wing, Roman walked steadily at her side. "Say you were with me," he insisted quietly.

"What?"

He stopped outside her door. Peering down the hallway, he made sure they were alone. Then he lifted his hand to her cheek once again. "If they ask, I will say I was with you for the entire night."

She held his stare. "They will call me a whore."

"They already do."

Bitterness spread on her tongue in the form of some miserable retort, but she bit it down. Roman was right. He hadn't said it to insult her, but rather to show her why such an alibi would be believed.

The world was always quick to believe what they already suspected.

If they pinned Vlacik's death on her, Vaasa had only two options: She was a murderer, or she was an adulteress. Only one ended in her execution.

Vaasa took in a deep breath, then pulled away from him, shocked to discover she was reeling from guilt. She didn't know how to look him in the eye and lie to him. To pretend she hadn't rushed back into Reid's arms the moment she saw him.

The relief she'd felt . . . that wasn't what she'd felt when she found Roman.

He let her go this time. Without another word, Vaasa slipped through the door and clicked it shut, leaning her back against it.

No footsteps sounded. Roman didn't leave.

He just stood outside her door, guarding the hall like any good ghost would do.

CHAPTER 22

A wrenching pull of magic broke through the haze of Vaasa's sleep. She sat up, ragged breaths spewing from her lips, and the motion was so violent she rolled off the couch and hit the floor with an echoing slam. Pain shot up her shoulder and side. She rolled onto her back, her thick quilt now tangled around her.

"Sleep well?"

Vaasa froze. Immediately she registered the rays of late morning light that filtered through the stained glass window, washing the floor in red, blue, and green. And that voice.

She turned her head and saw Ozik. He stood near the entrance to the entertainment space, dressed in brown breeches and a tucked-in white blouse with his formal blue Asteryan coat. His arms were crossed, a scowl firmly planted upon his face.

Her mistake registered at once, the events of the previous evening replaying in her head.

She had slept through their morning training.

"You certainly gathered enough attention coming through the main gates in the latest hours of the night," Ozik said. "Though no one seems to have a record of you leaving."

Vaasa pulled herself up, clutching the blankets to her chest. "I snuck out with my lead sentinel," she proclaimed. "It wouldn't be difficult for him to erase those records, would it?"

Ozik snorted. He uncrossed his arms. "Really, Vaasalisa, if you're going to commit cold-blooded murder, you should do so with a less scandalous alibi."

Vaasa's wide-eyed frown was the picture of shock. "What?"

Ozik tilted his head, assessing her. "You look genuinely surprised. Is it a ruse? I can never tell with you, I taught you so well."

"What are you talking about?" Vaasa demanded, rising to her knees and then to her feet. Fatigue racked her, but she pushed through it, clinging to her performance.

"Lord Vlacik was thrown out of a fifth-story window last night," he told her. "At The Lady Fortune."

The sight of his body crumpled on cobblestone would follow her for years, both a daydream and a nightmare. Her lips parted, then snapped shut. She raked a hand through her tangled hair. "He's dead?"

"Obviously."

"I had nothing to do with it," she said, pushing Reid's face from her mind.

Sarcasm coated his tone. "You seem positively bereft, though."

"Am I meant to mourn a monster?"

"Even monsters have funerals."

Vaasa stared at him, unsure of what to make of all these tidbits of seemingly useless wisdom. "Please don't harm Amalie," Vaasa said instead. "I'll come with you now to train."

But Ozik shook his head. "It's all right, given we're celebrating."

She arched a brow. "Celebrating?"

"The only high-ranking noble with knowledge of our magic is dead. You might have been forced to marry him if he'd gone to extremes to win your hand. So put on mourning garments, hang your head in solemn prayer at the Citadel, and then tell the people we are going to discover who did this. And tomorrow, we will breathe easier."

Vaasa almost gawked. Ozik had *wanted* Vlacik to die? Suddenly, she didn't think her alibi mattered at all to him. "Are we actually going to try and find out who did this?"

Ozik only shrugged. "If someone's imprisonment is convenient."

The next person to challenge them would find themselves guilty of a murder, then.

He walked to the door, his voice threading the air. "And anyway, everyone at The Lady Fortune wears masks, so how could we ever be sure? We only know one detail about the killer." Ozik turned to face her, his hand on the door. "They were wearing a sentinel's jacket."

It took every ounce of Vaasa's self-control to maintain her composure and keep her breathing even. Would she cause Roman's death once more?

As he opened the door, Ozik said, "We leave for the Citadel in twenty minutes. Mourning garments."

"You're in Asteryan blue," Vaasa replied.

He grinned and repeated her words, voice smooth as silk. "Am I meant to mourn a monster?"

Thick snow crunched beneath Vaasa's feet as she walked into the center of the city square, the Sanctum on one side of her, the Citadel on the other. She stood just in front of the iron pole at the center.

The clock tower on the Citadel chimed noon.

Nobles and merchants and workers all surrounded the platform she stood upon. Sentinels covered every inch of the square, eyes scanning the crowds while Vaasa and Ozik addressed the people. She rambled on, honoring the service Lord Vlacik gave to Asterya, speaking on the security of the city. Some listened, others were clearly waiting for Ozik to speak. It wasn't uncommon for him to deliver addresses on the throne's behalf; he was their closest advisor and served on their council, after all. He quickly took over, but Vaasa remained where she stood in a foolish attempt to make herself seem less like a figurehead.

When he finished, they stepped off the platform and marched into the Sanctum, the nobles following. Vaasa scanned the crowd, sighting

Lord Karev in the madness. His inky hair had gathered small flakes of snow in the places it burst from his fur hat. He was deep in conversation with someone. She veered from the throne room and started up the stairs in what she knew looked like an effort to avoid him. She passed Roman, cresting the top without looking back.

"Heiress," Lord Karev called. "A word?"

Vaasa looked over her shoulder, finding the lord already most of the way up the staircase. "Let him pass," she said to Roman.

Roman narrowed his eyes, but she held his gaze without budging. As was mandatory in a moment like this, Roman stepped aside, lowering his head to Lord Karev, who strode past him. The lord quickly took the responsibility of opening the door instead of allowing Vaasa to do so, his arm sweeping through the threshold. "You first, of course."

Vaasa gave an urbane smile as she stepped past him and into the large council room where many of the nobles would soon join them. A large table sat in the center, surrounded by at least ten chairs.

"You look positively lost in thought," Lord Karev said as he approached, so close that she had to crane her neck to meet his gray eyes.

She unclasped the cloak at her shoulders and swept it from her body, settling it neatly on the chair they stood next to. "So much to think about." She was careful to keep their proximity casually close, but had put enough distance between them to feel safe.

"A shame about Lord Vlacik," Lord Karev said.

Vaasa nodded. "A terrible crime. Though I suppose you were right about what you said the other night; he was frequenting the brothel."

His lips pursed, his cheeks still reddened from the cold. He leaned his hip against the table. "I suppose we all have our hidden tastes."

Her words from the night before, echoed back to her as a threat.

He knew.

Precisely as she'd assumed.

As she searched for a worthwhile response, she gave the appearance of a woman caught in a lie, but before she said anything, a small chuckle emanated from him.

And he thought he had her.

"An affair with your lead sentinel, how groundbreaking." Lord Karev slid farther onto the table, sitting entirely upon it now. Any hint of the charm he'd previously spun for her was gone. "Unless, of course, you had an ulterior motive for being there last night?"

He was pinning her into one confession or another: Either she'd been there enjoying the brothel for its original purpose with her lead sentinel, or she'd had something to do with Vlacik's murder. But if he already knew she'd returned to the fortress with Roman, it either meant the whispers had become widespread or he had eyes and ears somewhere in the fortress's ranks.

Vaasa shook her head. "I don't believe I know what you're talking about."

Lord Karev smiled wickedly. "Every idiot outside of this room is whispering theory after theory, but I know something they don't. Something *far* more interesting. I'm involved in a great deal of trade along the continent, and for the first time in my life, I met with an Icrurian salt lord last night."

Vaasa paused. This was not something she thought he would jump to.

Lord Karev continued, "What I'm trying to decide is if your presence last night was merely serendipity, or if it's no coincidence at all that you and he were in the same place at the same time. Either you're a murderer, or you're just like your father, because all the best players know serendipity is simply successful scheming."

While Karev might be brazen and perhaps unhinged, he certainly wasn't unintelligent, which Vaasa had known from the moment she laid eyes on him. If he had put together who Reid was, they were all dead. But he hadn't said as much. He was accusing her of many things, but a clandestine meeting with her Icrurian husband wasn't one of them.

Vaasa tried desperately to think on her feet. All the lord wanted was for her to think he had the upper hand, and no matter what he said, she had more leverage than he ever could: She could make him an emperor.

Vaasa put on a subtle meekness meant to soften her features. It was best he thought her afraid of him, or at least more powerless than she was. "We've found ourselves in a precarious position, haven't we, Lord Karev?"

The man looked smug. His body relaxed, ease pouring from his posture as he sat unbothered in front of her. "Why don't you explain it to me."

Vaasa ran her tongue over her teeth. Looking at the door, she pretended to check that no one was coming inside. To make herself appear nervous. He needed to believe himself cleverer, more connected, better informed. She controlled every aspect of her voice, broaching an almost *too* confident tone, one Karev would perceive as fabricated. As her trying too hard. "Would you believe my brother sent me into Icruria without a plan to make friends with the salt lords?" Vaasa asked, the lie coming as easy to her as breathing.

Lord Karev scoffed. "Your brother was a sniveling idiot. But I suspect that advisor of yours knew precisely what he was doing."

Vaasa paused for just one second. He had just provided her with a far easier lie than her brother spinning schemes, because it was a half-truth. She sighed in concession, tugging her hand through her snow-tangled hair. "All right, fine. Ozik asked me to make friends with the salt lords, and I did. When your friend mentioned salt the other night, I decided I would risk it. The man you met—I was trying to meet with him last night, as well. If I can deliver salt, I can secure the throne. But I had nothing to do with what happened to Vlacik."

Throne. All he needed was that one word.

Lord Karev smiled like the devil himself. "So you know the man?"

"I do."

"And what exactly is your intention with him now that trade has been cut off between Asterya and Icruria? What does Ozik want?"

She started to breathe a little heavier and gave a small frown, like she was losing control of the conversation. "Why would I tell you that?"

"Because I might be the only thing standing between you and a prison cell, Heiress."

She *barely* winced. This was a fine line to walk. Finally, she whispered, "So either I tell you the throne's secrets, or you're going to blame me for the lord's death?"

"That depends on what you can offer me. I can just as easily tell every noble out there that you and I were together the entire night."

There it was. An alibi and a marriage agreement in one fell swoop. She widened her eyes and looked down at the floor. "In return, you want a marriage agreement."

"I believe that is obvious," he said plainly. "And you can drop the innocent act. A man does not claw his way into a lordship without being able to read people. An innocent, vapid heiress wouldn't have listened to the bare bones of a conversation and then found herself in exactly the right place at exactly the right time. No. Your brother may have wasted you, but I certainly won't."

Vaasa ran her tongue along her teeth. "What do you want?" she asked, letting her own tone slip into bluntness.

"At today's council meeting, ensure Ozik nominates Roland Beránek to be warden of the prison instead of one of Vlacik's allies. I also want your connection to the salt lord. He doesn't trust me; our language barrier is too great. I suspect if you can help translate, a deal can be struck," he said.

So this was how Karev would give Sachia access to the prison. He was slowly untangling Vlacik's hold on the city guard, inserting himself instead. Vaasa was instrumental to his own plan, a missing piece he needed to slide into place. He planned to use her the way her father had, no matter how blatant or cruel. Vaasa crossed her arms—if she'd had her magic, she swore it would have hissed. Because this time, she was going to squeeze everything she wanted out of an arrangement like this. If she was going to be relegated to the schemes of men, she would weave a worse one all her own. "The man you met with won't be pleased with the breaking of Asterya and Icruria's trade agreement. He's selfish and motivated by money alone. My hope was to work with him to undermine the Icrurian forces. We win the war, and he becomes the wealthiest salt lord in existence. I believe *that's* a deal he will be interested in."

"To win a war, you need an army," Lord Karev stated.

And he had one of the largest mercenary armies on the continent. It was the only reason he held the power he did, and it was his greatest bargaining chip for an engagement to her. It was what set him apart as the head of the New Asteryan faction. Vaasa held his gaze, though she didn't bother feigning a smile. "I wonder where I might find a powerful lord with one of those."

It was positively carnal how he looked at her, the corners of his mouth rising with considerable pride. "In exchange for the throne, you get my armies and an alibi. It's a better offer than Vlacik ever would have made."

This was a part of her plan. Vaasa knew that, and yet her chest still constricted at the thought of going along with what he wanted. "Have an agreement drafted, then."

"Would we include last night's alibi in it?" he asked with such wickedness in his tone.

Vaasa only stared at him. "You can leave that part out."

Karev gave a small chuckle and leaned comfortably against a table. "I only have one concern."

"And what's that?"

Lord Karev looked at the door, gesturing with his hand to it. "Your lead sentinel. The moment we're engaged, you stop fucking him."

Vaasa reared back. "Excuse me?"

He smirked at her aghast expression. "If we're to be married, let us begin with the truth. I don't blame you your appetites, but I have no intention of ending up like Vlacik."

A fucking fool. Lord Karev thought she had no clue who'd committed that murder. He assumed he was smart enough to outwit her, to rise to power and overcome Ozik. Overcome her someday, too. All he had to do was convince her to marry him, and he thought he had won the game. But he was the prey, and he was the perfect choice for it: power hungry, gullible, and too full of himself to think he was either of those things.

Vaasa crossed her arms indignantly. "My lead sentinel is a means to an end. A way to visit the city and go where I please. He believes he has a chance at getting in my bed, so he does what I ask. But despite what you and everyone else seem to believe, I am not having an affair."

Lord Karev stared at her, gauging how much of that he believed. There was no sexual tension between them, no lust there for her to twist. In his eyes was only a craving for power. He stood, towering over her. "I am not the kind of man you need to seduce in order to get what you want. I have no interest in fucking you. I prefer my women with less . . . presence. But if you stand at my side, I will ensure you want for nothing. So if you need to go to the city, or you want a man thrown from a window, it's me you call upon going forward."

Never in her life had this much poison been spewed at Vaasa in such a charming tone. It was both an insult and a compliment, a transparent admission of the marriage he offered her. A marriage that, perhaps a year or two ago, she might truly have considered entering. In so many ways, Lord Karev and she were similar—maniacal, ruthless liars. There was a version of the world where he would have been precisely the man to overthrow Dominik. If she had been born power hungry, he would have been the bet she took.

But she did not want to rule Asterya. She wanted to dismantle it.

Vaasa pulled herself from where she leaned against the table, taking a few steps away. "Then I no longer need him."

Lord Karev nodded, uncaring about the space she'd put between them, and stood from the table. He beamed down at her, not a hint of attraction or craving in his eyes. It was all ambition that shone there. She was, just as she had said about Roman, a means to an end.

He started toward the door. "Remember what I said about Roland Beránek. I need him to be warden of the prison."

"I'll tell Ozik immediately," she agreed.

He peered over his shoulder. "I'll call upon you tomorrow. I'd like to meet with the salt lord sooner rather than later," he said before swinging open the door. He stared at Roman, then stepped past him as if the sentinel meant absolutely nothing to him.

Roman rushed in, looking her over, but she held up her hand. Ozik walked in just then, his curious eyes watching her. Vaasa stood up straight and strode to the door. "Nominate Roland Beránek as warden of the prison, and you've got your marriage agreement."

Ozik raised a brow. "You've made your choice?"

She stopped in her tracks, fury bright in her chest. She spat, "Don't pretend you ever gave me one."

Ozik chuckled, and Vaasa just kept walking, Roman following silently on her heels, grief pouring from him, unavoidable, undeniable.

As Vaasa walked back to the emperor's wing of the fortress, Roman kept his distance paces away. The moment they passed through the doors that led to the private hallways of this wing of the fortress, he stopped walking.

They were alone now.

Vaasa turned and released a small breath. The list of undesirable conversations she had no way to escape kept growing longer.

"Are you really going to marry that man?" Roman asked.

"What choice do I have?" She shook her head and dragged a hand through her hair.

Roman pursed his lips in contemplation. "Did you have Vlacik killed?"

Vaasa huffed an angry breath and placed her hand upon her hip. "Did *you*?"

He gawked at her. "I was inside the brothel for all of ten minutes—"

"And unaccounted for all of the minutes after. The murderer wore a sentinel's jacket, Roman, and you returned to the fortress without one. The guards at the gates saw you. It's all the nobility are talking about. It's precisely how Karev just cornered me into a marriage agreement."

Roman went still. Anger lanced his features, and she was once again struck by how quickly he morphed into a different person—a colder one. "So my mistake is the reason you have to marry Karev?"

Vaasa shook her head in frustration, a pounding headache stealing her patience. "Yes. Either I marry him, or he pins the murder on you and me. This is all I can do to protect you. To protect myself."

Roman ran his tongue along his teeth in contemplation, perhaps deciding if he believed her reasoning. "I'm sorry," he said. "Vaasa, I'm so sorry."

Her heart sank in her chest, this guilt burrowing so deep inside her she couldn't see a way to claw it out. It felt like no matter which direction she went, she couldn't avoid breaking his heart. "You need to be very careful, Roman. Karev wholeheartedly believes we are having an affair, and if you give him any hint of confirmation, he'll soon have all the power he needs to call for your head."

Roman looked down at his feet and cursed, fisting and unfisting his hands.

"I don't want to be the reason you lose everything again," she confessed. "I won't be."

Finally, a real truth she could give him—that she didn't want to hurt him. Not again. No matter what fears she held about him or what their circumstances had turned them into, that single thing remained true.

Roman met her eyes across the hallway. "Thank you."

Vaasa just turned and started away. "Summon me when Ozik has news."

It was only three hours before Roman knocked, his expression still twisted and guilt-stricken. He held a white envelope in his hands. "Roland Beránek has been made warden of the prison," he said. He extended a letter. "This arrived for you."

Vaasa took the envelope from him, inspecting the Karev family seal upon it. She popped it open with her finger, skimming it quickly. It was an invitation to visit the port together the following day.

And an official declaration of his intent to pursue a marriage agreement.

CHAPTER 23

Vaasa's hands shook as she held a glittering black wall in front of her. Her magic was more solid than she had yet seen it, able to take on shapes and forms at her command. It reminded her of what she'd seen Romana do, and something about that created a fissure in her. Her chest constricted. The thought of her coven was a knife in her gut. They had shown her only pieces of this, so careful not to push her too quickly, and Vaasa longed for that consideration.

Melisina was here in Mekës, yet Vaasa couldn't run to her.

She held Ozik's gaze from across the greenhouse. Nothing but spite and malice fueled her now. She had to be stronger, to become this man's worst nightmare. With each second that passed, the fury in her gut grew larger, more violent.

A hole in her wall of magic appeared, smoking at the edges, the magic losing its hold. Ozik growled in frustration. "Whatever it is you are thinking about, *stop*."

Vaasa tried to push it all away, but the more she denied her anger, the stronger it became. It crested. Her muscles tightened, and she let out a pained gasp, arms dropping so she could double over. The wall disintegrated into smoke and spread out from where she stood, hovering above the floor like fog on the water, crawling up the ocean-facing wall of the greenhouse and clouding it momentarily with black.

She took a sharp breath.

"Enough for today," Ozik said, disappointment apparent in his voice. He dismissed her magic in the room, absorbing it with ease back into his outstretched palm. She slumped, staring out at the churning sea, grateful this part of the greenhouse looked over the water and was positioned so that no one else could see inside.

A knock at the door drew her attention.

She turned to see Roman step in, and then her heart leapt into her throat.

Amalie.

"Your recent efforts are noted," Ozik drawled as he walked to the door. "Today not withstanding."

Vaasa could barely move, her eyes greedily drinking in the sight of her friend. No longer chained, her olive skin was unmarred, her brown hair clean, her body seemingly well fed. Roman softly let Amalie go, though iron still glinted at her wrists. There were two bracelets there, one on each wrist, though her hands were no longer bound. They must stifle magic, just like the chains, just like the rope Dominik had tied Vaasa up with. They had to, otherwise Amalie would have struck.

Vaasa stepped forward, but Amalie locked eyes with Ozik.

Ozik moved perceptibly slower.

Suddenly, rage leaked through the room like a scent in the air, deep and strong. There was a twisting to Amalie's face that Vaasa again didn't recognize. That softness, the ease and grace with which Amalie had always held herself, was absent. It was beyond a sense of resentment for a captor; what wound between Ozik and Amalie felt . . . older. Ancient, even.

"Come now, Roman," Ozik instructed, sidestepping Amalie to reach the door. She turned, watching him with unblinking eyes. "Let the women have their privacy."

"Sire—" Roman started.

"I said now," Ozik repeated.

Roman held Vaasa with his gaze, unflinching. True concern marred it. "I'll be just outside the door."

"Do you believe I would harm her?" Amalie spoke.

Vaasa's knees threatened to buckle. Amalie's voice was the same as she remembered it, no longer hoarse. Everything about her seemed . . . comfortable.

Roman didn't bother to answer the question. Instead, he slipped out the door and shut it.

Amalie looked at Vaasa with a small grin. "I don't think he likes me."

"Amalie," Vaasa whispered.

Amalie ran. Vaasa leapt forward and threw herself at her friend, the two colliding in an embrace that immediately brought tears to Vaasa's eyes. She pulled Amalie as closely as she could. "Tell me you're okay," she begged. "Tell me they haven't hurt you."

"They haven't hurt me," she assured. "Every other day or so, that guard or Ozik comes to ensure I'm fed, bathed, and given fresh clothing."

"They do?" Vaasa asked.

Amalie pulled back and met Vaasa's gaze. "They do."

Ozik was caring for Amalie? And Roman was helping? Relief and anger intertwined in Vaasa's body; on the one hand, it meant Amalie was cared for. On the other, it meant Roman had far more access to Amalie than he'd let on. Why hadn't he mentioned this?

Vaasa ran a finger over the iron bracelet, but since Ozik had taken her magic, she felt nothing, unlike in the prison beneath Lord Vlacik's knife. "They're in the city," Vaasa whispered, taking Amalie's arm and leading her deeper into the greenhouse. "Reid, Koen, and Melisina. I found them."

Amalie's brows rose.

"We're going to break you out," Vaasa said.

Amalie pursed her lips. Ever so quietly, she said, "I know."

What? Vaasa's brows slammed together. "What do you mean?"

"Veragi told me," Amalie murmured. "Or, at least I think it's her."

"The goddess has spoken to you?"

Amalie nodded. "This is the third time in my life I've heard her voice in my mind. Perhaps it's nothing but an illusion of my own making, but . . ." She shook her head in disbelief. "She told me to be patient. To bide my time. That help was coming."

Vaasa's mind reeled. Veragi, the goddess of witchcraft herself? The deity from which Vaasa and Amalie were granted their magic. "If I've learned anything in the past year, it's that plenty of the unbelievable is possible," Vaasa said.

Amalie sat down on the bench beneath the olive tree, the sage green of the leaves in such complement to the shades of brown in her hair. "Are you safe?" she asked.

"Me?" Vaasa took the spot next to her. "It's you I'm worried about. I've tried to sneak to the prison, I've—"

"Don't," Amalie told her. "I don't know how much time we have, and I . . ." She let out a small breath. "You need to find a way to kill Ozik, not spend your time fussing about me."

Vaasa dragged a hand through her hair, sitting as comfortably as she could. Ozik could walk in any moment, so she kept her voice low. "I haven't figured that out yet. But I found a note from my mother. It was meant to be paired with a necklace, but I think my brother hid it."

"A necklace?"

"My mother said it was the only thing that could protect me. That I shouldn't unite the pieces, because the cost was too great."

"What does that mean?"

"I have no idea."

Amalie let out a small sigh. "If I hear her voice again, I'll ask. Maybe Veragi will know."

Something like hope rose in Vaasa. The voice of a goddess—could it be true?

And if Veragi could speak to or through Amalie . . . Vaasa thought of Ozik's red eyes and shuddered. Perhaps only a goddess would know the answers about how something like that worked.

"Tell me everything you can," Amalie said. "I don't know how or why I keep hearing her, but perhaps there's something she wants me to know."

"Everything?" Vaasa asked.

"Everything we have time for."

Vaasa took a deep breath, this invisible weight lifting off her. *Honesty*, her mind whispered. And so she quietly uttered the truth.

That she had made a deal with the devil in order to keep seeing Reid.

That she was tugging on the cords of Roman's affection to gain access to Amalie.

That she was becoming the very thing she had always hoped to never be—

That the darkness was starting to seep its way back in.

Shame tightened her throat, but when she met Amalie's eyes, it dissipated to that small sense of self-forgiveness that her coven had taught her to embrace.

She could not hate herself when they loved her.

Truth bubbled from Vaasa's core as she began to speak every twisted detail of her current situation.

And with every word, her exhaustion lifted. Her fear. Her pain.

Amalie placed her hand upon Vaasa's, and for the first time since arriving in this city, Vaasa felt strong.

CHAPTER 24

That evening, Lord Karev called upon Vaasa to come into the city, saying he'd agreed to visit some of the local merchants who regularly traveled through his territory. *You are the perfect accompaniment*, he'd written in his note. *They will be so thrilled at their heiress's attention.*

Roman and a line of sentinels followed their carriage on horseback. As they rode through the streets, Vaasa pulled back the curtain to gaze out the window, and just as importantly to give the crowds an opportunity to see her with Lord Karev. Vaasa's heart reached north, begging for Mireh. Begging to dance in the Lower Garden and get lost in the stacks of the sodality. To view paintings and eat upon a patio. To be comfortable in a crowd.

She craved the sound of laughter and the conditions it needed to bloom.

Cold air stung Vaasa's nose as she left the carriage, the rancid smell of the port only mildly smothered by the crispness of the air. Cold waves battered against the docks, and Vaasa searched the docks with a keen eye, taking note of every ship that waited there, every channel one could take to leave it, and the precise location of the berths that could bring a hub like this to a screaming halt.

The ships in the harbor were mostly the same—unmarked, sails of different colors, constructed with the same Asteryan design that she had grown up around. Some were smaller and more adept at navigating the pirate-infested waters, while the other, larger ships likely took the longer path that hugged the coastline. A group of fishers tossed their catch down to waiting buckets, others lugging the buckets up to the fish market. All work stopped when people caught sight of them, though.

Voices rose at the swaths of Asteryan sentinels surrounding Vaasa, and Lord Karev approached, possessively placing his hand on her lower back. Vaasa fought the instinct to arch away from him. With his chin held high and a confident grin, he looked just as bold and arrogant as he had when he'd first arrived at the fortress. Just as charming, too, which she knew to be nothing but a facade.

"Shall we?" he beckoned her, letting the world's attention follow them as he extended her his arm once again, much to Vaasa's chagrin. She demurely lifted her thick skirts from the wet dock and kept walking, Roman and his sentinels about ten paces behind them. Lord Karev led them to the main square near the fish market, where bustles of crowds floated to and fro. Roman closed in, the rest of the sentinels and Lord Karev's guard following suit. Being the central market of Mekës, it was the loudest and most populated area, though Lord Karev quickly ducked into an empty, narrow street.

"You and the others can wait here," Lord Karev instructed Roman, who looked upon the lord like he couldn't ascertain why a command for Vaasa's lead sentinel had just come out of his mouth.

Roman gripped the pommel of his sword. "Where the heiress goes, I go."

Karev grinned wickedly, and Vaasa knew he meant his next words with each ounce of condescension she perceived. "She is with me, Sentinel. I'll keep her safe. Hold your post."

Roman met Vaasa's gaze, but her stomach tightened. "Hold your post," she told the group of sentinels, stepping closer to Lord Karev. "I'm safe."

Everything that left her lips now was a lie.

Without holding Roman's gaze for too long, she followed Lord Karev down the street. Still within their sights, the lord turned to face her, brushing a strand of hair from her face. She wanted to recoil. His gaze darkened with wicked triumph. His voice came low, meant for only her ears, as he stepped fully into her space. "I thought you had let the poor sentinel loose."

"I have," she assured him.

"And yet you keep him in your employ?"

Vaasa continued to force a tone of nonchalance. "He earned his title fairly; it felt too cruel to steal that from him, too."

A muscle flickered in Karev's jaw. "There must not be any doubt that my children are my own."

Vaasa wanted to hurl a knife at him. She bared her teeth, though to the world it looked like a perfect smile. "There will be no question as to the parentage of our heirs."

Lord Karev merely stared down at her, unconvinced. "There will be if he does not temper his reactions."

Vaasa shrugged, trying to make the entire conversation seem lighter than it was. "It's a fresh rejection. I'll speak to him."

"Sooner rather than later," he said. An order.

Vaasa nodded, lowering her eyes in an attempt to indicate submission. The more power she allowed this man to believe he had, the more secure she made him feel, the more likely she could bend him when necessary.

Lord Karev must have accepted her response, because he continued into a fabric shop. Vaasa paused, gazing around, Reid's words about where they were hiding coming to the forefront of her mind.

There, leaning against the counter with her light-red hair braided over her shoulder, was Sachia. Despite the beauty of the woman's face, she had dropped the facade of a merchant's daughter; tight leather breeches and the knife strapped at her waist immediately summoned suspicion. She looked like the kind of woman capable of throwing Lord Vlacik from a window.

Pirates.

That was how Lord Karev was able to fund his ample army; he was leveraging illicit trade to do it. Vaasa's heart pounded, though she kept her face frozen. She barely held herself from searching madly around the store for Reid.

"I thought you were lying when you said you'd bring the heiress," Sachia said. The woman carried an accent—not quite Icrurian, though familiar. It was from one of the long-conquered northern Asteryan provinces.

"I don't lie," Karev told the pirate. His eyes narrowed. "And she speaks fluent Icrurian, so there won't be any miscommunication."

Distrust pulsed between Sachia and Lord Karev, but the pirate didn't respond to the insult he'd just thrown her way. Instead, she stepped forward, inspecting eyes dragging along Vaasa's body. "So quick to jump to business." She extended her arm in greeting. "It's lovely to see you again, Heiress."

Her arm. Her *entire* arm, not just a hand.

Vaasa reached out and gripped the woman's arm in the formal Icrurian gesture. Sachia wrapped her fingers around Vaasa's forearm, squeezing tightly. One shake between them and the pirate dropped it, moving down a walkway lined with spools of silks that were stacked like towers upon the walls. It had been the smallest of gestures, but one that made Vaasa settle more comfortably into Sachia's presence. It was a symbol of friendship, of trust.

Vaasa inspected the spools of fabric, pretending to be interested, the corner of her gaze always watching Lord Karev. He walked with the same commanding stature as he did everywhere, and with each step he took, Vaasa inched farther and farther away. Distracted by the fabrics, or so it seemed, she wound her way to the farthest rows of the shop. Every shade of purple was here, the stacks of it so high that Vaasa could no longer see Lord Karev and Sachia.

A body came up behind hers, and Vaasa spun. Reid stood there, a finger over his lips, indicating a need for silence that Vaasa already knew. He was dressed in warm breeches and a thick wool shirt, which was a little tight on his shoulders and arms. Though likely borrowed, it was a harrowing sight to view the Wolf of Mireh in simple Asteryan fashion.

But he was here. He was inches from her.

She paused and took a deep breath. Just one. A single moment where her composure cracked. She silently choked, hand going over her mouth to keep the sound of an impending sob from breaking out. Her chest rattled with the pressure of keeping everything in.

Lord Karev and Sachia's voices drifted from the other side of the purple fabric stacks, still far enough away that she was hidden. Reid reached for her, his fingers landing beneath her chin, his thumb sweeping over her cheekbone to wipe away a stray tear. "We'll have none of that, Wild One," he whispered.

"Heiress," Lord Karev called, voice coming closer.

She turned the opposite way, blinking tears out of her eyes and gazing at the fabric as she walked without a hurry. When she looked back, Reid was gone.

"I'm over here," she replied, her heart in her throat.

Lord Karev came around the corner just then, gray eyes surveying the fabric she touched.

"Come," he said, gesturing to the back of the shop. She followed him through the winding maze of fabric until they reached a small door that had been left ajar. It led to a set of steep stairs that emptied out into a dim, lantern-lit basement room that Vaasa couldn't entirely see.

Her heart thudded wildly in her chest. Where had Reid gone? This could just as easily be a trap. Sachia ducked into the stairwell, and Lord Karev gestured for Vaasa to follow. And for a moment, Vaasa paused. But Sachia had given her a handshake only an Icrurian would understand. And Reid had said they could trust her.

Vaasa bit the inside of her cheek. No matter what, she didn't really have a choice.

Vaasa ducked through the door, eyes scanning her surroundings as she prepared to fight if necessary. Her winter boots thudded against the floor, and Vaasa looked up to find two men sitting at a table.

Koen... and Reid.

Everything centered on where Reid sat. His face didn't break at her entrance, no ounce of familiarity on his sternly taut mouth, but his eyes softened ever so slightly as he perceived her. To the left, there was another door. It must have been what he'd snuck through.

She remembered everything: every minute detail of the way he had come to know her and she had come to know him. How his hands felt on her waist when they danced, how he cut straight through her inhibitions and fears. Even the memory of it was enough to ruin the careful hold she'd placed on her body all these weeks. He was a threat to her numbness, he always had been. Willpower was the only thing keeping Vaasa from running to him. That, and Lord Karev, who sternly gripped Vaasa's elbow and guided her to the table.

Both Koen and Reid looked to where he touched her. Koen stood, cocking his head as if he was surprised to see her. "Vaasalisa," he drawled.

"Heiress," Lord Karev corrected harshly.

Vaasa chuckled as if the lord was just being protective. "Remi." She kept her tone friendly yet businesslike, especially as Koen extended her an arm. She switched into Icrurian, careful with her words in case Lord Karev was lying about his familiarity with the language. "Forgive him."

Koen held her gaze sternly. "I'll do no such thing."

Vaasa couldn't help her smile.

"Heiress," he said quickly, his Asteryan marked by an Icrurian accent that Vaasa was so deeply fond of.

Lord Karev pulled out a chair for Vaasa to sit in, and as she did, Koen said, "My guard."

He was using cut words, simple, easy. A way to pretend that the language barrier was greater than it truly was. Koen was fully proficient in Asteryan. For a moment, she was in awe of his propensity to put on a convincing act.

"I remember," Vaasa said in Icrurian, giving Reid a casual nod of acknowledgment before taking the seat Lord Karev had offered her. Her heart flew into her throat, and she translated the two words for Lord Karev, careful to keep his trust.

Amusement danced in the orange of Reid's eyes. While a dangerous game, perhaps it was easier to find amusement than to find truth; a coping mechanism, a way to tolerate what this situation had become.

One slip, and they would all be tied to that pole in the city square.

"We're here to discuss a line of trade, are we not?" Sachia asked in Icrurian, leaning back in her chair and glancing between everyone.

Once again, Vaasa translated. Lord Karev immediately jumped in, and Vaasa faithfully translated every word he said. She and Sachia did the majority of the language work, though Koen was smart in how he directed his questions to Vaasa instead, furthering Lord Karev's assumption that bringing in an Icrurian translator, not to mention the heiress, got him further with the deal. Vaasa didn't guide the conversation, playing well into the role of the meek heiress and letting Lord Karev think he was the brains behind the operation. He used her much like all the men in this city had; she was a tool, he the wielder.

They worked out the entire deal as if it were real—how they would utilize a network of Icrurian soldiers loyal to Koen, still going by Remi, and pirates outside Sutherland's reach that Sachia had a connection to. They would smuggle the salt through the blurred Icrurian-Asteryan border and into the frigid ocean near the Sheets. Lord Karev would then be able to sell it here in Mekës and the rest of Asterya, all for Sachia to take a cut of the profits. Aside from the initial profit of each sale, "Remi" would earn a substantial parcel of land upon the end of the war. The entire scheme was less sophisticated than Vaasa had expected of Karev, but she only provided subtle guidance and redirection when she felt it would make her seem interested, but never smarter than him.

"And in return for this connection," Sachia said, directing the conversation where she truly intended it to go, switching very clearly to Asteryan, "I want my brother."

Lord Karev leaned back in his chair, eyes glittering with intrigue, and Vaasa raised her brow. "Your brother?" Vaasa asked as if she didn't know.

"He is rotting in your wretched island prison as we speak," Sachia said. "Fighting for the nobles' amusement."

Vaasa's stomach tightened at the poisoned blade of her tone.

"You can pardon him, can't you?" Sachia asked her.

Warning bells went off in Vaasa's mind. Her words needed to be incredibly careful. "That power lies with the emperor," Vaasa said. Sachia must have known this would be the case—surely Lord Karev had told her that—but Vaasa still looked to her supposed betrothed.

"I'll have that authority soon enough," Lord Karev said.

Sachia tilted her head. "Are congratulations in order?"

Vaasa shifted in her seat, doing her best to avoid Reid's gaze, her only saving grace that he couldn't understand their shared Asteryan words. Koen didn't translate—it would undermine the need for Vaasa there as a translator.

"No formal announcement has been made, but yes," Lord Karev said. "The heiress and I will be drawing up a marriage agreement soon."

Sachia frowned. "I don't have the kind of time to wait for a royal wedding," she said. "I believe we've already earned your favor, haven't we, Lord Karev?"

The lord bristled slightly at her tone, eyes flicking to gauge Vaasa's response. The mood in the room shifted with Sachia's insinuation. He didn't realize that Vaasa already knew he'd played a hand in Lord Vlacik's death, so she blinked as if she didn't understand. Vaasa then flicked her eyes to Reid and Koen, who stayed in perfect character, neither seeming terribly concerned by this line of discussion. It was as if the two of them weren't involved at all. Sachia leaned forward, determination cut into every line of her face, and turned her attention to Vaasa. "If you cannot give me a pardon, then all I need is one night and for the city guard to turn a blind eye. Relocate them to another rotation."

With those words, light bloomed in Vaasa's mind. The brilliance of this plan . . . it was written by Koen, Vaasa was sure of it. She almost hazarded a glance at him. To do what Sachia demanded was to open up Vaasa's own occasion for escape. It created a window of opportunity for them all. But Karev had insisted on his own connection being nominated as warden of the prison, Roland Beránek. Karev had the prison in his pocket, situating himself perfectly to offer Sachia what he wanted.

Or to betray her.

Careful not to seem too eager, she turned to Lord Karev with a good idea of the words he wanted to hear. "I do believe a large celebration, like for a formal engagement, would be cause to move the city guard from the prison to the port, right? Certainly we could ask Roland."

Lord Karev slid those gray eyes to her, considering. "We'd have to announce our engagement soon in order to plan something like that."

Vaasa only shrugged, careful not to appear too eager or motivated. But she was far too aware of Reid and Koen's eyes on her. "Why put off the inevitable? The empire has been in limbo for too long."

"Then why not announce tomorrow?" Lord Karev challenged. "Invite all of the nobles to dinner. We can have the parade in a week."

The air squeezed from her lungs. He'd just backed Vaasa into a corner. If she refused him, he'd know she had a vested interest in what Sachia planned to do, or at least be suspicious. The immediacy of his request was in itself a challenge, even if it wasn't meant as one.

She held Lord Karev's gaze, knowing that Koen understood every word. That the moment they left this room, he would explain it all to Reid. She hoped desperately that Reid would understand, that he would know this was the best chance they had at making it out of this city alive.

"Tomorrow," Vaasa agreed.

Lord Karev grinned unexpectedly, not taking his eyes from Vaasa as he spoke. "We have ourselves a deal, Sachia. We'll host a formal engagement party next week, and that will be your opportunity. Get your brother and leave this city."

One week. She had one week to gain access to Amalie and find her mother's necklace. One week to solidify her own plans.

Vaasa nodded and reached across the table, placing her hand on Sachia's. "Why don't we meet you tomorrow night to celebrate?" She could hardly recognize the vapid tone of her own voice.

Even so, Sachia put her free hand to her chest as if she'd never been so honored, playing right into the scheme. She laughed, turning to Reid and Koen and switching to Icrurian. "Tomorrow night, we'll meet at The Lady Fortune."

Koen and Reid exchanged glances, and Koen gave a strong nod.

"He really doesn't speak Asteryan?" Lord Karev asked, eyeing Reid from his peripheral as if he were merely a lowly guard, unimportant. Reid had done a fabulous job of not trying to follow the conversation, even though Vaasa had a feeling the exchange would bother Reid tremendously.

Vaasa translated instead of Sachia this time, finally meeting the intensity of Reid's gaze for the first moment since she'd sat down. Reid tilted his head at her as she spoke in Icrurian. "No, not a word of it," Reid told her. "Though for the right woman, I would happily learn."

Vaasa fought her smile. "He says he does not, though he intends to," she told Lord Karev in Asteryan, and then quickly switched back to Icrurian. "I'm sure you could find someone willing to teach you."

The very corner of Reid's mouth turned up, and he nodded cordially, as if their conversation was built only of small talk. "Meet me tomorrow night, please."

She laughed. "Yes." Leaning to Lord Karev, she said in Asteryan, "He says he is interested in learning so he can speak to the women at The Lady Fortune."

Lord Karev huffed a bland chuckle, unimpressed. "Shall we?"

It tore at Vaasa's heart to stand from the table. To give one last parting glance to Reid before following Lord Karev up the stairs and back into the main fabric shop. She turned over her shoulder, meeting his eyes one last time, and despite them both, he winked.

Her heart thudded ceaselessly in her chest. Escape. She could taste it, feel it in the clutches of her hands.

"Heiress?" Lord Karev called.

Vaasa had a moment to recover. She turned just slightly and ran her fingertips along a spool of fabric as if she were mesmerized. "This purple wool," Vaasa mused, meeting the lord's eyes. "It's exactly my favorite color."

"Then you should have it," he said. Lord Karev gestured to Sachia, saying, "Add it to my credit."

It was a strange gesture, not inauthentic in its delivery, because Karev was getting what he wanted. She was useful to him, and the moment she ceased to be, he would run cold. Vaasa imagined this was precisely what it would be like to marry a man like Lord Karev—someone with whom she would build a dispassionate, though not entirely unkind, relationship . . . so long as she remained obedient. Perhaps in another world, it would have been the type her mother and her father shared. Allies, if not lovers.

Except her father had tortured witches, and her mother had spent fifteen years loving someone else.

"That is . . . generous, thank you," Vaasa managed.

He nodded with what she could almost believe was respect. "As I said, when you are by my side, you will want for nothing." As if the gift were something she couldn't have afforded herself.

Sachia summoned one of the older women who worked in the shop, telling them to package the spool. "I'll deliver it to the fortress, and perhaps we can continue discussions about that wardrobe," Sachia said.

Vaasa gave an approving nod. "Please."

Lord Karev extended his arm, something he didn't particularly have to do, given they weren't surrounded by anyone else. But the way he looked at her . . . it had softened, ever so slightly. Vaasa grinned, taking his offer and doing her best not to be revulsed as she settled into his side. "I see why Ozik finds you useful," Lord Karev said quietly. "That was well done, Heiress."

It was the closest to a real compliment that he would likely give her in private. As they exited, Vaasa found Roman waiting right where she'd left him. Just as Lord Karev wanted, she did not meet her sentinel's eyes. She waited until they climbed back into the carriage before she asked, "Do you do business with pirates often, Lord Karev?"

He ran his tongue over his teeth, looking speechless for the first time. It was odd to see him like this, and Vaasa immediately took advantage.

"I am the daughter of the continent's most ruthless conqueror," she reminded him. "People like us must stay in power one way or another."

Lord Karev let out a small chuckle and relaxed into his seat, as if she had just established something between them that had been the only part he didn't know how to navigate. "I believe we're similar, you and I," he said. "We share the same vision for our lives."

In so many ways, she wanted to say that she and he could never be the same. But as their carriage pulled away from the fabric shop, she wondered how much longer she could juggle these pieces before she had to cut out parts of herself to make room for what she was being shaped into next.

Schemer.

Chameleon.

Serpent.

Perhaps she was just as wicked as he.

"May we coordinate for tomorrow?" Lord Karev said, pulling Vaasa from her musing. "Dress in blue. We look powerful in blue."

The following evening, dinner dragged on, a boring affair of political pandering. Ozik was seated near Vaasa, in the same spot at the table that he had filled Vaasa's entire life. It was only the emperor's seat that remained empty, though every once in a while, Vaasa noticed Lord Karev staring at it. Vaasa sat where her mother had—perhaps presumptive, but at Ozik's behest all the same.

Anything we can do to make you appear inevitable is worth doing, he'd said.

It was halfway through dinner when Lord Karev stood from his table just next to the dais, meandering to the middle of the vast dining hall. He turned to face Vaasa where she sat. Dressed in the richest of blue jackets and black breeches, dark hair combed perfectly around his handsome face, he was the picture-perfect model of Asteryan royalty. With a brilliantly composed speech about progress and unity and carrying on the throne, Lord Karev turned to Vaasa.

She stood, lifting her glass and smiling. "Which is why, when Lord Karev asked me to be his wife last night, I humbly accepted."

The room erupted in what was evenly split between genuine celebration and fabricated cheers. The Old Asteryans were shaken, the New Asteryans emboldened. This conflict was far from over. It didn't matter if Lord Karev took the throne; the old guard would not share their influence so easily.

Which meant she saw a clear way to plunge the two factions into a civil dispute that would fracture any ruler's ability to summon a military large enough to challenge the Icrurian Central Forces.

Her father had been a brilliant politician, keeping both friends and enemies close to unite Asterya, and in another life, that would have been Vaasa's strength, too. But in this life, she would be the thing that broke it.

When the opportunity arose and the room plunged into celebratory dancing and cheer, Vaasa joined in. She embodied her roles as heiress and future bride, while Lord Karev was already on display as the regal, good-natured emperor-to-be. For hours they danced and smiled and accepted congratulations, but as any good noble knew, the first party was never the last one. Most of the people with real influence had already filtered out and gone somewhere else.

Roman lingered in the corner—no words exchanged between them, but no opportunity to slip away from him, either. If she wanted to make it to The Lady Fortune, she would need another way. She trailed Lord Karev to the back of the room, wine goblet in hand, and said, "Are you bored yet?"

He raised a brow at her, likely noticing the same things about the room that she did. Lord Karev handed his goblet to one of the servants who skittered by and took Vaasa's hand. He watched Roman, gauging just the right moment, and when Roman turned, Lord Karev pounced. "Now," he whispered, and pulled her out of the room like two newly engaged lovers. Lord Karev was the perfect excuse, the perfect alibi for her absence. Suddenly, her cavorting was appropriate—expected, even.

No longer a whore, just someone's future bride.

They fled through the Sanctum and out into the city square, Lord Karev waving down his carriage. He guided her in just as Roman burst through the front doors, anger marring his features. He ran toward them, face contorted in fury.

"Go!" Vaasa laughed as if she found the idea of cutting Roman this way to be funny.

She didn't. The hurt on his face was a knife to her chest.

"To the city," Lord Karev told his own hired mercenaries, who quickly signaled the horses forward. "Do not stop for the sentinel."

The carriage lurched, and they rode off before Roman had the chance to stop them.

CHAPTER 25

Reid waited with Sachia and Koen, hoping, praying, that his wife would make it here. He knew no one better at formulating a plan—surely she would find a way.

Masked women and men moved around the first floor, which had transformed entirely since the last time Reid had come here. Instead of an art gallery, it was set as a sweet-smelling garden, based off some Asteryan folktale about a demon and the bride he stole. Silver and gold chains hung from the ceiling with oil lanterns attached to each, washing the room in warm light. Winter jasmine threaded through those chains, creating curtains of falling flowers that resulted in pockets of privacy within the space. Pomegranates and bloodred roses decorated the tables, and all the women were dressed as if they were the bride themselves. Paint covered the exposed parts of their bodies, swirling to appear like vines.

Women hung over the seats near Koen and Reid, though just as Reid always knew his closest friend to do, Koen shied away from their touch or attention. Conversely, Sachia continued making friends with the workers, seeming entirely in cahoots. Reid knew this was a strategy to gain access to one of the third floor's private meeting rooms, which Sachia would happily pay for.

Reid could hardly focus on any of what they said, though. He kept picking up on little Asteryan words he was starting to memorize. *Heiress. Marriage. Lord Karev. Husband. Wife.* Hatred burned in Reid, low and simmering, but he kept his composure, or at least tried to. Koen had reluctantly told him of the outcome of their meeting; Vaasa had accepted an engagement to Lord Karev.

Reid had known it was coming, and yet it felt as though all that black powder had been stuffed into his chest and detonated.

Reid turned as a couple entered the room. Her face was covered by a mask built of crimson roses and pomegranate seeds, but he would know those indigo eyes anywhere. The costume she wore held similar imagery, the gauzy material of her dress thin and draping over her body, only acceptable in the warmth of a room. It reminded him of the detailed statues decorating the grander architecture of Mekës, particularly the ones on the Asteryan Citadel. While the bodice hugged her waist tightly, the bloodred fabric of the skirts fell as if carved from granite. A slit in the dress revealed the length of her leg, and Reid's jaw tightened at the sight. At knowing Karev had seen Vaasa in this dress first.

The bastard didn't even seem to appreciate the woman on his arm. Karev's eyes roved the room, seemingly counting the number of people he wanted to leave an impression upon.

"This ends in his death," Reid whispered to Koen, careful not to speak Icrurian too loudly. Though Koen assured him the new rumor was that pirates had killed Lord Vlacik, Reid knew well enough that story would change if their group became too suspicious.

Vaasa's eyes locked on Reid, then lifted to a woman who stepped behind his chair and ran her hands over his chest. Despite the way Reid wanted to recoil, he didn't. He couldn't. To plant even a seed of doubt in Lord Karev's mind would be dangerous for Vaasa. Reid had to pretend to be anything but interested in her.

But there was a heat in his wife's eyes that made him feel like the devil—the very one who'd stolen a bride and inspired the night's decorations. Vaasa watched where the woman touched him, and despite everything he knew about her, her lips turned down.

A break in her composure, even if only for a moment.

Reid stayed the course, taking measured sips of his wine. Koen looked away from them, and Reid followed suit. Sachia sat beside them, her eyes traveling over Vaasa and Lord Karev, then turned to him for confirmation. When Reid subtly nodded, she uncrossed her legs. "Third floor."

Sachia approached Lord Karev and Vaasa, her face obscured by a full-length mask. Given Sachia's breeches and tucked-in blouse, she blended in with the rest of the revelers quite perfectly. Someone handed Reid another drink, and he pretended to sip from it, focusing instead on Koen, who spoke with another man there. Koen was brilliant at small talk, and even though Reid couldn't fully follow the conversation, he knew enough about tone and body language to know the man Koen spoke to was enthralled in the conversation. Sachia walked back to their table, and two of the women pulled out chairs for Lord Karev and Vaasa, who were pretending to be anyone but who they were.

Lord Karev took the seat nearest them. "Good evening," he said in Asteryan.

Koen turned to the lord. The two exchanged words that Reid couldn't understand, and his lack of Asteryan infuriated him. Just like it had at the table when he'd listened to his wife without knowing what she said.

Powerlessness dragged claws down his limbs.

Lord Karev laughed at something Koen said, and as a woman approached and draped her arms over Karev's shoulders, handing him a goblet of wine, he said something with a confident tone, and Reid was able to make out the word. *Share.*

Whatever it was, Vaasa gave Lord Karev the most charming grin. He raised a brow at her, looking between her and the woman, and then Vaasa shrugged as if she were entirely unbothered.

She'd given him permission, he realized. Permission to go bed another woman.

Anger simmered in his body at the man's sheer disrespect. At the marriage Vaasa would have been relegated to had she never met Reid. He wanted to reach across the table and swear to her that it would never be that way between them, that the idea of sharing his bed with anyone else made him sick to his stomach.

He kept his hands to himself.

They all chatted, Vaasa casually sipping on her wine and tipping her head back in laughter. Her red-stained lips put on quite the performance as she smiled and spoke, eyes only drifting to him for moments at a time. Reid tried not to stare at her. Instead, he stayed quiet and watched the room like a diligent guard.

"And how are you this evening?" Vaasa asked in Icrurian, keeping her voice low so as not to garner any attention at the use of the language. Each day they spent in this city, the more Reid despised it.

He met her gaze. "Impatient," he admitted.

Lord Karev didn't seem to care that they spoke, not as he leaned into the curly hair of a beautiful woman whose skin had been painted as if she were a statue.

"Murderous?" she asked, a pointed question that simmered in his gut.

"This establishment brings it out in me," Reid confessed.

Vaasa furrowed her brow for a moment, and then said, "It was you? Not the pirate?"

Reid remembered it so clearly, though he hadn't made a show of the killing. Hadn't enacted any of the twisted things that had spun themselves out in his mind. He'd wanted to drag out the man's suffering like the slow inching of daylight. But instead, it was like the pinching of a candle, the way Reid took that man's life. Just like this moment, he hadn't understood the Asteryan that slipped from Lord Vlacik's lips, yet he knew it was a plea. It hadn't brought about hesitation. From a young age, Reid had not taken apologies from people who could never earn forgiveness.

"He sealed his fate, just like that one." He gestured with his head to Lord Karev.

Vaasa opened her mouth to retort, but Sachia interrupted in Icrurian, "Have you found a way for us to enter the prison?"

A subtle reminder that they could speak no further on a topic such as that. Not unless they were in private.

Vaasa carefully glanced at Lord Karev, but this line of questioning wouldn't be unfounded. He knew well enough they intended to infiltrate the prison island.

"Do you know if the prisoner we seek is still there?" Koen asked in Icrurian. He wasn't speaking about Sachia's brother, that much was certain. Reid watched Vaasa's expression drop to what he thought might be guilt.

"Yes. I have a plan to see her soon," she said.

"You do?" Reid asked.

Vaasa nodded.

Reid frowned. How exactly would she do that? He was about to ask, but Lord Karev said something in Asteryan that made Vaasa and Sachia immediately switch back to the same language. After a moment of what looked like explanation from Sachia and Koen, Lord Karev relaxed.

Eventually, Sachia stood, two women beckoning her and Vaasa away from the table. Vaasa looked wistfully over her shoulder at Lord Karev, playing such a perfect submissive fiancée, and Reid thought she'd asked *permission* to go somewhere. The act made his hand twitch beneath the table. Lord Karev pursed his lips, then gave an amused smile like he would to a child who he no longer cared to supervise. He said something at the table in a haughty tone as the women dragged Vaasa away, and everyone laughed. Koen was rigid as he did so. The lord didn't even bother glancing at where Vaasa walked.

Instead, his eyes trailed back to the curly-haired woman, the same one Reid had watched the man lust after the last time they'd been there. The moment Vaasa was gone, the woman whispered something in Lord Karev's ear.

Reid lifted his goblet to his lips, this time taking a heady sip. The men around them laughed, and Reid wanted to pull the dagger from his boot and thrust it through Karev's throat. But he had his opening when the lord stood from the table, nodding his farewell to the group and following the woman past the jasmine curtains and disappearing up a set of stairs opposite the set that Vaasa and Sachia had just ascended.

Reid waited with bated breath just long enough for Koen to strike up conversation with the people around them. He leaned in and muttered in Icrurian, "Third floor."

Koen lifted his goblet in farewell to the men around them, standing and following Reid to the far side of the main room. Laughter and a raucous farewell filled the air, the men likely encouraging them to go and pay for their fill. They ascended the stairs to the second floor, which was a mezzanine that made a horseshoe over the main room. Most of the first floor was concealed by the jasmine that hung around them, but pockets could be seen. Sachia appeared at their side, her mouth turned downward. "A man came in and she ran." Sachia pointed to a brown-haired man Reid didn't recognize who hung along one of the walls. He had dark breeches on and donned a borrowed costume jacket and a mask shaped like a crow's beak.

Sachia gestured to the opposite side of the mezzanine, which also contained a stairwell that would lead to the third, fourth, and fifth floors of the brothel. "We agreed to meet on the third floor, but she went further up."

"I'll find her," Reid muttered.

"Be careful," Sachia warned.

With his heart in his throat, he strode to the other side of the mezzanine and took the stairwell to the concealed floors above.

Reid searched a few hallways and climbed up three staircases before he finally sighted Vaasa. She was on the fifth floor, having changed her mask entirely, quietly testing the knobs of the doors as if she was trying to hide in one of the rooms. The one she jiggled was locked.

She turned, and their eyes met. Muffled moans and brazen cries of pleasure emanated from the rooms around them. This part of the building was not for socializing or cavorting with lords and pirates. It only made him pick up his pace as he approached her.

Vaasa looked over her bare shoulder at him, the stark red and black of her new mask in such beautiful compliment to the dress she wore. To the pale shade of her skin. She put a finger over her red lips as if to indicate that he should be quiet, and then whipped her head around, scanning both ends of the hallway. They were alone.

"Who is looking for you?" Reid asked on a whisper.

She shook her head, stepping closer. "It isn't worth talking about. He'll be here soon, we should find—"

"Why isn't it worth talking about?" Despite himself, insecurity lanced through him. He knew that expression—she was keeping something from him. "Who is he?"

Something hardened her gaze to exactly as she'd appeared those first weeks he'd known her—neutral, apathetic, even cruel. "It's my lead sentinel," she finally said, looking past him to survey their surroundings once more. "I left without his permission. And it isn't worth talking about because nothing matters except for our way out of here. Except for you and me and our friends."

She stepped around him to continue down the hallway, fleeing.

Reid clenched his jaw. His heart wouldn't calm. The voice in his head that felt he was going to lose everything that ever mattered to him screamed louder. He wanted a full explanation, not some veiled version of her circumstances. They hadn't gotten a real opportunity to discuss each element of the plan she was concocting, and tonight she had become *engaged* to someone else. "Except everything else *does* matter," he muttered, careful to keep his voice low. He spun to follow her. Two paths lay in front of them: a main staircase that led down to the lower floors where Sachia and Koen waited, and a roped off passageway they clearly weren't supposed to enter.

Reid hissed, "Vaasa, this deal with Karev, the things I am being forced to listen to and to see—"

"I only had to move this quickly because of your *murderous tendencies*," she said under her breath at him. "Karev blackmailed me. If I had denied him, he would have pinned the murder on me."

Reid's fists tightened. The ways in which they had been manipulated by that bastard—

Vaasa shook her head. "I told you to wait, to give me a few—"

Voices came from the stairs they were just about to walk down. Vaasa froze. Genuine fear overtook all the neutral, hard places upon her face. This lead sentinel of hers distressed her. Footsteps grew closer, and Vaasa's breath quickened. Reid did the only thing he could think to do.

He grabbed her wrist and pulled her against him, slamming his mouth into hers. Immediately he turned them, pushing her up against the wall and shielding her entire body with his own. No one could see her. No one could get to her.

They would have to get past him.

Vaasa froze for only a moment, and then fire ignited. She kissed him back with just as much gusto as he remembered from the first time he'd finally put his mouth upon her. Her hands flew into his hair and he groaned into her mouth, so easily falling into the image of two people stealing a moment of privacy among the debauchery. Reid pushed against her body more completely, feeling the press of her breasts against his chest, the smoothness of the thin gossamer she wore. He bunched his hands into the garment, placing pressure on the small of her back that forced her to arch into him.

The footsteps scurried past them, disappearing around the bend in the hallway. Logically, Reid knew this meant he should stop kissing her. That they should go to the third floor. But then her lips parted and her tongue brushed against his, and all sense of self narrowed to the taste of her. He took everything from that kiss that he could. Tongues tangling, hands dropping to grasp her backside, Reid thought he could very well lose himself if she let him.

He begged, "Tell me it isn't real with him. I need to hear it. I—"

"It isn't real," she swore against his mouth. "Nothing except *you* is real."

Reid opened his eyes to hers. She parted her lips, perhaps to scold him or to point out the ways in which he had become nothing but a jealous fool, but as their eyes met, whatever she was about to say was lost.

She grabbed his hand and fled toward the private hallway, ducking beneath the thick red rope.

"Where are we going?" he whispered.

"This is the madame's hallway," she said, pressing her back to the wall when they were out of sight from the main passageway and stairwell. Reid stopped to stand just in front of her, and she raised her hands to his chest, then wrapped them around the nape of his neck.

And she pulled him back into the searing kiss.

He kissed her with reverence and anger. His body was a rock beneath her hands. He was wound so tight. He couldn't believe he'd had to watch another man act as though he had a claim to her, act as though he had a right to this woman, when Reid had done everything and anything to earn her. Jealousy was an ocean inside him. Vast. Churning. He settled his hands on her hips. "Give me one reason I shouldn't kill that man tonight," Reid growled against her mouth, hands bunching in her dress as he slid his fingers beneath the long slit in the fabric and brushed against the soft skin of her upper thigh.

"Because you'd have to stop kissing me," she said back, leg lifting to wrap around his waist.

His fingers dug into her bare thigh, and he trailed hot kisses down her neck. "I *hate* this. I am going to lose my mind, Wild One."

"It's a lie," she seemed to promise him, eyes fluttering open for only a moment and then closing in contentment again the farther up her leg his fingers traveled.

Something carnal took over, some instinct he had that was perhaps fueled more by his ego than anything else. They shouldn't be doing this here, he shouldn't be near her where they could be found.

She was his wife. She was *his*.

"Forgive me while I remind you of that." Reid bypassed the fabric of her panties and slid a finger inside her. Vaasa moaned against his mouth, and he grinned at the readiness he found. "Already wet for me?" he whispered in her ear. He pulled in and out, curling his finger against her inner wall.

"Yes, you, you—"

Reid pressed his thumb to her center, circling the bud of nerves there, and she moaned before she could finish her sentence. Her hands fisted in his shirt. He slid another finger inside her and pressed, his free hand rising to dip beneath her neckline and cup her breast. His thumb and forefinger played with her nipple. His mouth found hers again, and she parted her lips for him. He took the invitation to sweep his tongue against hers, to kiss her as deeply as she'd let him while his thumb circled and pressed against her clit.

His body kept hers against the wall, even as her legs trembled, and he worried they wouldn't hold her weight.

He would.

His mouth brushed over her cheek, rising until his teeth grazed her ear. "You're going to come for me right here." It felt so much like a sin to have her in this position, and a brash part of him wanted someone to find them and see the ways in which he touched their heiress. See her head tip back as she fought a moan. *His, his, his*—the word echoed in his mind.

She didn't argue or push him away. He paid such close attention to the signs of her body, the signals that she wanted him. A rebellious fire lit in her eyes, and she whispered, "Make me."

Reid's breeches strained against his erection. His wife was always thinking, always rational and planned, but this was an abandonment of that survival mechanism. A submission to the instincts of who she was and what she wanted.

With *him*.

Her hips bucked, and he pressed her harder to the wall, locking her in place to make sure she couldn't move. He paid attention to the cadence of her breath, how it sped in desire instead of fear, how even as they did something they both knew they shouldn't, she drove him forward with the way her leg tightened on his waist. He watched the passageway in his peripheral, knowing deep down that she was trusting him to protect her. Trusting him to be her eyes so she could let go.

He pulled his hand from her bodice and tucked it beneath the hem of her dress, two fingers sliding inside her while he continued to use his thumb against her pleasure. She tossed an arm over her mouth and bit down on her own flesh.

"What would they think if they saw you like this, getting exactly what you want?" Reid asked so quietly. "Letting *me* do this to you."

She bit down harder, but he heard her muffled cry. She trembled and started to quicken around his fingers. She was rising for him. She had to be just as sunken into this fantasy as he was—the forbidden taste of it all.

She was doing so much pretending. It was a relief to give her something real.

He kept exactly the same pace, pulling in and out of her, teasing her while he did so. Her breath came quicker. Her body went taut. "I told you I was going to make you come in this hallway," he growled in her ear.

She cried out into her arm, the sound for his ears alone, and tightened around his fingers. Her knees buckled with her orgasm, but Reid caught her with his own weight. He plunged in and out of her, desperate to pull as much pleasure from her as he possibly could. She panted as he finally slid his fingers out. But then her hands flew to his breeches, and Reid tried to gain common sense, tried to grasp some part of him that knew the right thing to do was to deny them both this stolen moment. They were wasting time. They were—

Her fingers expertly undid the tie at his waist, and she dipped inside. She wrapped her hand around his erection.

All protest was lost.

Reid hiked up her skirts as she pumped him, a rebellious and thrilling smile on her face, eyes glittering behind her mask. It took him all of three seconds to place his hands at her thighs and haul her up so her legs wrapped around his waist, and then he maneuvered as strategically as he could to pull her panties to the side. When he felt her slick entrance at the head of his cock, he plunged himself inside her until he was seated to the hilt, mouth pressing over hers to contain her sounds.

He hadn't had her in all the ways he wanted to. Their night in Dihrah was just the beginning. He intended to have so much more. To discover everything about how she liked being taken, to know each word he could whisper in her ear to make her tighten. But right now wasn't about discovery; it was about reclaiming. Reminding.

Reid pulled out just enough to threaten a separation, but then he thrust into her again, and she buried her face in his neck with a gasp. He fucked her against the wall until her teeth sank into the fabric covering his shoulder. Until small, muffled cries of pleasure vibrated against where she bit him. With each stroke of his cock inside her, he felt his feet more firmly planted on the ground. Felt the truth wind between them like an unbreakable chain.

"Mine," he growled. "You're fucking *mine*."

Vaasa bit harder, and her teeth threatened to mar his shirt. And then he wondered if that was the point.

"If you want to mark me, Wild One, then do it," he told her.

Reid almost lost himself when she pawed at the black buttons of his shirt, undoing them until she could wrench the fabric from his shoulder. He couldn't help himself from picking up speed when she really sank her teeth into his skin, biting him hard, leaving a mark as if she, too, needed to know that in the wake of their distance, there would still be a trace of her upon him. He had used words and touch to remind her that he'd laid claim, but in the same fashion as he'd always known her, there was an edge of violence in how she expressed herself.

"That's right," he growled as he thrust into her again. "I'm still very much yours."

Vaasa groaned into his skin, and Reid thrust into her hard, pressure building in his cock with each stroke. He needed her pleasure again. He needed to feel it around something other than his fingers this time. She must have been thinking the same thing, because her hand snaked down her body and between her legs. Reid gauged her needs by the response he earned, settling into the speed and pace that caused her back to arch, that brought forth her whispered "Yes, right there, *please*."

She shattered around him, muscles clamping, and he didn't have the self-control this time to pull himself out of her. He finished with a stifled groan, and it took the very last ounce of his restraint not to let his voice out. She clung to him, thighs trembling, breath coming in quick spurts. "Vaasa, can you—"

"Get contraception?" she asked, likely realizing exactly what he did; this had been as impulsive as it could get. "Yes."

Relief flooded him, though a small lashing came from the voice in his mind that hated the times when he wasn't as responsible as he felt he needed to be. But then her voice floated between them: "When we are free of this place, I am going to lock you in our bedroom."

Reid grinned despite himself. "Going to break your little rule and let me take you in my bed?"

Vaasa bit her lip, a smile breaking the edges of her mouth. "It was a stupid rule."

Reid chuckled softly. Vaasa dropped to the floor and tugged her fingers through her hair, adjusting her dress while Reid tried to hide the evidence on himself. He handed her a handkerchief, and she did her best to clean up any remnant.

"Sachia and Koen are waiting," Reid whispered, though he hated that he had to say it.

A blush crept up Vaasa's neck, and he stifled his chuckle. Certainly, they would understand. "I'll go first," Vaasa whispered.

She darted out of the hallway, but just as quickly as he watched her go, the sound of her footsteps halted.

"Regína," Vaasa said, a name Reid didn't recognize.

A feminine voice spoke in Asteryan, sounding deeply apologetic. Vaasa spoke back. From the distance, Reid assumed someone had just come down the hallway he'd first found Vaasa in. But then Vaasa's tone sped up. Urgency coated her voice. Reid knew his wife's anger when he heard it.

And then her footsteps turned hasty, and he realized she was sprinting down the stairs.

Reid stepped out of the stairwell, but it was empty. He followed to the third floor, poking his head around the corner to see Vaasa push a man he didn't recognize away from her. He grabbed her wrist, and Reid almost stepped out on instinct, but then Vaasa twisted her arm to break the man's grasp. She stormed past him, and like a wounded puppy dog, the man followed her down the stairs.

It was the same man Sachia had pointed out earlier. Medium build, brown hair.

Her lead sentinel.

Reid pressed his back to the wall, fighting the urge to follow them. It took all his strength to keep his feet planted where they were. If he gave himself away, he gave her away, too. He had to trust that she could defend herself.

After waiting a few moments, Reid descended to the second-floor mezzanine, which was flooded with onlookers, each of them peering over the railing to view the commotion below. The first floor was covered in Asteryan blue jackets. Sentinels and the city guard. Customers fled the brothel in droves, crowds pushing to get out. To his left, he spotted Sachia and Koen, the two of them looking like every other spectator in the massive crowd that had assembled. He raced to them, and their eyes went wide. Koen breathed in relief. His Icrurian was low and quick. "The fortress claimed the heiress was abducted; they've practically shut down the city. I'd thought they found you."

Reid glanced down and scanned the crowd. There. Her red dress and mask gave her away, but only to him. Vaasa followed the same man Reid had seen through a set of doors that led to the entranceway, a crowd pushing all around her as if she were any other patron.

"Who is that?" Reid asked. "The man who took her."

"Roman Katayev, I bet," Sachia whispered. "Her lead sentinel. He's only come back to Mekës recently."

Reid racked his brain. Why did that name sound so familiar? A memory swirled in his mind, vivid and so prominent.

Years ago, there was a man. His name was Roman. I loved him, and Dominik had him killed.

That was what Vaasa had told him the night Dominik came to Mireh. The first night she had ever slept in Reid's bed. Certainly it wasn't the same man—that Roman was dead. Yet Koen and Sachia exchanged a glance, and it set Reid on edge. "What?" he demanded. "What don't I know?"

Sachia shrugged noncommittally. "There are rumors that he and Vaasa are having an affair. But I'm sure that's all they are. Rumors. The engagement will turn the tides."

Reid's mind raced. That had to be one of the hundreds of things Koen and Sachia had overheard in the city about Vaasa. There was so little else to talk about, and the circumstances of Vaasa's return would obviously garner gossip. It had to be untrue. He clung to what he knew of her; fought the voice in his head that told him he wasn't enough for her. That what he offered her wasn't enough.

After what they had just done . . .

"There are more rumors than truths," Koen assured him. "She is too close to power; people will repeat anything scandalous they hear."

Reid nodded, trying to absorb those words. Trying to convince himself of their truth.

"We need to get out of here before they start questioning people," Sachia said, gesturing with her head to the eastern stairs.

As they took the stairs and slipped out of the brothel with the rest of the swarming crowd, Reid glanced around, scanning the swaths of people, looking for one in particular.

But Lord Karev was nowhere to be found.

CHAPTER 26

"How fucking *dare* you," Vaasa seethed as she pushed past Roman in the entryway rooms of The Lady Fortune, not even bothering to change out of the dress she wore or return the mask. Adrenaline pumped in her veins. Her knees still felt weak. It was whiplash—to go from such hot desire to cold anger. She felt the remnants of her tryst with Reid all over her, and fear burrowed into her bones.

She couldn't let them find him. She had to get as far away from The Lady Fortune as possible.

It had been so fucking foolish.

Roman had shut down the brothel, had sent sentinels to swarm it in nothing but a brash show of power. There was no indication he knew who Vaasa had been with, or that she'd been with anyone at all. Only Regína had found her, and Vaasa had said she was hiding alone. Her breath was still labored, but that could be attributed to her sprint down the stairs.

She hadn't even gotten to say goodbye to Reid. Again. In that moment, it felt like she was on that platform at the Icrurian election being dragged away from everything she loved.

Roman had taken her from him. Resentment lit in her core, filling the spaces where her desire had been.

She trudged out the doors and into the freezing air, immediately regretting her choice not to change. Snow soaked the hem of her dress. Still, she had spent weeks in the island prison. She knew cold. She could survive, despite the utter uselessness of her dress in the frigid Mekës temperatures.

"Wait—" Roman said, then cut himself off.

A crowd gathered around the brothel, members of the city guard and sentinels in abundance, and Vaasa suddenly thanked her mask and costume for the veil of privacy it afforded her. If she didn't give herself away, these people wouldn't know who she was. She needed to seem like anyone but the heiress of Asterya.

"If you want to be with her, then be with her!" Vaasa snarled loudly enough for the people around them to hear.

Roman must have caught on to her intentions, because he put his hands up as if he were just an idiot man who had been caught with another woman. "Just come with me and let me explain."

"Why should I?"

The conversation they had now was real, though out of context. Roman slung off his borrowed costume jacket, a heavyweight fur-lined item. The fact that he had even bothered to change out of his sentinel's clothing told her that he'd intended to sneak her out all along. If he'd wanted to really expose her location, or if he believed she had actually been abducted, he never would've worn a costume. This was all to hurt her, to remind her that he had the power to make her miserable if he wanted to.

"You're freezing," he said, approaching the way a hunter approached prey.

Vaasa backed away from him, charging down the street while a group of people snickered at their lovers' quarrel.

Roman swore, chasing after her.

Vaasa turned down another street and kept the pace until she could duck into a very narrow walkway between two stone buildings. There was so little light and no people. Alone, her anger boiled over.

"You had no right!" she practically yelled at Roman as he sprinted onto the street.

Roman grabbed her bare arm, his face still covered in a mask. "Put on the fucking coat before you freeze to death."

"I've been colder," she reminded him. "Or have you already forgotten that I spent weeks in that prison?"

He winced, his grip loosening on her arm. "Just put on the jacket, please. What will the guards think if they see you in this dress?"

"That I fucked my new fiancé in a brothel," she spat at him.

Misery slashed his brown eyes like someone had taken a pick to the cliffs overlooking the sea, and she knew she'd been cruel. Good. She wanted him to hate her. She deserved it. Her rouge was likely smeared across her face, the remnant of a stolen tryst with a man Roman hated. A man he had no idea was in this city.

"You aren't going to let him touch you," Roman said, recovering just as quickly as he'd let the emotion show. "I know you won't."

"If you have it your way, I won't have a choice, will I?"

"Stop. Let me take you home, and then we can talk about this."

"There is nothing to talk about!" She pulled her arm out of his grasp. "You are on Ozik's side, not mine."

"I'll take you to her!" Roman snapped, tugging off his mask.

Vaasa went silent, and though she hated herself for it, the darkest parts of her smiled. She'd known Karev would be the thing that pushed Roman over the edge. To use him this way—it was a reminder of the evil she was well and capable of.

"Just put on the fucking coat, and I will take you to see your friend tomorrow night."

Vaasa gauged his facial expressions, searching for a thread of mistruth. When she found nothing but the desperate features of the man she had once loved, she let her shoulders fall. "If you're lying to me, I swear I will release you from your post."

It was within her power. Ozik would likely allow it, especially if she said it was Lord Karev's demand.

"I understand," Roman asserted.

Vaasa took the coat from his hands, slipping her arms into the fabric. Warmth coasted over her skin, and she sighed softly. She hated to admit how cold she was.

Roman reached for her. "Your feet are going to freeze. The hem of your dress is soaked," he said, eyes looking over the places the gauzy dress draped on her. "Let me carry you."

Vaasa touched her mask as if reminding herself that she was still hidden. That he couldn't see her face. Before she could argue, Roman scooped her into his arms and carried her through the snow like his own bride-to-be until they were closer to wherever he planned to claim he'd found her. Her body remained tense, her mind screaming that she was everything this city had once called her.

Gingerly, he set her down on the shoveled porch of one of the quieter taverns. Roman raked a hand through his hair. There was something so strange about his expressions, about the shaky way he held himself. "Take off your mask. Wrap the coat tighter around yourself."

When she did as he asked, he gestured for her to walk.

"Karev can't know," Vaasa reminded him quietly. "He can't know that I left with you."

"The men at the gate that night have been released," Roman said. "There are only two waiting for us, and they are loyal to me. They won't say a word to Karev."

She pursed her lips, once again wondering what Roman had done to earn a position with this much authority. Even before he'd been sent to die at the border as a punishment for their affair, his trajectory wouldn't have amounted to this.

"I have just as much interest in keeping this private as you do."

Vaasa sighed in resignation. She took every step silently until he led her around the corner where a single carriage waited, manned by two guards who kept their eyes down.

Vaasa loaded into the carriage, and when Roman followed her in, she didn't argue. They needed the windows closed where he couldn't be seen. The carriage lurched forward. They sat in silence. Vaasa stared at the closed curtains. After a few minutes, Roman's voice came low. "Things would be infinitely different if I had it my way, Vaasa. You know that."

"I know," she whispered.

"Tell me you have thought of a way out of this marriage. That you've got something up your sleeve, and this is just a way to protect yourself. You have a plan, you always do."

Vaasa pursed her lips as if contemplating. "If you mean what you say, that you'll take me to see my friend, then yes. I have something up my sleeve."

She was going to break his heart. When she fled this city with another man, it would leave him in shambles, and there was nothing she could do to change that. She was a witch. The wife of the Icrurian headman, the very man she had just fucked in the middle of a hallway. *Catastrophic* didn't even begin to describe the consequences they would have faced had they been caught, so she supposed this outcome was still better than that. And yet, she had gotten a dirty thrill at the thought of subverting all their expectations, at embracing the very thing they tried to insult her with. *Whore. An Icrurian's plaything. Not fit to rule.* At least in that moment, she didn't have to pretend any longer.

Because she *wanted* it. She wanted her life with Reid more than she had ever wanted anything, and this time, she wasn't going to flee from those desires. No amount of fear was going to leave her lonely. She would fight and claw and kill if it meant she got to go back with him.

She looked across the carriage at Roman, and she accepted him as a casualty. She couldn't convince him to stop coming back to the things that hurt him—Asterya, her. They were the same. This nation had sent him to be a prisoner of war, and yet he'd returned.

She was in love with another man, and still she thought he would chase her. That he would never release the image of her he'd made up in his mind.

"We'll go to the prison tomorrow night," Roman said.

"Thank you."

Vaasa stared at the curtains of the carriage once more. She could only hope Roman followed through.

"Funny, you never seemed to get caught sneaking out when you were younger," Ozik said as Vaasa walked into the greenhouse.

Her stomach rolled, the silphium Roman had obtained in the early hours of the morning causing her abdomen to cramp. She'd taken it there in front of him, if only to seal his desperation. Her muscles ached. Everything felt sluggish and sore. The lack of sleep would eventually catch up to her, but what other choice did she have? Daytime in Mekës was boring and useless. It was only under the cover of night that the true city came out. "Mind your business," she said to Ozik.

He chuckled. "Snappy today."

Magic flooded her body, no longer a small trickle that he controlled in order to allow her to acclimate. He simply opened the lid, and the force careened across the cord that bound them. This morning, she didn't hesitate. It didn't pain her, and her breath stayed steady.

Vaasa immediately shot the magic out of her hands, not bothering to wait for it to transition from smoke to wolf. The creature lifted its head and sniffed the air, then lowered its nose to the gravel. It stalked forward, and this time, Ozik took a careful step back.

"Why can Veragi magic be fueled by others when corporeal magic can't?" Vaasa demanded.

Ozik kept his eyes on the wolf. Their link didn't sear the way it used to, though it tugged, and she knew her magic was being capitalized on. Perhaps he was using less power, or he didn't want it to hurt, or she had just gained enough control to block out his side of the bond.

This time, when the Miro'dag took shape, Vaasa didn't twitch.

He rolled his shoulders and said, "Corporeal magic has limitations that sentimental magic does not, while sentimental magic has consequences that corporeal magic does not. Take the Imros coven, for instance, who can manipulate metal. They are not haunted by their magic, nor does it threaten to kill them the way Veragi magic once threatened you. But an Imros witch cannot use their power without metal. They must be in the presence of the physical thing that fuels them."

Vaasa summoned more magic, relief in her bones at the ability to use it. She hated that one of the few times of day she genuinely looked forward to in this fortress had to be spent with Ozik. When she let it run free, the magic sharpened on the wolf, and it grew larger. When she focused, she felt it shift within her. Those glowing white eyes and sharp teeth, just beneath the surface of her skin, their beings seemingly one. "And Zetyr magic is limitless? Anything you will it to do, it will do?" she asked.

"Only with a clever bargain," Ozik confirmed.

"But death is a part of your deity's description. Why?"

"Because prey is far easier to catch when it asks you for a favor."

He only ever spoke in maddening riddles. Vaasa stared at Ozik, her mind absorbing his words with the same diligence she had once listened to him lecture. All those pretty gems of information were worth nothing if one wasn't willing to mine them. "You never say your deity's name. Why?"

Ozik pursed his lips, and she wondered for a moment if she'd caught him off guard. "Remember what I told you: The deities are monsters, and the more people who believe in them, the more power they have."

It reminded her of her earlier conversation with Amalie—the hope that rose in them at the thought of Veragi. Was that misguided? "So what? You don't believe in your own deity?"

Ozik shrugged, leaning back against the olive tree. The Miro'dag swayed back and forth. "All questions have answers, but not all of those answers are known."

"Or perhaps not shared, even if they're known."

He smirked at her implication that he was hiding something from her. "Do you feel more powerful now? More in control?"

She gritted her teeth and stared at one of the black stone statues, the morning light catching on the golden threads of granite within it. The answer to this question felt traitorous to herself. *Yes.* Instead of responding honestly, she said, "How would I know? I can never hold on to it for an extended period of time."

"Hmm," Ozik muttered. "Keep it, then."

Vaasa's brows slammed together. "What?"

He lifted from the tree, cleaning his coat of any dirt with the palms of his hands. "I will be gone for a few days, so you needn't come here until I return. If you succeed in keeping our little secret, we can discuss you having broader access to your power."

Hope rose in her, but fear followed. "Gone?" she sputtered. "Where could you possibly be going?"

"Mind your business," Ozik said, echoing her words from earlier. He walked past her, making for the door. Across their bond, the Miro'dag diminished, and she felt the leeching of power as it dimmed.

"So that's it for today?" she asked.

He looked over his shoulder and grinned. "No, Vaasalisa. Your work has just started. Let's see if you can keep this little game with Karev going without revealing the truth: Two witches rule Asterya."

Vaasa gawked at him.

"Don't be out too late," Ozik warned.

And then he crossed into the other room of the greenhouse, leaving her standing there in shock. She swore it was a silent blessing, almost like Ozik knew precisely what she intended to do.

But that couldn't be right. He wouldn't allow her to visit Amalie in the prison.

Would he?

By the early afternoon, Roman resumed his post. Vaasa had not spoken at length with him—no more than the necessary interactions to arrange their visit that evening. Ozik's warning rang in her mind, as if he was clearing her way to the island, aware she intended to go. But unless Roman had told Ozik, she didn't see how.

Unless he had some way of accessing her mind across their bond, a thought that made her shudder.

When someone knocked on her door, she assumed it was Roman with further questions. Yet when she opened the door, she came face to face with... Sachia.

And Melisina.

Vaasa laid eyes on the high witch of Veragi and thought her entire body would sink to the floor. It took every crumb of willpower she had to keep her face neutral. Still, she scanned Melisina's silvery-blond hair, her stunning green eyes, the laugh lines around her eyes and chin. *Melisina.* She was here.

Sachia held a stack of multicolored fabrics over one arm and a seamstress's satchel in the other. Behind her, a guard carried a spool of purple fabric. They were flanked by multiple guards, Vaasa realized, who all seemed to be looking at Roman for permission.

"Heiress," the pirate said, sketching a bow. "I thought you were coming to the shop this morning. I came to see if you were sick." Sachia illustrated her facade perfectly in a utilitarian dress with an iron-and-leather belt. Expensive, still looking the part of a merchant's daughter, yet not just for fashion. Her red hair was plaited over one shoulder, and her mossy eyes danced with mischief.

Clever witch.

Vaasa smiled wide, gaze floating to Roman, who watched their interaction closely. "No, I'm not sick. I just overslept, I'm sorry."

"I wasn't aware you had summoned an outside seamstress," Roman said. "Do you not prefer the fortress attendants?"

Sachia glowered at him so brilliantly that Vaasa had to hold back a laugh. "Perhaps if they were as talented as my family, this line of discussion would be worthwhile."

Roman crinkled his brow. "Who is your father?"

Sachia put her hand on her hip. "Havel Jaroš. Who is your father?"

Roman flicked his gaze to Vaasa, perhaps looking for a way out of the conversation he had gotten himself into. Vaasa pretended to stifle a laugh, then let that small chuckle out, trying to seem like she and Sachia were more familiar than they were. That this entire arrangement was harmless. "I met Sachia the other evening and fell in love with her family's work. We made these plans days ago, but it must have slipped my mind. Forgive me?"

Roman ran his tongue over his front teeth, but at her amicable words, he conceded a respectful dip of his head. "Heiress." He turned to dismiss the group of guards waiting behind Sachia.

Vaasa ushered Sachia and Melisina into the entertaining room, and Sachia gazed around, wide-eyed. When Vaasa shut the door, she let out a small breath.

Melisina opened her arms, and Vaasa threw herself into them.

"My girl," Melisina whispered in Icrurian, her voice wrapping around Vaasa and squeezing as tightly as her arms.

Something in Vaasa gaped open, a wound that this place delivered over and over and over. Melisina was here, in the same place Vaasa's mother had died, showing her more affection than any member of Vaasa's family ever had. Tears welled in Vaasa's eyes, and she fought the urge to sob. "This is dangerous," she whispered back, the use of Icrurian a stark relief in her day.

"What's a little danger in the grand scheme of things?"

Vaasa pulled back and stared at Reid's mother. "I cannot tell you how happy I am to see you."

Melisina placed her hands on Vaasa's cheeks. The cool touch of Veragi magic brushed Vaasa's skin. "We are going to bring you home. To bring you both home."

Home. The word settled in Vaasa's chest, her heart a map, a pin splitting through parchment right where Mireh was. Marking it forever with a title that the very ground she now stood on had never earned. Home: A place. A feeling. A people.

"I'm going to see her tonight," Vaasa said. "I have a way into the prison. She's cared for and uninjured, at least. That much I know."

"You must be careful. Things don't feel the same. Something is brewing," Melisina said.

Vaasa didn't know how Melisina could sense something like that, but if she had learned anything during her time in Icruria, it was to trust the instinct of her high witch.

"What's down here?" Sachia asked, meandering toward Vaasa's mother's hallway, and Vaasa's heart rate spiked.

She stepped forward. "Don't."

Sachia raised an eyebrow.

Melisina placed a hand on Vaasa's shoulder, and Vaasa looked over at her. The high witch's eyes dipped to Vaasa's hands, and she gasped. "You have your magic?"

Vaasa looked down and cursed, immediately snapping the magic back within herself.

Melisina pulled back, staring at her in awe. "How have you become so adept at that?"

Heart thundering in her chest, Vaasa looked around as if an attendant would be there any moment, but they were alone, as safe as they could possibly be. "I have so much to tell you," Vaasa whispered.

Melisina walked to the couch where Vaasa had been sleeping and sat down, hands on her knees. "Do tell."

She walked to Melisina and sat upon the floor in front of her, knees curled to her chest. Vaasa didn't know where to start, but the moment she found words, everything came flowing at once. She recounted everything: Ozik's connection to her, the notebook she had found in her father's office, her suspicions about her mother's necklace. She told Melisina about the red eyes and the dark ancient thing she could feel on the other side of her connection to Ozik. They discussed Ozik's morning trainings and the strides Vaasa had managed with her magic, the way Ozik urged her to feed on other people's emotions, and the frightening confrontation they'd had in the hallway.

Melisina's hand flew over her mouth, then fell after a moment. "That is dark magic," she whispered. "After feeding on others, do you not feel burned-out? Consumed?"

Vaasa shook her head. "It's . . . easier, actually."

"Have you considered that you might be channeling Ozik's magic in the same way he is channeling yours?" Melisina asked. "Because fueling Veragi magic with an outside source is incredibly difficult. I have only accomplished it once or twice in my lifetime, and it left me sick."

Vaasa's lips parted, then closed. Channeling Ozik?

A bargain goes both ways, he had once told her.

She hadn't once considered that she was leeching magic from him the way he was leeching from her. But then she remembered Ozik's outburst in the greenhouse: *Get out of my head!*

"You might be right," Vaasa murmured. But that hadn't been a part of their bargain; she'd given up her magic, not him. Yet she felt it: The cord that bound them tugged at her then, as if her own body could confirm the suspicions. She pictured it coated in her own dark Veragi magic, tendrils of smoke wrapping around it. The longer she had been here, the more she'd gotten used to the feeling of their bargain. Now that her magic was back at her command, even temporarily, all her senses were heightened. "Look at this." Vaasa stood and guided Melisina down the hallway her mind and body had finally somehow deemed as safe into her father's office.

Melisina gazed around, wide-eyed, at all the books. Vaasa unlatched the secret compartment in the desk and pulled out Dominik's notebook, scurrying to where Melisina stood. The high witch looked down upon it and watched as Vaasa flipped through the pages, landing on the one that held the intricate drawing of her mother's necklace.

Melisina let out a small hum. "She did not wear this in Mireh."

"What can you tell me about her time there?" Vaasa asked.

"It was brief," Melisina said. "She only had interest in a cure. But she practically lived in our library, reading books at every hour of the night. She never seemed to gain control; her magic was more unpredictable than even yours."

Vaasa wondered if her own mother had bargained her magic to Ozik in the same way Vaasa had. If the unpredictability of her mother's magic had perhaps been due to whatever a connection with Ozik offered. "Do you think she could have been channeling Ozik?"

Melisina merely shrugged. "I don't understand how your bargain works, so I can't say. But one day, I woke to her gone. She left a note asking for a marriage agreement between you and Reid. I brought it to him, and when news of your mother's death swept the continent, I knew the only way to save your life was to heed her request."

Vaasa trembled despite herself. Her mother's last act in Mireh had been to find a way to send Vaasa there. To give her some semblance of safety. She'd also tried to protect her with this necklace, yet another thing Dominik had stolen from her.

"She left me this note." Vaasa unfolded the parchment, showing Melisina the Asteryan writing. She translated, "'A wedding present. There is so little I can pass down to you other than pain. But I can give you this: my necklace. It is the only thing that will protect you from him. Whatever you do, stay in Mireh and do not unite the pieces. The price is far too great.'"

Melisina darted her eyes between the note and the drawing of the necklace. "Who is 'him'?"

Vaasa's fingers tightened on the notebook in frustration. "Ozik, Dominik. I don't know. But the necklace isn't in here. I don't know where Dominik hid it, but he never brought it to me."

"Hmm," Melisina mused.

Vaasa pointed at the stone drawn in the center of the necklace, her finger tracing the raw lines of it, particularly on the right half. "It looks broken. And Ozik wears this ring that holds a similar stone. I'm beginning to wonder if they are two halves of a whole."

Melisina sighed in frustration, shaking her head. "I wish there were more of us. That all of our texts hadn't been burned in the fallout of the war. I swear there are a thousand puzzles that could be solved if the pieces hadn't been erased by the ambitious and the frightened."

Vaasa closed the notebook, letting it hang at her side. "Ozik keeps saying that the Witches' War was more about the deities than it was about the covens. That without any witches behind them, the deities can be defeated."

Melisina's eyes lifted, a warning laced in the way she laid her hand on Vaasa's shoulders. "Ozik is like any other person with power. He will only teach you what it serves him for you to know. He can tell the story of history however he pleases."

Vaasa's heart sank. It was a fair assessment, and the way knowledge sat at her fingertips but couldn't quite be grasped felt like a noose around her neck. "Do you think . . ." She shook her head, the idea so outlandish even she couldn't entirely believe it.

"What?"

Vaasa worried her lip. "What if Ozik is a deity? What if that's why he didn't die when I stabbed him?"

Melisina shifted her weight and then leaned on one of the chairs. "I don't know. I think you'd need to find the necklace before anything else, though."

"There is one place I haven't checked," Vaasa confessed.

Melisina quirked a brow.

"My mother's room. I . . ." Vaasa trailed off, trying to control the panic that squeezed her chest. "I haven't been able to walk down that hallway. It's where I found her. Where I inherited my magic."

Melisina closed her eyes in a shared understanding and sorrow.

"I can't do it. But you can," Vaasa realized. She ran to the desk and put the notebook back, latching it. "You can go in there."

"Come," Melisina said, gesturing to the door. Together, they left her father's office and returned to the entertaining room, finding Sachia laying out swatches of fabrics upon the floor. While Vaasa knew it wasn't to serve the purpose they claimed, it at least kept up the ruse, should any attendants walk in.

"It's there," Vaasa whispered, raising her hand to point. She didn't often stare at the carpet or down the walls any longer because even as she did so now, her throat closed. "The room on the left," she managed.

Melisina extended Vaasa a hand. "Together," she said.

Vaasa shook her head, tears already pricking her eyes.

"One witch is a problem," Melisina whispered.

A tear, unbidden, rolled down Vaasa's cheek. "Please. I can't."

Melisina spoke again, still so soft, so gentle. "A coven is a nightmare."

Vaasa looked at the woman, the many roles Melisina filled seeming to spin around her. Mentor. High witch. Mother-in-law. And it had been so long since someone had offered her a hand with such pure assurance, since a moment of progress had been coupled with kindness instead of pain.

Hatred for Ozik spun itself out in Vaasa's body. For the things he had stolen from her, for the tactics he used now to teach her. As she stared at Melisina's hand, it was as if Vaasa stood in the witches' tower of Mireh. As if air came easy and warmth floated throughout the room. The same choice Melisina had given her from the very start: Walk forward together or stay standing still. Not an ounce of judgment to be had for the direction Vaasa took.

Hands shaking, she took Melisina's outstretched palm.

Melisina curled her fingers around Vaasa's and squeezed. "Even slowly, forward is forward."

And then they began to walk, Melisina leading and Vaasa trailing her. Her body tensed, and panic caused her breaths to speed up. She took one step. Another. Faintly, Vaasa knew she was shaking.

She stopped. Stared.

The memory appeared fresh in her mind. The body on the floor. The jade of her mother's dress. The sunken cheeks and scent of rancid burning flesh in the air. In Icruria, it had been easier to picture the world as turning, to feel time as it passed. But here, in this city, time stood still. It froze on the moment she'd found her mother and hadn't moved past that place. In so many ways, these weeks had presented her with snippets of the past like dogs barking on her heels. Roman. Lord Karev. A path to the throne. All choices she might have made had she never known Icruria. Had she never known love and a coven and the way comfort could be found in the hearts of others.

Vaasa felt so desperately lost.

She looked up at Melisina, who still held her hand with a firm grip. Reassurance emanated from the high witch's eyes.

And so Vaasa looked at the hallway, and the world began to turn again.

She saw her mother's body disappearing. The jade dress disintegrating into ash that blew away with the cold. The rug clearing of blood and that one single moment being replaced by every moment after.

Feet walking down the hallway.

Light reflecting on the walls, signaling the turn of night to day.

Time moving, spaces changing, and life continuing past the moment it felt like it had stopped.

She didn't think this place would ever feel clean. That she could ever stare down the entirety of it without considering what had been found here. But with the feel of Melisina's hand on her own, Vaasa thought it was possible to see the place as more than just one thing. It was possible to acknowledge what it had been, and then let it become something else, too.

Just like herself. A liar, a manipulator, and also someone who would do anything for the people she loved. A person who months ago would never have taken Melisina's hand. Who never would have looked Reid in the eyes and told him she loved him.

Now those words could roll right off her tongue.

Her body no longer needed to function as the scene of a crime.

She took another step forward. And then another. It wasn't a confident stride or a commanding march by any means—her body shook with every inch she moved—but she walked. Vaasa walked until her hand was on her mother's door, and she turned the knob before she had a chance to stop herself. Before she could overthink.

Inside was a four-poster bed, white chiffon drapes hanging from each top corner and shielding the quilts in a veil of blurred white. Along one wall was a light birch armoire, the natural knots of which had been sanded out to leave a uniform beige. The chambers were untouched, as if her mother would rise from that bed any day now. A place Dominik hadn't dared to overthrow. Vaasa glanced around, and it all felt less scary than the hallway.

It still felt sacrilegious to search through every crevice and armoire. Yet Vaasa did it. She parsed through each one feeling as if she were overturning a grave, and even more so when her hands came up empty. There was no necklace. Not in the pockets of Vena's dresses, not in the bottoms of her drawers. It was not under the bed or slid beneath the rug.

She looked up at Melisina, who gave a solemn nod. "It's okay to stop looking here now."

Vaasa sighed in defeat. "I'm running out of time."

"We must leave this place, that is the priority."

Vaasa took one last look at the room and then prepared herself to step back into the hallway. She moved quickly, holding her breath, her magic jostling to life as she sped back into the entertaining room.

Sachia was waiting, leaning against the wall. "Anything?"

"No."

"So what's your big plan, consort? How are you getting to the prison?" she asked.

Vaasa pursed her lips. "My lead sentinel has agreed to take me."

"And you believe it'll work?"

Vaasa walked back to her father's office, her magic more under control now, her panic waning. "I believe of all my options, it's the most likely to work."

"I agree," Melisina said as they both followed her into the office again. Sachia glanced around, taking it in the way Melisina had.

Meanwhile, Vaasa sat down on the desk, fiddling with the hourglass her father had always left perched at the edge. "I'm going tonight. I'll chart whatever path he takes me through and relay the information. Those are the guards we'll have positioned elsewhere on the night we decide to break in. After tonight, I'll have more information." She eyed the small iron statue of the owl on the shelf near Sachia and stood. "There is a passageway here that leads to an apartment in the city." She pulled the latch, and it creaked. Vaasa pressed on the door, and it opened to reveal the dark walkway Vaasa had taken to the brothel.

Sachia gawked with childish delight, and Melisina stared into the darkness. "This is how you've been getting into the city," Sachia said, immediately crossing through the threshold and doing a full turn in the passageway. "Creepy."

"I'm going to write down the location of the apartment. Meet me there tonight. If you're stopped, I'll have a promissory note drafted saying you've been granted use while you craft my wedding wardrobe," Vaasa said. "I'll tell you everything I find."

"You really are clever," Sachia mused. "I'll bring Reid with me tonight."

Vaasa stared at her for a moment, her heart speeding up at the idea of seeing Reid. "Why are you doing this for me? For us?"

Sachia shifted her weight, then shrugged. "Believe it or not, your wolf is a rather . . . stand-up man. Plus, Melisina told me I have to in order for her to train me."

Vaasa turned to her high witch, who watched both girls with curiosity. She gave a simple shrug.

"You're a witch?" Vaasa asked.

Sachia crossed her arms. "Is this an interrogation, or are we going to take your measurements so I can at least pretend to be making you a better wardrobe?"

Vaasa let out a genuine chuckle of surprise. Despite herself, she almost liked Sachia. "You have no more ties here, then?"

Sachia gave a small grin. "No. When I have my brother, I'm going to run from this city and never look back."

Vaasa bit the inside of her cheek, deciding whether or not to trust the pirate. Eventually, she conceded. "You have a thing for strays, don't you Melisina?"

Melisina laughed, and the sound of it sloshed into the cracks that had taken residence in Vaasa's chest. Today, she saw Melisina. Tonight, she would see Amalie. Reid.

Vaasa said, "Your brother. What is his name?"

Sachia pursed her lips. "Micha," she said. "His name is Micha."

"What did he do?" Vaasa dared ask.

Sachia leveled her with a stare. "Nothing. I defected from Sutherland's inner circle, so Vlacik had my brother tied to the iron pole and whipped. Now he fights practically to the death for the nobles' entertainment."

Vaasa looked down the cold passageway. "I see why you wanted Lord Vlacik dead."

"Your husband killed him before I had the chance. But it was me who pushed his body out of the window."

Vaasa winced. "Wearing a sentinel's jacket was smart, I'll give you that."

"Not as clever as you would have done it, I imagine."

"I would have made him suffer for far longer," Vaasa admitted.

Sachia gave a slow nod. "As long as you aren't like your brother, you and I are going to get along fine," Sachia said. "Now let's go. I have a feeling that sentinel of yours is going to check my work."

CHAPTER
27

The moment darkness bathed the blue rugs and stone hallways, Vaasa slipped from her room and found Roman waiting, just as he'd promised. In the winter, night fell early on Mekës, and Vaasa had every intention of taking advantage of that.

The two walked through the night, and they didn't speak about the evening prior. Didn't speak about the full day she'd just spent with Sachia and Melisina. In secret, she had basked in the feeling of her magic. Had spent all afternoon releasing it, hoping that would be enough to quell it for tonight.

Vaasa was dressed in royal blue breeches, the same ones the sentinels wore, her hair pulled up and folded tightly at the nape of her neck. She donned their coat and even a fur hat. Though the disguise was a bit bulky, it would do. Colder and colder the air became, the hallways narrowing until they found the large staircase Ozik had stopped them on last time.

He wasn't waiting for them. She'd considered that outcome, had weighed it as a possibility. Relief came quick, her magic seeming to duck back into herself as if it no longer felt the need to be alert.

Roman reached a heavy door at the end of the servants' halls. He used an iron key—one of many—on the small metal loop he kept latched at his hip. Vaasa made a silent note of the key's shape, tucking the information away.

He turned to her. "Are you ready?"

"I'm not actually jumping from the bridge," she told him. *A rite of passage*, Roman had called it the day he and his friends had leapt over the side of that bridge into the frigid waves, as every sentinel in Mekës someday did. It was a dangerous initiation into their ranks, but one Roman had passed with flying colors. "We just need these men to believe I am."

He gave her a brilliant smile, one that would have had her heart melting ten years ago. He gently pulled a brown sack over her head, completing their disguise, and dragged her into what Vaasa could only assume was a smuggler's den.

"We've got a jumper!" Roman exclaimed, and the guards waiting all cried out in unison. Roman didn't have to explain himself to the men stationed at the private entrance and exit—they were his friends, Vaasa quickly realized. Men who felt a kinship to him for their roles in this place. Though she couldn't see through the gauzy sack he had pulled over her head, she heard everything. She could feel them all—their ease, their humor, even their hunger. Magic stirred in her body.

The sentinels didn't question him as he dragged her into one of the skiffs used to carry goods back and forth from the prison. Vaasa tripped over the lip, and Roman let her stumble, not daring to break their characters as she slammed into the boat. Her knee collided with the bench and she bit her tongue, but she stifled her grunt of pain. Her magic lurched, but she clamped down on it.

The men around them hollered with laughter.

"You think an unbalanced lad like that's going to survive the jump?" one of the guards asked.

The others kept laughing, tossing out their own jokes. Vaasa used her hands to guide herself up and onto one of the benches, keeping silent and hanging her head as if she were embarrassed.

"Says he wants to try," Roman said as men presumably pushed the skiff into the water. "Who are we to deny him the embarrassment?"

The men threw out their agreements, some mocking, some more sincere. Their voices faded as the boat rocked in the water, the smell of brine and fish stuffing up Vaasa's nose. Eventually, Roman tucked his fingers under the brown sack and pulled it from Vaasa's head. He smoothed out the strands of her hair that flew around her face. "You did well," he said.

She scanned their surroundings. They paddled into the Iron Bay, wind rocking their boat. "You sounded just like them," Vaasa remarked.

"It's just a language among men," Roman clarified.

Vaasa quietly looked out at the water, at the lights of the city at the shore, and thought that she knew plenty of languages, and *men* who didn't speak like that. Waves lapped at the side of their boat, the ocean churning with the cold, salt water spraying up and onto Vaasa's face. She pulled her borrowed sentinel's coat tighter around herself as Roman rowed. Minutes felt like hours. She remembered this trip feeling shorter when they'd forced her to return to the fortress.

The island grew closer, larger, more ominous. Roman maneuvered their boat to the backside of the prison, aiming for the Last Crossing. As she eyed the towering bridge, she thought of the night Roman had made the jump. Of the way he had snuck into her room afterward, cold and emboldened, and it was the first time she had ever taken him into her bed.

She looked at him then. He tilted his lips into a remembering grin as he spotted those very same lights, this unexpected memory coursing between them as he felt more familiar to her in that moment than anyone in Mekës ever had.

But the man who sat before her now . . . he was no longer that person.

"It's a foolish tradition," she chastised him.

"It earned me you," he said in return.

With an amused shake of her head, she let the comment pass. He pulled into a dark crevice beneath the bridge. It must be the place all the sentinels went when they wanted to jump. A weak spot in their rotations, or one they purposefully ignored to make the leap itself possible.

He tied their boat off on a small wooden post that had been dug into the ground there, likely by other sentinels. She heard the jingle of keys in Roman's hands, and she wondered—did he have the ability to get Amalie out of her cell? Surely Ozik hadn't provided him that kind of access.

Roman jumped into the frigid water without a care for the cold and then reached for her waist. He lifted her up and out of the boat, putting his arm beneath her legs and keeping her from getting wet. Once on the sand, they took care to stick to the dark places and slunk up to the prison.

Roman gestured toward a rickety, terrifying ladder that had been built into the cliffside. Wooden planks were spread at different lengths and widths, makeshifts thing that sent a small tremor through her. She hated heights. Still, he insisted she go first, so she started the climb. Vaasa held her breath, fighting back the magic that still churned like the ocean.

Vaasa hauled herself over the sharp lip, silently thanking the lack of snowfall today. She scrambled to her feet, pressing her back against the remaining cliffside next to an opening to a small tunnel. The guards must have created a passageway here. Roman climbed up and stood next to her, pressed almost chest-to-chest with her on the narrow ledge. "Are you ready?" he whispered, holding up the brown sack again. When she nodded silently, he slipped it over her head.

Taking her elbow, he guided her into the tunnel. "Stairs," he said under his breath. He guided her up, never slipping, while Vaasa had to focus in order to keep her balance. He still held her elbow tightly, keeping her upright. Faintly, she heard him unlatch either a door or a gate. She did her best to memorize the feel of everything around her, knowing she would need to communicate this all to Sachia.

The eerie quiet of the island made Vaasa shiver, but it was more than just the cold. Roman gripped her arm, pulling her around a corner suddenly and closing a door behind them.

"Got a jumper?" a voice asked.

"Staněk, what did you do to get tunnel duty?" Roman asked, a light laugh following his words.

"I don't mind a boring post," Staněk responded. "I value glory far less than getting to go home."

"Fair point," Roman said, and he kept walking.

"No shame in seeing me again, boy," Staněk called after them. "Don't rush the jump. You can always try again."

Roman tightened his grip on her elbow. "You hear that?" he said, speaking before Vaasa had to respond, alleviating her of that problem.

She nodded, stumbling on a stair purposefully, and Roman held her upright even so.

"Get your nerves under control," Roman snapped as he pulled her around the corner, one last part of their roles before they were officially out of earshot. A few more steps and Roman stopped. He removed the brown sack from her head, folding it and tucking it into his jacket. Vaasa immediately glanced around at the dark tunnel they had carved into the island, the steps beneath her feet nothing but slippery stone. One door lay in front of them. Roman slid it open and glanced around, then gestured her forward. "This way."

Vaasa stepped into a minimally furnished common room, one she realized was likely reserved for guards when they took a break or if they waited between shifts. At this time of night, it made sense that it was empty. Men were either on shift or they were home.

"Careful," he reminded her, "and stay behind me."

Roman led the way, and it wasn't lost on Vaasa that he knew precisely where Amalie's cell was. He'd been coming here at least every few days.

They entered a narrow stairwell with stone walls seeming to close in on them, and without so much as hesitating, Roman began to climb again. They went up five floors, the steps beneath them becoming less slippery the higher they went. Apparently, people didn't go up this far all that often, because boots hadn't worn the steps down yet. A wooden door took them into the fifth level's hallway. Trying not to peer around at the familiar wood-and-iron doors, she kept her eyes on the back of Roman's jacket. Every thread of brightness woven into the blue was dimmed in this lightless place. Her body remembered everything—the iron, the cold, the delusions.

When he slowed, Vaasa stared at the thick wooden door he'd stopped in front of. She shimmied past him and approached, her heart in her throat. Quietly, she peered through the iron bars. "Amalie," she whispered.

Amalie jumped up from where she sat on the floor. "Vaasa?" She ran to the bars, her face now visible.

"Don't stand too close," Roman warned.

Vaasa shooed him, practically pressing her face into the iron. "Are you all right? Have you . . . given any more thought to what we talked about?"

Vaasa knew Roman was listening, so she chose her words carefully. But she had to know—had Amalie spoken to Veragi again? Did she have any information about the necklace?

"Yes, I—"

Amalie's voice cut off.

Vaasa pressed harder into the bars, magic biting at her insides as she tried to calm herself. "Amalie?" Vaasa whispered.

Amalie tilted her head. Blinked.

Her eyes bled to white. Bright, glowing like the moon, like the wolf that had grown from Vaasa's darkest moment. Vaasa sucked in a breath, and then Amalie's hands flew up, her fingers snaking around the bars. They opened in invitation, curling in a beckoning call, and on the tips of them was the faintest trace of black mist.

Whoever this was, it wasn't Amalie, Vaasa was certain. The thing that looked back at her was no human, no being of this world. Bright white eyes, the same she'd seen in her conjured wolf, the same she'd seen in every manifestation.

Something in Vaasa's bones told her she knew this magic. Knew this force, even when she couldn't see it, even when she couldn't access it within herself. There was no reckoning powerful enough to take this familiarity away, because the magic existed within Vaasa, too.

"Veragi?" she whispered.

The goddess smiled in what looked like relief.

Roman moved to block Vaasa, but before he had the opportunity to stop her, Vaasa gripped the iron bars. Veragi's hands closed over hers, and faintly she heard Roman hiss her name. But his voice was drowned out by the sudden onslaught of magic. It ripped through Vaasa, unforgiving, down her spine and through her limbs, tearing and pulling. Mist wound around her neck and then plunged down her throat and nose, the sensation muddling her mind as it wrapped around it and squeezed. Pain seared through Vaasa, but just as quickly as it came, the agony abated. Behind her eyes was the image of something that started blurry and then took perfectly clear form.

Vaasa stared at her mother.

Vena Kozár paced in a hallway, staring down at her hands as Veragi magic consumed them. She twisted her fingers into fists, holding them close to her body, trying to breathe. Vena's head whipped to the side, and Ozik approached. He looked around them as if checking to be sure they were alone.

He took Vena's hands in his. *It hurts*, Vena whispered.

I know, love, Ozik whispered back.

The images Veragi sent shifted, turning in on themselves until Vaasa stared at the greenhouse. It spread out in front of her as if she were standing there herself.

Ozik led Vena into the structure, the olive tree towering above them, the stone statues all around them. Vena graced Ozik with a smile the world had rarely ever looked upon, one Vaasa herself had hardly seen. The two exchanged words Vaasa couldn't hear. Vena turned and lifted her hair, and Ozik fastened something around her neck, whispering to her all the while.

The black stone necklace.

On his hands, small black veins writhed. Ozik closed his eyes. His face contorted in pain. When he opened them again, red flashed until gold bled through the crimson in a smothering wave. The black veins on his hands snapped back, leaving the youthful skin of the advisor

Vaasa knew. Ozik paused there, holding the necklace, staring down at Vena as if he looked upon his entire world.

Once again, the images shifted and turned. Fear pounded through Vaasa, fear that wasn't entirely her own. It was a miserable kind of adrenaline as Vaasa's vision leveled out. She stood in the hallway of the emperor's quarters, her mother fleeing down it. Her hand lifted to her neck, but there was no necklace there to hold.

Ozik lifted his hand and twisted his wrist, and in front of Vena, the Miro'dag took shape.

It struck.

Vaasa swore she screamed as she watched it all happen—watched her mother sink to the ground in a pool of jade fabric, watched the life dim in her eyes. Watched as the Miro'dag feasted upon Vena Kozár like she was nothing but a soul to consume.

Ozik turned, and his eyes glowed bright red. There was no sign of gold any longer.

The vision spun. As it all leveled out, Vaasa stared at . . . her brother.

He clutched the necklace in his hand.

Vaasa was a mere ghost, a fly upon the wall, as Dominik slid back the lid of their mother's sarcophagus. Located in the grand mausoleum that sat sturdy in the center of the city, Vaasa remembered the day her mother's body had been laid to rest next to her father's. She had just learned of her impending marriage to Reid of Mireh. Fury had shadowed the entire ordeal.

And now, there was Dominik, his fist clutching the necklace's iron chain as he stared down into the sarcophagus. Vaasa couldn't see her mother's body, but she remembered the etchings of snowdrops the makers had carved into the sides of her coffin. Their mother's favorite flower.

Rage simmered in the harsh tug of Dominik's features. He placed the necklace in the sarcophagus and then grimaced. All of a sudden, his eyes went wide, and he reared back—

His gaze snapped up, and even though consciously Vaasa knew this wasn't real and that he couldn't see her, fear flooded her veins. It was as if he stared into her soul, as if he were still alive and crawling toward her with a knife again.

Vaasa was thrown back into herself, the vision disappearing on a snap. Veragi released Vaasa's hands, and Vaasa lurched backward, stumbling into Roman as he wrapped his arm around her waist and tried to tug her away from the cell. Nausea swept over her in a roiling wave. She fought to keep her magic settled, to prevent it from leaking onto her hands. Vaasa doubled over, curling in on herself as Roman tugged at her shoulders to try and get her to stand. Loss and anguish made a home in every crook within her.

"Let me go," Vaasa croaked, fingers still clinging to the bars.

The bright white of Veragi's eyes drained, and Vaasa gasped as her best friend's body crumpled into an unconscious pile on the dirty prison floor.

CHAPTER 28

"No!" Vaasa cried.

"Quiet," Roman commanded in her ear. He tugged on her body and hauled her away from the cell. Feet slipping on the slick floors, Vaasa fought as he dragged her down the corridor, kicking her legs like a toddler. "Get ahold of yourself!"

Everything she had just seen played in her mind, wicked and strong and seemingly unending. Over and over, the vision swirled.

Her mother had loved Ozik, enough to give him access to her power. And he had murdered her in cold blood. That dark power consumed him—it must have fed on Vena's magic the way it now fed on Vaasa's.

Their escape hinged on her finding the necklace; she was certain. Dominik had hidden it in their mother's sarcophagus. It was a place she could gain entry to.

"Promise me you'll make sure she's okay," Vaasa begged.

"I promise," Roman swore. "But we need to go, *now*."

Vaasa's instinct snapped into motion. She forced her body to turn and run, and then Roman sprinted behind her into the stairwell. Something sounded from down the stairs, and Roman froze. Guards. "Run," he told her. "We can't be here."

Wrapping his hand around hers, Roman broke into a sprint, and Vaasa forced her feet to move. They took the stairs to the fourth floor, Roman smoothly inserting the key and hauling them through the door. It took only two steps until Roman pressed his back against the wall, waiting and listening. Vaasa hoped she would hear the people on the stairs open and close a door, leaving the stairwell empty so they could escape.

Vaasa breathed in. Out. Roman worked on a door next to them, sticking keys in and frantically trying to turn the lock.

The footsteps sounded on their level, and Vaasa knew the people were coming through the door immediately in front of them. Roman must have figured that out, too, because he unlocked the latch to what Vaasa assumed was a supply closet next to them. He pulled her unceremoniously through it, landing them in a room with little to no light. Immediately, she registered that the space around her was larger than any supply closet could be. She didn't know where they'd gone. She could hardly focus on the tight grip Roman kept on her hand. She needed time to consider what she would say to him, how she would frame what she'd seen.

Darkness covered every inch of space around them.

Footsteps sounded outside the door. They came closer and closer.

And then they passed, going farther down the hall until Vaasa couldn't hear them anymore.

Neither she nor Roman dared to speak. The silence was an echo onto itself, as daunting as the approaching footsteps had been.

"What just happened?" Roman finally whispered into the night.

Vaasa shook her head in confusion, her magic riling when she couldn't see or escape. She hadn't come upon an explanation yet, a way to twist this. Her heart pounded mercilessly in her chest. Her pulse thrummed in her own mind.

"*Vaasa,*" he demanded.

"I don't know," she hissed through her teeth.

"You're lying," Roman snarled. He stepped into her space, his body looming close enough that she could see the outline of his once-comely features. Their breath mingled. Something in his eyes darkened as he looked upon her. As questions furrowed his brow. Distrust wove into the harsh pull of his mouth. "I watched it, Vaasa. I watched what that magic did to you—yet you live. Who is Veragi?"

Vaasa's throat threatened to close, a lump sitting inside it at hearing the goddess's name. She had taken Amalie over, had shown those images to Vaasa *through* Amalie. Emotions filled Vaasa to the point of bursting—Roman's, hers. Her magic needed escape. "I don't know," she swore.

Roman raised his voice. "Honesty, Vaasa. You promised me honesty!"

She covered his mouth with her hands. "Be quiet!"

Silence coursed between them, the uncomfortable kind that set her on edge. This silence was deafening. It twisted her fear and amplified it.

She looked past his shoulder, her eyes having adjusted to the darkness, and made out the shape of a table. Vaasa's hands dropped from Roman's mouth, and she stepped past him, more of the room becoming identifiable.

There were iron chains attached to the wooden table, and a small counter space at the back of the room. Vaasa crossed to it, looking at sharp tools crafted of metal and wood. Torture devices. Vaasa turned away with her hand over her mouth. She faced the center table and inspected those heavy iron chains. Reaching out tentatively, she touched them.

The iron hummed on her fingertips, and she pulled away, recognizing the material as the same one Lord Vlacik had confined her in. Dread pooled low in her stomach. She knew this room.

She turned to Roman, who watched her closely, his eyes inspecting her in the darkness.

He had the key.

Bile rose in her throat. *Water, water, water,* Vaasa thought to herself. Melisina's voice filled her mind, a memory from the day she had hidden beneath a table and her coven had crawled under it with her.

Whatever form the magic takes right now, picture it as water. It is trickling and flowing, slipping back down to its home.

She darted her gaze to the door, but there was no way out. Roman stood in the path. Something deep inside her cracked, a fissure rooted in the past.

He had the key.

"How long were you working for Vlacik?" she whispered.

Roman opened his mouth to speak but then snapped it closed. His fist clenched at his side, and then a hand raked through his hair.

Vaasa dropped her voice to a low demand. "How long?"

She didn't believe an ounce of the guilt that racked his face. The part he was playing . . . it was that of the yearning lover. But that wasn't true. Vaasa didn't think he loved her at all.

Every moment she had lied to Roman, he had been lying to her.

Roman dropped his arm, and his voice turned sharp. Cruel. A brutal tone lacking any of the warmth she had once known of him. "For about two years, before you concocted some way to have him thrown from a window."

Shock stole her breath. Her mind worked out the timeline on a wheel. "You were here before I was sent to Mireh. You were here when my parents died."

He had been in the city before their deaths, and he hadn't come for her. He hadn't found a way to see her, to let her know that he was still alive.

"I clawed my way back to this city on a pirate ship," Roman confessed. "Vlacik was the last connection I had here from my youth. Both of our fathers had died, and he was a lord with enough power to get me the connections I needed to survive here."

Vaasa wanted to vomit. It wasn't Ozik who had brought Roman back—it was Vlacik. "You knew what he was doing to me?"

"No," Roman asserted with a strong step forward.

Vaasa backed up, trying to put as much space between them as she could. Roman watched the movement and his mouth turned downward. "I knew what he did to witches. After what I've seen, what I've been through . . ." Roman shook his head. "I take no qualms with it. Whatever your mother passed down to you, it has been excised."

A prisoner of war. Roman had been in Wrultho under Ton's reign, had likely seen more brutality than Vaasa could imagine. What had they done to him? Who had this life turned him into? "He tortured *people*, Roman. Witches are people."

"Every soldier tortures people, Vaasa. That is a fact of war, which is probably something you should get used to, considering you're at the core of one."

"He tortured *me*," she whispered.

A small snarl escaped him. "And if I had known that, I would have killed him myself. I don't know how you orchestrated—"

"I didn't orchestrate his death!" Vaasa hissed.

"Then what were you doing there at the brothel? What the fuck are you and Ozik doing in the greenhouse every morning?" Roman shook his head in disbelief. "You're looking at me like you can't believe I deigned to tell you a lie when mistruths are all you have offered me."

"You know Ozik is a witch, right? You watched what happened in that stairwell."

"Of course I do."

"So only some witches deserve to be tortured?"

Roman released a chuckle. "Ozik deserves a knife through his heart, and if I have anything to say about it, that's what he'll get."

Vaasa narrowed her eyes. "How did you earn your position as lead sentinel?"

Roman crossed his arms. "That was part of Vlacik's demands. He wanted me close to you."

It was like a cold rush of water thrown on the back of her neck—of course. How hadn't she seen it? It was no accident when he'd found her in that hallway, nor when he returned to the very place she had once spent nights in his arms. He went there not because he wanted to see her, but because he wanted to take advantage of her. He believed her desperate and lovesick enough to seek him out, to trust him.

He'd been right. She had been moments away from telling him

everything, from indulging in that piece of her youth that she so badly wanted to cling to. The little glimmer of love that had once grown so large in her mind because it had been taken from her, and she'd never been given the chance to leave it first. "You were telling Vlacik things about me? Spying on me for him?"

"Not a single thing that mattered," Roman swore. "I told you that first night that I am here for *you*, and that hasn't changed."

"Are you one of Sutherland's men?" she demanded. "Is that how you have access to this room? Is that the pirate you allied with in order to come back here?"

Roman stared at her for a moment, and then crossed his arms. "Yes. I was on a job for him until Vlacik had me reassigned here."

Vaasa didn't dare move. Her power jostled to life, risking exposure. Roman uncrossed his arms and stepped toward her, and she had nowhere to go. She stumbled, and her back hit the table.

"He found me in the Loursevain. Put me on my first crew three years ago. I fought and murdered my way back to this city. But I was nothing when I stepped off a boat; just an escaped prisoner, a soldier who deserted and paid the price. I swore I was going to be somebody worth an empire. Worth you." Roman shook his head, as if he could hardly stand to relive the memories. "But then you were married off to another man, and there was nothing left here to save. So I helped Sutherland take the city guard, and then the prison. And when Sutherland told me Vlacik wanted to overthrow Dominik, it was a cause I could get behind. But then you came back, and Vlacik offered me access to you, Vaasa. *You.* The only woman I have ever loved. I was staring at a chance to have everything we ever wanted, and I took it."

In front of her, he morphed. No longer the young sentinel, no longer that initial taste of rebellion that made her believe life was larger than the role her family wanted her to play. She remembered the thrill of the first time he'd kissed her, the intensity of doing something deeply forbidden. And yet when she looked at him now, all that enchanted romanticism was just . . . gone.

What remained of their young love was cold and silent. A dead thing that he was pounding upon the chest of. He was yet another power-starved man who wanted to sacrifice her at the altar of his ambitions. He did not love her; he loved the idea of winning the Asteryan heiress.

Cruelty clawed at her throat, begging to be let out, begging to steal the air from him the way he'd stolen it from her. And suddenly, she didn't care if she broke his heart. She *wanted* him to break.

"You are a coward," she snapped.

Anger twisted his features into that unrecognizable enemy. "I'm the coward, am I?" Roman stepped into her space.

Vaasa recoiled, her body remembering what had happened to her upon a table like this. What those chains were capable of doing to a witch. Roman didn't drop her gaze. His hand settled upon her waist, ignoring the way her body tensed.

"Stop," Vaasa managed.

Roman's voice came low. "I spent *years* infatuated with you, and when I finally earned a place in your bed, I was willing to be anything you needed in order to keep just a taste of you. *That's* when I was a coward. Because I'm not who you chose, am I? That was a brutal, ruthless man who takes what he wants without an apology. And you can't even say that you didn't love him."

Desire, harsh and cutting, painted his features, and Vaasa didn't care to look at it. She almost wanted to let her magic out to play and watch what her wolf could do to a man like this. Here, in this moment, backed against a table, violence bloomed in the dead of winter. "Stop, Roman," she whispered.

"Tell me that's what you truly want," Roman said. His hands tightened on her waist. "Because I don't think it is."

Vaasa held her chin high. She refused to tremble in the face of him, refused to show an ounce of her fear. Roman leaned in, his lips just inches from hers, and Vaasa's heart pounded painfully in her chest. Panic soared in her veins. She swallowed, doing anything she could to keep it down.

"I can offer you anything Karev can, anything that *wolf* can," he said so quietly, his words and breath coasting between what little space separated them. "I can be a weapon, you just aren't wielding me."

Her hand against the table behind her slid a fraction until her fingertips brushed the chains. Her magic winked out, and relief came cold and sweet. Rationality broke through the haze of her anger, a stark reminder of where she stood and what she had to lose.

She couldn't alienate Roman. Not now. Not yet. He could turn on her at any moment, and it was only through his mechanisms that she would travel freely within the city. He could clear the way to the mausoleum, to her mother's sarcophagus. He had access to Amalie and Sachia's brother. He was a stress point for Lord Karev, one worth keeping.

Every step forward had to be intentional. This, above all else, was critical.

I can be a weapon, you just aren't wielding me.

With a small breath, Vaasa released the chains, her magic flooding her stomach. She stifled it. Instead, she lifted her hands to his chest, her fingers curling in the lapels of his jacket, hiding the tips in case any magic leaked out. "I understand why you did it," she whispered. "If I had been given a way back to you, I would have taken it, too. No matter how sinister."

He looked between where she touched him and up into her eyes.

"I didn't know you were alive, Roman. If I had known . . ." She closed her eyes for a moment, honestly remembering what it felt like to believe he was dead. The guilt she had carried, the self-loathing that had festered because her love for him had been the final nail in his coffin.

"I should have told you sooner. For that, I'm sorry."

Vaasa opened her eyes. Tilted her head. "No, you're right. I want someone who's going to fight. Someone who's going to claw their way to the throne and slaughter anyone who tries to take it. Since I cannot earn it myself, I was willing to let Reid of Mireh be the person who claimed it for me. Perhaps Karev, if that's what it took. But . . ." She shook her head. "I didn't know you wanted it, Roman. You never told me that you did."

"I want it," he said with such satisfaction it made Vaasa sick. He lifted a hand to push back a tendril of her hair, fingers lingering on the side of her throat. "I want *you*."

She curled her hands tighter against his chest. "I can't touch you. Not yet."

"And why is that?" he demanded.

"Because when I touch you," she whispered, pushing his chest so he ceded space, forcing him backward until her arms were entirely extended. She breathed easier. The part she had to play came freely now. She looked him square in his eyes. "There will be no lord or advisor in my way. There will be you and me and a throne and nothing else."

She lifted her hands from him then, an ugly darkness curling in her stomach. She hated herself. She hated the words she had just spoken. In many ways, she was no different from Ozik. But Vaasa could only see one future, and it wasn't here in Asterya.

She would *never* forgive him.

At her small display of willingness, Roman closed his eyes and his body relaxed. A starving man who had just been offered a crumb, yet confused it with a feast.

"Tell me what you saw tonight," he said. "Complete honesty, Vaasa. I'm tired of being left out of your plans."

Vaasa spoke instinctually, careful with her phrasing. "My friend showed me a weapon. Something my brother put inside my mother's sarcophagus. Something I think he hid in hopes I wouldn't be able to protect myself against him or Ozik."

Roman ate her words with the same ferocity he was swallowing her lies. "You're going to need to retrieve it, then."

"I am."

"I can arrange for you to visit the mausoleum privately. You're entitled to grieve your parents without a host of sentinels in the room; no one will think twice."

"Tomorrow," she said, time winding down around her as she considered how much had passed since they'd ducked into this room. Melisina was waiting for her. Reid was waiting. They would coordinate everything tonight. Once they had the necklace, they would need to flee as quickly as possible.

"Tomorrow," Roman agreed quietly. "And then we will decide how to rid ourselves of Lord Karev."

She nodded, hoping with everything she had that he would be sated long enough with an almost, a someday.

He stepped forward and ran his thumb along her cheekbone. She kept her hands behind her, one on the table, the other within inches of the chain. But then he dropped his, tentatively brushing her wrist until he lifted her hand to his chest. "You can touch me, Vaasa. We are alone."

Vaasa swallowed a deep breath and then lied as naturally as breathing. "History has a terrible way of repeating itself." She hoped the words would remind him of exactly what he had to lose, positioning her as the rational one between them.

His face softened. "It won't, not this time."

"I can't," she whispered. "*I* can't survive it a second time. Karev will kill you if he finds out who you are. Who you work for. What we plan to do together."

Roman pursed his lips, but at her outright refusal, his hand slipped from hers. He backed away, and Vaasa stifled her look of relief. He pressed his ear to the door, listening for the sounds of people coming or going. With a gesture of his hand, Vaasa carefully crossed the room. Magic still bit at her insides, and she pushed it down, her adrenaline slowing to a manageable pulse.

The hall was empty. They were silent as they snuck back to their pinnace, pretending Vaasa was merely a sentinel who had failed to gather enough courage to jump from the Last Crossing.

And when she made it back to her quarters, she rested her head against the door for a moment. Relaxed.

She had gotten a taste of it all—had been reminded precisely what came alive inside her when Reid was near. Without him, the coldness within her came back swiftly and without mercy.

Until she was back in his arms for good, there was no line she would not cross. No lie she would not become.

A plan unfolded in the darkest recesses of her mind, and it was all the worst parts of her. Yet those parts were the very reason she had survived this long. They had been built upon the back of this place, had been necessary. That darkness had served her and might continue to serve her if she played her cards right.

She had a choice, after all.

She could be one of two things: a prisoner in a fortress of her own making, or a wolf they had let into their house.

CHAPTER
29

Vaasa reached the end of the dark passageway that connected the fortress and her family's apartment. She pressed upon the back of the false bookshelf wall. Her grandfather had kept a reading room here, and if Vaasa had the time, she might have explored every book he had chosen to keep private. Instead, she launched into the hallway and came face-to-face with Reid, who must have heard the sound of her opening the concealed door.

"It was Veragi," Vaasa blurted, just as Reid gathered her up and into his arms. Cool magic poured from her hands, the dark mist expelling from her body the moment he held her close. The moment she felt safe enough to allow it do so.

"You're okay?" he asked into her hair and then pulled her to arm's length to inspect. "What happened?"

"Did you see her?" a voice tumbled down the hallway. Koen's.

Vaasa looked past Reid to see him standing at the end of the hallway, eyes more alight with hope than she had seen them yet. He adjusted his spectacles, and Vaasa thought he might be trying to soften the intense tightness of his shoulders, but it didn't have the effect of making him seem relaxed, only anxious.

"Yes," she said, stepping around Reid and walking to Koen. "But . . . Veragi possessed her somehow. She showed me images of my mother and Ozik."

Melisina gasped. "The goddess communicated with you?" She sat behind Koen on the couch in the main family room. Her hand covered her mouth. Vaasa crossed the room and took the spot next to her, avoiding Sachia, who was fast asleep beneath a blanket on the opposite couch. Reid's eyes traveled to where Vaasa sat, but he didn't beckon her over to him. He sat on the ground instead, just in front of the fireplace that raged with a much-needed warmth, and pulled his knees to his shoulders.

Vaasa nodded. "Amalie's eyes glowed white, like your horse and my wolf. She never directly spoke to me, only showed me images. But I had to touch Amalie to see any of it."

Melisina breathed heavily, gaze drifting around the room like she was caught in her own thoughts.

"Have you ever heard of something like this?" Reid asked Melisina.

"All I have been able to read are the tomes still left in the Sodality of Setar and the Sodality of Una. Every other coven is a mystery. But yes, there are a few records that survived the burnings during unification, some of which discuss a witch's ability to communicate, and even harbor, their deity," Melisina said.

"Is it only those of us with sentimental magic?" Vaasa asked.

Just then, Sachia stirred awake, sitting up and glancing around the room. Her eyes went wide at seeing Vaasa, and she sat up entirely.

Koen, who stood just behind the couch, arched a brow. "Sentimental?"

"Magic pertaining to the spirit or the inner world, instead of magic that deals with the physical," Melisina said. "These are old terms."

"It's what Ozik calls it," Vaasa chimed in.

Koen furrowed his brows and came around the settee, sitting opposite Reid on the floor.

"So, your magic is sentimental?" Sachia asked. "What would he call mine?"

"Corporeal," Vaasa said. "Magic that requires an element or physical object present in order to manifest. You can't manipulate metal that isn't there."

"But your magic is fueled by your emotions?" Sachia asked.

"Precisely," Melisina said. "I never heard Freya classify magic this way, but the witches of Una do. Veragi witches lack even more resources than other covens. We were hunted for centuries, and our histories were burned long before unification."

Freya was Vaasa's great-grandmother and the founder of the Veragi coven in Mireh. Before her, Veragi witches had been scattered and on the verge of extinction, considered to be wielders of dark magic and often ostracized because of it. Vaasa couldn't imagine what the world would look like if the magic-less Icrurians hadn't burned all their texts and records. If Icrurian unification hadn't cut the covens off at the knees.

She supposed, though, that it would have led to a world in which the witches ruled, not the magic-less. Icrurian unification had ended the Witches' War and allowed for the covens' fragile existence, even if some cities were still hell-bent on purging their witches.

"I've never heard the witches of Una refer to it as that," Koen said, bringing Vaasa back to the here and now.

"You wouldn't have," Reid reminded him. "Even less likely, given your foremanship and relation to the headman. The only people the covens distrust more than each other is the state."

Koen shook his head. "Foolish."

"Necessary," Melisina argued. "The last time witches were weaponized, they almost went extinct."

"They pitted their own covens against each other," Koen rebutted.

"Enough," Reid said, interrupting them both.

This dark side of Icrurian history was somewhat foreign to Vaasa, as she had spent her time in Dihrah falling behind in her classes. What early education she'd gleaned here in Asterya hadn't been about magic at all—it had been about the Icrurian exchange of power, which was so different from Asterya's. She let out a small breath, running her fingers through her hair at the same time that Koen pulled his knees to his chest.

Sachia let out a frustrated breath. "So, you believe it's possible? That Amalie could be carrying Veragi as we speak?"

Melisina pursed her lips, her tiredness apparent in the way her lids started to droop. "Anything is possible. I've told Reid from the very start that I suspect this is larger than any of us; this is about something that occurred long before unification. There is history woven into the fabric of everything, and I don't believe these circumstances are an exception."

Vaasa had the strange sense of being overwhelmed, much like she used to feel at the beginning of learning about magic. She'd had less than a year of actual studying and training with Melisina. There was so much she didn't know.

"Tell us what you saw," Koen said to Vaasa.

Vaasa told them everything about her interaction with Amalie—the white eyes, the relief on Amalie's face when Vaasa accurately identified her as Veragi. The vision of her mother and Ozik's affair, the bargain they made that gave him access to Vena's magic. Then, she told them of the mausoleum and her brother hiding the necklace inside her mother's sarcophagus.

Sachia tucked her blanket up to her chin. "So, before we can leave, you need to visit the mausoleum? To take the necklace?"

"What do you believe this necklace will even do?" Koen asked.

Vaasa bit her lip. She didn't know. "There must be a reason my mother left it for me. She said it would keep me safe, and now that Veragi has sent me on the path to find it, I believe it's a weapon of sorts."

"Whatever its role, it must be found," Melisina agreed.

"It's the last thing I need to do before we escape," Vaasa confirmed. "And Ozik is away from the fortress right now. I need to act quickly."

"I just need to pinpoint where in the prison my brother is," Sachia said, voice churning.

"My lead sentinel will find him," Vaasa said. "I promise."

That was all the information she gave, confusion and shame

burrowing into her body at the pieces of Roman's identity that she kept hidden. She just needed to speak the truth to Reid first.

Sachia's eyes glistened at the edges. "We won't need Karev, then?"

"No, we won't."

The pirate gave a slight smile. "Thank you."

Vaasa wondered how many years Sachia had been beholden to the whims of these Asteryan lords. What deals she had made to survive, and what they had cost her. In that way, Vaasa and Sachia were shockingly similar. "You're welcome. Do you still have access to the black powder you smuggled in?"

Sachia frowned, but it was Koen who spoke next. A small thrill laced his tone. "You have a plan to use it?"

Vaasa gave a sharp nod. "The night of the engagement party."

Koen leaned forward, a conspiratorial gleam in his eye that brought a smile to Vaasa's lips. "Tell me everything."

Vaasa woke with a start, her mind not entirely registering where she was. Yet the moment she smelled salt and amber, she knew. Reid's chest was pressed to her back like it had been for so many nights in Mireh and Dihrah, before she'd ever given in to her desire of him, and for just a moment, she allowed herself to revel in it. They slept on the couch in her family's apartment, a blanket warming their bodies. The others had gone back to the fabric shop, but Reid had stayed. Her magic leaked onto her hands as her throat tightened. How many nights had she wished for this? How many times had she shivered on the floor of the Mekës prison picturing herself just as she was now? Safe. Warm. Loved.

She took in the lightless rugs, how no rays of early morning sun broke through the curtains, and let out a small breath of relief. The stillness of the night drenched every corner of the apartment, and the fire continued, a churning red and orange glow visible in the coals. Burned, but not out. Vaasa gingerly turned in Reid's arms, prepared to bury her face into the crook of his neck and just lie there, when she felt him stir. His eyes opened softly and met hers.

"You should sleep more," Reid whispered, his hand stroking her side. Touching her with reckless abandon, perhaps simply because he could. "It's only been a few hours."

"I don't sleep well at night," she confessed.

It was a jagged truth. The hours between midnight and dawn made her restless. She couldn't remember the last time she had slept soundly through them. There was such tender worry in the crease between his brows.

The sight of it summoned something unfamiliar in Vaasa, and despite herself, tears sprang to her eyes. She'd grown up in an apathetic city; no warmth lingered here. So when she looked upon comfort, she still didn't entirely know what to do. That much of her hadn't changed. She remembered the false words she'd spun to Roman in the prison, the subtle insinuation that she wanted him, and all the lies she told added up to a dagger at her own neck.

Roman's betrayal wounded her somewhere deep. She was still trying to wrap her head around the fact that he'd been working for Lord Vlacik—that he'd been in Mekës before Vaasa had even left for Icruria. No matter what he claimed, it meant he'd only come back in pursuit of her throne.

After he'd been sent to the northern Asteryan border, the memories of him had become dark around the edges—she'd forced them to be. But there were times she had taken solace in the idea that even here in Mekës, a glimmer of love could be found. She'd clung to it, and he'd proven her wrong.

She squeezed her lids shut to try and dismiss her impending tears, but they wouldn't leave. The weight of sadness racked her ribcage, and the resilience she'd tried to carry started to chip away.

It wasn't that she loved him. It was that the final piece of brightness here had turned against her, had twisted into something terrible.

"Let it out," Reid whispered while his hand skimmed up and down her side in a subtle attempt to calm her.

One rogue tear slid down her cheek. She hated that she felt this way. Her magic churned with the ferocity of the Iron Bay, like waves curling in on themselves and crashing against her insides.

"Reid, I need to tell you something," she whispered into the dark.

He was still beside her, but not rigid. "Then tell me."

"I told you once of a man I loved when I was younger, a man Dominik had killed."

Reid let out a breath. "Roman."

"Yes," she said reluctantly. She sat up just a bit, her hair falling around her face as she met his gaze. "He's . . . alive. He's my lead sentinel. He was working for Vlacik, for those pirates."

Reid didn't move. He only stared up at her, never breaking their gaze. And then he said, "Back home in Mireh, I would have waited years more to have you. There were only two things that would have ended my pursuit. If you told me you did not love me, or if you told me you loved someone else."

Vaasa's throat tightened to the point of pain, the ball of her emotions lodged there. Another tear slid over her cheek.

"So tell me now, because I value your truth, and because I always want you to live in it. I am not a man you ever need to lie to."

"You are the only person I love." She dropped her forehead to his, closing her eyes. Relishing in the closeness of him. "I want to be your wife, of my own free will, of my own volition. Not for salt, not for freedom, not for anything other than the unalterable truth that I am yours until I cease to pull breath."

A part of Vaasa knew she was going to fall apart, that there were details they should try to fit together and potential outcomes they should anticipate. But she was so tired of living in what this city made of her, of spending all day in her own mind. "Please," she begged into the minimal space between where her lips ended and his began. She crossed that distance, pressing her mouth to his, lifting her hands to run over his shoulders. She needed this—to be touched in a way that was not menacing, to be close to someone she knew would not put a knife through her back. To be the version of herself she so desperately wanted to be. The version of herself that was his. "Tell me you still want that, too. That in the end, it's just you and me. That you will want me beyond your ten years as headman, that you will need me for more than power."

Without a hint of hesitation, Reid rolled so that he was above her, one leg on either side of hers. He kissed her so gently it bordered on torturous. She didn't want gentle. She didn't want kind. This place sharpened each of her corners, and she couldn't even protect herself from it. Her magic churned in her abdomen and melded with a kindling heat, the taste of Reid heady on her tongue. It was all she could do to ground herself now—to smother this pain with the feel of him, to sate this longing with his taste. "Of course I want more," he whispered against her lips. "You are not the blood of war. You are everything that happens after for me."

Anything she had ever felt for another dwindled into smallness. It paled in comparison to the enormity of what this man summoned from the depths of her—something she'd thought she would never once feel.

That she could trust every piece of her being with another.

That she wanted to.

Vaasa was greedy with her hands as she slipped them under his shirt. She kissed him so desperately, she thought she would be lost. Her nails scratched the hard muscles of his stomach. She wanted to drag her teeth along them, a thought that ignited more passion in her body. Fire blazed in her core, and she couldn't believe how her desire consumed her. She bit his lower lip, and a sound emanated from the back of his throat, tongue sweeping through her lips to tease her. The intensity of everything she'd experienced speared through her, and she couldn't contain it anymore. Her fingers dug into the skin of his back as she clawed at his shirt's hem, trying to haul it off him.

Reid lifted enough for her to accomplish her task, his eyes going alight with the sight of her being so wanton. He grabbed ahold of her leg and maneuvered it so he was entirely between her thighs, looming above her, strong hands coasting over her hips and up to where her blouse tucked beneath her breeches. She stared up at his half-naked form with nothing short of reverence. The sculpted lines of him looked just as she remembered, only accentuated in the dim firelight. She caught sight of the small bite mark she'd left on his shoulder during their last encounter, and it sent a thrill through her. The strength sewn into his broad muscles reminded her of the way he worked oars upon Icrurian ships, the way he could lift her with ease onto his desk in the High Temple, how she'd been so fucking foolish not to take advantage of every opportunity to have him that she'd been presented. All that time wasted.

"What are you thinking?" he asked softly, his hands hovering above her stomach with the hem of her untucked shirt balled in his fist.

She bit her lower lip. "I should have fucked you on our wedding night."

A smile formed on his face. "Oh, Wild One," he laughed, pulling up on her shirt so she had no choice but to arch her back. His mouth dipped to linger just above her breast, his eyes looking up to meet hers. "If you had let me fuck you on our wedding night, you never would have left."

He kissed her through her shirt then, teeth grazing over her nipple, leaving the fabric wet. He'd done this to her on the Settara as they made their way to Dihrah, just days before the election, just days before everything was lost. Vaasa dug her fingers into his hair, needing to be reminded that he was real. He was here for her. "You sound awfully confident," she said.

"I am," he insisted. His teeth grazed over her covered breast again. "You want to know why?"

"Why?"

His voice hummed along her skin. "Because you aren't the only one who's good with knots." With one hand, Reid pulled her shirt over her head until the fabric was bunched on her arms and twisted, causing the sleeves to tighten around her wrists. Before she could register what he was doing, he looped the shirt onto the decorative arm of the couch, sliding it between two thick crevices of wood so the fabric was secured behind her head. She pulled, but she couldn't release herself. Her arms were trapped.

Vaasa's breath hitched, and her eyes went a little wide. Faintly, she felt the cool mist of her Veragi magic as it played on her bound wrists.

Reid smiled like the devil. "You're at my mercy now."

Vaasa could hardly breathe. Reid lowered his head to her now naked breast and took her nipple into his mouth, sucking until she let out a small gasp. He switched to the other side, flicking his tongue until she squirmed. Vaasa let her low moan unleash, finally alone with him, finally able to make whatever sound she wanted. His lips brushed the sensitive skin of her neck, hands roaming along her shoulders. His eyes roved over everywhere he touched, fingers brushing the base of her neck.

Faintly, she realized he was inspecting her—going slowly in order to look for wounds. Scars. He was going to find them. Yet she couldn't stop herself from arching into his touch. His breath was so warm. Her collarbones, the swell of her breasts, each of her shoulders—and then he paused.

His fingers ran over the slightly raised lines on her upper arms where Lord Vlacik had cut her. Such fine, delicate work that man had accomplished with a blade. Reid's eyes met hers, and she shook her head. He had to know she wasn't able to handle those memories. That they needed to stay buried.

"You want to forget?" he asked in that low voice of his, somewhere between a growl and a plea.

"Everything except you," she confessed.

"Hmm." His lips pressed hungrily to her collarbone again in a way that told her he would oblige her. That despite his innate ability to cut right to the center of things, he had no intention of pushing her now. His thumbs scraped over her nipple, his mouth following, the warmth an indication of his desire to take away her pain. He was giving them both what they wanted: her an escape, him an assurance.

His fingers hooked into her breeches, and he tugged them down her hips. She lifted herself from the soft cushion of the couch, and then they were off, tossed to the floor. Sitting on his knees, Reid took in the view of her body beneath his. His eyes snagged on the shirt that still bound her to the couch. To the subtle outpouring of magic that Vaasa assumed had swallowed the entire wooden arm where he'd secured her blouse. His large hands rested on her bent knees.

"Perhaps I should keep you right here," he said. "It's an awfully tempting view."

Vaasa licked her lips, anticipation and heat swirling in her lower abdomen and blazing between her thighs. From this angle, he looked more powerful than she had even fantasized. There was something intoxicating about being at his whim, yet an unexplainable trust wound between them; he would not hurt her. He had always paid attention to the signals of her body, and with the way he watched her every twitch, she knew he was doing so now.

His hands gripped more tightly on her knees, and then he spread her legs wider, watching her expression closely. She breathed heavier. Vaasa closed her eyes, but he tsked, squeezing her legs. "You're going to watch what I do to you. Otherwise, I would have covered your eyes, too."

Vaasa's lids flew open, and she met his demanding, hungry gaze. She had known he would be good, that the sex would only serve to make her want him more, but she hadn't expected this. Their first night together, he'd been cautious with her. He hadn't revealed the darker truths of his desires and the way their intimacy had the opportunity to develop. It was as if their time apart had sped it up; in the wake of their urgency, he was taking what he wanted with abandon.

"Then stop waiting and show me something worth watching," Vaasa teased. She tugged at the blouse, testing its grip.

Amusement danced in his features as he ran a hand up the inside of her leg, fingers brushing against the panties that covered her. He swept over them, her skin beneath the fabric incredibly sensitive, and there was something heady about the almost touch. His head lowered to the inside of her knee, his mouth brushing her bare skin. "What is it you want to see, Wild One?" he asked just before he grazed the inside of her thigh with his teeth. "Tell me."

The words bubbled up in her, an unexpected shyness accompanying them. But when he stopped sweeping his thumb over her panties and his lips paused their descent, she knew he would go no further without instructions. "Your head between my thighs is a good place to start," she whispered.

He grinned. Slowly, he worked her out of her panties, pulling them off with a tug. Spreading her legs again, his mouth continued up her thigh. "Like this?"

Her body hummed in anticipation. "Yes," she breathed softly.

Warm breath coasted over her center, and Vaasa's chest rose and fell at a quicker pace. Desire coursed in her veins with every time he almost tasted her, his teeth dragging against her hip bone and down to her thigh again. She struggled against the blouse tying her wrists, the uselessness of that feat only making her excitement rise.

He peeked up through his lashes. "Remember what I said. Eyes on me."

Vaasa nodded, panting now.

Reid pressed his tongue to her core, and Vaasa practically bucked; she was so sensitive now. He pressed an arm to her waist and held her locked against the couch as his warm tongue slid along her. Seeing him pleasure her was one of the most maddeningly sexy things she'd ever seen, and it became easy to comply with his wishes that she watch. Vaasa let out a desperate moan, arms straining at the confinement, her hands balling into fists as heat spread in her abdomen. He kept his ministrations, hastening the speed, flicking his tongue in an unrelenting rhythm. Using his body, he spread her legs wider until they were hooked over his shoulders. He groaned into her with hot breath. His tongue worked her, every muscle in her body ricocheting against the other. She moaned his name, and his free hand dug into her hip. She rose for him, climbed so high. It felt so good, so right, so—

Release shattered through her, and her body lurched forward, the arm of the couch creaking so much she thought she'd break it. But then she sank back into the cushions, and a vulnerably loud beg fell from her lips. "More, please, Reid, please—"

Before she could finish her sentence, he tugged down his breeches and spread her legs again. He entered her in one swift thrust, and she arched off the couch at the fullness. Reid met her gaze, and his eyes darkened. Lust drenched his face.

A dirty thrill went through her. She held tightly to the blouse around her wrists. She'd always heard he was ruthless, violent, a warrior. She hadn't seen him reveal that part of himself fully. Maybe he thought that was what she needed. But it wasn't; she needed the unrelenting one, the merciless one, the man who took what he wanted.

She held his gaze and said, "I want you to fuck me like you wanted to that night I put a knife to your throat. Punish me for having ever left your side."

He loosed a low sound of approval and then pulled out of her. His hands grabbed ahold of her hips and spun her until her breasts pressed into the warm couch. He pulled her up to her knees, forcing her to arch her back, her hands still bound in front of her. One of his hands grabbed her ass while the other held tightly to her hip. He used his knee to spread her wider, and then he buried himself inside her in one stroke, his body slamming into her backside.

Vaasa moaned his name into the cushion and he thrust into her, *hard*. He did it again, and again, and again, and she went dizzy with pleasure as it built in her core. He leaned over her, his chest pressed to her back, his breath warm against her ear as he worked in and out of her. "Do you know how many times I've wanted to have you like this? To fuck you from behind?" His fingers dug into her waist, gripping her to the point of pleasurable pain. "Even when I wasn't supposed to. It took every ounce of my self-control not to bend you over that couch you insisted sleeping upon."

Thrill flooded her veins, the thought of him doing just that a once unspeakable fantasy.

"But I am so tired of being patient, Wild One," he growled. "You are *mine*."

Vaasa cried into the couch, pleasure barreling down her spine. "Reid, Reid—"

A throaty moan broke through his lips as he thrust into her again, and it summoned an inextinguishable excitement. Especially when one of his hands gripped the knots that kept her arms secured. He slid the knot off the arm of the couch, releasing her, and forced her to lift until his chest pressed to her back. He was so deep inside her she thought she'd orgasm for him right there, but then one hand snaked up to her throat and wrapped around it tightly.

"Is this what you need?" he asked. "To know I'm losing myself inside of you?"

Vaasa whimpered, the sound of his voice doing unfathomable things to her. *This*. This was what she wanted. Needed. There was so much pent up inside her—he was a safe place to let herself loose. "Touch me," she commanded.

He nipped her ear. His free hand slipped between her legs, and he played with her, thumb circling her core over and over as he thrust in and out, his other hand remaining possessively on her throat. He hit that spot inside her again and *again*. The feel of him sent lightning up her body, and she squeezed around the length of him.

"You're going to come for me again, aren't you?" Reid asked.

"Yes," Vaasa moaned. "*Yes*."

"Then do it," he commanded. "I want to feel you nice and tight."

Heat spread from her abdomen out, her entire body going taut as she found that release he demanded of her. A second orgasm washed over her, and this time she didn't muffle her desperate cries of satisfaction that melded into his name. He rode her through it, wringing every ounce of pleasure he could from her body. He held her pinned against him, and he thrust harder, his body racking with his own release. His hand dropped from her throat, and for a moment he just held her, the two of them breathing deeply.

He pulled out of her, and they cleaned themselves up, escaping to the nearest bathing chamber.

"Just another hour of sleep," she whispered, curling up on the couch again with Reid.

He pulled her back against his chest, resting her in the crook of his body, and ran his fingers through her hair. "It's all right. No one can find us here."

Without another word, sleep took Vaasa under.

CHAPTER
30

Exhaustion beat through Reid in a way it hadn't since he was young and traveling with his father through eastern Icruria. During his conscripted time in the Icrurian Central Forces, he had charted hundreds of waterways at his father's side. Sometimes, the work required sleepless nights in the tumultuous, undiscovered branches of the river. Even then, in the darkness, he'd had a beacon that made the impossible seem possible: his father. Here in Mekës, another uncharted terrain with far more twists and turns than the rivers Reid had conquered, he was without that beacon. He had been for years now. Timeless years, changeless years, ambitiously empty years. In the past few months, that light had become the woman he sent back down a shadowy corridor.

Back to another man. To a pirate, to the nemesis of someone Reid had just begun to trust. He had to tell Sachia; it was another enemy they shared, another chance to solidify their loyalty to each other. Their aims were the same once again.

Reid tried not to consider the extent of it. He didn't know what had plagued Vaasa upon discovering the love of her youth still alive, but if he let himself linger on the thought of Roman too long, his rage would become untamable.

His fear.

The main square was only a few blocks away from the apartment, and at this time, it was bustling with the people who worked the local mercantile. He blended into that crowd easily. Just another few blocks away, the port released the last of the morning ships into the bay for their fishing expeditions or welcomed back the merchants who had only just arrived. He swore this city never slept, even if its streets always felt cold and lifeless. Such an antithesis to the world he had grown up in. While Mireh was always full of people who stayed out late or frequented the establishments on the Settara, they were friendly. It was a way to spend their free time. Here, it was only work that pulled people from their beds. It made walking unseen through the crowds easier than expected—no one met each other's eyes or acknowledged their neighbors.

Reid turned the corner to the fabric shop and halted.

The street was swathed in blue. City guards created a pool of coats that surrounded the fabric shop, and every instinct Reid had spent his life honing kicked into gear. He kept his hood pulled up, thankful for the dusting of snow that made it practical, and folded his body into the crowd that stood watching the event. Someone was dragged from the shop. All Reid got was a glimpse of brown hair and spectacles.

It was Koen.

His stomach folded in on itself. Reid closed his fists, counting the guards that surrounded Koen, considering any path he could take through the crowd in order to reach him. There was no way. He would be outnumbered in seconds, dead within minutes. He considered himself a strong fighter, but there were at least ten men surrounding Koen.

His only option was to go in the back. To see if there was any way to save his mother.

Reid sprinted, aiming for the alleyway at the back of the row of buildings that contained the fabric shop. Snow crunched beneath his boots. He couldn't even feel the cold. As he turned down the ally, someone burst through the back door.

Blond hair, terrified jade green eyes.

"Mom." Reid skidded to a stop in front of her, hands gripping her shoulders while he inspected for wounds.

"Sachia is in the basement," his mother gasped, grabbing Reid's arms. "She forced me to run—she wouldn't let me use my magic."

Reid couldn't explain the relief that barreled through him, the sheer gratitude. If his mother had wielded magic, every cover they had would be at risk.

"We have to go back for her," his mother demanded.

Reid threw open the door, and they plunged into the back of the fabric shop, to the very last row of tall spools. The fabric shielded them from anyone's view, but the shop was eerily quiet. There was a small hallway and a set of stairs that led to the basement, and Reid raced to the door, his mother hot on his heels. He heard a voice behind it, and ever so quietly, he turned the knob. He slid through it, tiptoeing down the hallway that would lead to the main basement room, pulling a knife from inside his warm coat.

There were only two voices, and they spoke Icrurian. Like Sachia wanted one of their group to understand what she was saying.

Sachia's voice came panicked, quick. "I don't know what you're talking about."

"Don't play stupid," a man's voice spat. Not anyone Reid had heard before, but his Icrurian words were thick with an Asteryan accent. "Answer me. Are you doing business with the heiress?"

Reid inched down the hallway, his heart in his throat.

"Yes," Sachia confessed.

Reid's stomach lurched. With a look to his mother, he slid to the edge of the hallway, just enough to peer into the room, hoping with everything he had that the man wasn't facing him. Ready to pounce if the man was.

Sachia was pressed to the wall, the man's hand wrapped around her throat, a blade pressed to her abdomen. Reid couldn't see anything but the man's back, swathed in a blue coat, but he recognized his stature and the short cut of his brown hair.

Roman. It had to be. It was the same man who had dragged Vaasa out of the brothel.

Reid tightened his grip on his knife, fury boiling his blood. He couldn't kill the man—not if it meant ruining their chances of getting to Amalie and to Sachia's brother.

Roman pulled Sachia forward and then slammed her into the wall. She gave a small grunt of pain.

"Is Reid of Mireh in the city?" the man demanded.

"No," Sachia swore.

"Then why does Karev believe he is?"

Desperation rode every word Sachia choked out. "*I don't know.*"

"What did she hire you to do?" Roman asked.

"I was supposed to sell Karev black powder; the heiress helped broker the deal."

The man paused. He leaned in closer to Sachia, his knife still pressed to her throat. "Do whatever she says, or you and your brother are dead." He sheathed his knife and threw Sachia to the floor with a slam. Reid backed into the hallway to avoid being seen, but he listened carefully. His mother stood at his side, quiet as a mouse, her hand on his arm.

Roman's boots sounded on the floor, the stairs, and then the door to the main part of the fabric shop slammed.

Reid jumped out from the hallway and rushed to Sachia, his mother right behind him. Sachia's eyes went wide with relief, but she clutched her throat. "I didn't—" she gasped down breath. "I didn't tell him anything, I swear. That man works for—"

"I know," Reid said shakily. "Vaasa told me last night."

"Are you all right?" Melisina whispered.

"I'm fine." Sachia curled in on herself in a way Reid had never imagined her doing. Desperation seemed to physically weigh down her spine as she pulled her legs to her chest and rocked. "We need to leave this city, Reid. Everything Vaasa has planned, it needs to be moved up. Roman knows who I am, and he'll sell me out to Sutherland."

"Why did they arrest Koen?" Reid asked.

It was his mother who spoke, ancient rage threading her soft voice. The kind of anger that promised retribution. "Because they thought he was you."

CHAPTER 31

Vaasa wore all black.

With a gossamer veil covering her face and silk gloves up to her elbows, she entered the city's mausoleum. Roman hadn't taken her here himself, but it was no matter. One of the other sentinels had arrived, and with him, a carriage.

Though the sun still shone outside, the mausoleum was dark, save for the ever-present glow of candlelight and the kaleidoscope of color cast upon the floor by stained glass windows. The black granite building itself was stark against the city's landscape, statues that had caused Vaasa to shiver when she was younger carved into the front face. Her footsteps echoed on the stone floor. It was entirely empty of staff or visitors; the fortress sentinels had seen to that.

She stared up at the single statue that guarded her Asteryan ancestors' resting place. Looming in the center of the arching entryway, large wings burst from the back of an otherwise human figure who bowed their head in prayer. Andrej Kozár, the first of her family line to hold the Asteryan throne, and the man her father was named after. His ashes were incorporated directly into the stonework she gazed upon now, the custom a remnant of the old coastal kingdom of Asterya before her grandfather expanded to Mekës. They burned the bodies then, and the most important of figures were enshrined within the limestone the Asteryans used to mine before her grandfather plucked iron out of the mountains. It was he who insisted on a change in tradition; his sarcophagus remained at the highest point in the room, the first of their line to be preserved instead of burned.

And on the step below him, side by side, were the next: her father and her mother.

And the step below them, her brother.

Vaasa stared at the sarcophagi. The space next to her brother was not filled, having been reserved for his wife who never came to be. Dominik had avoided the possibility of an official heir for most of his life, undoubtedly afraid that the moment that child was born, there would be another who could usurp him.

More importantly, there was no space reserved for Vaasa. It was expected that she be laid with her husband elsewhere, and if she never married, she supposed she would have burned like the old Asteryans. Perhaps turned into the most useless of statues. Even in death, she would be apart from her family. Relegated to the periphery because she was a tool, never an inheritor. She realized it was only if she married Lord Karev that she would be laid to rest on the step below the rest of her family. Her only path to eternity in this room was a marriage to another.

The thought made her blood boil. Made her wish to topple Andrej's guardian statue and let the candles light the tapestries decorating the wall. In her mind's eye, she watched smoke fill the room. Watched the stained glass shatter from the heat and the stones crumble. Finally engulfed. Finally returned to the fire the way the old Asteryans had once mourned their dead.

Magic crept along the floor around Vaasa's feet, the black mist leaking from her hands, and she didn't bother to contain it. She wanted it to spoil the sanctity of the room. Wanted it to coat every surface.

Her footsteps echoed as she crossed the threshold past Andrej's statue. She climbed each platform using the stairs that split the center, all the levels empty until the top. She slowed next to Dominik's sarcophagus, unable to gaze upon it closely. Yet her magic hummed. It spilled from her in large waves of black that rose and fell like smoke, the force skittering over Dominik's resting place. She swore she heard her power hiss. Guilt twisted her stomach, and it didn't matter how much she told herself there had been no other choice; his journal flashed behind her eyes. It was a dichotomy—her memory of him and those drawings. It assigned him both beauty and violence, leaving her somewhere caught in the middle.

She took the next step, and then the next. Magic licked the stone beneath her feet. She landed upon her parents' level and swore her heart lurched in an attempt to escape her own chest. She had never come here, not even after her mother's demise. She couldn't bring herself to.

Vaasa turned, gazing down upon her mother's resting place. A large stone box, the lid and sides decorated with etchings of snowdrops. They covered the stone in long, twirling vines. Carefully, Vaasa ran her fingers over them, tracing some of the tangles. Tendrils of her magic kissed the stonework.

Gripping the lid, she pushed with all her might, just as she'd seen Dominik do in the vision Veragi had showed her. The stone creaked with the slide of the lid, and Vaasa's magic ducked into the crack it made. There was a coldness on the edges of it that almost made Vaasa stop, a distinct sensation of terror that climbed up her throat.

But she pushed until her mother's preserved face was revealed. Those sharp features, enshrined precisely as they had been when Vaasa found her in that hallway. Cheeks sunken, just a collection of skin and bones. She dropped her eyes to her mother's neck, and there it was: the necklace. Dainty iron links that were bound to a raw, black gemstone in the center, the rough edges of which made it seem as though it had been broken off from a larger part. The necklace had been draped upon Vena's delicate throat. Vaasa eyed the clasp.

Tentatively, she reached for it. Her fingertips brushed the iron, and she gasped as every ounce of magic in her body winked out. Like it had with the ropes they had bound her with beneath the colosseum and the chains they had used on her in the prison. The same ones still encircling Amalie's wrists and throat.

Vaasa pulled her hand back. Magic flooded her body once more, and she could feel *everything*. This was how her mother had stifled her magic. How Vena Kozár had gone years without being discovered as the witch she was. She had used this chain to block her own connection to Veragi.

The hours Vaasa had spent bound beneath the colosseum in Dihrah had been excruciating enough. The weeks in the prison without her magic had driven her to the point of hallucinations. Yet her mother had to have worn this every day for *years*.

Vaasa stared wide-eyed at the stone in the center of the necklace. It was a strangely alluring gem, the onyx color so black it swallowed all the light around it. Despite herself, Vaasa reached for the necklace again, hissing when she touched the chain. She quickly undid the clasp and pulled the necklace from her mother's body.

The moment she did, color crept from the top of Vena's head, glittering black, coating her face and neck and shoulders. Right before Vaasa's eyes, Vena Kozár turned to . . .

Stone.

What Vaasa stared down at was stone.

She reeled backward, panic cinching her chest as her hands covered her mouth to prevent a horrified scream. Still, Vena's body hardened to glittering onyx, veins of gold and silver running along what used to be skin. It was uncanny, the resemblance. The immediate connection to . . .

The statues in the greenhouse.

Vaasa's magic roared around her, released in a whipping wind as fear shot down the cords that bound her to Ozik. Cords that had felt distant these past two days, perhaps because they had been coated in her magic instead of his oily power. Vaasa approached the sarcophagus with bile churning in her stomach, her hand still on her mouth. She closed the lid, nausea climbing up the back of her throat.

Her other hand clutched the raw black gemstone of the necklace. Something shifted in her body.

The cords that bound her to Ozik twisted and tightened, and the energy from the pendant shot up her finger and arm. It filled her entire body with a power that was both familiar and new, a whisper of her own magic wrapped around Ozik's, her shadows and his oil mixing into something Vaasa had never felt before.

And then a story wrapped around her and pulled, plunging Vaasa into another vision, but this time . . .

She saw the world through Ozik's eyes.

CHAPTER 32

Two days before Ozik's Evocation, he crept through the thick forest outside the walls of the city of Wrultho, light on his feet, careful not to make a sound. He took one step. Two. Three.

A small squeal emanated from the sage green bush in front of him, and then Ellena sprinted out from behind it. Ozik cut to the right and chased her, careful to always be a step behind, until she burst through a wall of branches into their small, sacred clearing, marked in the center by a towering olive tree—the tallest in the area.

Ellena threw her small body against it, spreading her arms over the long trunk and squealing in delight.

"You are far too fast," Ozik told her as he feigned exhaustion, placing his hands on his knees and taking exaggerated deep breaths. Then he approached, running his hand upon his daughter's inky black hair, braided around her head in a coronet.

From their left, Ellena's mother Julianna emerged through a small path between trees, holding her shimmering black bow in her delicate fingers. With the other hand she clutched a rabbit, a small red stain upon its underbelly, a product of the arrows that Julianna had surely conjured. Her midnight hair fell from its containment in messy strands around her face, her cheeks blushed the same color he'd memorized from the first moment he met her. He wanted to make her blush like that again, to be the reason warmth coated her cheeks. Wrapped in a turquoise-blue dress, Julianna's bare feet were stained from the forest floor, and though that same dirt smeared along the side of her leg and even a small streak across her face, she was still the most beautiful woman Ozik had ever laid eyes on.

At her side, a slinking fox made of the same wisps of shadows as her bow curled around her legs, darting in and out of the tree line in playful gestures. The bow in her hands scattered to just licks of smoke on her wrists while Julianna's fox leapt into the air, dissipating on the wind into glimmering streaks of black.

Dark magic ran through Julianna's veins, one of shadows and smoke that could suffocate the very light out of a room. Because though she was sunshine, Julianna had always been eclipsed. She was born to the goddess Veragi, just as Ozik had been born to Zetyr.

Others called Julianna a curse, but to Ozik, she was a summoning.

He stepped toward her, but as he did, her eyes registered the movement. She stepped back. This was his plight: to love a woman greater than he'd ever known before, to be the father of her child, and still not have her.

Ellena ran to Julianna, and as she did, the rest of the world slipped into irrelevance. Ozik had known women all his life, but never in the way he'd known his daughter. Before he'd laid eyes on the tiny creature with his same liquid-gold eyes, he had known only one thing with certainty: The world was his for the taking. But upon knowing his child, the axis of that world shifted.

It was no longer his to take, but rather his to give.

Together, they sat beneath the olive tree while Ellena braided strands of wild grass with vivid pink flowers. Ozik fiddled mindlessly with the black stone embedded in his ring—an anchor to his Zetyr bloodline, the only surviving bloodline for generations. Zetyr witches had been hunted to extinction. No one knew how Ozik's father, Laus Vichardi—an imprisoned criminal, no less—had come to claim the magic. Laus had emerged from the catacombs beneath Wrultho with an anchor, a Zetyr talisman. Some said he'd made a deal with the devil, others said he had been chosen by the deities themselves. What they did know was that it was Ozik's mother, a witch who hailed from Ohros, the goddess of fate and sight, who had given Laus the ultimate bargain: her magic, in exchange for a son. It had given him a well of raw sentimental magic to draw from, and with it, Laus had vanquished the reigning Zuheia coven and conquered the city of Wrultho.

Yet Ozik had long learned that the *how* of things never mattered so much as the *why*.

And the why was simple: because of Ozik. For the Ohros witches had the gift of foresight, and his mother knew that to take this path was to deliver them all to greatness. It was on Ozik's thirteenth birthday when the Ohros witches confirmed his mother's vision and declared he would be the most powerful Zetyr witch in history. And on that day, his father had taken the enormous black stone anchor inlaid in his dagger and split it in three. One for him, one for his wife, and one for Ozik.

That was the first day he heard Zetyr's voice in his mind. He had heard it every day since.

As they watched Ellena weave, Julianna was quiet. There were times like these, where she seemed lost in her own mind, and then her eyes lifted to his. Bright light shone from behind her irises, a sign that her own goddess spoke in her mind. They were the same, her and him. *Divine*, born into a power unlike any other, a mouthpiece for their deity. Just as Ozik had heard the voice of Zetyr since his father gifted him his anchor, Julianna heard the voice of Veragi. She convened with the goddess daily.

The white light in Julianna's eyes dimmed, and she opened her mouth to speak, but then closed it.

"What is it?" he asked softly.

Julianna only shook her head. "We should go home."

Home, to the house Ozik had built for them outside the city walls, where the river met moss and wildflowers did not have to hide from insular men. Ozik looked at Ellena, who would never receive his Zetyr magic. Instead, she would inherit her mother's. It was the only reason Laus Vichardi had allowed the child to live; she was a girl, and that at least categorized her existence as a disappointment instead of a threat. The time Ozik could see Julianna and Ellena had grown shorter with every season; each year Ozik came closer to his Evocation, the less tolerant of a Veragi woman and a bastard child his father had become. Last year, his father had insisted the visitations cease altogether. He had demanded Ozik focus on more *permanent* things.

And so Ozik loved them in the shadows of the forest, beneath the leaves of an olive tree.

This half-life—it would all be over soon. When Ozik emerged from his Evocation and he had the complete anchor, Ozik would change every tile in his estate to suit their desires. The kitchen would shift, the rooms would overturn, the bathing chambers would be whatever colors Ellena declared.

Then he would marry Julianna. Somehow, he would convince her. He would honor her in the way she deserved for having brought Ellena into this world. Ozik didn't care if Julianna's magic marked her as cursed, if she would never offer him the same bargain his mother had offered Laus. Ozik would be strong enough. He was destined to be the most powerful Zetyr witch in history. There was a reason Zetyr spoke to him directly before he even inherited his magic.

"It's time," Julianna said, black mist curling around her fingertips as she brushed them over their daughter's shoulder. Ellena looked at Ozik with a somber lowering of her eyes. Goodbye did not suit either of them well. Still, she was an obedient girl, so Ellena rose from the grass and wandered, never farther than their hidden paths, her dainty hand dragging along the bushes and flowers. Ozik walked her to their home's gate just as her hand splayed toward a bush of white bell-shaped flowers.

Ozik blocked her fingers. "Tisel, dear, is more deadly than a blade. A quiet killer, quick as a breath."

Ellena's small hand shot back to her chest, the other curling around it. "Sorry, Papa."

"We're almost there," Julianna whispered, taking Ellena's arm and guiding her through the gate.

Ozik said goodbye to his daughter silently, with a shared look only they two could understand. When he looked at her like that, the world around them went silent. But then she slipped through the gate, and Julianna, too, and though his heart lurched to follow them, all Ozik could do was grip the bars and watch.

His guard sat atop a horse at the edge of the forest, faithfully awaiting Ozik's return.

"All is well?" his guard asked.

Ozik nodded.

They traveled through the mighty walls of Wrultho and back into the great city, going directly to the center where Ozik's family estate was built. More guards lined the perimeter of the great Zetyr stronghold, but in the throes of his historic Evocation, Ozik had already begun to plant a seed. The guards knew his father had an expiration date, and so he had slowly, inconspicuously turned them to his own needs. The men protecting this home would bleed for him—for Ellena and Julianna, too, when he commanded it. Because his father could be many things: a ruler, a witch, a king in his own right, but he could not be Divine, no matter how hard he tried.

When Ozik ambled back through the door of his father's estate, a part of him remained in that forest. *Two more days*, he repeated to himself. *Two more days.*

That evening at dinner, Ozik sat at his father's table with a renewed sense of possibility. Raucous laughter filled even the corners of the room as most of the inner city tried to squeeze into their grand dining hall. *Two more days*, Ozik continued to tell himself. Such words were enough that when his father cracked a joke with Ozik as the punch line, it merely rolled off his shoulders. Yet when someone else laughed a little too hard, they were met with the keen puncture of his father's stare; it was only the great Laus Vichardi who could mock his own heir. He boisterously told fables of his greatness, slouching in his chair and using exaggerated hand movements to add emphasis to his tales, the golden dagger containing his anchor strapped to his side. Behind him, his Miro'dag swayed back and forth, its crimson, beady eyes overlooking the entire room. The creature was a manifestation of Zetyr magic, a henchman that could do his father's bidding. Every sentimental witch could manifest one, even if they took different forms. For Julianna, it was a fox.

Sitting at his father's side, white hair falling down her back, was Ozik's mother. She smiled upon him, her golden eyes so similar to Ellena's. To his. At her neck was a dainty necklace, her small portion of their family anchor stark against her pale skin. In mere days, the dagger would be his for the wielding, the necklace his to bestow upon his own wife. Ozik would not waste his power the way his mother had, would not gallivant about the way his father did. He would do the very thing he had been born to, the thing Zetyr was leading him toward: He would unite the cities of Icruria under his name, under *his* bloodline. Wrultho would be but one city that bowed to the Vichardi line. That bowed to Zetyr. The magic-less rebels would have no footing then, and any coven who defied him would fall.

Ozik stood, walking around the room and mingling with their visitors. He preferred to stay close to the walls, to know what was at his back at all times. The room only grew fuller as dancing began, and Ozik wanted nothing to do with it. He stepped into the hallway, but a voice drawled from behind him.

"You reek of the forest."

Ozik turned to find his father standing there, gray eyes that matched his aging hair narrowed upon him. "What do you want, father?" Ozik asked.

Laus ambled forward, the guards standing at the door slipping into the main hall at Laus's gesture to do so. "Does she smell of dirt, too?"

Ozik's heart began to pound. Laus knew where he'd been that afternoon?

"Don't look so surprised," Laus said. "I see everything. I haven't given you my magic yet, Ozik."

This is the way it had grown between them; what was once a

prideful gaze in his father's eyes had soured. In many ways, Ozik had humiliated him when he'd come to Laus asking for shelter for Julianna and Ellena. Ozik was barely seventeen at the time Julianna's stomach had started to swell, and to bear a child with a Veragi witch was in itself an indignity. But Ozik knew the truth; it was not disappointment that had stolen the pride from Laus's gaze.

It was envy.

Every year they came closer to Ozik's Evocation, the more Laus saw his own life fade into irrelevance. Ozik had to pretend he did not want this family; to cast his daughter and the love of his life aside so his father would allow him to take their family's Zetyr magic *willingly*.

That was the key. Zetyr magic could only be passed down through a bargain from father to son. Once Ozik had it, he could do whatever he wanted with the power. And he knew what he wanted.

His father would rot in the river then.

"I have finalized your marriage agreement with Diana's family," Laus said. "We intend to announce it tonight. It's best you come inside."

Diana. An Ohros witch, just like Ozik's mother.

"She is willing to sacrifice her power?" Ozik asked, disbelief riding his words. "Her family wants that?"

Laus sneered. "You know how the sentimental magics can be, especially when inherited so young. Diana is wildly powerful, but she is capricious and cannot tell the difference between a hallucination and a vision. It is a favor to relieve her of her burden, just as it was for your mother."

Ozik scoffed. "And if I do not want to spend my days bedding a mad woman?"

"Have you not already bedded a mad woman? Given her a child?"

"You know nothing of what you speak," Ozik warned.

"No, Ozik, *you* know nothing. I have been patient enough with your ignorance. Your choice is simple. Come inside, accept the marriage agreement, and in two days' time, you will ascend to the position

I have created for you. Or I will rid us all of your bastard child and whore witch, and you will inevitably do as I say anyway."

Ozik grit his teeth, his anger a scorpion, his righteousness the stinger.

"Your mother is waiting," Laus said before he turned and opened the doors.

The raucous crowd screamed and stomped their feet as Ozik followed his father into the room. As Diana, with her tight emerald-green dress and wild blond ringlets, stepped forward to meet him. Ozik looked into her cloudy eyes, and her brows twitched, the smallest furrow. And then her irises cleared, whatever vision she had just seen gone to her now.

Ozik danced with Diana, his hands heavy. His father watched on with an expression that was never quite satisfied, but his rage had quelled at Ozik's compliance.

And then when the night was coming to an end, his mother walked him to his room. Nimble fingers unlatched the necklace at her neck, and she placed the links in his hand, curling his fingers around the small portion of the black stone anchor. The smallest of the three pieces. "I know it is two days early, but give this to Diana when you are ready," she whispered. "It will . . . help her, as it has helped me."

His mother squeezed his hands and then left him standing there.

And Zetyr's voice floated through his mind, ancient and all-knowing. *Your future is yours, Divine. Do not give your power away so callously.*

Will this protect her from my father?

That is a piece of me, the voice said. *Its wielder carries my strength and protection.*

Ozik stared down at the necklace, his fist tightening around it once more. And he knew what he needed to do.

As the afternoon sun started its descent to night, the last that Ozik would ever have to wait, he met Ellena and Julianna in the same place at the edge of their home. Julianna wore a long dress, only offering a glimpse of her legs for Ozik to feast upon. Something in him stirred; she had always had that effect upon him. When she was near, he could practically *taste* magic.

After five rounds of hide-and-seek, Ellena sat with her legs curled beneath her, her small fingers diligently braiding together pieces of grass while she caught her breath. Once more, she wove in small, pink flowers. Her black hair was braided away from her face in that unique way Julianna always accomplished, and her golden eyes stayed entirely focused upon her task. Julianna crouched in front of Ellena. "Go inside, dear. It's time to say goodbye."

Obediently, Ellena stood and bid Ozik goodbye, another sorrowful moment that Ozik would put an end to in just a day. Ozik wrapped his hands around the bars of the gate surrounding their house. Ellena shimmied through, but before she darted into the house, she reached back and pressed something into his palm.

It was the bracelet she had woven the day prior, the little pink flowers tied securely by small knots of grass.

"For you," Ellena said, then she disappeared into the home.

Ozik's eyes began to water.

This time, Julianna didn't follow Ellena directly inside. She halted by the gate, waiting until Ellena had shut the door and could no longer hear them. Squeezing her eyes shut, Julianna took a breath, but her dark power leaked onto her hands. She shook them, trying to rid herself of it, but it only grew.

"Dearest," he whispered, tucking Ellena's bracelet into the pocket of his cloak and capturing Julianna's hands in his own. Her black mist crawled along his skin. He didn't recoil the way others did. He liked how it felt on his skin. He wanted to taste it. To taste her. To steal away whatever caused such turmoil tonight. "What is it?"

"I went into the city today," Julianna whispered low. "I heard about your engagement."

Ozik kept his expression neutral. "It is not what it seems."

Julianna knew well enough that Ozik needed to marry someone

eventually. That he had been a man of great power with a fate as sealed as the catacombs beneath their city, at least until she had unraveled it. When he'd finally taken her to his bed, it was the first time he had felt that his life was his own for the shaping. That the prophecies were true, and that he could have anything he wanted because of it.

The flickers of Julianna's magic were enough to tell Ozik she was on edge. That her emotions were running too high. He couldn't help the way he bloomed at the idea that this bothered her.

That she didn't want him to marry someone else.

Her midnight-blue eyes watered. She squeezed them shut, then looked away from him. "I'm leaving. I'm taking Ellena with me."

"What?" Ozik barely processed the words.

"She isn't safe. Not from your father, not from anyone. Veragi has told me to go. It's time, Ozik."

Ozik stiffened. "Stop. Tomorrow, I will become the most powerful witch in the city. The most powerful witch on the continent. The Ohros witches have said so."

Julianna took back her hands, and the loss of her skin against his left him cold. "And with all of that power will come a host of enemies. People who will take her from us both in an attempt to harm *you*. A wife who will carry an undying vengeance at you having a child with someone else. With someone like me."

"I dare them to try," Ozik snarled. "And I told you, it is not what it seems. I have no intention of marrying that woman."

Julianna wiped a stray tear from her face. Steeled her expression in that unfathomable way of hers. The strongest woman he had ever known. "Ellena cannot be fodder in the cross fires of your future. Surely you know that."

Ozik shook his head. Reaching out, he gripped the gate just so he would have something to hold on to. "You can't go anywhere; I won't allow it."

Juliana tilted her head, dark magic swirling up her arms in menacing threads of black. "You have always been bold, Ozik, but never so painfully wrong."

The pulses of her magic filled the space around them. Julianna didn't take kindly to his commands, not in the early days of knowing her or any of the days that followed. Perhaps that was part of the allure—she was not like his mother, or Diana, or any other woman he had known.

"Go," she demanded. "The sun is setting."

"Jul—"

"I said *go*," she snapped. Her magic flew from her in tendrils, a warning if Ozik had ever seen one. He had not known Julianna at her lowest, but if it was anything like the other Veragi witches he'd read about, he didn't want to be near her if she lost control.

But he also didn't want to send her back to their daughter like this.

Julianna turned and walked toward the house. Ozik touched the necklace in his pocket. She could see reason if he just showed her his version of the future. The things he knew that the Ohros witches did not. The truths that they could never see, because they lived inside Ozik.

"Marry me," Ozik said.

Julianna stopped in her tracks, just in front of the house. She wrapped her handwoven shawl around her shoulders tighter, staring at him like she wasn't sure she heard him correctly.

"Marry me," Ozik said again. He couldn't help himself. He walked through the gate and up the pathway to the house, giving her all the time she needed to back away.

But she didn't.

Ozik swept a strand of hair away from Julianna's eyes, savoring the feel of his fingertips against her skin. She had never let him back in again, not after she'd learned she was with child. Seven years pulsed between them, and he had longed for her in every single one.

Julianna pulled away. "Don't. Don't say things you do not mean."

He caught her hand with his own, tugging her back to him. He used his free hand to pluck the necklace from his pocket and display it for her. "I mean it. I mean every word," he assured her.

There was a hardness to Julianna after what he'd put her through.

The way her life had been forced into a box of Ozik's making. She could not find work. She could not marry someone else. All she had was what he had given her, and his gut twisted when he thought of the consequences she paid for both their actions. He wanted so desperately to soften her once more.

And at the sight of the necklace, soften she did. Tentatively, she reached, running her finger along the links.

Any trace of the dark Veragi magic on her fingers and wrists disappeared. She gasped, pulling her hand back. "Ozik, what is that?"

"It is part of my family's anchor," he told her. "It binds you to me, and through me, to Zetyr. My god will protect you. If you wear this, my father cannot harm you."

Julianna's breathing sped up. "Ozik—"

"I mean it," he interrupted. "Don't leave. I don't think I will survive it. Take this, and then when I earn my father's magic, marry me."

She inspected the links of the necklace, the small black stone within it. The raw edges, the piece broken from a larger chunk. "When I touch it, I cannot feel my magic. It goes silent."

Ozik furrowed his brow and watched as Julianna's eyes lost focus, as a subtle white glow emanated from them. She came back to him almost instantly, her eyes lifting to his.

Something so unreadable crossed her features.

Her voice came out a whisper. "You cannot marry me. You need magic, Ozik. Someone to fuel your power."

He didn't understand or deign to guess what Veragi had just spoken to Julianna, but she wasn't running. She wasn't asking him to leave. He curled his fingers around the necklace and put it back into his pocket. "Then I will make it so. I will find someone willing, for surely I have something that they need. And until then, bargain with me." His hand brushed up her arm and curled to her waist, pulling her into him. She didn't push away.

And so he took a risk. "I will offer you a kiss for every one." He dropped his mouth to within inches of hers, almost kissing her, almost tasting her, until he pressed his lips to her neck. She sighed in his arms.

He trailed his finger along the curve of her ribcage, up to the neckline of her dress. He drew a line where the fabric met the skin of her breast just as his mouth brushed her ear. "A touch for each agreement we make."

She curled into him, her body loosening with each word. Her magic coasted around them in tendrils of black. With the skim of his fingertips along her collarbone, she shivered.

"Be my wife," he whispered again. "I will keep you both safe. We will give Ellena siblings. Brothers. Heirs. The most beautiful family this world has ever seen."

He had the distinct fear that she wouldn't believe him. That she would shirk his words and his intentions because that was the fair thing to do. It was what he deserved. In every way, he had failed her.

But not anymore.

His fingers curled around the nape of her neck, and he pulled back just enough to tilt her face up to his. Tears welled in Julianna's dark blue eyes, an admission of vulnerability he had not seen from her in years. "And if the city does not agree?"

"I am the city," Ozik told her. "And the people will fall to their knees."

She was at war; he could see it in the rise and fall of her breath, in the way her fingers curled tightly into his shirt.

"You have given me the world. Let me give you a lifetime," Ozik whispered.

At his words, she closed the space between their lips. Her mouth met his, and Ozik groaned low in his throat. He tangled his fingers into her hair. And he kissed her. He kissed her with seven years in the making, with the heat of every moment he'd looked upon her and could not have her. There was no comparable happiness. It did not get bigger than this moment. She fisted his shirt and pulled them to the door, their bodies pressing to the house he had built, until she fumbled with the knob, never breaking their mouths apart.

He gathered Julianna up in his arms, the feel of her body summoning a memory from so long ago. A memory of hope. Of need. Of breathless fate that could be molded into whatever Ozik wanted it to be. He would give anything for this woman. For their daughter. "Let me in again," he begged against her mouth. "Let me worship you like our gods intended."

She tugged him through the threshold, the two of them practically falling into the small house. Passing the hallway that led to Ellena's room and plunging straight into Julianna's on the opposite side. The four walls were small yet limitless—quaint, but more like home than he had ever felt on his vast estate. As he slowly peeled off Julianna's clothes, as he kissed every inch of her skin, he didn't care for the dead or the living or the concept of fate at all. He thought he could make it himself, as he always thought when he was with her.

And when he buried himself inside her, when she blushed at her nakedness and then moaned with her pleasure, he thought himself an oracle in his own right.

As they lay together, she turned in the crook of his body, his chest to her back. She swept the hair from the nape of her neck, making room for the necklace. An invitation, an agreement. As he latched the clasp, he pressed a kiss to where it settled on her neck.

"Say yes," he whispered into her hair. "Say you'll marry me."

And that look on her face when she finally gave herself over to him, when she whispered yes and agreed to the future he'd written, burned into his mind. The image held a place there, a home, unmoving and equally unforgiving, for the rest of Ozik's life.

CHAPTER 33

It was agony—absolute *agony* that pulled Vaasa from her vision of Ozik. The magic in her body twisted like chains around her organs, yanking in every different direction.

Get up, a voice snarled in her mind.

Her eyes flew open. She was lying on the smooth mausoleum floor, her fingers digging into the stone steps, coldness seeping into her bones. If she hadn't known better, she would think she was still in the prison. That everything until now had been some twisted, torturous dream that Ozik had sent her.

Reid wasn't real.

Melisina had never come.

There was no way out.

But it was still the mausoleum she stared at. The necklace lay inches from her hand. She must have collapsed. Her head was fuzzy, and it pounded with the increasing pain of whatever her connection to Ozik caused. She sat up, rubbing at her temples, taking in her surroundings once more. She stared down at the necklace on the floor, at the stark black stone in the center.

It was the same stone. The same piece of raw gem that she had just seen in that vision. Set in a different chain and pendant, sure, but the same anchor.

The creak of the mausoleum door opening caused Vaasa to tense. The statue of Andrej still guarded the room, yet there was movement just behind it. Something stirring in the shadows.

That movement forced her instincts into action, and Vaasa gripped the necklace and stuffed it into her pocket. The moment it no longer touched her skin, magic flooded her system once again. Vaasa gasped, pulling the dark tendrils back into her body with a heaving effort.

Footsteps echoed on the stone floors, and then a figure came into view. Dark hair and menacing gray eyes highlighted his attractive face, his mouth turned into a grimace.

Lord Karev.

"I've been looking everywhere for you," he said, tilting his head in that predatory way of his. "I was surprised to hear you were visiting your family's mausoleum when so much commotion was happening in the city."

Vaasa stood, her legs only slightly wobbly beneath her, and her magic hissed a warning in her ear. The cords that bound her to Ozik tugged again, and his voice whispered in her mind, *Do not let him know of your power.*

Vaasa almost lost her composure. *You . . . can hear me?*

Pay attention, he hissed.

Lord Karev started up the stairs that split the platforms of the mausoleum in half, his menacing grin growing wider as his eyes devoured the fear that certainly showed itself on Vaasa's face. Heart pounding, she considered the ways she could take to escape. He blocked the stairs, but she could jump from platform to platform if she kept her balance.

She stepped carefully to the side, traversing the top level, trying to casually open a path to the exit.

He followed, blocking any chance she had. "Before we go, I have a few questions."

Get out, Ozik said in her head.

Without hesitating, Vaasa bolted across the platform nearest her and jumped to the one below, careful with her weight distribution so she didn't slip on the slick floors. Lord Karev sprinted to the same side of the mausoleum, no sarcophagi in his way, all the levels below Dominik empty of burial monuments.

"A quick little heiress," he purred, jumping up to the next platform and closing in on her.

Vaasa turned and ran the other direction, leaping for the stairs as her only final option. She took them as quickly as she could, the skirts of her black dress threatening to tangle around her legs, and she saw the exit. Sprinted for it—

Lord Karev jumped into her path.

Vaasa's heart thudded in her chest, and her magic lurched in her stomach. She skidded to a stop. He was too close. She didn't stand a chance of escaping him, not unless she let loose her magic. It was an irrevocable decision to reveal her power—

The moment of hesitation cost her.

Lord Karev's hand whipped out and curled around her neck. Vaasa tried to scream, but he squeezed tighter, pressed harder, until he cut off her airway.

If there is any trust between us, let it be now, Ozik's voice rang in her mind. *Do not use your magic. He will kill you if he knows you are a witch.*

Panic sliced down her spine, and Ozik's words echoed in her ears like the chiming of a clock. Lord Karev pulled her against his chest, his free hand fisting in her hair and cranking her head back so it was pinned to his shoulder. "You've been keeping secrets, haven't you, Heiress?" Lord Karev snarled.

Vaasa's lungs screamed for air. Her body locked up. She clawed at his wrists, her nails digging into his skin. His hiss of pain came low as a sticky wetness trailed over her fingertips—blood. He kicked the back of her knees and she crumpled, waist slamming into the platform nearest her. Her ribs screamed in pain, but his grip on her throat was lost, and she sucked down air. Then he was on her, her arms locked against her body as he settled one knee on either side of her hips, baring his considerable weight on her lower back to keep her in place.

"The new warden of the prison had some *interesting* things to say about one of his inmates, someone your sentinel seems to visit often," Lord Karev said in her ear. "Why don't you tell me what you know about Icrurian magic?"

Vaasa's stomach turned over on itself. She used any last ounce of self-control to keep her power contained. The new warden of the prison, put in place at his behest—of course. It was a misstep. An utter miscalculation not to assume the next person in charge of the prison would quickly discover Amalie and her connection to Vaasa.

She thrashed what she could of her body, but Lord Karev fisted his hand in her hair again, pulling until a sharp pain spiraled across her scalp and she cried out.

"Did you know that Reid of Mireh was arrested this morning?" Lord Karev asked. "You've been playing me like a fucking fool, letting him masquerade as a salt lord all this time."

Vaasa stopped breathing of her own accord. Those words sunk claws into her, rattled her bones. Reid of Mireh, arrested. That was where Roman was. She was sure of it. Bile crept up Vaasa's throat. She was going to vomit.

It was over. Any leverage she had, gone.

Calm, Ozik willed her. *Keep calm.*

Ozik knew.

"Listen to me *very* closely," Lord Karev said, emphasizing his words. "You have feared for your life ever since Lord Vlacik's death. The moment you saw Reid of Mireh, you came to me like a good little heiress, and I summoned the city guard. You are going to watch his execution with a smile on your face, and in the name of strengthening Asterya for this war, we are going to appeal to the church for an expedited wedding. And then you are going to tell me every single thing you know about magic. Do you understand me?"

"Yes," she sputtered, her voice cracking.

"If you ruin this for me," he warned, low and deadly, "I'll hang you from the Sanctum myself. You and I could have been allies. I want you to remember that the next time you think about double-crossing me."

Vaasa stayed absolutely still, and to her relief, Lord Karev's weight lessened on her. He loosened his grip on her hair. His fingers left her scalp. Magic filled her body like a well, and she choked it back.

She should attack him. Kill him right where he stood. Vaasa rose from the smooth floor, shaking, and measured the space between them, wondering how many steps it would take to reach him, how much power would be necessary to choke him the way he had just choked her. Yet all that came was measured breath as her mind spun. Worked. As she did her best to survive this very moment as unscathed as she could.

If she let out her magic, she had no choice but to kill him, and there wasn't a soul in this city who would believe she hadn't done it. Not when it was only her and him in this mausoleum. They were looking for a reason to burn her at the stake. The city thought too much of her, the nobles too focused on the rumors they'd all whispered.

Power twisted in her gut, the cords that bound her to Ozik growing thicker, more menacing. They hummed with her rage. It all mixed in her body, the oil and the mist, the two power sources seeming to come alive. She felt him there at the other end, felt his power as if she could wrap her hands around it and pull.

As if it was hers to wield.

The door creaked. Vaasa whipped her head to the entrance. Roman sprinted in, looking more frantic than Vaasa thought possible. She held her ground, the fog of rage swirling in her mind.

His sword was drawn, and he looked between Lord Karev and Vaasa.

"Don't worry, Sentinel," Lord Karev drawled, his voice echoing through the stone chamber, far sturdier than before. "She turned in the Icrurian scum herself. She's been safe in this room with me while we waited for the city to clear."

Tears pricked at Vaasa's eyes, but she didn't say a word. She just stared at Roman. His gaze dipped to where she touched her neck. "Reid of Mireh was working with others," Roman confirmed, only speaking to Vaasa. Delivering a report not to the lord, but to her. "I'm told they fled the scene."

Sachia. Melisina. Koen. Vaasa couldn't dare ask for clarification. Only one thing was clear: Lord Karev had orchestrated the arrest. He had somehow put it together.

She'd been a fool to believe two Icrurians could stay hidden in this city for long.

Vaasa's chest rose and fell with her measured breaths. She had so little information, any assumption would be its own risk. Instead of spiraling, she schooled her features. The necklace in her pocket grew heavier. The tangled mess of magic in her body started to expand. She would need to play every second correctly if she intended to survive. If she had any chance of getting this necklace back to Amalie.

With a salacious grin, Lord Karev stepped toward her. Vaasa twitched.

Roman took note of it. And like every time before, he said nothing. He did nothing. Not even as Lord Karev gripped just above her elbow, fingers digging into her muscle sharply. What was meant to be a guiding touch quickly transformed into a drag, and Vaasa stumbled over her feet. He pushed open the doors, and cold wind slammed into Vaasa's face.

The moment they were in sight of the other sentinels, Lord Karev's touch softened, and he caressed up her bicep before strolling away to where his own carriage waited.

Vaasa filled her lungs with biting air, fuller with each step he took away from her. He climbed the stairs of his carriage. On the left, her own carriage waited, manned by two fortress sentinels. The same ones who had taken her and Roman back the other night.

Men who were loyal to Roman.

"Heiress," Lord Karev called, leaning out of his door with a tight grip on an iron handle.

Everyone around them turned to hear Lord Karev speak, and she understood the title to be a summoning. A demand. Vaasa halted, fist clenching. She lifted her eyes to meet his.

"I'm delivering our execution order tonight," he said. "The Wolf of Mireh loses his head tomorrow."

Our. Despite the rage that curled in her body, the sheer temptation to untether her magic and show this man what real power looked like, Vaasa nodded. She could kill every man in their vicinity. Could smother the breath from all their lungs. If she didn't find a way to escape, this was how she would spend the rest of her life.

Roman approached but kept a healthy distance, likely aware that any proximity in front of Karev was the quickest way to be dismissed. Somehow, in the span of a few days, the lord had situated himself as the holder of the crown. It didn't seem to matter that he wasn't legally emperor or that they weren't married—the moment this city was presented a nobleman with a semblance of a claim, they bowed.

Vaasa swallowed her fury. Longing burst through a dam within her; to be who she was before she'd come back here, to climb into Reid's bed, to feel the trickles of magic upon her skin. She wasn't certain if anything would be different, if their ending would have changed, but if she had just let herself love him, she would have had Reid for longer. She knew it now just as much as she'd known it on that platform staring up at Ozik.

But memories did not make the pain of loss worse. They made it worthwhile.

She should have loved him with every tremor of fear, with every quake of her cowardly bones. She should never have left him this morning.

"Tomorrow," Vaasa managed through the tightness of her throat.

Lord Karev smiled with fabricated approval. "I believe we're going to have a wonderful marriage."

Vaasa bit the inside of her cheek so sharply, the metallic tang of blood trickled onto her tongue.

Lord Karev shut the door to his carriage, and even standing in the snow, Vaasa could not feel the cold. She kept her teeth gritted; it prevented her magic from making an uninvited appearance. She wasn't certain that she'd be able to keep it down—not like this.

Not anymore.

Roman ushered her into the waiting carriage, and despite the eyes upon them, he loaded inside with her. Panic reared in her stomach, and her magic stuffed up her throat. Vaasa shook her head, desperate for him to leave. Roman ignored her unspoken protest and slammed the door shut, locking both of them inside.

She was going to lose control over her power.

Vaasa shoved her hand into the pocket of her dress and gripped the necklace. Her magic choked to nothing and a dull hum throbbed in her fingertips. The tension in her body eased, even if only a fraction, and she forced herself to take deep breaths.

"Did he hurt you?" Roman demanded.

Vaasa pulled her knees up to her chest, rocking backward on the seat and curling into the corner. She couldn't do this right now. She couldn't have this conversation, couldn't think of anything beyond Lord Karev's words. She wanted Reid. She wanted warm air and salt and the Icrurian sun. But they had him. They were going to kill him.

"Answer me, damn it!"

Vaasa's eyes flew open and she hissed, "Yes. He choked me and pinned me to the floor."

Tears welled in her eyes, and one slid down her cheek, no longer a ruse. She batted it away with her free hand. Part of her felt sick at saying out loud what had happened in that room. It was too vulnerable, too raw. Roman didn't deserve to see her pain. But he needed to believe her pain was due to Karev, not because of Reid.

It took a moment, but Roman eventually muttered, "I should have been there. I didn't think he would come for you so quickly."

Vaasa closed her eyes. All sense of energy drained from her. She couldn't mask the blaring pain in her ribs or the tenderness of her throat. Her free hand rose to it, brushing along the reddened skin where a bruise would inevitably bloom.

"Was he telling the truth?" Roman asked. "Did you really turn in the Wolf of Mireh?"

Vaasa considered her options, pain extending up the hand that touched the necklace. She opened her eyes. Roman gazed at her from across the carriage with this glimmer of something, like he knew a piece of information that she didn't. Like he knew the answer to his question already.

"No," she said on instinct, trying to remind herself what was at stake if she estranged him. "I had no idea that Reid of Mireh was here."

A small breath from Roman caused Vaasa to tense. There was no telling whether he would believe her, if those words would exonerate her or not. "You need to know something."

Vaasa sat up a little. "What?"

"I went to see that pirate you've been meeting with. Sachia," he said.

Vaasa closed her eyes. There was no use continuing to argue, to lie, given Roman's connection to Sutherland.

"Sutherland has been searching for her for months now," he confessed. "He wants her dead."

Vaasa clung to the necklace in her pocket, to the only lifeline she had that would prevent her magic from destroying everything around her. She opened her eyes and stared at him across the carriage. "Did you kill her?" Vaasa asked bluntly.

"No. And I won't, not so long as you have a use for her. I know about the black powder. I assume you're setting a trap for Karev."

Vaasa uncurled just slightly, keeping her hand in her pocket. "That was Karev's trade proposal, not mine."

Roman scooted forward on his seat, extending a hand and placing it upon her knee. It didn't seem to matter that she was curled in the corner of the carriage or that she had already drawn back from his touch. His voice dropped to an almost indistinguishable whisper. "Tell me you found the weapon we can use against Ozik. That you have a way of eliminating them both."

Vaasa pulled her gaze from where he touched her. "I found it."

Relief softened his features, loosened his grip upon her knee. "What is your plan, Vaasa? Let me in. Please. Karev, Ozik, all of it."

Vaasa pursed her lips. Carefully, she unfurled, though she was careful not to force Roman to remove his hand from her knee. Instead, she turned so her body was at his mercy, so she appeared as the vulnerable woman he wanted her to be. "You won't tell Sutherland?"

Roman slid from his bench and came to his knees before her. "He is in the prison, has been for months. I am loyal to you," he said, keeping his hand on her knee, the other raising to graze her neck where Karev had hurt her.

"I don't want you to be complicit," she whispered.

But he shook his head. "Stop trying to save me, you're only making it more dangerous."

Vaasa hated herself, but she leaned into his touch. If Reid was arrested, she would use every weapon in her arsenal to get him back. She didn't care what it cost her. "I'm planning an assassination," she confessed. "In exchange for her brother, Sachia's crew will do the dirty work. Ozik and Lord Karev will die. You and I will narrowly escape. It's meant to happen on the night of my formal engagement party."

Roman's lips parted. Closed. "Did you know that she was housing Reid of Mireh?"

"No, I swear it," Vaasa whispered, hoping he might be delusional enough to believe her. "I met a salt lord, but that's it. Karev met him, too. But Reid of Mireh was nowhere to be found."

Her words seemed to confirm something to Roman, some detail she didn't know clicking into place. "That's why you insisted on going to the prison. To help Sachia find her brother."

"Yes."

"You should have asked me," Roman said.

"I didn't know if I could trust you yet."

Roman curled his hand around the nape of her neck, still on his knees but rising enough to meet her almost eye to eye. His touch was gentle now, not a trace of a threat within it. "And now?"

"And now I know you'll do anything it takes to help us win the throne," she whispered back.

"Anything," he confirmed. Roman stared at her, his eyes wild with fury and desire. Revulsion twisted in her abdomen, her hand still clutching that necklace with everything she had as he leaned closer. As his mouth approached hers.

No, no no, she thought.

He brushed her lips with his own, and Vaasa fought her body's natural reaction to tense. She let him kiss her once, twice, and then she prepared to rip their mouths apart, to make some excuse about how she couldn't risk this when everything was coming to a head.

But the carriage lurched, and Roman released her, backing up to his seat like a frightened animal. Vaasa looked down at her lap, putting a hand over her mouth as if she were surprised.

"No one will know," Roman swore quietly.

Vaasa lifted her gaze, grateful for the space between them, the lingering taste of him brief and unwelcome. But it had to seem stolen, like some small thing she had allowed herself. She forced her body to stay open to him, as though the brief kiss had brought them closer, not further apart. "Has Ozik returned to the fortress?" Vaasa asked.

Roman frowned. "Ozik never left. He's been locked in his quarters for days, hasn't come out."

Vaasa sat up fully. "What?"

"He claims to have a flu," Roman said.

Vaasa clamped her lips together, confusion rattling her to the bone. Slowly, she released the necklace, careful to control the tide of magic that swept through her. Her breath caught, and she winced, placing her other hand on her throat, pretending it was only the pain. The magic stretched her skin, sunk claws into her abdomen. She didn't want to breathe.

But she did.

Vaasa reached for that connection between her and Ozik, feeling for the cords still knotted around her insides. It was a shimmering beacon. Her own magic brushed upon it, and as Vaasa followed it, she allowed the channel to open the way she had a few times now. She waited.

And then it slammed across their bond, that miserable, awful keening. A tormented cry that echoed in her ears. All Vaasa could see in her mind was the curve of Julianna's smile, the vivid pink of the flowers Ellena had strung together in a bracelet. Everything Vaasa felt and heard and saw was washed in vibrant crimson. The color smothered the cords. Vaasa squeezed her eyes shut, sure she could hear Ozik screaming in the haze of it all. Wetness rolled down her cheeks. She couldn't be sure if they were her own tears or if they were Ozik's.

Something was terribly wrong. She needed to find Ozik.

"Vaasa," Roman said.

She shook her head, tucking herself in tighter. "I'm just—" She swallowed. "Scared." She wasn't sure she could even form words through the wrenching of her soul.

"We'll get you back to the fortress," Roman promised.

Ozik, she whispered in her mind, just like she had in the mausoleum. *What happened to them? What happened to Julianna and Ellena?*

The cords tightened. The screams went quiet. Cut off, like someone slammed the door on the room where the sound emanated. Silence echoed in Vaasa's mind. She breathed and breathed and breathed.

Ozik? she whispered across that binding.

His voice was a mere whisper in time, an exhausted push of breath. *You are not the only victim of a bargain, Vaasalisa.*

Vaasa ran as best as she could into the greenhouse, nausea sweeping over her, the moment Roman left the emperor's wing. One of his many guards trailed her, but when she entered the greenhouse, he waited dutifully outside.

The necklace still sat in her pocket. The last rays of light bathed the ocean, the room dimming but not dark yet. Her eyes immediately landed on the black stone statues, tracing the lines of gold threading them. She put her hand over her mouth, the image of her mother in that sarcophagus unfolding in her mind.

She searched the statue nearest her, the round eyes of a woman with her delicate hand over her mouth. Drapes covered just one of her shoulders, cascading down her body to pool on the floor. Magic bubbled in Vaasa's veins and here, in the greenhouse, she let it out. Black tendrils of power seeped from her fingers and wrapped up her arms. Lord Karev's attack had left her no time to process what she'd seen.

To decide if any of it was true.

Ozik, so in love it was sickening. He'd had plans. A family. A *child*. All in an ancient version of Icruria, of Wrultho specifically. The precise location Vaasa's father had targeted in Icruria. He'd struck an economic deal with Ton of Wrultho and ultimately betrayed him, cutting off Wrultho's water source and sparking conflict at the border. It was the first step to conquering the city.

That was Ozik's doing, not her father's. Vaasa was certain.

There were three parts of this anchor, three pieces that Ozik's father had broken. One in the necklace in her pocket, the other in the ring Ozik wore. The third, Vaasa bet, was in Wrultho.

The dagger.

The pieces her mother said not to unite.

Vaasa looked up at the statue and wondered if everything she'd once made up about them was true. People with stories of their own, lives they had lived.

"The cost of a broken bargain," Ozik's voice said from behind her, but something was different about it. It carried an ancient tenor—a deep, echoing rumble. Like it had in the hallway when she and Roman tried to sneak to the prison the first time.

Vaasa froze. Turned.

His hands were in his pockets, his white hair brushing his shoulders. Shadows warped his otherwise smooth, pale skin, which had lost most of its natural color. Drained was the only way Vaasa could describe it. Far past how she'd seen him on the platform at the election. His blackened veins were stark against his pale skin, his eyes so bloodshot they might have well been red. Muted was the golden hue he had given to Ellena, the color he had inherited from his own mother.

An Ohros witch, capable of seeing visions of the future. The goddess of fate and sight.

Ozik *had* aged compared to the version of him she'd seen in the vision, but not nearly enough. A young man then, barely older than a teenager, while now he seemed to be middle-aged. He was still aging, even if it was happening very slowly.

"That's what you did to my mother, then?" Vaasa whispered. "To all of these women?"

"All of these witches," Ozik corrected. He stepped further into the greenhouse, eyeing the statue nearest Vaasa that she had been staring at. "A Cota witch, the goddess of wind and sky. This coven was the fourth I drove to extinction."

Vaasa watched every step he took, careful to place herself away from him. As he drew closer, she backed away. Her magic leaked freely onto her hands, which she refused to dip into her pockets. If the anchor strengthened or weakened him, she couldn't tell. "How?" Vaasa asked. "How did you drive entire covens to extinction?"

He chuckled at her defensive pose. "It used to suffice, the game of bargains. People took them freely. It was so simple to offer them that one thing they wanted and to watch regret pool in their eyes when they realized the cost."

Vaasa noted the word *cost*, her ears ringing with it. The magic in her sharpened. It clawed at her abdomen. She held it back, careful to keep her control, terror pulsing in her mind.

"The last of a bloodline, dead at their own hands, chasing a selfish dream or a lost love. It's always those two things, you know. Without fail. Love or power, it's all anyone wants." He gazed up at the statue Vaasa had been staring at, running his hand along the crook of the woman's elbow. "Without a witch to their name, a deity can be sealed away. Cota has been sealed for two generations."

Sealed. Not dead.

"How does one seal a deity?" Vaasa asked.

His lip curled in anger. "Ask Veragi."

Vaasa's brows threaded, this strange sense of understanding striking her like lightning. Ozik was not himself. He behaved and spoke the way he had on the stairs the night she had put a knife through his throat and he did not die. Vaasa latched her gaze on Ozik's hand. On the ring.

His anchor. The thing that connected him to his Zetyr magic. *Divine*, he had called himself and Julianna. But he had spoken to Zetyr long before he'd ever inherited that ring—like Amalie claimed she had spoken to Veragi.

It was such a wicked turn of Ozik's lips, the way he smiled at her. He curled his fingers on the statue. "You know, that little anchor in your pocket... your brother hid it, just like I told him to. He begged me for one of his own, and the stupid boy thought I'd given it to him. He wore that clawed ring everywhere, no idea it was just a useless stone. He never understood why he couldn't do what you and your mother could."

Vaasa's lips parted in confusion, and she furrowed her brow. Her final conversation with Dominik churned in her mind, and she remembered that in the catacombs beneath Dihrah, the first question he'd asked her was how she had learned to manipulate the curse. She had thought it was because he wanted her to die, that he was angry she hadn't. "Dominik was trying to learn to wield magic?"

"What else do you think Lord Vlacik wanted to discover? The two were insatiable, so desperate to harness the power of deities they didn't even believe in."

Dominik had worn that ring until the moment he died. Until the moment Vaasa killed him. And he'd thought it was an anchor that would protect him.

"A scared little boy, just like your power-starved father, making bargain after bargain as he ravaged a continent. Your grandfather mined all the steel, but your father was determined to do more. To conquer magic, of all things. Ozik's fear was so visceral every time your mother revealed herself."

Vaasa sucked in a breath. He spoke about himself as if he wasn't Ozik, as if...

His crimson eyes, glowing just like Amalie's had, though hers had been white.

When she'd connected with Veragi.

And then it all clicked. She should have realized it sooner. This was not Ozik she looked upon. This was the being she had faced on the stairs on the way to the prison, the thing that kept trying to break free of a body that contained it.

Ozik wasn't a god. He was possessed by one.

"Zetyr," Vaasa gasped. "You're *Zetyr*."

Vaasa filed through every moment she'd spent with Ozik, trying to categorize them, trying to reconcile the two different beings she'd been presented with. In her youth, he had been constant, and she could cling to no memories of his mortality faltering. But these past few months, each time he vacillated between crimson and gold, it was their fight for dominance in the same body. Ozik pushing through, reclaiming control, only to be lost in the red again. Ozik's control had deteriorated, and quickly.

This is what she'd seen on the other end of their bond. That red pool, the cavern in Ozik's mind, the ancient thing that seemed to be emerging from within him.

It was Zetyr.

The corners of Zetyr's lips curled up. "In the pursuit of extinguishing my enemies, a man like your father is the perfect red herring. He did all of the searching for me. Uncovering witches one by one, making them ripe for the slaughter. The deities who betrayed me will pay for their crimes, despite Ozik's valiant efforts. You know, he used to serve me so willingly, before your mother came along."

Vaasa took a step away from him, her mind reeling. Ozik had left breadcrumb after breadcrumb for her to find. The torture in the prison, a way to strengthen their connection and show her what her father and brother had done. The training each morning, allowing her to glimpse Zetyr without knowing it. The nights when his pain raged across the cords that bound them.

His entire scheme of making her a figurehead, all to highlight what her father had been turned into. Every language she spoke, every political system she learned, every history lesson packaged in words with double meaning. He had taught her how to find the answers, how to observe.

Her father's office.

The notebook.

The necklace.

Their bargain.

You were never trying to steal my magic, were you? Vaasa whispered into her mind. *Our connection helps you hold him at bay.*

Ozik's voice murmured in her head, quiet, seemingly far off, yet distinguishable nonetheless. *You are far cleverer than anyone has ever given you credit for, even me. But especially your father.*

Tears welled in Vaasa's eyes as she gazed upon Zetyr, at the hateful contortion of a face that did not belong to him. "What bargain did Ozik make? What happened to Julianna and Ellena?"

Zetyr tilted his head with such menace as he said, "Without fail, *love or power*. One cannot have both. And as you've been told a hundred times, love is a useless thing."

He dropped his hand and started toward her.

Vaasa backed up and pulled her knife from her waistline. The weapon felt heavy in her hands, tangible, real. Despite it, she shook. She stumbled back again.

He was a *god*. What use was a blade?

Zetyr laughed at her display. Vaasa's gut twisted with the inhuman sound. "Shall we use that knife to execute the Wolf of Mireh?" Zetyr taunted.

Vaasa's heart lurched. This sounded nothing like Ozik—it wasn't strategic, it lacked depth, was missing that inherent double meaning. Before he could get closer, before he could get his hands on her, Vaasa dipped into her pocket and grasped the necklace. Her magic winked out, but she pulled the anchor from her pocket and held it out between her and Zetyr, hoping, praying, that it would do something.

Zetyr froze.

He halted in his steps, his face contorting in rage, and the gold in his eyes grew brighter. Clearer. The webs of blood within them retracted, and Zetyr shook his head, resembling a wild animal. The black veins in his neck receded. Vaasa stepped forward, and his knees cracked against the gravel.

"Good," he gasped, his voice leveling out, breath filling his lungs. His head hung. "Well done, Vaasalisa. Well done."

He took a large breath and lifted his face up, not a trace of red in his eyes any longer.

Ozik.

Vaasa clutched the necklace in her shaking hand. The hum of the iron links worked up her fingers, reminding her of the magic that wanted so desperately to get out.

Kill him, her mind thought. *Kill him now.*

Rage flooded her veins and all her reasoning, all her careful planning, was lost. She dropped the necklace into her pocket and let her magic spring to life. Instead, she did exactly as he'd once told her to do.

She struck.

Vaasa launched a wave of magic across the greenhouse, the edges sharpening into a glittering wall that slammed into Ozik. He flew backward and hit the olive tree, sliding to the ground in a slumped-over version of himself.

Immediately, the cords within her tightened. Ozik's head snapped up, his eyes so clear, his skin pale and unmarred.

But he pulled back on her magic, was taking it away again, he was—

No.

In her haze, she felt as if she grasped her hands around those cords and pulled back. Nails sinking into the power, with all her might she fought against the stealing of it. It felt as if the rope had slipped through her fingers, so she tightened harder, grit her teeth, tugged more. It was hers.

It was *hers*.

Ozik smiled.

Something on the other end of their connection gave.

Magic poured into her in a tidal wave, her anger and fear and desperation swirling in her veins like a heady wine. It was red and black, mist and oil, a combination of both their power. That shimmering bond between them overflowed like a well, and she let it fill her, let the strength of it fuel each ounce of magic that sprung to life in her body. The wolf tore from her bones, more real than anything she'd ever conjured. Every placement of its feet, every stone beneath them, she felt so distinctly. She dug her own boots into the ground in tandem with the manifestation.

It growled, prowling forward.

Vaasa wanted to kill him. There was no space for sympathy, no thoughts to consider Julianna or Ellena or why Ozik had done any of this. She had never hated someone like she hated him—it was a depth of rage she hadn't thought herself capable of.

Unleashed, the wolf sprung forward and tackled Ozik to the ground. He grunted as he slammed into the stones, and Ozik spun, trying to thrash the wolf off him. It dug its teeth into his face, and Ozik *screamed*. She tasted his blood, felt the slickness of it on her own tongue, and the metallic tang lit up the part of her that was entirely capable of violence. It felt as it had when she'd taken Dominik's life. It was *her* kill. *Her* choice.

It was the part of her that was capable of great horrors to get exactly what she wanted.

Ozik roared in his rage and pain, and she thought, for just a moment, that she had done it. That she was finally going to kill him. And then his voice whispered in her mind. *A shame to only have one third of a thing, isn't it?*

Vaasa stumbled backward.

Call off our magic, Vaasalisa.

Vaasa hauled the magic back inside herself. Not just her magic— his, too. Melisina was right. She was channeling Ozik.

She forced her body backward, stumbling, mind reeling. She had one piece of the anchor in her pocket, but it wasn't enough. She needed all three pieces. *That* was how she killed Zetyr.

Her mother's note unfurled in her mind: *Whatever you do, stay in Mireh and do not unite the other pieces. The price is far too great.*

What was the price? What was her mother trying to warn her about?

She thought of Ozik's bloodshot eyes, of the veins showing beneath his skin. Perhaps that was the cost: To wield the anchor was to give oneself over to it entirely, to slowly lose control of your mind and your heart and your humanity. The anchor of the god of souls could do no right by the person who held it.

That was what Dominik had sought, the reason Lord Vlacik had tortured her. It had taken Ozik, a man capable of such incredible love, and turned him into a vessel usable by Zetyr due to his father's bargain. Maybe that was what Vaasa's mother had seen. Maybe she had watched a man she'd loved for fifteen years become a beast.

The wolf disappeared. The tang of blood remained on her tongue. Ozik lay on the ground for a moment, his chest rising and falling. Vaasa hit her knees. The heel of her palm dug into the sharp cobblestones as she gripped them to keep herself from falling face-first. She stared down at the glimmering stones beneath her hands and tightened her grip upon them.

What did it matter if she'd finally figured it out? If she knew precisely the way to kill him and escape her bargain? The bargain itself meant nothing, not now. He had taught her exactly how to use it to her own advantage. He didn't want their magic linked so he could wield her power—it was so that she could wield his.

"Did you do this to my mother?" She begged for an answer. "Did you link your magic to hers just so she could fight off that deity inside of you?"

"Yes," he confessed from where he knelt on the ground. He leaned forward, his hands on the gravel, his back rising and falling with breath.

"I hate you," she spat, not even sure she believed him.

"I know," he whispered. "But I have given you everything you need to finish what she couldn't."

Ozik had turned Vaasa into what her mother had been, a tool to fight his battles. And Reid was going to die anyway. He would be executed on the iron pole in the middle of Mekës. Ozik had given her nothing—all he'd ever done was take. He'd taken her mother, her life in Icruria, and now . . .

"Do something," Vaasa demanded, her voice edging with violence. "We had a bargain, Ozik. Reid's life for my magic. So *do something*."

Ozik rose. Black oil slathered his face, one of his eyes sealed closed as he rolled his shoulders, his jacket tattered and frayed. The skin of his cheek peeled back and dripped black blood.

But all traces of red were gone.

Slowly, the wounds on Ozik started to heal. His skin sewed together, his bruises faded, all evidence of her attack disappeared with each breath he took. He leveled her with his gaze. "I sent Karev to arrest the wrong man."

Vaasa froze. "What?"

"Reid of Mireh is waiting in your family's apartment as we speak. It is his friend that Lord Karev arrested."

Vaasa scurried to her feet, but as she caught her balance, Ozik's tired voice drifted across the greenhouse.

"In the quest for your hand, I've situated the lords perfectly to be conquered by Icruria. They are on the verge of a civil war, and Karev is the single person holding them back. And because I am the one who taught you to steal thrones, this is something you already know."

It had all been a trick. A brilliant, terrible scheme. She had been just as much a pawn as the men had. She just hadn't realized why. "Why build an empire you plan to break?"

"Because when you carry the power of a god for as long as I have, conquering a nation is a worthwhile goal . . . until you fall in love. When you do that, there is no higher purpose than delivering the world to your partner's feet. Your mother asked for an empire, so I gave her one."

Vaasa curled in on herself. *Your mother saw a spider, so afraid of being crushed beneath everyone else's feet.* What would being married to a man like Vaasa's father do to a woman? To spend a lifetime in the shadow of men who saw her as nothing but a pawn to further their own ends?

Perhaps it wasn't her father's evil that Vaasa had inherited, but her mother's burden.

"You want to destroy Asterya," Ozik continued. "And I will help you. But in return, there's something you must do for me."

Rage coiled in her with such intensity, Vaasa went dizzy. "Another bargain?" She shook her head. "No."

"I was twenty-four years old when my father unsealed Zetyr from his tomb." Ozik dragged in a breath, a sorrowful rattling. "Every day he grows stronger, and it won't be long until I can no longer hold him back. The witches in your coven are the only ones who can reseal him. He won't stop until he kills every single one of you, just like he did your mother."

Vaasa stopped breathing.

"I never laid a hand on her, and I never would have," he swore. Vaasa had never once thought she could find sincerity on Ozik's face, but there it was. She gazed at nothing but a shattered man. "When I fell in love with your mother and realized what it would mean to reseal Zetyr, I gave her that necklace. A simple chain that stifled her magic, and something else she never understood: a third of my family's anchor. A talisman powerful enough to hold off Zetyr and circumvent the consequence of breaking a bargain."

Vaasa's lips parted in shock. The necklace in her pocket could keep her alive. It could prevent Ozik's bargain from killing her? That was why he had trained her. Why he had shown her the pathway to channeling his magic—it was a breaking of their bargain, but she held the necklace, so she survived. "Why not just release her? Release me?"

"You cannot be released from a Zetyr bargain once it has been made. The terms must be met. So I armed her with the only thing that would grant us more time."

Vaasa grit her teeth. "And she didn't know?"

"Not until that summer she went to Icruria. She began in Mireh, but she soon fled to my homeland, to the place where the last third of the anchor is hidden. Wrultho."

Vaasa's breaths came heavier. She stared at the olive tree in the back of the greenhouse, at the very thing Julianna and Elena had once sat beneath. This entire place, a relic of the life Ozik had lost. He had carried it with him, had grown it here in Mekës like a torturous testament to his past. "What happened next?"

Ozik looked down in shame. It was perhaps the first time she had ever seen him reveal such a thing to her. "I have spent hundreds of years carrying two pieces of my family's anchor, and for a time, that was powerful enough to hold off Zetyr. But when I gave your mother the necklace, it meant limiting my own protection. And one night, I couldn't fight him. I . . . lost control. I told her to never take off the necklace, but she was trying—"

Ozik stopped speaking, his hand upon his throat as if he could hold back his emotions.

"She was trying to give it to me," Vaasa said.

He closed his eyes.

The weight of what he told her bore down heavy in the air, smothering Vaasa. Her voice wavered, sadness coating every word. "You aren't the reason she's dead. I am."

Ozik shook his head, dropping his hand. "Don't ever say that again. I am, without a shadow of a doubt, the reason your mother is gone. If she had never loved me, if I had never learned of her magic and tried to trick her into resealing Zetyr, she would still be alive."

Tears pricked Vaasa's eyes. Ozik couldn't guarantee a thing like that; the magic might very well have killed Vena Kozár even if Ozik had never intervened. Of this, Vaasa knew intimately. It was when Vena removed her necklace, when she tried to hide it for Vaasa, tried to give Vaasa something that would protect her—

Vaasa covered her mouth with her hand and choked back a sob. The image of her mother turning to stone lapped ceaselessly against the walls of her mind. "She tried to give me the one thing she knew would save her own life."

"I know you have doubted your mother's favor; I have seen it since you were a child. But to love you openly, to show you any affection . . . it would have put you in danger. You were your father's daughter, but you were caught between two people who could not stand the life of the other. Your mother wanted to tell you what was coming, wanted me to train you, but your father wouldn't allow it. He was hell-bent on finding a way to cleanse you of what he believed was a curse. *That* was when the torture of witches began."

Her father knew. He'd known that Vaasa would someday inherit the magic crawling beneath her mother's skin. "He conquered a continent in search of a cure?"

"When your mother inherited her magic and your fate became clear, your father demanded you be able to read any book you came across, to converse with even the eldest of history-keepers. If there was a way to eliminate magic from his bloodline, from *you*, he believed you would find it. Your parents were complicated people, Vaasalisa, but you must understand that they loved you and your brother, even if the only way they knew how to show it was how their parents had shown it to them."

Tears slid down Vaasa's face. Every language, every nation, every violent upheaval that Vaasa had been forced to witness, was in pursuit of saving her life. Her family had been fundamentally fractured, and now here Vaasa was, alone and still standing with the remnants of their choices in her hands.

And the remnants of her own.

Vaasa stared at Ozik, shocked that she could feel such pity wrap around her ribcage, such sorrow and compassion for a man who had calculated every moment of these weeks with precisely this exchange in mind. To steal her. Train her. Use her.

He was no better than her father. Selfish, ambitious men.

And once again, she had no choice but to bend to their schemes.

"Fine. State your bargain," she said.

Ozik didn't smile. Even though she knew he had been leading her to this exact moment every second she had been back in Mekës, satisfaction was nowhere on him. Not on his face, not in his voice. "I will help you and your friends escape this city if you will go to Wrultho and finish what your mother could not."

Vaasa's fists opened and closed. It was all she could do to stop herself from twitching. "What is the cost of reuniting the anchor? Why wouldn't my mother do it?"

"Because," Ozik said, voice leveling out, "in order to reseal Zetyr, you have to kill me."

CHAPTER 34

Reid waited for her.

He swore he had spent his life doing exactly this. Even when he didn't know her. Even when he didn't realize she was coming. He had been moving through life in precisely the same way he paced in her grandfather's library now: aimlessly, not understanding why he took the steps he did, just knowing he had to put one foot in front of the other.

The secret door unlatched.

Reid froze.

Vaasa burst through, her breath labored, her wild eyes searching.

They landed on him.

A sob burst from her chest at the same time Reid threw his body across the room. He scooped her into his arms as she wailed, her chest racking with her tears, and Reid's own eyes watered at the sound. Pain emanated from her in waves. He ran his hand through her hair over and over. "Shhh," he whispered. "I'm here. I'm here."

"I thought they found you," she cried.

"They didn't," he said. "But they have Koen."

She pulled back, tears staining her face, her eyes red with

exhaustion. At that moment, Reid's mother came barreling into the room, her eyes wide. His mother practically toppled Reid over as she pulled Vaasa into her arms.

Vaasa started to cry again, the release of her emotions so intense he thought she would rattle the building. Her guise of neutrality had completely fallen. There wasn't even an attempt to put it back up. Reid's mother whispered to her over and over, the two rocking back and forth.

Vaasa took a breath as she came back to herself. She looked around the room, likely feeling who was missing, just as Reid did. "Do you believe he's alive?" Reid asked, voice so low.

"He's alive," Vaasa said. "And I have a way to get him out. To get everyone out. But Sachia has to work with Roman."

Reid's brows slammed together, and his mother stepped away from Vaasa. "Roman?" she asked.

Vaasa nodded. "I'll tell you everything, I promise."

Sachia walked into the room then and crossed her arms, standing beneath the doorway. "What do I have to do?" she asked.

Vaasa set her lantern down on the desk, the light illuminating the sharp plane of her face. Her mouth was turned down in a grimace. "That plan we discussed, we need to move it up to tomorrow. Gather your crew and get the black powder. Roman is waiting for you at the Sanctum."

CHAPTER
35

The city thrummed around her. Vaasa had known this citizenry to be difficult to excite, but today, the streets were filled to capacity.

Their open-top cart hit a pothole, and Vaasa tried not to jolt too obviously. Lord Karev sat at her side, chin held high, and the city roared with each wave of his hand. They had paraded through the streets for two hours, people clogging every direction and alleyway, but as the last hour of sun reigned in the sky, the execution was imminent.

At her side, Lord Karev was the picture of the future emperor, reminding her in many ways of how her father had looked on days such as this. Poised. Immovable. The perfect combination of aristocracy and violence. His dark hair and bedroom eyes complemented the deep royal blue of his jacket. It was a trick of the gaze, a symmetry between him and the hundreds of city guards who lined the streets. Lord Karev had never served a day of his life as a soldier or guard, had never worn those particular coats, but he wanted to exude the image of someone who had.

The cart rode through large crowds as people ran to feast their eyes upon them. She wanted to cover herself, to hide from their judgmental stares and the circus calls, but Vaasa waved despite her desire to run. Gloves covered her hands and arms in snow-white, the same pure shade swirling up the hem of her Asteryan blue gown. Vaasa squared her shoulders and smiled, wondering if every person around them could see through this foolish facade.

The narrow streets were difficult to navigate with this many onlookers, forcing the carters to direct the horses down the wider ones. The snow falling from the sky picked up in intensity, and Vaasa wiped the cold droplets off her cheeks.

Despite her sweeping cloak, Vaasa shivered.

Their cart arrived just in front of the Sanctum. Sentinels lined the pathway as Lord Karev guided Vaasa from the cart and down the steps that would lead to the first floor. Sentinels opened the doors for them, and they were ushered into the main vestibule, both curving staircases that led to the second floor covered in nobles and their honored guests. The gallery was stuffed to the brim. All around them, each important family mingled, treating the events of today like a celebration. The offices in this building provided the perfect lookouts over the grisly scene.

She hated every person in this room.

Roman and a host of fortress sentinels followed them inside, partnering with the city guard to defend the nobles. Most of them had their own hired mercenaries. At their entrance, all voices went silent, and everybody in the room turned to them.

In tandem, the nobles bowed.

Lord Karev smiled the way any good emperor would, a mix of power and humility pouring from him. His footsteps echoed on the black-and-white marble floors as he guided Vaasa farther into the room by her elbow. Her magic begged to bite the hand that held her. She pictured it then, teeth sinking into Lord Karev's throat the same way his hands had wound around her neck. She gazed out at the room one more time, her heart thudding with reassurance, not a wisp of hatred leaking onto her smiling lips.

He would regret every moment of this day. They all would.

Ozik approached Vaasa and Lord Karev, dipping his head and

interrupting her violent daydreams. She tried not to tremble. The connection between them hummed, and his golden eyes were clear of any red. Her gaze darted to his hand. The raw, jagged black stone winked at her. One-third of a thing, not powerful enough to contain a deity. She wondered how long the two anchors, the ring and necklace in tandem, would have been enough. If that was why Zetyr had never been able to break through during Vaasa's youth. But surely he had been there, simmering in Ozik's mind, playing some role in the expansion of Asterya's empire.

Perhaps when Ozik had given Vaasa's mother the necklace, it had been the beginning of the end of his control.

"The future emperor and empress!" Ozik exclaimed.

The room erupted in cheers. It was only the Vlacik family who stayed silent, a furious disapproval written in how they glanced among themselves and scowled. Lord Karev stepped forward with one hand raised, and the room quieted. Vaasa forced herself to watch him with the expression of someone taken—someone just as enthralled as the rest of them. His voice boomed through the vestibule. "Today, we put an end to this Icrurian conflict with the rightful execution of the Wolf of Mireh!"

The room erupted once again. She met Ozik's eyes, which watched her so carefully. Every twitch of her body had to be exact; she was hyperaware of her magic, of keeping it at bay. Lord Karev walked through the crowd, greeting the heads of families, suddenly paying attention to both the Old and New Asteryans. They all groveled at his feet, and then at Vaasa's, fabricated compliments spewing from their faithless mouths.

The crowd parted, and they ascended the stairs on the right side of the building. They would view the execution from the Emperor's Suite, a room on the top level of the Sanctum that overlooked the square and the iron execution pole. The suite had sat empty since her father's death, but Vaasa had watched more than her fair share of executions from that room, sometimes stepping out onto the narrow balcony when the weather permitted. Her father had sometimes addressed the crowds from the space, the width of it only large enough for one, maybe two, bodies. She pictured him there, expressive hands waving as he drew every eye in the square.

When they reached the top floor, Roman used his keys to open the door for them. It was perpetually locked, a small security measure her father had taken.

Only one way in and one way out, and it always required a key.

The Emperor's Suite was immodestly sized, the wall facing the city square built of glass. She eyed the doors that opened to the small balcony, tracing the blue curtains and long silver ropes that dangled from them. Today, the curtains were wide open, a substantial pile of rope on the floor of either side. She trailed the rope to the mechanism that controlled it at the back of the room. Built of iron, it was sturdy, able to hold far more than the weight of curtains. Dominik had swung from those ropes as an early teenager, immediately eliciting their father's ire.

Vaasa walked to the windows, running her fingers along the thick glass. Behind her, Lord Karev dismissed Roman from the room.

"I'll be just outside the door, should you need me," he told them both.

On the first night he'd come into her room, Roman said he had met Reid in the war camps. He had watched the arrest, had spoken to Sachia. He *knew* the man being tied to that pole wasn't Reid of Mireh, and he had allowed her to believe it was.

"Go downstairs," she instructed. "Find Ozik."

"What—"

"Your future empress just gave you a command," Lord Karev bit.

Roman grit his teeth. He tried to make eye contact with her, but she just stared out at the execution square, keeping her eyes on the clock tower, doing everything she could not to aggravate the scowling lord in the corner. Everything hinged on her perfect behavior.

The door closed, and she was alone with Karev.

Vaasa stood next to the glass, holding tight to her rage and her violence, the only movement in her body the way her finger tapped against the glass. Each press in time with the hand on the clock.

Vaasa peered down with her heart in her throat. Below, the crowd began to part the way fish did when a predator was near.

She sucked in a breath. Her eyes caught on Koen's head of brown hair. He was dragged in chains to the iron pole by at least ten sentinels.

He lifted his spectacled eyes to the sky.

Surely, he knew they were coming for him. Ozik had assured her that Koen was alive by his own orders.

Guards began to wrap chains around the pole, and on the far-left side of the square, a member of the city guard ostentatiously sharpened his blade. Vaasa knew the shape of that man's body, despite the mask that covered his features—a security measure always taken by the executioner, lest someone's broken family come seeking revenge. Every instinct she had homed in on Reid as he sharpened a large blade over and over.

Vaasa kept her eyes peeled, her chest rising and falling with her breath. She stared straight out at the square as the hands on the clock moved closer to the hour. Vaasa's voice threaded the air around them as she watched each *tick, tick, tick* of the clock.

"You're going to forgive me one day," Lord Karev said, his voice approaching from behind until he settled into a spot near where she stood, gazing down at the city square. At Koen. "You'll wake up and realize the absurdity of your treason, and then you'll find yourself thankful for a partner who saved you from yourself."

Vaasa kept her eyes glued to Koen as they secured him to the iron pole. "You know, my lord, you have the same flaw my brother did."

Lord Karev chuckled with such little care. "And what's that?"

Vaasa turned, meeting Lord Karev's amused gaze. Likely, he'd believed the same whispers that Roman had, the ones that pinned Dominik's death on Reid. He wouldn't consider her smart enough or well versed with a blade. "Confidence," Vaasa said. "He did not believe I would kill him, either."

A thick brow rose on Lord Karev's face, a thread of fear replacing the haughty gratification that had overcome him from the moment he'd found her in that mausoleum.

Vaasa gave a serpentine smile. "That isn't Reid of Mireh," she confessed. "He was the bodyguard."

Lord Karev's expression dropped, first bleeding to confusion, then melding into rage. He opened his mouth to speak, but the clock struck the hour, the chimes of it pealing in the air.

Cracking booms rattled the Sanctum, one after the other, and screams reached all corners of the city square.

Vaasa released every ounce of her tethered magic into the room.

CHAPTER 36

Reid sprinted through the madness of the city square, eyes on the iron pole looming next to the ocean. Explosions rang out from the Sanctum, one by one, black powder ignited by members of Sachia's crew who had laid the sort of firetraps that would put even the Icrurian Central Forces to shame.

People screamed as they fled the square. Guards watched Reid pass as they, too, ran, fires breaking out along the side of the building. Explosion after explosion knocked the scaffolding down. Donning a stolen blue Asteryan coat and the mask of the executioner, there were only mere seconds more that Reid could continue to blend in.

He only needed twenty feet to reach Koen.

He caught the eye of a city guard who noticed which direction Reid's body turned, and the man unsheathed his weapon the moment Reid stepped forward.

Reid lifted his sword and ducked, narrowly avoiding the swing of the guard's blade. He spun and plunged his sword into the man's kidneys, then twisted, spinning his body to stab another guard in the side. He didn't have time to appreciate the bloom of red on Asteryan royal blue. Swinging his sword in tandem with his steps, Reid roared as he sprinted at another man. Steel clashed with a ring in the air, and the sound of it settled with familiarity in Reid's bones.

He might not understand Asteryan, but this was a language he spoke.

Reid spun his blade around the sword of the opposing guard, disarming him with a quick movement of his wrist. The sword clattered against stone, and Reid dragged his own across the neck of the guard. The man fell with a macabre splatter on Reid's boots. He leapt over the body, people screaming and fleeing from him, and members of Sachia's crew emerged from the crowd. Flames swallowed the back half of the Sanctum. Reid distinguished carefully between those that ran *at* him and those that ran *around* him. Just as it had been in Innisjour, it was only the fools that faced him who met the blood-slick end of his blade. Yet he was on the verge of descending into the version of himself that didn't care for human life, that was capable of killing anyone and anything that stood in his way. He clung with shaking hands to the person his father wanted him to be.

In front of him, the final guard stood, the only thing standing between Reid and Koen. The guard lifted his enormous broadsword with strong arms and a frame that stood as tall as Reid did. The man snarled something vicious in Asteryan, and Reid bellowed with laughter as his opponent brought his blade up. Too heavy. Too wide. A blade like that was never meant for battle—it was built for a gruesome show, one Reid was moments from stealing. The man swung down. Reid dodged and then performed a perfect riposte, moving his blade far quicker than the city guard had time to counter. Reid sliced through the side of the guard with a middle blow, and his sword sang with the cutting of fabric and flesh.

The guard roared in pain and sunk to his knees. Reid gave one last swing, and his blade lodged in the side of the man's head. All life drained from his eyes.

Reid reached the iron pole, and Koen railed against the chains that bound him. "Are you all right?" Reid yelled over the chaos.

"Oh, just *fine*," Koen muttered as he struggled against the chains with only half his body. Blue and purple bruises shadowed his face, and every time his left shoulder moved, Koen winced. He'd been beaten at minimum, likely worse.

"You should have told them you weren't me," Reid insisted as he started to tug at the iron chains that secured Koen to the thick pole.

"They would have killed me regardless. No use in taking you with me to hell."

"Hell is the last place you'll go," Reid said. He growled in frustration as he continued to work the chains. He started pulling at them, cursing, "These *fucking* chains."

"Move!" Sachia's voice rang in the air as she leapt onto the platform. Dressed in a utilitarian dress, her red hair braided over her shoulder, she was back in the part of a merchant's daughter today.

"Oh, thank the gods," Koen said.

"Cover me," she bit at Reid.

Reid grabbed his sword again just as Sachia slid to the spot in front of Koen. Her hands hovered over the chains. She bent her fingers and slashed downward. The line of links broke. The chains unraveled and clattered to the ground.

Koen stumbled from the pole and clutched his arm, letting out pained breaths. "Shit," Sachia said. "It's broken, isn't it?"

Rage coated Reid's tongue. They had broken Koen's arm.

And then more explosions sounded, this time coming from the port.

"Please tell me you have a plan," Koen begged, staring as debris and fire and smoke wafted into the ocean.

"Yes, we have a plan," Sachia insisted. Two members of her crew jumped onto the platform. She barked her commands. "Get Koen to the ship and make it to the prison. Find my brother. We'll meet you there."

No. She should go to the ship, too. There was no guarantee they would both make it out of this alive, and she needed to see her brother. That had always been her plan. "Sachia—" Reid started.

"There is no time, Wolf, and I'm not leaving you. Let's go!"

Sachia jumped from the platform and into the crowd. Reid stared after her, paralyzed for a moment at the sureness he'd just seen in the pirate witch. She easily could have abandoned them all there and made it out of this conflict. In so many ways, that was the most advantageous choice for her.

Yet she hadn't. She'd gone running after Vaasa without hesitation.

A member of Sachia's crew helped support Koen, and his friend leaned against the man with a pained look on his face. Reid turned to the docks where their tenders were supposed to be waiting. Fire swallowed the mooring in incredible blasts of red, orange, and yellow as various ships launched into the ocean, people fleeing toward the larger ships anchored further out in deeper water. The Iron Bay was a mess, boats narrowly slamming into each other as some tried to make it out to sea while city guards rushed in to try and save their own water vessels. They had targeted the quickest of the Asteryan ships in hopes of easing their escape.

"You can make it?" Reid asked the pirate holding most of Koen's weight.

Koen scoffed at him. The pirate nodded sternly.

The Red Corsair was waiting. Koen could manage. Reid turned to face the Sanctum, the place his wife was trapped, and then his jaw dropped.

"Tell me that was part of the plan," Koen said.

Reid shook his head.

"Holy *shit*," Koen hissed.

CHAPTER 37

Glittering black power burst from Vaasa in long, angry tendrils, and the glass windows around them shattered. Lord Karev slammed into the wall. Fear wafted in the air, a source Vaasa greedily stole from, the strands of her magic growing thicker, longer. The Sanctum shook, and then another boom sounded from the far side of the building, and Vaasa stumbled a step.

She didn't have time to hesitate, to figure out what was happening below them. She needed to stop this execution, and she needed to ruin any chance Asterya had at building an army. Ozik had made himself clear—if Asterya survived, Zetyr would be at Icruria's doorstep in no time.

Lord Karev used his hands to lift his torso, his leg bent at an unnatural angle from its impact with the wall. An agonized cry escaped his lips as he tried to stand. His eyes darted between the rattling door and where Vaasa stood near the window.

He was prey backed into a corner. He knew he wasn't going to survive her.

He yelled for help, and Vaasa scoffed as she walked forward. Her magic poured from her hands, the release of it heady like wine. It grew in her abdomen, soaking the ties that bound her to Ozik. His own power sat there, ripe for the taking. She pulled from it, her magic rising, the floor around her covered in black mist. "There is no one coming for you, Lord Karev."

He tried to drag himself along the wall, his breaths flying in and out of his chest. Fear was the only thing on his once-handsome features.

"What are you?" he asked through gritted teeth.

Vaasa tilted her head, shifting the raw magic around her into serpents that slithered across the floor. Their hisses rose in volume like a chorus. "Unhinged," she said, stepping forward. "A whore."

Tears streamed down his face.

"*Cursed.*"

The magic at her feet grew larger, taller, spinning in on itself until her wolf took form. The air tasted of fear and anguish, of cowardice, and it only sharpened every minute detail of her manifestation. The glittering black wolf stood at least waist-high, its edges crackling like fire, purples and greens and blues swirling in black. It was an extension of her, an energy she could feel outside herself as easily as she felt it inside herself.

"You will never be emperor," Vaasa swore.

And the wolf pounced.

Lord Karev threw up his arms in a futile attempt at defense, and the wolf sank its claws into his torso, toppling him onto the floor as it latched its teeth onto his shoulder. The lord screamed in agony, his pain a tangible thing that Vaasa could feel along every inch of her skin. It was heat, life, energy. It made a home in her.

She tightened her fists, and the wolf snapped its teeth into the side of his neck, ripping out a chunk of his throat. Blood sputtered from the wound she'd dealt. Lord Karev's eyes went blank, death finding its mark with as little hesitation as Vaasa had shown. Blood pooled around the body, crimson soaking into Asteryan blue.

The wolf dissipated.

Vaasa's hands shook, images of her brother flashing through her mind, and nausea rolled in her stomach. But she remembered the weight of Lord Karev's body. The coldness of the floor he had pinned her against. The sheer helplessness he had wanted to instill.

It wasn't enough.

She sprinted to the pile of rope next to the curtains, tugging them back to Karev's body. She wrapped the rope around Lord Karev's torso and over his shoulders, making sure it would hold, using the same knot she'd once used to tie Reid to his headboard on her wedding night. Her small, vindictive touch.

Someone crashed through the door behind her. Roman's voice rang across the room, panic so clear in his breathy tone. "What the hell are you doing?"

She dragged Lord Karev's body to the shattered balcony door. Sucking down a breath, she hauled his weight up and tossed it over the side of the building. The rope whizzed by, and Vaasa watched the mechanism from where she crouched, out of sight of the square, her breath caught in her lungs.

The rope went taut, and the mechanism squealed, lurching, but it held.

She caught one glance of the city square, just one, and her breath stopped.

It was chaos. People screamed and ran in every direction. Smoke billowed in the air. The black powder they'd planted the previous night had set off perfectly.

Vaasa turned, meeting Roman's eyes. He shouldn't be here; if he'd followed her command, he would have been far enough from this room to make returning impossible. "They all saw you down there, right?" she asked. "You have an alibi?"

"That's why you sent me away," he said. Roman's body relaxed. The power-hungry, love-twisted fool. He approached her, though his demeanor remained tentative, as if he still questioned whether she would turn on him next.

Her eyes dipped to his waistline, snagging on his keys, and then back up. Vaasa hastily removed her blood-soaked gloves, making a show of it by contorting her face into disgust. She threw them to the floor and backed away, as if she were unsure how she had just done what she'd done, as if she was not the kind of woman capable of such violence.

And then she looked at Roman. She crossed what little space remained between them and sank into his body, purposely shaking just enough to seem as though adrenaline had overtaken her. He held her despite the initial distrust he'd displayed, and to solidify his cooperation, she whispered, "Get me out of here, Roman."

Without hesitation, he took her blood-soaked hand, and they sprinted into the hall. His footsteps echoed on the staircase with her own, screams still bouncing across the first and second floors, and Vaasa's heart beat in her chest. She made it halfway to the second floor, but it was filled with a panicked crowd, everyone pushing to get down the final set of stairs and out of the building. No damage was done to this part of the Sanctum, but no amount of planning could have predicted where the crowds would run or whether the exit would remain open. She needed to lose Roman in this crowd, needed to—

Roman's hands wound around her waist, and he tugged her back up the stairs. Vaasa slipped. Her back arched at the impact of sharp stone, but still Roman forced her to stand. She turned and ran with him—it was her only choice. If she fought him here, she might not be able to make it through the crowd quick enough to outrun him.

On the third floor, he pulled her through a door and into one of the antechambers that served as a waiting room. Art covered the walls and continued to a painted ceiling, gold embossed into the image. It was empty, just as the connected offices would be.

The connected offices, which led to the . . .

Servants' tunnels.

Her magic bit at her gut, instinct roaring to life. Vaasa followed him through the door into the council chamber and burst through another hallway that led to the offices on this floor. She spotted a door that led to one of the servants' passageways built into the Sanctum. A piece of iron could be slid across it when the council wanted privacy, sealing the tunnel, the only exit out the other side of the building. She sprinted toward it, her hand *just* brushing the knob, when Roman wrapped his hands around her wrist and pulled. She spun, and he hooked an arm around her waist, hauling her against him.

"If you go in there, you'll burn," he told her. "The building is going to come down. I don't think we have another option; we have to go out the front."

To do that meant to bring him right to Reid, and that was a risk she would never take. Vaasa stared up at Roman, and she tried. She tried to find any of the love she had once held for him, tried to latch onto the younger version of her that would have done almost anything for him. But even that part of her cried out in resistance.

He had betrayed her, like everyone else in this worthless city.

She made up her mind.

"Roman," she whispered with a false reverence.

He looked down at her like she held the world in her hands, as if he believed that all his past sins could justify these very means, as if his name from her lips was vindication enough.

She held his gaze with such severity and confessed, "Reid of Mireh is in the city, and he's waiting for me downstairs."

Roman's brows slammed together. "What?"

"He orchestrated this attack. He's the one who murdered Lord Vlacik. I thought he was the only way to get rid of Lord Karev, and he promised to help Amalie escape. I didn't think you would do it."

"Vaasa—"

"If I go out the front of this building, he's going to force me to leave with him."

Frustration contorted Roman's face, his thick brows pressing together and his jaw so tight he could have bent iron with his teeth.

"I can't go with him. I can't go with Reid of Mireh."

"Why?" Roman demanded, tightening his grip on her. "Why tell me this now?"

Vaasa parted her lips. And then she put a hand at the nape of Roman's neck and pulled his mouth down to hers.

Roman froze, then hauled her close. Vaasa's heart slammed against her chest. Every muscle she had begged her to stop. She didn't want him, didn't want to kiss anyone but the man waiting outside in the square.

Liar. Manipulator.

Serpent.

She thrust her hands into Roman's hair and kissed him as if she meant it. Her hands slid down his shoulders and to his waistline, pulling herself to him, hands seeking as she bit his lower lip. He groaned, his tongue snaking into her mouth, and she fought the urge to gag. She guided herself back against the wall, letting him press her to it while her other hand caught the knob of the door. She twisted.

And then she threw her entire body against Roman's, shoving him as hard as she could as she opened the door.

She threw him inside, their mouths parting, and he stumbled backward into the servants' tunnel.

Without hesitating, she slammed the door closed and hauled the iron bar down, locking it.

His fists pounded against the door, a bloodcurdling scream emanating through it, but Vaasa looked down at her hands.

At the set of keys she'd taken from his belt as she kissed him.

She shoved those keys into her pocket next to her mother's necklace and ran for her life, leaving her past—and her guilt—locked behind that door.

CHAPTER 38

Hesitation was the most likely of murderers. Esoti had taught Vaasa that, and as she raced through the Sanctum, that training snapped into place. She scurried down one of the flights of stairs that had emptied out and spilled into the city square. She was covered in blood with a panicked look on her face, a host of guards charging straight toward her.

She ignored every single one. Her head whipped around as she searched the crowd for the man in the executioner's mask. She had to find him, had to . . .

There.

Reid scaled a waist-high wall near the Citadel, keeping his balance with each precise step he took. His head lifted.

Their gazes collided.

Vaasa darted forward, but one of the city guardsmen caught her. He grabbed hold of her waist and restrained her, violently hauling her back. She thrashed and screamed. He cooed at her as though she were mad, as though her attempt to bolt was nothing but panic, and it was his responsibility to save her from herself. "Heiress, please," he grunted. He must not have made the connection yet, must not have pinned Lord Karev's death on her.

To the left, Sachia broke through the crowd, only prevented from reaching Vaasa by the line of city guards who blocked ordinary Mekës citizens from the rest of the nobility that fled the Sanctum. They were creating a path out for *them* before anyone else, leaving the rest of the people to burn or choke.

Every ounce of fear and torment that haunted this place melded with the rage already boiling inside Vaasa. The ground wept with the hundreds of deaths from the past two generations, the tang of their blood still marking the stones. It was an energy that had never left the square. She had felt it each and every time she walked between these two buildings. Her senses were so heightened, so keen.

Magic detonated from her with the same force as the explosions.

Veragi magic slammed into the Sanctum and shattered the remaining windows on the first floor. Colorful shards of stained glass exploded in every direction as wails pierced the air. It sliced through skin and sinew, cutting into the bodies of the people who tried to contain her. The ones who tried to run before anyone else could. Through every desperate noble who had crowded behind the city guards for safety, thinking themselves exempt from the violence they had always imposed on others.

People dropped, one by one, her magic slicing them where the glass didn't.

High-pitched shrieks cut the square, everyone's fear a palpable thing. It only fed into her power, only doubled and tripled every ounce of what she felt. Glittering black mist rose from the ground and circled her, spinning like a tide pool. Vaasa emerged from the pulsing cloud of her magic, shadows circling her body.

Their terrified echoes of the word *cursed* swirled in the air.

Every guard that ran at her fell; magic shoved down their throats or slid like a blade along their necks. She was going to decimate the square. She would kill every person who stood in her way.

They stared at her with horror in their eyes.

Good.

Magic spread like poison on the ground, crawling up the bodies of the nobles it touched. No mercy lived within her, not as she attacked the very people who had watched and sneered as she was dragged through the city. Their calls came to the forefront of her memories. All her life, they had used her and prepared to trade her, as if she weren't human. She was, after all, only someone's daughter.

Her power rose higher, and she began to pull from Ozik's side of the bond. With the anchor firmly in her pocket, she was protected from the consequences of their bargain, could take his magic at will the way he had been using hers. In glittering, maddening red, power poured into her. She devoured it. The taste was silken on her tongue—these people's pain, their anguish, their terror.

They had celebrated the idea of executing her husband today, turned it into a performance to sate their bloodlust. They had whispered all those cruel things, imposed their own identities upon her, never knowing who she truly was.

Not cursed.

Witch.

She was going to bring down the whole city. She would bury herself if it meant she could bury them.

Black mist rose around her, blocking out the setting sun, snuffing out light and sound and anything alive. They couldn't reach her. They wouldn't dare try. They were all too afraid of what she was.

And then Ozik's voice threaded her mind from some far-off place that she didn't know or feel. *Do you remember when I told you that I do not lie?*

Vaasa held her breath. *Yes,* she whispered back.

I made a promise to your mother, he said. *The first one-sided bargain I made in a very long time. I swore to her that I would keep you alive. So you must run, Vaasalisa. Please don't make a liar out of me.*

A tear slid down Vaasa's cheek. Everything she felt crested over her. The more that she fed from the things outside her, the more unstable she felt. It was a gift to perceive everything—people's emotions, their intentions, the subtle changes in everything they thought. It allowed her to predict everyone's next move.

But it was a danger, too. Because right now, she was drowning in all of it.

And then someone broke through the mist.

A large frame with eyes of orange and black, hidden beneath an executioner's mask. Their gazes locked. Faintly, she knew that she could accidentally kill him. That this magic was too far gone, her rage and guilt and grief and pain muddling the lines between rationality and reactivity.

But Reid of Mireh did not look afraid.

He breathed. His chest rose and fell. Her magic adjusted, it made room for him, it welcomed him inside the prison she'd created for herself. A place where she could harm everyone, and no one could touch her.

It let him in. *She* let him in.

He met her where she stood. His hand raised and settled on her cheek. "Let it go," he whispered. "Run with me. Live with me. Let me give you everything the world should have given you sooner."

Her magic stuttered. She gained a semblance of control over her body, like her weight had a foothold on the stones beneath her again. She looked at what she could see of Reid's face, at the familiar curves and lines of it. And then suddenly she was there again, on that platform at the Icrurian election, their future playing out behind her eyes.

A future she could have, if she only let herself.

Vaasa took a grounding breath, then with everything she had, hauled the magic back within.

It slammed into her body as if she'd been thrown from a great height. She screamed in blinding pain. She stumbled back and fell, hands scraping the stones beneath her, tearing through her skin.

Reid hauled her to her feet as she gasped down air, the pain transforming into a sharp awareness of her surroundings.

"Run for the port," Reid commanded. "I'll guard your back."

Vaasa took off in a sprint. She panted, arms pumping, the people in the square parting and fleeing from her. The sentinels and city guard were all behind her now, all dead or dying or injured. She looked over her shoulder to see Reid running, someone hot on his heels, and they raised a sword.

A scream broke from her lips.

Red hair came flying from the left, and the man went tumbling to the ground, steel clattering, Sachia rolling with him until they hit the wall Reid had perched on earlier. The pirate sprang to her feet and ran, leaping over a body as she went, blood dripping down her face.

Reid's hand wound around Vaasa's and tugged. She raced to the edge of the square, past the platform that held the iron pole. They scaled the sea-facing side of the Sanctum until the fiery port came into view.

A loud whistle sounded from their right, and Sachia darted toward the stone parapet that lined the ocean. Reid led Vaasa that way. Their footsteps pounded against the stone. Sachia threw herself over the parapet, body dangling by her hands, and then dropped.

Vaasa's stomach hit the parapet and she peered over. A small tender floated in the water just feet away, far enough from the flame-consumed port that they had a clear path out into the bay. Sachia swam to it.

"Go," Reid instructed.

Stone cut into Vaasa's waist as she pulled herself over the side of the parapet and fell, the icy water below soaking into her dress as it swallowed her. She broke the surface with ease and kicked. The hem of her gown tangled with her legs, but she swam as well as she could, crossing the mere feet until she reached the boat. Arms came down and hauled her up, the dress heavy and threatening to pull her back, but she finally slid over the side.

"Get down," Sachia commanded as the boat rocked, two people Vaasa didn't recognize reaching for Reid. He was up and over in seconds, and then Vaasa hit the deck, rolling beneath a bench seat. She shivered. Reid rolled into her, clung to her, their breaths coming in and out in tandem. Blankets were thrown over them as the tender carved a path into the Iron Bay.

CHAPTER 39

Vaasa waited. She could hardly think as the boat rocked on the waves, heading for the prison. Her mind spun as magic clawed at her insides, seeking more to feed from. She reached into the pocket of her dress and gripped the necklace with a barely audible sigh, one of her fingers dragging along the set of keys she'd tucked next to it. Relief flooded her—they weren't lost.

Her magic sputtered out at first contact with the necklace, her body quiet for a moment though dread curled low in her stomach.

The last of the day's light broke through the smoky haze as Vaasa's blankets were pulled off her, revealing the sky to her once again. Sachia sat on the seat across from them, and Reid sat up. He hauled his executioner's mask off.

They weren't being chased, then. The port was distracted, engulfed in flames.

Sachia started rummaging through one of the storage latches, pulling out a bundle of clothing. It was a uniform meant for a sentinel. "Change into these."

Vaasa tucked her hand into her sopping pocket and then unfurled them, displaying the keys. She wondered for just a moment if Roman had managed to escape. The thought of him burning, the sound of his screams . . .

"Wait," Sachia said. "Are those the keys to the prison?"

"I don't know everything he had access to, but I think so. In case you struggle with your magic, we have a backup plan."

Reid stared at the keys as Sachia took them from Vaasa's outstretched palm, but he didn't ask questions. Sachia turned the keys over in her hands, then folded them tightly within her fingers.

"Ozik cleared the guards," Vaasa added.

Sachia's brows rose. "If he's going to betray us, now is the time."

Ozik wouldn't. He couldn't, not now that a second bargain lived between them. Vaasa dipped into her pocket and grabbed ahold of the necklace, her magic winking out now that she touched the iron links.

I want you to kill me, Vaasalisa.

Her mother's warning blared in her mind—that the cost was too high. This was the piece of Ozik's request she hadn't yet put together. What would it take to kill the vessel of a god?

Shivers racked her body. Reid lifted the blanket to her shoulders, affording Vaasa what felt like an inconsequential privacy. Cold air assaulted her as she quickly shucked off her bloodstained dress. She pulled the wool uniform on and basked in the immediate warmth, then shoved her feet into boots before slipping the necklace into a buttoned pocket of her pants. The moment she released the necklace, magic returned on a breath.

Vaasa hauled the large, heavy fabric of her dress over the side of the boat, leaving it for the ocean to claim. Any guard would take one look at her and know she wasn't a true soldier, but it was still better than trying to make it through the prison in a blood-soaked gown.

Reid lowered the blanket. "We'll follow the plan we set originally."

"*The Red Corsair* is waiting out in the bay with the larger crowds," Sachia said before turning to the ocean and away from where Reid was undressing. "Koen's arm is broken and he's been beaten, but he's alive. He's with Melisina on the ship."

"Everyone's alive?" Vaasa asked, hope rising in her with the wicked churning of her magic.

"Everyone's alive."

"Thank you," she said, her hand coming up to clutch her throat on instinct. Everything was happening so quickly, she could hardly keep up. Smoke billowed into the sky from the fire in the Sanctum, and despite trying to shove guilt aside, she imagined Roman's screams.

"Was it you? Did you kill Lord Karev?" Sachia asked suddenly.

Vaasa met the pirate's eyes. She nodded.

Sachia's jaw dropped. "You hung him from the Sanctum?"

Vaasa chewed on her cheek, wringing her hands nervously as she stared at the lip of the boat. Each moment that passed felt like a lifetime. She slid her eyes to Sachia once more, reluctantly answering. "I only did to him exactly what he threatened to do to me."

Reid went still at her side.

"Shit," Sachia muttered.

Their boat approached the Last Crossing, hugging the shadow of it. Only a sliver of yellow fought for dominance in a blue-faded sky, indigo blue revealing stars above them. Four figures appeared from under the sturdy columns of the bridge, and Vaasa's heart leapt into her throat, but Sachia let out a sigh of relief.

"Crew members," Reid assured her with a quiet murmur. She turned to him, and his broad shoulders and chest stole her vision, clearing it of anything else. Magic poured from her hands, and she didn't bother trying to keep it down this time. He dipped his gaze to the magic, then back to her eyes, giving that amused smile that had once driven her to the brink of madness. Then he darted over the lip of the tender and into the water just as Sachia jumped in, the water coming to their knees.

Strong arms hauled Vaasa up and out of the boat, Reid tightening on her body and legs like he wasn't going to let her go; water didn't dare to touch her. He walked her all the way to the shore, setting her upon the rocky beach. There was a purposeful look on Reid's face, all determination and task, and the sight of it reminded Vaasa precisely who she'd fallen in love with.

"Lead the way," Sachia commanded under her breath to Vaasa while two of the men beached the tender.

They ran under the cover of twilight, hauling themselves up the ladder one by one, the cold filling Vaasa's lungs as she sucked down air. The guard who normally watched the cave entrance was nowhere to be found; the prison was a ghost town. All the guards had likely been assigned to the execution or had gone to the port, leaving only the bare minimum here. Ozik had done precisely what he promised, and the thought gave life to further panic in Vaasa's body. Still, the only way was forward, and so she descended into the cave.

Reid stayed just behind her, his fingers brushing against the small of her back. It was empty. No one.

In front of the door to the sentinels' break room, Vaasa slid to a stop, fumbling with the iron ring of keys until she found the one that opened it. The small group swarmed inside, finding two guards waiting, and the three members of Sachia's crew took their lives before they could scream.

They sped into where the prisoners were held, the stone walls seeming to groan with the captives. It filled Vaasa's ears like the waves of the ocean. Ducking into the stairwell, they started up to the third floor, which was where Roman had told Sachia that her brother would be.

Sachia burst through the door. "Micha!" Sachia yelled, pain and desperation coating each syllable. "Micha!"

Nothing.

"Micha!" Sachia yelled again, relentless. She began looking through the bars of every cell, the other members of the crew doing the same thing.

"Sachia!" one of the crew members yelled.

The pirate sobbed, throwing her body toward a cell on the left side. Darkness bathed the sullied floor, but Sachia didn't seem to care. She didn't seem afraid. They fumbled with the keys for two, three, four tries until Sachia cursed and ordered everyone to step back. Her hands extended, and she twisted her wrist sharply. The lock squealed, then clicked, the training she had done with Melisina paying off. Sachia threw open the door. She rushed in and dragged a smaller body out, Vaasa crouching to meet them.

He had red hair like Sachia's, eyes the same stunning shade of green.

Except those eyes were open.

Unmoving.

His body did not twitch. He was pale, skin stuck in a lifeless pallor, his lips blue. His young face was contorted in pain.

A bloodcurdling scream broke from Sachia. Vaasa braced herself for the sound of guards, stumbling back to Reid's side with her hand over her mouth.

Sachia slammed her hands against her brother's chest as she attempted to resuscitate him. Over and over she tried, tears falling to his frozen body relentlessly. The keys lay motionless on the floor next to her.

Reid stepped forward, but Sachia growled, baring her teeth like a wild animal. "Do not touch my brother."

Tears flooded Sachia's eyes and rolled down her face. It was a connection Vaasa couldn't relate to, yet one she understood. The pirate's pain infiltrated the air around them. Sickness crawled up Vaasa's throat as she watched Sachia search her brother for any signs of life. There was nothing that could undo what had been done.

Sachia whispered to him, "I'm so sorry."

The door behind them burst open.

The pirate turned, looking down the hallway as three guards ran into the hall. Rage lit the green of her eyes, and Vaasa felt it when magic pierced the air. Sachia stood as if she held no weight. Her arms rose and every metal bar set in the prison cell doors around them shook. Reid's eyes went wide.

With a shrill squeal, the metal snapped from the doors and flew through the air, impaling each of the guards.

They hit their knees as Sachia sprinted forward. She drew a blade and ran it across each of their necks in succession, not slowing between slashes. Sachia heaved in breaths as blood bathed the prison floor. Her knife dangled from her fingertips.

Vaasa knew the look in Sachia's eyes, knew what it was to be out of control. "He did this," Sachia seethed. "Karev murdered him."

He'd likely done it that morning, given the freshness of the body. Punishment for her involvement with Reid and Koen.

Karev had died too quickly. Circumstances necessitated such a thing, but the thought would not cease in Vaasa's mind. She should have dragged it out, should have made him suffer for each violent press of his hand and his orders.

Sachia threw herself back to the floor at her brother's side, her hands shaking as she ran them over him. Members of her crew surrounded her, some of them speaking to her, but she snarled, "I won't leave him! I won't."

One of the men with curly black hair looked at Reid, his tender brown eyes wet. He picked up the keys and handed them to Reid. "Go. We'll meet you at the cliff entrance."

Reid gave a solemn nod. "Be safe, Jonáš."

Vaasa did her best to stay focused, to stay the course. "This way," she said, weaving her fingers through Reid's and forcing her legs to carry her down the hall. They were headed to the fifth floor when the sound of pealing bells filled the air. "Shit," Vaasa cursed.

"What is that?" Reid asked.

"A distress signal. Any guard left on this island will know the prison has been breached." They were going to have to fight their way out.

Vaasa sprinted to Amalie's cell. Hands snaked out of the bars like the curling legs of a spider, and Vaasa knew whatever she faced was not Amalie.

Vaasa looked inside and found eyes white as snow staring back at her.

"Veragi," Vaasa breathed.

The goddess nodded.

Vaasa fumbled with the keys again, putting one into the lock. It didn't work. Neither did the next one. Or the next. Vaasa couldn't breathe. Roman might not have even had the key to Amalie's cell, maybe he'd never been able to—

The lock clicked.

Her heart sank. He'd had the key all along. He could have let her or Amalie go at *any* point, and time and again, he'd chosen not to. Vaasa ripped the door open. Amalie's body stood there, the chains around her wrists and neck tarnished. She was well cared for, but the iron manacles on her wrists looked rusted.

"Fuck," Reid whispered from behind Vaasa.

Veragi stepped forward like she had all the strength in the world. "Help me get these off of her," Vaasa demanded as she started pulling at the chains.

Without hesitation, Reid lifted his sword. "Move."

Vaasa scuttled back as Veragi spread her wrists as far as they could go. Reid swung down, his sword cracking against the chains, and the tarnished links fractured. They slid to the floor.

Darkness burst forth from Amalie's body, tendrils of magic licking the air in angry snaps. Reid jumped out of the way as a miserable keening broke from Amalie's throat. The glowing white of her eyes grew brighter, and Vaasa lifted her arm to cover her vision. In seconds, it was over, and Vaasa stared at her best friend.

Only it wasn't her best friend. It was wild, white eyes. There was no trace of Amalie staring back at her.

"Is she alive?" Vaasa whispered.

Veragi met Vaasa's gaze and gave a strong nod. "I would not kill her." The goddess's voice threaded the air, a dark and powerful Icrurian that reminded Vaasa of Melisina.

"We need to go," Reid urged as the door on the other side of the hallway was thrown open. Three guards sprinted toward them. Veragi's head whipped their way. Vaasa startled. She looked *nothing* like Amalie. Gone was the kindness, the warmth, the care. All that remained were harsh lines and malice that caused even Vaasa to step back. Veragi lifted her arms with grace and squeezed her hands. Magic flew through the air, whizzing toward the guards, solidifying into sharp points just before it made contact. Those edges pierced their chests.

Their bodies halted and sank to the floor.

The magic disintegrated into black smoke, wisping out from the dead guards like steam off tea.

Vaasa stared at Veragi, and all she could think of was Julianna.

"This way," Reid said, clutching Vaasa's hand and running back to the stairwell entrance, neither of them having the time necessary to ruminate on what they'd just seen. She held tight to Reid's hand, and they fled back down the stairwell and out the same door they had taken to enter, sprinting down slippery steps with as much skill as they could manage. Snow fell from the dark sky, cold drops of it splashing off Vaasa's cheeks. She looked over her shoulder to see Veragi following, body uninhibited by the weeks in this prison, by the things that had been done to her, by the cold.

Sachia and the rest of her crew were pressed to the cliffside, staring down at the ladder they had used to climb up. "Shit," Reid growled, looking down at the space below the bridge. It was littered with lamplights. Guards swarmed the ladder, at least fifteen, too many for them to fight.

"This way," Vaasa yelled, trailing the perimeter of the cliff until they landed on a pathway that led to the Last Crossing. If they could get across the bridge and take one of the boats on the other side, they could get out. They'd have to fight their way through, but there were likely fewer guards on the administrative side of the island, all of them having run into the prison with the pealing of the bells. In the distance, fire still raged along the Mekës coastline, flames lighting the black sky.

Footsteps pounded behind them, the sound of Asteryan commands blaring through the snow as guards chased them onto the bridge. Sachia and her crew swarmed behind them—

Vaasa's stomach turned over on itself, and suddenly, fire erupted within her.

She *screamed*.

Her knees cracked against the ground. Magic tore from her very bones. The world flipped and scorched her from the inside. Reid howled her name, his hands wrapping around her waist and trying to pull her up as the guards closed in on them. Vaasa couldn't get up. It was the most excruciating the magic had been since the very first moment she'd bargained it away, her muscles torn and her body ripped apart in defiance of the force being stolen from her. Vaasa wailed again, fisting her hands in her hair as agony eliminated all other things from her mind. A splitting crack boomed from the left, and Vaasa gasped, falling onto her hands despite Reid's grip.

"Going somewhere, Vaasalisa?" came Zetyr's ancient voice.

CHAPTER 40

Veragi screeched, a bloodcurdling, angry cry. It was not Ozik who stood on the opposite side of the bridge, just like it was not Amalie who stood at Vaasa's side. The sheer enormity of power emanating from both deities bounced around the bridge, making even the air feel heavier.

Run, Ozik's voice curled into her mind.

Remember our bargain, Vaasa hissed across their bond, her hand still clutching her abdomen.

One breath. Two. She lifted her chin. Zetyr stood across the bridge in front of all the guards. Crimson glowed in his eyes, entirely consuming the pupils and whites, just like Amalie's were coated in white. Dark webs protruded upon the skin of his neck and cheeks.

And on his knees in front of the deity . . .

Roman.

Vaasa's heart dropped into her stomach. The guards behind them fled, emptying from the bridge with terrified shrieks. Zetyr raised his hand and twisted, pulling his fingers into a fist.

The roar of the Miro'dag sounded behind Vaasa. The terrible screech of the creature caused her body to lock. The cracking of bones echoed, and Reid cursed, still holding tightly to Vaasa. She didn't look. She didn't need to see them to know the Miro'dag had killed the guards. Zetyr had eliminated the people who knew of his magic.

"The demon is blocking our path," Reid growled in her ear.

There was no way off this bridge. Either they faced Zetyr or they faced the Miro'dag.

Vaasa put one leg beneath her, then another, standing to her full height at Veragi's side.

"Vaasa—" Roman choked, then went silent as Zetyr grabbed his shoulder.

Those glowing red eyes landed on Veragi, who stood next to Vaasa and Reid with a dark scowl painted across her lips. The bridge stretched between them, but the distance started to close as Vaasa held Roman's pleading eyes.

"Finally, we meet again, sister," Zetyr purred at Veragi. "Tell me, will your witches save you now?"

He threw his arms forward, and Vaasa lurched as the cords between her and Zetyr tugged. The magic he wielded was incredible, far more than Ozik had ever taken from her. Power pulsed down the bridge, a stream of red flying toward them. Veragi stepped forward, and a glittering black wall rose into the air, blocking the assault. It dropped, and he struck again, and again, and again. She blocked each attack with a raise of her arms.

Zetyr cackled into the sky and screamed, "No tomb can hold me forever!"

Vaasa forced her shaking hand into her pocket and took hold of the necklace. Her magic extinguished, and she gasped at the relief, even as it hummed against her fingers. Her head snapped up to see Zetyr shake his head like a dog.

He couldn't access her magic when it was dulled. It might not be enough to stop him, but it was enough to cause him to falter.

The crimson in Zetyr's eyes sputtered, gold leaking through, and his face contorted in rage. Ozik was fighting. Even right now, he was *fighting*. The anchor upon his hand was the only lifeline he had left.

Strike! Ozik screamed in her mind.

Vaasa burst forward, her fingers clutching the necklace, and Reid let loose a strangled holler as she broke from his arms. Reid's steps pounded behind her. Roman screamed for Vaasa to stop. But she had already faced this. She thrust the necklace forward and Zetyr roared, stumbling back and away from Roman. That glowing red sputtered, gold breaking through entirely, and Zetyr's body—*Ozik's* body—convulsed with his fight.

A flash of bright white lit the bridge and shadows whirled around them, growing, shifting, flares of magic so dark they swallowed any light. Veragi's power shot at Zetyr. Glittering black mist curled around him and gripped like a vise. His body slammed into the bridge and dragged toward them as if a rope had been tied to his leg and pulled. His screams pierced the air. The shadows writhed over him, snuffing out each of his senses, burying him in magic like a tomb, his limbs going rigid in the senseless void.

Except for his hand, his *ringed* hand, where the licks of magic could not penetrate. They kept trying, but each time the tendrils dipped to the black stone ring, they recoiled. Something about that ring scared them off, as if they were fingers touching a flame.

"Holy shit," Reid cursed from behind her.

Vaasa whipped her head to Veragi.

The goddess lifted from the bridge, rising into the air over the ocean. The whites in her eyes pulsed, and a wicked cry broke from her lips. A scream that sounded so much like Amalie's. The goddess held Zetyr down, but only for so long. It had to have been using everything Veragi had.

"Jump!" Vaasa screamed to Sachia, whose crew was dragging her to the edge of the bridge, eyes wide at the goddess. Sachia took one look, waited one second, and then flung herself over the ledge.

Vaasa met Reid's eyes. "Go!"

Reid stood there, gaze on her, and shook his head. "Not without you. Not this time."

Zetyr lay beneath the swaths of Veragi magic, unmoving within his binds. If she released the necklace in her hand, it was possible Zetyr would harness her power again, that he could use it through Ozik's connection to her.

She couldn't wield.

But if she took Ozik's ring, it would remove the last semblance of a defense he had against Zetyr.

Magic sharpened around her. Veragi's power. A tendril lifted and then dropped like a blade, severing Ozik's hand at the wrist. Veragi snarled at the body on the bridge as it began to convulse. To fight.

Veragi's message was clear—take the ring, no matter what it cost.

"I need the ring," Vaasa panted. She sprinted forward, eyes on the ring, the necklace in her hands—

Someone moved into her path. She skidded to a stop, meeting Roman's pleading eyes. "How could you do this?" he screamed, and then his voice dropped to a strangled plea as he looked past her to where Reid stood. "Was any of it real?"

She saw the desperation in his maddened brown eyes, remembered every fracture of kindness and love that had once lit up his face as he looked at her. Fear had made a home in him, too—fear of loss, fear of powerlessness, fear of his entire existence being stolen from him just because he had loved the wrong woman. It was the sort of despair that would cause a man like Roman to do something he could never take back. To lock her in a prison, if that was what it took to save his own life. In a way, he had already died for her once. After what she'd done today, she didn't think he would do it again. "No," she said. "I guess that makes us both liars."

Veragi faltered in the air, her arms shaking, and Ozik's body convulsed. Zetyr would not stay down much longer. A terrible peal sounded on the other edge of the bridge, and Vaasa's heart jumped into her throat.

It was the Miro'dag. It was behind her. Near Reid.

Again.

And she had a choice. She had a choice to win this fight, to get the ring, or to turn around and change the outcome this time. To save him.

"Don't," Roman begged.

With one last look at Roman, Vaasa spun on her heel.

Love or power; she knew precisely who and what she would choose.

The Miro'dag took form, Zetyr finding his grip on his power again, and Vaasa sprinted. "Reid!" she screamed as she threw the necklace, the links of it disconnecting from her fingertips, sending him the very thing that could save his life should Zetyr rise.

Agony, wicked and dark, filled Vaasa's lungs and broke from her in an ear-piercing scream.

Not just pain.

Magic.

It flooded into Vaasa's stomach, into her veins, drowning her, smothering her. Her muscles tightened as they sewed back together, weaving with the force in her bones, a well inside her filling to the brim like a hole had been dug into the ocean. It was gruesome and all-consuming.

It exploded.

Magic burst from her in tendrils of darkness, the familiar black mist flooding the entire bridge as if someone had blown out the moon. It stole the air, the sound, the light. It stole everything.

And in her mind, Ozik's voice whispered, *You are more powerful than I could ever have imagined.*

The stones beneath Vaasa's feet shook, and magic—her magic, his magic—morphed at her command, following the call of her heart. The commands of her soul. Four legs. White eyes. A howl that crashed into every corner of the continent. Vaasa's feet dug into the ground. She lifted her arms. The mist enveloped her hands and her wrists. She was *untouchable*. She was pure power. She was a wildfire, a monsoon, a life-altering natural disaster.

Her wolf ran at the Miro'dag, snarling, and Vaasa followed with her steps in tandem and her heart beating wildly in her chest. It chased away the cold, the fear, the longing. The magic filled every empty, miserable piece of her that had chipped away into a chasm these long weeks. Everything she had withstood. Those who had tried to control her. Lord Vlacik, Lord Karev, Roman.

Her wolf grew with each step, reaching the height of the Miro'dag and the size of Melisina's horse, and just as Ozik had taught her, it struck. The Miro'dag screamed as the wolf sank its teeth into its throat. Metal coated her tongue as if she could taste the blood, taste the rip of flesh and the accompanying tearing of Zetyr's magic. Vaasa kept going. She lifted her hands and urged her manifestation onward. It tore into the Miro'dag with an unforgiving rage. It remembered, just as Vaasa did, what had been taken from her.

The weight of Reid's body in her lap.

When he ceased to pull breath.

The wrenching away of her magic.

She wanted it all back.

The Miro'dag extended its webbed wings, and as it had done in the colosseum of Dihrah, it winked out of existence. Her wolf stood snarling. Oil dripped from its mouth, the manifestation clearer than it had ever been. Vaasa heaved air into her lungs. Her knees wobbled. When she stumbled, arms wrapped around her waist, and she fell into Reid's weight. "I've got you," he promised.

He hauled her to the edge of the bridge, and she took one last look at the opposite end to see Veragi's eyes dim and her body plummet downward, directly into the water. The same ocean Reid now hauled her toward.

"Jump!" he screamed.

She glanced across the bridge one final time, her gaze meeting Roman's.

And then Vaasa flung herself off the side.

For a moment, all she heard was the roar of wind in her ears. Her stomach flew up and into her throat. Then the sound of Roman's scream broke through the air, and the glacial ocean swallowed her whole.

CHAPTER 41

Ice sank into Reid's veins.
 The cold was so stark, so suffocating, it took a moment to realize he was still alive. Black water raged around him, turbulent, the sea roaring with its power. Reid plunged down into the freezing abyss, falling into its unforgiving depths until the world around him went quiet.

Through all that violence, there was a moment of peace. A moment where he was aware of Vaasa's hand in his, of the fact that she had jumped, that she had never let him go.

And then the tide ripped them apart.

The world sped up, and frigid water broke through his mind's calm. Reid's body screamed against the impact of the ocean. His lungs strained for air. His back slammed against the rocks and arched with the impact.

He broke the surface and sucked down breath but was quickly pulled back under by the waves. He had minutes before the freezing water killed him. Before it killed Vaasa. Before their bodies slowed and stopped, unable to cope with the cold. He had hoped this wasn't trading one death for another.

Reid launched his body through the water. He kicked and swam, cutting the waves like a razor blade, determination filling him where the peace had been. Water blurred his vision, stung his eyes, but he pushed through the waves with each ounce of strength he still had.

He whipped his head around and found Vaasa clinging to Amalie's body, whose white eyes had ceased to gleam. She was limp in Vaasa's arms, and his wife dragged her through the water, both of them struggling to stay afloat. A tender quickly approached them. Panic rose, but then red hair bobbed from the side of it. Members of Sachia's crew reached into the water and plucked out Vaasa and Amalie.

Reid forced his arms to move even as waves crashed over his head. His hands slammed into wood, and then Jonáš grabbed at his arms and pulled. Reid's shoulders ached against the pressure. Hands pawed at his legs, then grabbed ahold of the fabric of his stolen breeches in a death grip.

With one more tug, Reid flew up and out, midsection slamming against the lip of the boat and promising a bruise. He tumbled over and into the space between benches, staring up at the sky as he heaved in breaths. Blankets were immediately thrown on him.

Sachia looked to Reid at the same time Vaasa gripped the side of the boat, her knuckles going white. Magic licked the wood around her hands. She stared up at the bridge, at the body standing so close to the edge.

Roman.

Something broke on Vaasa's face: fear, betrayal, and then . . . guilt. He didn't know what happened in that room, how Lord Karev had ended up swinging from ropes in the public square; all he knew was that his wife shook. She couldn't tear her eyes away from where Roman stood on that bridge.

Reid leaned into her, and she went rigid. Magic dipped over the side of the boat. More blankets were tossed at everyone, an almost useless counter to the ice, but it was just enough. Reid's gaze roved over Amalie first, who was laid down in the center between two benches, eyes closed, unconscious. It still didn't make sense to Reid—how long had Veragi been there? What had she done to Amalie? All this uncertainty felt heavier than the water-soddened clothing—he knew nothing.

Vaasa's magic curled over the lip of the boat and leaked into the water around them, covering the ocean like fog. Reid shivered and rocked, keeping his eyes on it as it extended far past their boat. As it covered the waves in nothing but pitch-black smoke.

"What's happening?" one of the crew members whispered, eyes caught on the tendrils of magic rolling over the ocean.

"Get us out of this water," Sachia snarled to the men rowing.

The boat picked up speed, cutting through the magic and waves.

The black mist on the ocean writhed. It was a thick layer, eerie and creeping, spreading all around them. Vaasa's chest rose and fell. She stared at the bridge, then Amalie, then back to the bridge. Reid placed his hand under her chin to softly turn her face to him.

"Eyes on me, Wild One," he whispered.

She exhaled, finally looking at him. There was hurt, even vulnerability, on her face, her mask slipping ever so slightly for him. But she still steeled herself in that infuriating way of hers, and this time he understood it.

This was the only way she knew how to survive.

"Reid," Sachia snapped.

He whipped his head to where the pirate pointed, to the group of five or so Asteryan naval vessels that plowed through the water toward them.

"Shit," he cursed.

"Faster," Sachia said, still rocking back and forth slightly to warm herself.

The ships behind them gained speed. Reid pulled Vaasa closer. *The Red Corsair* came into view in front of them, grand and beautiful, red sails billowing in the icy wind. Someone stood on the edge, a silhouette of strong shoulders and a wild mass of blond hair that blew in every direction. A thick cloak draped over her body. She paced in front of the railing, then froze.

His mother.

Their boat bumped against the side of the ship, and a rope ladder careened down the side. Koen peered over the ship, and even in the dark, Reid could see the way his friend's eyes locked on Amalie. One arm was in a sling, the other holding a spyglass. "More blankets!" Koen yelled the moment he was aboard.

"Go," Reid said, hauling Vaasa up and forcing her to climb.

Vaasa was out from the blankets without a care for the cold. Their small boat rocked, and Vaasa gripped the ladder, hauling herself up each step. Her foot slipped, causing Reid's heart to shoot into his throat, but she caught her balance and kept gaining height. Hands reached down and gripped his wife's shoulders, hauling her up onto the ship, and she tumbled out of view.

"Go," Sachia told him.

He stood and the boat rocked, but he pulled Amalie up and over his shoulder, leaving himself only one arm to climb the ladder. It was all he needed. Reid hauled himself up despite the way his frozen limbs fought each strain and pull of muscle. He carried himself and Amalie up as quickly as he could, lifting the witch into the waiting arms of the crew members at the top. Koen reached with his uninjured arm. Reid pulled himself onto the deck at the same time a female crew member ran with Amalie's limp body into one of the private quarters—Jonáš's, Reid realized.

"Our exit is blocked," Koen said, pointing to the other side of the Iron Bay, where the Asteryan city guard had created a line of ships. A barricade to anyone exiting the bay. No doubt they were looking for him. For Vaasa. Reid whipped his head to the only unimpeded exit, the place the Asteryans had never been able to navigate by ship, a place only pirates dared to go. A passageway no doubt crawling with the very pirate crews that wanted Sachia dead. An enormous iron statue guarded the entrance, Vaasa's grandfather's face lit in the moonlight, but no boats blocked the path.

The Loursevain Gap.

"*Move!*" Sachia barked as she threw herself onto the deck. "We're going to have to go through the Gap."

The boat lurched, and panic broke Reid's position. He chased Sachia across the deck, glancing back at Vaasa for a moment before asking the pirate "Are you sure about this?"

"I have to be, it's the only fucking way out."

"Sachia—"

"What?" she snapped.

"Are you okay?"

She skidded to a stop. Pain unraveled on her face, and after a moment, Sachia turned to the sea and screamed into the air, her grief pulsing around them in a terrible ache that spun around the ship.

The Red Corsair lurched toward the Loursevain Gap, and an explosion rang from behind them. Reid turned to see a large metal ball slam into the ocean near them, a splash ringing.

Another explosion. Sachia lifted both of her hands and curled them into fists sharply. The ball of metal flew to the left, careening into the waves.

The five Asteryan ships still chased them. He had a sinking feeling they would follow them into the Gap, that this chase would last for longer than they could survive it. He surveyed the entrance, the ships that now raced to block their path, and caught his gaze upon the imposing iron tower thrusting a sword into the sky.

"Bring down the tower," he said on a breath. "We have to bring down the tower."

He turned to Sachia, who slowly pulled in breath. In and out. In and out. Her magic might be their only chance.

"The tower!" Reid yelled.

Vaasa stepped forward and silently extended Sachia a hand. Magic coated it, spilling from Vaasa and coating the deck just the way she had coated the ocean. His mother joined her, both witches holding out a hand for Sachia to take. The pirate looked at them. Her eyes darted between their outstretched offers.

"Together," Vaasa said to her.

"Together," his mother said.

Sachia gripped their hands.

Vaasa's magic spread from her body. She walked past them all, her hand still in Sachia's, who led Reid's mother behind her. The three witches ascended the steps to the highest deck, walking as far out onto the bow as they could go. Sachia turned to the tower, eyes locked on the rendering of Vaasa's grandfather. The man who conquered this port and set the Asteryan Empire in motion.

Power rumbled around them. The sound of it echoed through the bay in a deafening crack. Sachia lifted her arms, palms facing the metal towers, and then she cranked her hands like she'd done to the locks in the prison. She adjusted her palm, honed that very magic Melisina had been teaching her, pushed it further and further outside herself.

Reid's mother extended a hand and lifted it slowly. Her shimmering black horse grew from the shadowy fog darting across the water. It aimed for the tower. Vaasa touched Sachia's shoulder. Melisina touched the other. The power around them doubled. Tripled. A tsunami of its own.

Their ship broke into the gap. Glittering black magic hit the coast and climbed the tower like ivy.

Sachia screamed with her anger as they passed the statue. Her agony slammed against the iron tower, echoing through the bay just like her voice. Reid felt every inch of it—the sorrow, the love, the unceasing need for revenge.

To deliver precisely what had been taken from her.

And then his wife's eyes glowed crimson.

The same color as Ozik's, as the Miro'dag. He took a step forward, but the magic around her sharpened. It lifted from the water in tendrils that shifted and moved. Black, glittering ropes, the edges of them smoking and writhing.

Reid looked to his mother to find . . .

Her eyes glowing red, too.

And then Sachia's.

The witches held each other, their magic splintering the air in a wave of mist and rippling wind. The ship passed the tower, the narrowing of water, the entrance to the Gap. The iron tower groaned as it tilted at Sachia's command. The foundation of it bent until the metal itself simply . . . snapped.

The tower fell with terrible speed into the Gap. The metal struck the ocean, and a gigantic wave slammed their ship forward. Reid stumbled with the impact. The iron statue bobbed for only a moment, then one side of it dipped beneath the water.

It successfully blocked the Loursevain Gap—had closed off the entrance and made it impossible for another ship to follow them through, at least until it finally sank beneath the waves. It bought them up to an hour.

The glow of Vaasa's eyes extinguished first, then his mother's.

Sachia finally turned, and her eyes went soft, her body slumping.

As Vaasa stumbled backward and pulled Reid's mother with her, all three witches crumpled to the floor. Jonáš's voice rang out around them, commands tossed in every direction as the cliffs on either side of the Gap rose to swallow them.

The boat soared into the night, every whisper of magic around them going utterly silent.

CHAPTER 42

Vaasa was far too restless; her body ached, and her lungs felt tight, her mind reeled like a spool of ribbon come undone. Hours passed, no sign of another ambush or that anyone had managed to chase them into the Gap. It was cramped in the hull of the ship, hammocks strung on either side of their small quarters, a round table in the center. Melisina was with Amalie, who still hadn't woken. Koen slept.

Reid sat at the table in their tight quarters, refusing to rest unless Vaasa did.

Her schedule had become one of a ghost—night was the only time she'd been free for a long while, and she couldn't force her body to rest.

Zetyr. He had taken over Ozik's consciousness in the end, had pushed Ozik somewhere in the back of his own mind. And she had channeled that deity's magic. Had been able to extend the power past herself and through the other witches as they entered the Loursevain Gap. The oil still coated her insides. Her mother's necklace now sat in her pocket, tucked tightly into a pair of warm winter leathers that Sachia had given to her.

A hand brushed her shoulder. Reid's. She turned to where he stood behind her, and he gestured with his head for her to follow him. They took the ladder back up to the main deck, and early morning sunlight bathed the wood. He walked to the bow where a set of stairs led to a small upper deck above the captain's quarters, much like Vaasa had sat upon when he'd first brought her back to Mireh. There were maybe ten paces of space around them, but it was enough to approach the railing of the ship and look out into the widening river.

Their speed was incredible. Vaasa knew that on any other ship, the journey would have been untenable. It was by Sachia's magic alone that a ship this size was able to move with such speed and agility. The iron hinges she had crafted to propel the oars allowed it to switch directions in mere seconds, and there were mechanisms underneath the ship that could be lifted by Sachia's will, allowing it to coast through the shallow meanders that beached other people's vessels. The witch must be utterly exhausted, though perhaps this schedule was one she was used to. Vaasa had a feeling that Sachia wouldn't truly rest for days to come.

Maybe years. Maybe never.

Up here, Vaasa felt the motions of the boat more distinctly. She didn't mind. She leaned against the iron railing, letting the cold air bite at her cheeks. In this leather armor, she was comfortably warm. Golden light flickered along Reid's carved jawline and threw shadows against the railing he leaned back upon. She lost her breath for a moment. Was she really here? Had she actually done it?

For one terrifying second, she thought her mind or Ozik might have played a trick on her. An illusion or some other form of torture. She breathed in and out, fighting against the thought. Her hand curled around the railing. Magic darted over and under the metal.

Vaasa wasn't certain the Asteryan navy would continue to come after her at all. Especially as she looked upon the jagged cut of canyons that jutted out on either side of the Loursevain Gap, snow piling atop the ledges at higher elevations. She could see up the side of the mountains, at the marbling of black and brown that cut through the rock and dove into the river like the roots of some ancient tree. Treacherous and steep, the cliffside mirrored the ones surrounding the fortress in

Mekës. With each sharp bend the water took, Vaasa felt more assured that a full naval force could never navigate this. At most, it would be mercenaries who chased them, and they likely couldn't be rallied in time to cut off *The Red Corsair* before it reached the top of the river.

So long as they made it through the gap alive, they might stand a chance at reaching Innisjour.

Adrenaline bled out of her, replaced by a stiff tiredness that threatened to pull her under. Reid peered at her out of the side of his eye. "Something happened between you two before you left, didn't it?"

Vaasa closed her eyes. There were a thousand things she had to tell Reid, but she was afraid words would fail her. She knew she owed him an explanation. "I betrayed him in the end," she said, though she knew it was more of a consolation prize. "Locked him in the servants' tunnel of the Sanctum and left him there to burn."

"Oh," he muttered. It wasn't of disbelief, or accusation, or anything other than acceptance. Vaasa looked down at her hands, at the magic she had no interest in stifling. Not after everything she had just lived through. No. The magic would breathe before it was taken from her again.

She had to breathe before everything was taken from her again.

"Can we rest now?" she whispered.

Perhaps it was selfish to even ask such a thing, but when a softness took Reid's mouth and eased the worry lines of his forehead, she thought it was okay to live in ignorance, at least for a few hours. He looked at her so tenderly then, perhaps in a way she didn't deserve. "Yes," he said.

She followed him back into their group's sleeping quarters, her muscles growing heavier and heavier with each step. Reid climbed into a hammock, and despite the movement of it, she slipped into it with him. His arms wrapped around her, his body pressed to hers, and she breathed. Just breathed.

Vaasa closed her eyes.

And then there was a small tug somewhere in her core, a strange summoning down the line of her connection to Ozik. On instinct,

Vaasa reached for those cords, the ones still very much tangled in her body. Their bargain wasn't broken, though seemingly more direct, as if she now knew each curve and twist of the string. A pathway she could easily navigate.

There you are, Ozik's voice drifted through her mind. Distant and quieter, but still there.

Vaasa went rigid. Reid shifted next to her, but he didn't speak. He only trailed his fingertips up and down her arm in an effort to calm her, ignorant of the advisor's voice inside her mind.

Is it really you? she asked Ozik.

For now.

Then he went quiet. Vaasa squeezed her eyes shut. She felt the shape of the necklace in her pocket. Ozik had given her everything he'd promised—they'd escaped, and Asterya would likely crumble into itself before it ever had the chance of fighting Icruria.

And now, she was supposed to reunite the pieces of the anchor. To reseal Zetyr in his tomb. A second bargain now lived between them—her freedom for her agreement to do the very thing her mother couldn't. To unite the pieces of the anchor and vanquish Zetyr once and for all, killing Ozik in the process.

The thing her mother had said was not worth the price.

Vaasa didn't believe that Vena Kozár had left her children in Zetyr's path simply because she'd loved Ozik too much to kill him. Her mother had been just as steadfast as her father in this way; between love and power, they would both choose power. Vaasa was certain of it. Which meant there was another price, another reason her mother had not wanted to unite the anchor. Something Ozik hadn't told her, because he knew it would stop Vaasa, too.

So, Vaasa had left Ozik's ring on that bridge.

Without it, she could never unite the pieces. She could leave Ozik to be ravaged, leave the Asteryan nobles to contend with a god none of them believed was real. Whatever havoc Zetyr wreaked, it could only serve to weaken Asterya.

Vaasa had no wish to know what that price of reuniting the anchors was. The way to survive a broken bargain now lived in her pocket, after all. She would tell Reid to bring them back to Mireh, to take advantage of the ruined empire Vaasa had left in her wake. Once they won the war, she would decide what to do with Ozik. With Zetyr.

She shifted in Reid's arms, panic building in her throat. For a while, she tried to focus on the rise and fall of her own chest. But then she felt Ozik again, stronger now. Something shook on the other side of her bond with Ozik. Magic pulsed around her, within her. It flooded down the cords that bound her to him, until his voice was inescapable, begging to be heard. It was only screams, as if Ozik was locked behind a wall.

Ozik repeated something over and over, though Vaasa had the strange sensation that he wasn't speaking to her. She listened closely, distinguishing the words the best she could, until they finally rang clear.

Remember our bargain.

And then he went silent, his presence completely gone, like a candle extinguished by the wind.

EPILOGUE

Ozik distinctly remembered the night of Vena Kozár's death; even trapped in the back of his own mind, he had felt the bond between them extinguish. Their bargain made null. Ozik had been there in that hallway, watching the world through his own eyes but unable to move. Subject only to Zetyr's whims. Ozik had not held her in the last moments she pulled breath, hadn't whispered a promise that he would find her in whatever came next, whether it be another world or another lifetime. That silence had haunted him every day since. The sheer *nothingness* that had existed on the other end.

It felt much like losing a limb.

The night Vena Kozár was taken from him, he had fought Zetyr until her last breath. When she was gone, Ozik had sunk into himself. For months, he had lived in the back of his own mind like a coward, grief-stricken and sick, while Zetyr ravaged the Asteryan empire. The god of bargains and souls had surfaced before, but never with the kind of autonomy Ozik had granted him after Vena. Zetyr had twisted Dominik into the boy's darkest potential, had spun fear into his mind of Vaasa's intentions to overthrow him. Had sicced brother upon sister in the deity's first attempt to kill her.

He wanted every Veragi witch dead, for they were the ones capable of sealing him away.

By the time Ozik had beaten Zetyr back into submission, it had been too late. Dominik's plans were in motion, deals had been struck with the foreman of Wrultho, and the Icrurian election had been infiltrated. He had tried to guide Dominik into different choices, but the path had been carved, and all Ozik could do was find a way to help Vaasa survive it. They'd visited Mireh, and despite the lies Vaasa had tried to spin, Ozik had known she could finally control her magic. That whatever the witches in Mireh had taught her was working.

And he knew this was his last opportunity. He would likely never again be so close to a Veragi witch, and if anyone was capable of re-sealing Zetyr, it was her.

So this was worth it. Ozik sat there, a prisoner in his own mind, a spectator to his own life. Zetyr had taken control, and Ozik's only hope was sailing on a ship into the Loursevain Gap.

Roman Katayev approached the dais where Ozik's body sat. Ozik felt each of Zetyr's movements: the twitch of his eyebrow, the cocking of his head. It was as if Ozik had committed the motion himself, though it was entirely against his will. A complete disconnect of his own intentions from his body, yet trapped here all the same. Witnessing. Hearing. Knowing. By now, the red in Zetyr's eyes had faded. The bulging black veins had burrowed once more beneath the surface. Those things were only symptoms of Ozik's resistance, and Ozik could no longer fight. Zetyr was perfectly camouflaged, as he'd been in those months after Vena's death.

A man walked at Roman's side. Tall and burly, with a jagged scar running vertically upon his neck. His blond hair was unkempt, but his face was shaven, a strange contradiction that Ozik had never been able to place about this particular pirate. Perhaps he wanted the world to see that scar. It didn't matter; Zetyr had already manipulated Captain Sutherland the same way he'd manipulated Vlacik.

But Zetyr did not know the stakes for Roman. Ozik's dealings with the sentinel had been one of the things he managed to keep from

Zetyr. So swift, so brief, one single bargain lived between them that Zetyr had never caught on to. It had been brokered in one of those rare moments when Zetyr was locked so deep in his tomb that he had no access to Ozik's world.

Ozik felt sick at the sound of his own voice, of the dark tenor it had taken with this deity's occupation of his body. "Sutherland," Zetyr greeted the pirate captain, rendering Roman as nothing but a scorned lover who would chase Vaasa into hell if that's what it took to avenge her abandonment of him.

Captain Sutherland looked up. He had just spent the past few weeks locked in the Mekës prison, courtesy of Lord Karev and the new regime he had established in the prison. No doubt, Roman had set Sutherland free. Ozik needed very little to know the truths of people—to see their faults. Roman's was his delusional loyalty. He followed even the worst of people into battle.

"We intend to depart now," the pirate king said, his Asteryan accent thick. "They will be lost beneath the waves."

Zetyr looked down at where Veragi had severed his hand. Though magic had healed him in kind, this time, the goddess had a left a mark. An ugly, jagged scar that extended around his wrist like a bracelet. Proof of his vulnerability. Proof that Zetyr, and therefore Ozik, could be killed. "Bring me back the necklace and the ring, or do not bother to return," Zetyr stated.

The ring. But Vaasa didn't have it.

Roman gazed upon the deity, seemingly without a clue it wasn't Ozik he spoke to. Yet Roman's gaze turned assessing, even if just for a moment. The sentinel had always been smarter than he seemed, more resourceful. He had witnessed Ozik's struggle against Zetyr in the hallway the night Vaasa had attempted to slit Ozik's throat. He knew the magic that plagued Ozik made him less like himself.

Roman's gaze darted down to the empty finger on Zetyr's hand, where the anchor no longer lived. Just as quickly as he'd looked, he met Zetyr's eyes once more.

It was the only chance Ozik had.

Ozik screamed in his own mind, used every ounce of strength he had left to send one phrase across the planes between them, to force one thing up his throat and out of Zetyr's lips. He said it over and over and—

"Remember our bargain," Zetyr spat angrily, communicating the words Ozik was trying to say.

In exchange for Roman's position as lead sentinel, he had agreed to do one thing above all else: Keep Vaasalisa Kozár alive. If she died, so did Roman.

It was the only promise Ozik had made to Vena Kozár that he would not break. To save her daughter, no matter what it cost.

Pain shot through all that was left of Ozik, and exhaustion overtook him. Zetyr beat Ozik back until he couldn't even see out his own eyes. His senses went dark, and he hid in the burrows of his magic, in the place that Zetyr had occupied for hundreds of years before Ozik's father had set him loose. The place Ozik had built inside himself that fateful day when he'd sealed Zetyr into his own body.

Around Ozik, the dark walls of the tomb of Zetyr rose higher and higher, a perfect replica of the one waiting for Vaasa in Wrultho. Next to his feet, a red pool of magic swirled. He had shown Vaasa this place, this darkest recess of his mind, so she knew precisely what to look for when she was strong enough to channel his magic entirely.

If she wanted to, she could find him here.

Ozik sat upon the ground next to the pool of magic, dipping his fingers into the crimson water. And just as he had after Vena's death, Ozik faded into obscurity, having lost his fight against Zetyr.

He was unsure when, or if, he would ever rise again.

ACKNOWLEDGMENTS

What I never expected about publishing is that it's actually the second book, the book *after* your debut, that throws you for a loop. Writing this book has been a marvelous challenge filled with all the ups and downs that come along with this industry, but to say I wasn't prepared to write a book while others perceived my debut novel is an understatement. There's quite a lot of people who made it easier, though, and for all of you I'm incredibly grateful.

To the influencers and authors who embraced me with kindness, I'm forever grateful. Thank you to the team at Saga Press who loved my debut novel enough to publish it, and then were willing to let me keep publishing books. When I first conceived of this series, it was a duology. It was only in writing *The Wicked and the Damned* that I realized this story would be more effectively told over the course of a trilogy, and my gratitude is unending for the opportunity to tell it that way. So much happens behind the scenes in publishing, so thank you to Amara for helping bring this story to life, and to Savannah and Christine for helping me share it with the world. To everyone at Saga and Simon & Schuster, thank you.

Sam—I will literally never stop talking about how much I adore you. I'm so glad I have you in my corner. No one understands the immense amount of work an agent does until they see them in action, and I hope you know I deeply admire your enthusiasm, kindness, and talent. You're the best champion of my stories, and I can't wait to keep telling them with you by my side.

Noemie, who is both a critique partner and a fabulous friend, thank you for reading this work and giving me the feedback necessary to make it the best story it can be. Without you, I never would have had the courage to expand this world into what it needed to become. Robby—it's been such a joy to foster a friendship with you, and I appreciate your encouragement and support as I underwent publishing my sophomore novel.

Jacob, I once again owe you a whole page of friendship gushing. Thank you for coming over at the drop of a hat to help me organize index cards all over my table into some semblance of an outline. You're an amazing thought partner, and the lore of this world has been shaped by our friendship. I am so grateful for you.

Erin—thank you for letting me spoil the entire story so I could pick your brain and for giving me the courage to expand this into a trilogy. Hopefully there were still some twists here you weren't expecting, and I'm sorry for when I inevitably spoil the next book, too. Your friendship means the world to me, and I wouldn't be who I am now without you.

To all of my friends who have offered emotional support during this journey—Emma, Kristi, Brittany, Spencer, Mikey, Maria, DeeDee, and Marissa, I am so thankful to have you in my life. To my amazing Unhinged and Uncorked book club, thank you for helping me love reading books, despite the way publishing makes me want to hate them sometimes. Thank you to my parents, my brother, and every other member of my family for your support while I pursue this career. I hope I'll continue to make you proud.

Lucas, I love you so deeply. It's an honor to rediscover the world through your eyes. Ben, you are an amazing father and partner, and I love spending my life with you. Thank you for everything you do to help support this career and make room for my art. I love you.

And finally to Shasta, the dog we adopted at nineteen who saw me through college, grad school, the start of both of my careers, and my entrance into motherhood; who was with me for the first manuscript I ever finished; and who passed halfway through the drafting of this story. Losing you brought me to a halt. I don't believe I will ever fully recover. I still manifest you in my mind, even if you don't lay at my feet beneath my writing desk anymore. I know you're waiting with a pair of my old running shoes, and I can't wait to see you then.

ABOUT THE AUTHOR

REBECCA ROBINSON is a fantasy romance writer based in Northern California. During the day, she works as an administrator at her alumni high school. By night, she's an avid reader, writer, and consumer of all things art. She is the author of *The Serpent and the Wolf* and *The Wicked and the Damned*.